BIRDS OF PREY

AMADO V. HERNANDEZ

BIRDS OF PREY

TRANSLATED BY
ESTELITA CONSTANTINO-PANGILINAN

To my parents, Attorney and Mrs. Romualdo Constantino, in grateful recognition of their inspiring example of perseverance, kindness, and integrity spiced with a dash of humor.

–Estelita

*"FOR THE GIFTS OF THE EARTH
ARE MEANT FOR ALL"*

–Ecclesiastes

CAST

MANDO PLARIDEL—a guerrilla who recovered Simoun's treasure from the Pacific Ocean; a socialist leader

ANDOY—before he became Mando Plaridel

DOLLY MONTERO—daughter of the wealthy Montero family; beautiful, modern, fickle

PURI—a farmer's daughter; the loveliest maiden in the barrios of Hacienda Montero in Central Luzon; cousin and sweetheart of Mando

DON SEGUNDO MONTERO—landlord and head of a smuggling syndicate

TATA MATYAS—an old revolutionary who lived in a hut in the Sierra Madre; later, Mando's foster father

DR. SABIO—scientist and intellectual; president of Freedom University

MAGAT—fearless leader of disciplined guerrillas in Southern Luzon; friend of Mando Plaridel

"THE PRESIDENT" (Different from any resident of Malacañan)

SENATOR MALIWANAG—nationalist legislator

SENATOR BOTIN—opportunistic legislator

CAPTAIN PUGOT—former Japanese collaborator who became overseer of Hacienda Montero

GENERAL BAYONETA—treacherous military man; Son Tua's son-in-law

GOVERNOR DOBLADO—a corrupt head of a province

PASTOR—farmers' leader and father of Puri

MANG TUMAS—aged leader of the tenants of Hacienda Montero

DANOY—young leader of the farmers

ANDRES—Makapili leader during the Japanese times; associate of Mando and Magat after the war

RUBIO—labor leader

COLONEL MOTO—head of the Japanese forces in Manila during the Occupation; lover of Dolly Montero

DOÑA JULIA—wife of Segundo Montero

SON TUA—Chinese millionaire who became rich from contraband goods

PONG TUA-SON—bachelor son of Son Tua; an architect

LIEUTENANT WHITEY—American pilot; Dolly's boyfriend

CAPTAIN GREEN—another American pilot

LILIBETH—friend of Dolly

MARTIN—guerrilla companion of Mando

KARYO—guerrilla companion of Mando

BISHOP DUMAS—a poker player

JUDGE PILATO—a poker player

IMAN—a reporter for the *Kampilan*

DOÑA NINAY—wife of Governor Doblado

TINDENG—mistress of Governor Doblado

SANTI—another reporter

HELEN—jewel agent in Paris

MIKE—American agent of Mando

COLONEL MOSCA—a Latin American diplomat

It was late in 1944. The Imperial Japanese Army in the Philippines was about to collapse. Each day saw the growing resistance of the Filipino guerrillas, the strengthened resolution of the towns-folk not to give aid to the enemy, and the scarcity of food and basic necessities. Nevertheless, twenty million unarmed citizens, weakened by three years of hunger, sickness, and maltreatment, remained subdued by half a million rifles and bayonets. The Philippine situation proved the saying that a hero becomes braver when wounded.

The promise of President Roosevelt and General MacArthur had not been fulfilled. Other than occasional raids by a few U.S. planes, the Philippines was still at the mercy of the cruel bow-legged conquerors. But the country had not given up. So that when Bataan and Corregidor fell in April and May 1942, the resistance of the masses spread throughout the land, to the Sierra Madre in Luzon, to the forests of Mindanao, to the shores of the Visayas: on the hills, the plains, the fields, the rivers, the lakes, and the caves of the archipelago. In the hearts of the descendants of Lapu-Lapu, Rajah Soliman, and Andres Bonifacio smoldered raging volcanoes.

One afternoon in September, three men who could hardly walk reached a hut in a secluded spot at the foot of the Sierra

Madre. Darkness had driven away the last rays of the sun, and the hut looked like a part of the mountain and the woods. Like a huge nest sheltered by the dense trees leaning against a hill, it overlooked the vast Pacific Ocean up to where the sea met the sky. It was twilight and darkness had covered the forest. That cloudy afternoon, the sun would peep out only for a while, for it had rained continuously. From noon to dusk, the three men trudged through fifteen kilometers, crossing rivers, cutting through thorny vines, stepping on stones, being bled by leeches.

At their second call, a voice answered. "Friends," the leader answered for the group. They went up to the house without waiting to be asked.

"Tata Matyas," the leader greeted the old man who peeped through the door.

Tata Matyas stood with his lips parted, trying to identify the visitor's voice. Looking closer, he recognized Mando and welcomed him.

The young man was five feet, ten inches tall. Despite his fatigue, the muscles of his arms and neck were like raw rubber. He had shiny bronzed skin and a beard of several days' growth.

"It's me, *Tatang*,[1]" Mando answered him respectfully, wiping his right hand over his dirty face.

"When was your last visit, Mando?" asked the old man, glancing at the two companions.

"About four months ago," Mando recalled. He introduced his guerrilla comrades Karyo and Martin.

"Come in," said Tata Matyas.

The three slumped on the floor of the bare, narrow room. Tata Matyas lit an oil lamp made of half a coconut shell and placed it in a hoop with a cord attached to the bamboo rafter. The light fell on the faded pictures of Jose Rizal and Andres Bonifacio, the two foremost Filipino heroes.

---

1 tatang—father

"You are very tired," observed the old man. "You seem to have walked quite a distance."

"That's true, sir," agreed Mando, adding, "The Japs attacked Sampitan."

Tata Matyas was startled by the news. He stared, waiting for further explanation.

"They caught us by surprise," continued Mando, "We were almost wiped out."

The old man shook his head, aware of the serious implications. Sampitan was the last headquarters of the Filipino guerrillas in that part of the mountains of Luzon, in southwestern Tayabas (now Quezon province) north of Bicol, a barrier to anyone attacking the general headquarters in Infanta. The surprise attack on Sampitan showed that they were trying to take Infanta where the submarines of the Allied Forces had been anchored since the middle of 1943. In this hidden rendezvous were loaded arms, medicines, and other war supplies. From Infanta, the supplies were distributed to the guerrillas in southern and central Luzon, and some places in the Visayas.

Mando described the bloody encounter in Sampitan. They were not only surprised, but outnumbered.

Carrying his rifle, Mando had sought cover and fired back. But he ran out of bullets and had to escape. It was suicide not to retreat. Martin and Karyo, who had retreated unarmed, met Mando in the forest.

From his first hiding place, Mando saw some guerrillas board two motorboats. They had not gone far when bullets rained on them. Many fell, but some dived. Mando could not find out what happened to them, for he had to move when he ran out of bullets.

The sudden downpour saved the three guerrillas. Apparently, the Japanese no longer followed them and had turned to the siege of the headquarters. The guerrillas followed a path and lost themselves in the wilderness. Led by Mando, they sought their way where the trees and vines were thickest. Their journey was slow and dangerous.

"You must be starved," said Tata Matyas after Mando had related the grim event.

"When have guerrillas not been hungry?" the young man remarked. The old man understood, for he knew that the guerrillas in the mountains were lucky to have even one square meal a day.

"I have cooked the rice, but I should cook some more and fry some dried *talakitok*.²"

"Salt will be all right," said Mando.

"Dried talakitok!" Martin clucked and gulped. "How much rice did you cook?" he joked.

"With my appetite, talakitok tastes better than *lechon*,³" Karyo said frankly.

"We're lucky you have dried fish," remarked Mando.

Tata Matyas explained that he had caught two large talakitok and some mudfish with his traps in the rice fields below and he had been eating his catch for several days.

"We shall eat in a short while." He went to the kitchen.

The small house was divided into two. The door opened into the kitchen, which was separated from the rest of the house by a wall of dried *anahaw*⁴ leaves and woven bamboo slats.

The hut was supported by ten rough but sturdy wooden posts, each about a foot thick. The roof was of *cogon*.⁵

Tata Matyas built the house himself many years before the war and lived there alone. The past years, he could be seen going to the barrio, but lately, vendors from one town brought his needs.

---

2 talakitok—a kind of fish

3 lechon—roasted pig

4 anahaw—a kind of palm

5 cogon—a kind of grass

During the war, the hut had frequent guests. Most were guer-rillas passing by while the roads were "hot." The safest path was through the dense forest. Tata Matyas' hut served as temporary refuge from the law or the enemies of freedom. There the refugees rested and shared the food of the kind old man. Some gave donations; others left with a "Thank you." Tata Matyas showed the same hospitality to anyone who sought lodging. He would cook his last ganta[6] of rice for anyone who needed it. Or when there was no rice, he always had a supply of kamoteng-kahoy.[7]

Mando had stopped by Tata Matyas' hut several times. The first was more than a year before, while on his way up the Sierra Madre from a town south of Manila. He was with a group and a guide. According to the guide, the old man was a revolutionary. He had fought against Spain and the United States and stayed in the mountains after the independence issue lost to American power. While some leaders of the *Republic of Barasoain*[8] surrendered and some became outlaws, Tata Matyas stayed in a secluded town at the foot of the mountain. When those who refused to bear arms were persecuted, he disappeared, as if swallowed up by the caves. However, after many years, when he was almost forgotten by the public and by the authorities, people who wandered in the wilderness of Sierra Madre brought news that Tata Matyas was alive and well. He had become an "old man of the mountains."

The second and third stopovers of Mando at that hut were four months ago, when he brought an important note to the guerrillas on the plains and later when he went up to the Sierra Madre. He was alone then. He and Tata Matyas came to know each other and

---

6 ganta—unit of measurement equivalent to around three liters

7 kamoteng-kahoy- cassava, a root crop

8 Republic of Barasoain—a government formed in Barasoain, Malolos, Bulacan by the Filipino leaders after they overthrew Spanish rule

exchanged views. Mando briefly told his life story. An orphan, he was serving a rich family in Manila and was sent to school as payment. His schooling stopped during the Japanese Occupation. He joined the outlaws when his master betrayed him to the Japanese.

The two men talked about many current topics: the meager help from sympathizers, the widespread poverty on one hand, and the wealth of the collaborators on the other.

"If I were your age," sighed Tata Matyas, and he looked into the distance. "In my youth, I joined two struggles," he recalled. "Now with my age, this is all I can do." And his face was clouded with sadness.

He was referring to the welcome he offered guerrillas and other unfortunates on their way to or from the mountains.

"If I were you, I'd find the means to support the national movement without counting on unreliable sympathizers." He sighed and continued, "People have become greedy and self-centered— giving only when they get something in return. In a conflict, they usually side with the winner, even if he is in the wrong and even when the victim is a relative." He sadly shook his head. "Ah, if I were your age, Mando." Mando couldn't help asking why.

"What would you do if you were me?"

Tata Matyas didn't answer at once. He went to an old chest of thick, hard wood in a corner of the room. Slowly he opened it and drew from the bottom an ordinary *tampipi*.[9] Mando could see its contents—three or four books, a few pamphlets and papers yellowed with age, a bolo, and a dagger.

Tata Matyas chose a book, closed the tampipi, and returned it to the chest. He went back to Mando.

"*El Filibusterismo!*" exclaimed Mando.

"Yes," answered the old man, "the second novel of our hero Rizal, printed in Ghent, Belgium in 1891." He looked steadily at

---

9 tampipi—a native suitcase

the guerrilla before going on. "Here, in this book, is what I would do if I were your age. How old are you now, Mando?"

"Twenty-four, sir."

"In your prime," said the old man, as if admiring a rare thing, "a bright hope dreamed of by those lost in darkness. You're more mature than I was when I joined the revolutionaries."

When Mando made no comment, he asked, "Have you read this book?"

"Yes, sir, also the *Noli Me Tangere*," Mando replied without hesitation.

"Yes, the *Noli* was published in Berlin, Germany in 1887. Rizal's first novel."

The young man's eyes shone with pride.

"What did you read in those two books?" Tata Matyas' voice was vibrant.

Mando thought awhile before answering. True, he had read the two famous novels of Dr. Rizal, more than once, and he knew the plots and the main characters. But he was taken aback by the question. He felt like an unprepared student being cross-examined by a teacher, but he showed no hesitation.

He spoke slowly and quietly when he saw the old man looking at him steadily. "I have read about the illness of a nation and the instability of the government during Rizal's time—the corruption of leaders and the ignorance and oppression of the masses."

"Right!" agreed Tata Matyas. "You have read them." Then he asked, "Do you remember Simoun?"

"The new Machiavelli," Mando remarked, "Yes, Simoun— Juan Crisostomo Ibarra in the *Noli* who became Simoun in the *Fili*."

"What else do you remember about Simoun?"

"From his adventures in foreign lands, Ibarra—now Simoun— returned, a rich and powerful man. He brought an iron chest full of priceless jewels."

The old man opened the book and looked for several passages about Simoun. He said, "Here is Simoun," and requested Mando to read. Mando read aloud.

Simoun told his sorrowful story. He returned from Europe thirteen years ago, full of hope and happy illusions. He was to marry the girl he loved. He was ready to do good and forgive those who wronged him so long as they left him in peace, but this was not to be. Secret hands hurled him into the whirlpool of uprising plotted by his enemies. He lost his reputation, position, love, prospects for the future, freedom, everything, and escaped death only because of the heroism of a friend. Then he swore revenge. With the ancestral wealth, which had been buried in a forest, he fled abroad and went into trade, took part in the Cuban wars, helping now one side, now the other, but always to his profit. There he met the general, at that time, only a major, and won his confidence in the beginning by lending him money. Later, they became close friends because of certain crimes, the secrets of which were known to the jeweler. By dint of bribes, Simoun secured for him the assignment to the Philippines. And once in the country, Simoun used the general as a blind tool, impelling him through insatiable greed to commit all manner of injustice.

Then, he asked Mando to continue.

"I had returned to these islands summoned by the vices of the rulers. In the guise of a merchant, I have gone from town to town, opening doors with money. Everywhere, I've seen greed in its most abominable forms—hypocritical one time, shameless the next, always cruel, fattening on a dead social system like a vulture on a corpse. I asked myself why the corpse

didn't distill in its entrails some infection, some venom, some deadly virus that would kill the loathsome bird. But the corpse let itself be torn to pieces and the vulture had its fill. I couldn't bring this corpse back to life and turn it against its oppressor.

On the other hand, its decay and total disintegration were taking too long. So it incited even greater greed; I facilitated its satisfaction; and injustices and abuses have multiplied. I have encouraged crime and cruelty to accustom the people to the thought of death. I fostered insecurity to drive them to seek the most desperate solutions. I crippled business so that the country, impoverished and ruined, would no longer have anything to fear. I whetted appetites for public funds. When this didn't prove enough to make people rise, I wounded them in their most sensitive spot and made the vulture insult and pollute the very corpse on which it fed."

Mando's throat was dry when he stopped reading. Tata Matyas declared, "Simoun failed because he was driven by desire for revenge, as Father Florentino said. Sin and evil cannot be washed and cleansed by other sins and evil deeds. The country was not yet prepared; besides, a country gets the government it deserves."

"But the government can be changed, overthrown, or it can disappear," Mando commented, "but the nation goes on. Experience has shown that the evil of a government often rouses a country to turn and break its chains. That's what happened to Spanish power in the Philippines and will surely happen to the power of the Japanese."

Tata Matyas agreed, but he cautioned, "If we don't make mistakes and if the youth become our real hope. This is what I am thinking of regarding Simoun's wealth, laid by Father Florentino at the bottom of the Pacific."

Mando reflected and said, "I thought Simoun was just a creation of Rizal's imagination."

Tata Matyas smiled at Mando's skepticism and shook his head. "Everything Rizal wrote was true," he finally declared. "Although Rizal did not call them by their real names, his characters were actual people, not figments of the mind." He added, "Don't you believe that Captain Tiago, Fray Damaso, Cabesang Tales, Sisa, Huli, Maria Clara, Elias, Filosofong Tasio, Isagani, Basilio, and Ibarra or Simoun were real people who lived during Rizal's time?"

"I do," Mando conceded, noting that the old man was getting heated. "Otherwise why should he have aroused the hatred of his enemies? Besides, this usually happens in an occupied country. Its story is buried and forgotten, its lovely folklore and its heroes. Later, they become only myths like Bernardo Carpio, Mariang Makiling, and others. How many still know the heroism of Lapu-Lapu, Soliman, Dagohoy, Diego Silang, and his wife Gabriela?"

"What you said is obviously true," agreed Tata Matyas, repeating, "All that Rizal wrote is true. We saw it then; now you, the youth, are the witness." He added, "Nature is taking care not only of Simoun's wealth. Where is the money of the Revolution of '96 and '98? It has disappeared, swallowed by the earth, since the fall of the Barasoain Republic. Perhaps secretly buried in the wilderness. Look what happened to the silver money of the Commonwealth before Manila was left to the Japanese—thrown between Manila Bay and Corregidor. You must have heard that, with the Japanese position uncertain, Yamashita is thinking of stashing away the wealth he stole from the Philippines. More or less, that is similar to Simoun's jewels. If our history were to be written later on, it would be considered fiction."

Mando stared at Tata Matyas, looking for possible signs of senility, for the old man was in his seventies. He saw not a trace. The revolutionary was in full control of his faculties. Tata Matyas continued:

"Truly Mando, if I were your age, I would not hesitate…"

"To do what, sir?"

"Dive for Simoun's wealth."

The young man was astonished. "I would dive for it," repeated Tata Matyas.

"But Tatang," Mando groped for words. "Do you…?"

"What?"

"Do you believe that Simoun's wealth was really thrown into the ocean by a priest?"

Tata Matyas gave an understanding smile as he answered.

"Father Florentino was not a foreign priest," he explained. "He was a holy Filipino priest. My grandparents knew him. My father told us the story related by his father before the trouble in Cavite…"

Briefly, Tata Matyas told the story of the good priest, scion of a rich and well-known family. "He had no natural inclination for the priesthood and had planned to marry his lovely sweetheart. However, he was persuaded by his mother who had promised the Archbishop. As a priest, he was respected and liked by all. Not long after, he decided to retire to avoid being implicated along with the other Filipino priests in the Cavite uprising of 1872. He retired in a house where Simoun later hid himself and died. Father Florentino did not care for money nor worldliness, unlike many Spanish friars," he concluded.

Mando admitted that Elias and Simoun were among his idols. He regretted the lack of information about them, just like Rajah Soliman and other early heroes.

"That is the usual strategy of conquerors, as you say," explained Tata Matyas. "They wipe out all the proof, even traces and memories, if possible, of the noble sons of the conquered country. They want the newly conquered to get used to the condition and ways of a slave."

Mando promised to study and prepare for diving for Simoun's jewels. "I need to know more about this," he said.

Tonight, the old revolutionary and the young guerrilla recalled their conversation as if it were only yesterday. That was four months ago.

II

The rice and fried fish disappeared in no time. For Mando and his companions, the meal was both lunch and supper. After clearing the table, the old man asked his guests if they wished to retire, for they had a tiring day.

"There are mats and pillows. Spread out the mats and rest." Mando got the rolled mat of *bangkuwang*[1] near the old chest and spread it on the floor. Right away, Mando and Karyo lay down. After stretching and yawning, they both fell asleep and were soon snoring.

Mando didn't go to sleep. He went outside as if drawn by an irresistible force. He smelled the fresh cool breeze common to such heights and saw through the branches the full moon casting a silver glow on everything it touched.

"Why don't you sleep, Mando?" Tata Matyas called from the door of the hut.

"I am just enjoying the beauty of the night. Who would have guessed that such bad weather would be followed by a night such as this?"

"The darkest night gives birth to the brightest dawn."

Mando looked at the sea—so vast and silent. The sky mirrored in it was silvery gray, yet the sea was bright green, like a carpet of

---

1 bangkuwang—a coarse, fibrous aquatic herb used in mat weaving

melted emeralds. Every time a fish jumped, a chunk of emerald would break into a thousand tiny chips of glittering diamonds which were swallowed up at once by the giant darkness.

Suddenly, the moon hid behind the clouds as if it felt the growing coldness. Mando returned to the hut and saw Tata Matyas seated at the doorway.

"When I see the silver moonlight and the emeralds and diamonds of the sea, I am reminded of the jewels," Mando said. "I recall our long talk about the *Fili* four months ago."

"Ah, Simoun's jewels," sighed Tata Matyas. "The only difference is that you see only an illusion, whereas Simoun's jewels are real…"

"Buried at the bottom of the ocean," whispered Mando.

"No ocean is too deep to dive in," observed the old man.

Mando was standing on a wide rock, which served as a stairway to the hut, but Tata Matyas did not move from the narrow doorway. It seemed that the old revolutionary didn't want to end this conversation with the young guerrilla.

"You were once my age," Mando tried to speak calmly, so that the old man would not think him disrespectful. "Why didn't you dive for Simoun's jewels then?"

Tata Matyas smiled bitterly, but when he spoke, there was no bitterness in his voice.

"I'm glad you asked," he said. "You should know why, instead of thinking I ask others to do what I didn't in my prime."

"I didn't mean that," Mando protested.

"Your question was valid, don't try to take it back," insisted Tata Matyas. "Diving for Simoun's treasure has been on my mind for several decades, beginning in 1898. And that is the real reason I settled in this place. But, when I saw the revolution betrayed by the very people who should have supported it, when surrender became the mark of patriotism and continuing the struggle was called treason, I gave up my plan and told myself that it was better to keep the wealth safe at the bottom of the sea."

The old man stood up to let Mando pass. "You think it is time to recover the wealth and use it?" asked Mando.

"More than ever," he answered quickly.

"Why?"

"Because the enemy is more heartless now. The country has suffered too much from poverty and conquest. And there are good men – you loyal guerrillas – who should use this wealth."

"But Tatang, Simoun's wealth is great for one person, but too small to save a country that is the victim of modern warfare," Mando pointed out. "How much would this be? A few millions in cash, not even enough for a warship and a few airplanes."

"I didn't say it was enough to win or finance the war. Not money alone nor arms are the key to victory. More important is the courage of a nation that refuses to kneel and bow before the conqueror. I meant that Simoun's wealth is a valuable tool. It can be used to destroy or to build. If it were in the hands of your movement…it would be used, Mando, not for this war, but afterwards, in times of peace, for the Japs won't last much longer…"

Tata Matyas stopped when Mando muttered his doubts. "Our headquarters were destroyed and the three of us barely escaped," Mando said, doubtfully. "Perhaps the Japs are on their way to the guerrillas' general headquarters at Infanta. I fear that…"

"The headquarters were destroyed," Tata Matyas cut him short, "but you are alive and so are the others. Losing a battle is not defeat. Didn't the enemy occupy Manila, snatch Bataan and Corregidor? They have governed for three years. But tell me, isn't Filipino resistance more spirited now than at the outbreak of the war? When the USAFFE surrendered, the country had to defend itself so that it was decisive and effective. During Napoleon's time, he attacked Spain and Russia and occupied a large territory. But he did not really triumph even for a day. This is what is happening to Japan in the Philippines; her days are numbered."

"Unfortunately, a lot of whom the nation counted on have sided with the enemy," Mando said, gritting his teeth.

He was thinking that if he had not escaped, Don Segundo Montero would have had him killed by the *Kempeitai*.[2]

"Don't think too much about the cowards and the traitors," advised the former revolutionary. "Why grieve over the ebb and flow of the water, the falling of leaves, the flight of the summer birds during winter? That is nature, my son."

"Is treachery natural?" asked Mando, full of loathing.

"One of man's weaknesses. In any group and for all time, remember that there are always the chameleons and the opportunists. Jesus had only twelve apostles, yet among them was Judas. Even his chosen disciple denied him thrice when he was cornered. Big events are like floods; they sweep everything that is frail and weak, but the strong posts and sturdy trees remain steadfast. As long as a nation has men ready to kill or be killed for their country's honor and freedom, that nation will not become a slave, even if it is defeated and occupied by a stronger force."

"But these traitors should be exterminated like snakes and other poisonous creatures," Mando stressed.

"Their treachery shall be their own graves," explained Tata Matyas. "Besides, the circumstances make the traitor just as the occasion makes the hero. Don't think that anyone is born a traitor or that one starts out a hero. Many who have turned traitor in times of crisis were considered patriots in better times." He paused, trying to recall something before he continued.

"That happened to us during the Philippine-American War. When they saw that the tide was turning against the Republic, some of Aguinaldo's own ministers went to the enemy. To excuse their treachery and cowardice, they cited the salvation and peace of the nation. Naturally, they were called patriotic by the new masters and were rewarded. They were given high positions, lands, and other opportunities. Those who did not surrender became traitors to the foreign government, were branded outlaws and blamed for

---

2 Kempeitai—Japanese military police

various offenses. Those who fled to the mountains or refused to kiss the American flag were either jailed or exiled, like Mabini, Ricarte, and other heroes. Others were hanged, like Macario Sakay and his companions."

His face was bitter as he recalled an ugly chapter in the Philippine-American War, which was repeated during the Japanese War against the Americans and the Filipinos.

"That is why I did not return to the town and I live like a hermit here in the Sierra Madre," explained Tata Matyas. "I was failed by history. But you…"

"That might happen to me, too."

"No, Mando. You are young and your path is clear. You can avenge the victims, the slain. You will be the hope and support of a new life…You, the youth…"

"Tata Matyas, who among our heroes are your models and idols?" Mando asked. "Rizal or Bonifacio? I think it is Rizal because…"

The old man quickly answered.

"All heroes should be honored: Bonifacio and Rizal, also Burgos, Plaridel, Mabini, Jacinto, Luna, also Aguinaldo for some of his qualities. All were noble and all served the motherland. But neither can we deny that one is better than the other. For me, the three cornerstones or foundation of Filipino heroism are Rizal, Bonifacio, and Mabini. Rizal was the martyr and guiding spirit that raised the prestige of the Malays; Bonifacio was the strength and courage that broke our chains and bound the people into a true nation; while Mabini was the brains that set up the First Republic and proved that Filipino leaders in government could equal anyone in brains, steadfastness, and love of country. Plaridel and Jacinto also had rare qualities, but these were also possessed by Rizal and Bonifacio.

"Then, sir…" Tata Matyas made a sign that he was not yet through.

"But a hero's nobility is not his alone," he went on. "I shall repeat what I said a while ago—that the circumstances create the traitor just as the situation helps to make the hero. For example, the treacherous killing of Bonifacio and the later attempts to denigrate him, lessened his deserved glory. If Plaridel had returned to the Philippines before the revolution, as he wanted to, and had been able to lead the revolutionaries, he would have been our number one hero. But unfortunately, he died of tuberculosis in Barcelona. Look at Rizal; he knew that the uprising was near, because Bonifacio had sent Dr. Valenzuela to him in Dapitan, but he refused to join. Instead, to prove to Spain that he had nothing to do with the Katipunan, he asked to be sent to Cuba as a surgeon in the Spanish medical team in the Cuban revolution. Was he not on his way to Havana when he was seized and returned to Manila? The friars and the Spanish authorities here refused to forgive him for his attack in the *Noli* and the *Fili*. Besides, they were afraid of the intellectuals. They expected to subdue the bolo of Bonifacio's Katipunan, but the ideas of Rizal's two books would spread, not only in the Philippines but to Spain and Europe. Thus, Rizal was fortunate even in death. For, if he had not been shot at Bagumbayan and had not become a real martyr, he might have become just like Trinidad Pardo de Tavera, Fernando Canon, and other learned Filipinos. Look at Aguinaldo; if he had been killed at Palanan and not captured by General Funston with the help of the Macabebe, he would be above Rizal and Bonifacio, and the nation would forget the slaying of the Katipunan Supremo and General Antonio Luna. Someday, I will tell you of the nobility and tragedy of Macario Sakay."

As Mando listened to Tata Matyas' story which he seemed to be reading from the pages of history, colored by his own views and analysis, the more he admired and respected the old man, who was so well-informed and noble, despite his life of seclusion in the Sierra Madre. Tata Matyas should be the model for the New Filipino, Mando thought.

"I've reached life's sunset, my son." Tata Matyas held the young man's arm, which he felt to be hard as steel. "Yes, I am old, while you are in your prime. You are a sun newly risen. I admit you were not wrong in thinking that I am counting on you to realize my dream. I don't talk like this to everyone. I have faith in you, and I believe that it is not our time but yours, which the noble priest meant."

"What would you have me do, sir?" asked Mando with his eyes fixed on the old man. It seemed that he had resolved to follow the wishes of the old nationalist.

"I told you once what I would do," said Tata Matyas, "if I were your age and in the face of the nation's situation."

"Ah, yes, Simoun's jewels!" Mando guessed what the other had in mind.

"No other," agreed the old man.

Tata Matyas moved carefully between the two sleeping men, opened the old trunk and again got the native suitcase. Karyo and Martin slept on. Tata Matyas returned to Mando who was leaning against the wall. He looked on as Tata Matyas opened the book to the last pages. When he found what he was looking for, he handed the book to Mando.

"The last time you came, you read about Simoun, his desire and scheme, and why he failed. This time, read the part narrating his death and how his iron chest was thrown into the ocean by Father Florentino," requested the old man.

Mando looked at the passage and read. Mando's voice was soft and clear.

> The patient was dead when the priest approached. He knelt and prayed.
>
> When he stood up and gazed at the corpse, he saw extreme grief, the result of a purposeless life, which he would bring beyond death. The shaken old priest muttered.

"May God have mercy on those who led him from the right path."

Mando paused but Tata Matyas asked him to go on.

Meanwhile, the servants whom he had called were praying the requiem. Father Florentino took from its hiding place the famous iron chest containing the fabulous wealth of Simoun. He hesitated for a moment, then calmly went down the steps with the iron chest towards the cliff where Isagani often sat gazing at the ocean.

Mando took a deep breath before going on. Karyo moved but didn't awaken. Martin snored loudly. Tata Matyas looked steadily at the young man who was reading.

Father Florentino looked below. He saw the waves of the Pacific Ocean kissing the rocks roaring and shining like fire in the moonlight. Like a handful of diamonds scattered by a genie from the depths. Father Florentino looked around. He was alone. Then he threw Simoun's iron chest into the ocean. It turned several times before hitting the water. The old man saw the splash of the water and heard a gurgling sound. The water closed and swallowed the immense treasure. He waited a while to see if the water would throw it out, but the waves moved on as if nothing but a tiny stone had fallen into its depths.

Tata Matyas cleared his throat. Mando read up to the end.

"May nature keep you, in its depths, together with the corals and pearls of the limitless seas," said the priest, stretching forth his arms. "If for a noble and high purpose you should be needed by man, may God suffer you to be taken from the ocean depths. Meanwhile,

you shall not cause evil, you will not buy injustice or provoke greed."

It was late when Tata Matyas and Mando ended their talk. The next morning, the three guerrillas said goodbye to the old man of the mountain.

III

The three had no definite direction when they left Tata Matyas' hut. For the time being, they would go wherever their feet led them. Just the same, they followed a path leading away from Sampitan. They wanted to reach the guerrillas' general headquarters at Infanta. From their position, the shortest way was through Sampitan. But because of their experience the day before, returning to that garrison was suicide.

Mando told Martin and Karyo that they had to go down to Laguna or cross to Rizal. From there they could move slowly to Infanta. There was another way from Bulacan, but it was too far from southern Luzon. In Laguna, they could make their way through the hills and forests once they reached Longos or Santa Maria. In Rizal, they could also inch their way to Infanta from Baras and Tanay. In these towns were footpaths made by guerrillas and outlaws.

On the other hand, they had no idea which places or routes were held by the Japanese and which were in the hands of those who refused to surrender. They should inquire, feel their way, and be cautious, for the situation changed from day to day.

So they stopped from time to time, for there was no need to hurry. They could never reach Infanta in less than a week, not even if they should walk from sunup to sundown.

Their first problem was food. For several miles around, there was no house nor people. That was why Mando was surprised when he suddenly tripped on a stone marker engraved with the initials of the proprietor of the vast rocky land.

"So someone owns this place," he exclaimed.

"Really?" Karyo was puzzled.

"There are lands registered in the name of every big shot," sneered Martin. "Only we have no land except the mud on our bodies." And he looked at the dried mud on his feet and arms.

"But I'm sure," observed Mando, "the only one who reached this place was the surveyor. The man with the initials on the marker can't come here; it can't be reached by car."

"If he tries to climb this height, he will surely roll straight down the ravine," guffawed Martin.

"But they don't have to come here. They have many servants among small fry like us," answered Karyo.

"Ask where those rich people are," Mando said sharply. "I bet most of them are in Manila, enjoying themselves with the Japs. While we…"

"Because we don't like the Japs," growled Karyo.

"Because we are not turncoats," Mando was angry. "We don't wish to act like slaves."

"The chameleons want to stay in power forever," said Martin.

"Everything has to end," remarked Mando.

"After the war, they will surely be on top again," Martin spat out. "Pshee!"

"Over my dead body," Karyo threatened.

"The nation cannot be fooled all the time," answered Mando. "We were fooled by foreigners for four centuries, but this won't happen again, no more…" His voice was hard, then he sighed. "But now, powerful Filipinos are the ones fooling the country."

"If a dog gets used to being muzzled…" said Martin.

"The moment the muzzle is removed, the first to be bitten is the one who chained it," said Mando.

"In these times," Karyo said, "the chained dog is lucky because it is fed. Friends, if you are not yet hungry…" And he got up from the rock where he was sitting. The three walked silently in single file. Suddenly Karyo stopped at the mouth of a riverbank and…

"There!" He pointed to the guava trees teeming with fruit.

Karyo and Martin raced to climb the trees. They ate in the trees and threw Mando some guavas. They picked ripe and half-ripe ones and placed them in their pockets. They had their fill of the guavas.

"We'll have food till tomorrow," Karyo said happily.

"Until you have a stomachache," remarked Martin.

In reply, Karyo twirled a large ripe guava round his fingers.

"One guava with seven holes." Then he finished it off in two bites.

When full, they looked for a waterfall and drank the clear water, then walked on.

Darkness befell them in the forest; so they walked faster to reach the plains before night, if possible. It would be hard to pass the night up there without shelter, because of danger from snakes. The leeches would crawl and suck on their bodies, causing wounds and bleeding.

The moonlight was tearing off night's veil when they reached a riverbank. The river was swollen, and the waves were swift.

The three decided to stay there till morning. They sat on the ground and ate guavas.

"Even dried-up guavas satisfy," jested Karyo as the seeds of the guavas made a grinding sound on his teeth.

"At this moment, all I ask for is a whole fried chicken," Martin said before biting a half-ripe guava.

"All I ask for is a bed without pests," wished Mando, and he stretched on the ground with his head pillowed on his palms.

He got up hastily, rubbing his hard legs, shoulders, and nape. As soon as he laid down, he was immediately attacked by a swarm of insects.

Martin and Karyo sat restlessly because insects were crawling over their feet and wherever their bodies touched the ground.

After gathering bamboo twigs and dried leaves, Mando took from his shirt pocket a box of matches wrapped in cellophane and made a bonfire.

"It is all right to make a fire," he remarked, remembering a guerrilla regulation. "There are no Japs here anyway."

"If only we had dried fish," said Martin, "It would be delicious roasted over that fire."

"Roast the guavas," suggested Karyo.

"See, the insects are gone," Mando remarked happily, lying down again near the fire.

But as he looked up at the moon, he saw how quickly it was covered by clouds, and darkness swiftly spread like a black veil thrown by a giant from the bending forest. In a short while, Mando felt the raindrops, slow at first, suddenly thick and fast, and soon rain fell in torrents.

The three squatted with their backs to each other. They had an untimely bath and suffered from the intense cold. Tired from walking the whole day, without food except guavas, wet the whole night and without sleep. This was not the first time they endured such hardship.

"It is hard to love one's country," sighed Mando when the rain abated.

"If I had known that life in the mountains would be like this, I would not have left the stone house."

"Stone house?" asked Karyo.

"Jail," said Martin.

"You were jailed?" Karyo sounded concerned.

"More than once! First, I wounded someone; next, I was accused of stealing," Martin narrated without a blush. "But what's wrong with that? I had a debt; I paid for it. The contemptible ones are the shameless who are free to commit grave crimes daily against their fellow men, against society and the government. Yet they are called honorable," Martin said angrily.

"Rizal's prophecy has come true," Mando agreed. "To be honorable, one has to go to jail first."

"The way I see it," said Karyo, "bad and good depends on whether one is caught or not. You are bad when you are caught; you are good as long as you don't get caught."

Martin protested, "One should be judged according to his true self, not according to the cover, just as a fish is judged by its flesh and not its scales."

"I wish it was so," answered Karyo, "but this is not what happens. Because the skin and scales are exposed and seen. Often, even if the flesh is rotten, this is not noticed."

"I am bad, I admit," confessed Martin, "but I'm no hypocrite. I joined the guerrillas to save myself. Is there a safer place for an escaped convict than among the guerrillas? Here are all sorts of people, good and bad. No one will scrutinize you. No one will ask where you came from. As long as you are ready to fight, you pass, and you get arms. If they don't have weapons, it's up to you to get them. Better if you bring arms."

Karyo, a true country boy, had a different tale.

"I became a guerrilla," he said, "because the Japs raided our town. My pregnant wife was killed when they machine-gunned the place. I am an unschooled laborer, but I love my wife and our country."

The two asked why Mando became a guerrilla. He was young and intelligent. Surely the Japanese would want him to be a collaborator. Why did he go to the mountains? Why did he join the fight?

"I am a Filipino," Mando said simply. "Isn't that enough reason?" he asked. He did not relate how he barely escaped from the anger of the Kempeitai when they raided the meeting place of a group of students gathered to relay the real news about the war.

These contradicted reports in the papers hawked by the newsboys, as "newspapers with false news."

In their minds was the bitter truth that many Filipinos, men and women, were helping the enemy in various ways. Mando would not forget that his own master had reported him to win the favor of the Japanese.

The three men huddled back-to-back patiently, endured the torrent, which finally subsided to a shower.

All were wet but got some warmth from each other. For a while, they forgot their discomfort during the lively exchange.

When the moon peeped out again, the only sounds in the surrounding stillness were the flow of the water and the wind among the leaves. After a while, they dozed off. Their drooping heads rested on their knees.

The first shafts of sunlight awoke them. The sky was bright and clear. The weather was fine, and the river had receded. There was not a trace of the ugliness of the past night.

They shook off their fatigue in different ways. Mando ran backward shadowboxing. Then he lifted rocks with outstretched arms. Mando developed his unusual inborn strength with regular exercise and the study of karate.

Along the shore they found some coconuts left by the rising waters the night before.

"God's gift," Karyo remarked happily and began picking up the scattered coconuts. They opened the coconuts with sharp stones and sipped the water.

"Sweet," commended Martin, "Good! We'll have 'rancho' for two days."

"Who says anyone will starve on this land?" Mando said mockingly.

"In the city, *taksan-taksan,*[1]" observed Karyo, "for they have no coconuts or guavas."

---

1 taksan—Japanese word for many

Then they split the coconuts, scraped off the white flesh, and munched on the contents.

"Before I left Manila," Mando told them, "small pieces of coconut meat were roasted like corn by the roadside and sold at twenty pesos per piece. They are called *kastaniyog*[2] and served as breakfast for many."

"Coconut is an excellent product," boasted Karyo, who was from a coconut region. "Besides food, it is the source of almost everything."

"It is truly wonderful," agreed Mando. "Just look at this coconut. Its meat is better than the contents of the heads of many of our present Filipino leaders."

"Our leaders' heads are not empty," objected Martin. "Only, they are full of ashes."

"For me," Karyo concluded, "what a leader should not lose are his balls. A leader without balls is not a man."

Mando and Martin agreed. Martin added:

"If you want, let's see who has the biggest," he challenged and the three laughed. "Let's see who is the most manly."

Then they saw two monkeys masturbating. "There is your cousin," Karyo kidded Martin and the three laughed.

"Do you know what I'll do when the Americans return?" asked Martin.

"What else? Clean their shoes, of course," Karyo teased him.

"That's where you're wrong, pal," declared Martin and flexed his arms. "I'll grab two American girls and get both of them pregnant in a month."

"Would they pay attention to a dark person like you?" mocked Karyo.

"Oy, American girls are crazy over *Pinoys*.[3] Ask the Pinoys from California. That's why there are frequent fights between

---

2 kastaniyog—coined from castañas (chestnuts) and niyog (ripe coconut)

3 Pinoy—slang for Filipino

Americans and Pinoys. The moment the white woman has a taste of the Pinoy, goodbye to the damned boyfriend."

"That might be a tall tale," remarked Karyo.

"No kidding, do you know why the American girl likes the Pinoy?"

"Why?"

"Because he is circumcised, smooth like the head of a top," boasted Martin. "White men are not. They have raincoats like the monkeys we saw."

Mando and Karyo guffawed at Martin's comparison.

"But among our fellow Filipinos, many are not circumcised," remarked Karyo. "How many did I operate on at the guerrilla headquarters; some were even married. The Visayans and the Bicolanos were envious of the Tagalogs, so they got circumcised."

"Maybe the whites think it is alright to be *supot*[4] as long as their children's noses are pointed," said Martin.

"Once I saw a picture of the statue of Hercules, the strongest man, and just think about it– he is supot," agreed Mando. "But Jesus Christ was circumcised."

"Maybe that's why Magdalena liked him and jilted Judas," declared Karyo.

Their jesting stopped when they saw the clear water of a spring. They ran and dived to drink.

---

4 supot—not circumsized; literally, "encased"

IV

The river, which last night had been a fierce, forbidding monster, was now like a tame carabao, quiet and calmly waiting for its rider. After a breakfast of coconut meat, they took the leftovers and crossed the river. They faced another day's walk.

The place they passed was like a door closed behind them. To the left before them were hills and forests and to the right were thick vines, which were like prison bars. Above, the clouds were turning red as fire, emitting burning arrows. Mando thought of the gap between those who helped the enemy and those who not only refused to help but fought back. He saw the image of resistance in himself, Martin, and Karyo, in Tata Matyas, in the guerrillas whom he saw swimming in the ocean while being chased by Japanese bullets, and in the corpses of those slain in the garrison at Sampitan. On the other hand was the collaborator, one of whom was Don Segundo Montero, the haughty Monte of Manila and Nueva Ecija – landlord, producer, businessman.

When the footsteps of the Japanese Imperial Army resounded in the suburbs, Monte was among the welcomers. In front of his car, a huge flag of the rising sun waved in the wind. He respectfully greeted the head of the occupying troops and declared that he was ready to serve and obey. He was backed up by his family in this subservience. His wife Doña Julia and his daughter Dolly offered no objections. Mando recalled several bitter experiences. He had just turned twenty-one, living as a servant in the palatial residence of the Monteros'. He was nicknamed Andoy. He had no wages except for his food and a measly allowance. He served Don Segundo and the whole family and often the little time he had for his studies was spent doing errands. Some days, he was a servant; other days, he was a gardener. Sometimes, he was sent to buy household items; at times a driver for Doña Julia, or a house-boy to clean Dolly's room. Dolly, the couple's only child and the apple of their eye, was about to graduate from an exclusive girls' school at the outbreak of the war. Andoy was often slapped and abused by the family even when he was grown-up.

The day before, when Mando was asked why he fled to the mountains, he said he was a Filipino and that was enough reason. But in his heart, Mando knew there was a reason deeper than he cared to reveal.

Andoy or Alejandro Pamintuan, who later became Mando Plaridel, had driven Don Segundo's car outside the city to the head-quarters of the commander of the Japanese Army. The USAFFE had left Manila. When they arrived at the temporary GHQ of the military staff, Don Segundo leaned back in his car and ordered Andoy to go down and inquire.

A mean-looking soldier with a rifle stood at the gate. Quietly, Andoy approached and greeted the soldier in English. He was startled when the soldier slapped him twice. Then, shouting *kura, kura*,[1] he was about to hit Andoy again. Andoy nearly forgot him-self and was about to use his strength and knowledge of karate, a skill relatively unknown then. Fortunately, a Japanese civilian arrived and intervened. He asked the soldier what happened, then explained to Andoy why he was so treated. The soldier was angry because Andoy did not salute him and his speaking in English seemed a challenge.

---

1 kura—Japanese term used for giving orders

Afterwards, the civilian approached Don Segundo's car and accompanied him inside. After fifteen minutes, Don Segundo came out looking pleased.

Apparently, Don Segundo's trip was successful; he won over the Japanese officer. However, he couldn't forgive Andoy for the incident at the gate, which almost ruined his mission. All the way home, he heaped abuses on Andoy, calling him a fool for not bowing before the Japanese. He was a slowpoke for not studying Nippongo as soon as the war broke out. He regretted spending on Andoy's schooling, for he was dumb, surely inheriting this trait from his stupid ancestors and peasant parents.

Andoy was furious, but he controlled himself. He was patient by nature and not used to talking back. Then, he had no idea he would ever kill anyone. He remembered how Don Segundo had also abused his late father. Andoy's father was then Montero's driver. Andoy's mother was the laundry woman until she became bedridden.

Such heartlessness and abuse naturally aroused similar feelings or caused festering wounds crying for a desperate cure. Certainly, there were enough reasons to drive Andoy more than the soldier's slap, to leave the Monteros and join the outlaws, but there was a more serious cause. He learned that Don Segundo had reported him to the Kempeitai as a worker for the guerrillas. He was tempted to kill the Don, but thought better of it and escaped instead.

He was disgusted when he saw how servile the couple were, groveling before the Japanese. He felt that even in his lowly state and poverty, he could never do such things. He did not realize then that the Monteros were not moved by admiration, a liking, or affection for the new master. Rather, it was fear of losing wealth and comfort. Desiring to maintain the status quo, they debased themselves. Just like those similarly favored before the war, their shameless weakness was exposed in these times of trial, so that they readily exchanged human dignity for favors from the enemy.

When he joined the outlaws, he changed his nickname Andoy to Mando. The former Alejandro Pamintuan became Mando Plaridel. And Mando he remained.

As the shadow cast by the sun's rays among the branches and leaves fell on their path that morning, these sad-angry memories crossed Mando's mind.

He told himself that, while it was hard for a person with a conscience to help the Japanese, living in the hills was a greater physical punishment for anyone. He was like a hunted beast without shelter from sun or rain, uncertain of food. The only certainty was hunger. And the uncertain hours of rest.

Climbing up and down the steep inclines, with no foothold except sharp stones and thorny vines, when a slight misstep could make him plunge into the yawning unfathomable abyss. Bravely crossing wide rivers and being carried by the strong current. Or walking on the slippery trunks of palm trees bridging that river. Wading across marshes and being sucked down with each step as by quicksand. Cutting across the tall cogon and *talahib*[2] whose sharp leaves bit one's flesh. In the afternoon, finding one's body covered by land and water leeches, clinging until they drowned in the blood sucked from one's body. Tired from walking the whole day, and wet, for in that section of the mountain range and the forest, there was hardly a day when it didn't rain, even when the August sun was shining on the plain.

If no charitable soul offered boiled rice, eaten with rock salt or cooking oil for viand, one made do with guavas or coconuts picked along the way. Many days not even an unripe guava could be had.

Luckily, Mando and his companions saw smoke as the sun leaned towards the west. They walked towards the tiny hut. A couple lived there alone. An iron kettle was set on stones.

_____

2 talahib—a kind of weed

After Mando introduced them, they were invited in. After a while, they went to the brook nearby to wash themselves. The old man lent them clothes so they could wash their own.

On their return to the hut, some kamoteng-kahoy were smoking on a *bilao*.[3] This was what the old woman had been cooking.

Kamoteng-kahoy, in the city, became the food of the poor during the war. It was enough to stick it in the ground in the backyard or *kaingin*[4] and it would quickly grow and bear fruit without much tending. After some months, its roots bore flesh like the sweet potato or *tuge*[5] which was soft and delicious when boiled. During the war, it took the place of rice and bread.

The old woman also served ginger tea sweetened with honey. This they drank from smooth halves of coconut shells.

"This is the first time I've tasted this," said Mando. "Coffee and tea are a far cry to this."

"We lack many things here," said the old man. "But we have some things not found in town."

According to the old man, the town capital of Diliman ten miles away was held by the Japanese, who had a strong garrison. Soldiers from this garrison raided nearby towns to make the townsfolk feel their presence. Then, the phrase "There are Japs" was bad news to the townsfolk. It was like saying, "There are evil spirits," or, "There are bandits."

"Do the Japs come here?" asked Mando.

"Seldom," answered the old man. "Sometimes they order the felling of trees or ask for wood, stone, or lumber. But they never stay until dark."

The old man related that the Japanese had recently been sent to the town from the provincial capital. Reports had reached them

---

3 bilao—flat native basket

4 kaingin—a burned clearing in a forest

5 tuge—a kind of root crop

that guerrillas were using the town as passage to the mountains, so they decided to post a watch.

"But the townsfolk are the ones burdened," explained the old man. "So they were obliged to evacuate here. Many moved to other towns. The Japs vent their anger over their failure to catch the guerrillas on the peaceful civilians."

"There are really guerrillas in town, aren't there?" asked Mando.

"There are," affirmed the old man. "But how can the Japs tell who are the guerrillas? Anyone who arouses their anger is caught and beaten up and forced to plead guilty. Once they admit their guilt, they are made to squeal; anyone whose name is mentioned suffers too. In the end, the stool pigeons and those whom they reported are all beheaded. Just like killing chickens."

"Poor folks," Mando shuddered.

"There seems to be a sword hanging over everyone's head," said Martin.

"Perhaps they hold *sonas*,[6]" declared Karyo.

"They often do that in some towns," said the old man. "Once, some Japanese soldiers got drunk and had a brawl. They reported that the outlaws attacked them. The next day, there was a sona of the area around where the fight had taken place. Everyone was herded to the old schoolhouse and locked up without food or drink the whole day. The Japs searched their houses and took anything they wanted. Bolos, axes, knives, daggers, scissors, clocks, money, jugs, goats, chickens, eggs, rice, bananas, and other things."

"After robbing every house within the area – for this was plain robbery – they then turned to the people in the schoolhouse. There was a man supposed to be from the place, said to be a Makapili

---

6 sona—the Japanese practice of cordoning off an area and rounding up the residents

with a *bayong*[7] over his face with holes over the eyes. He pointed
out the supposed guerrillas," the old man sighed.

"That's the 'evil eye,'" said Martin.

"Everyone fingered by the traitor was separated from the
group," the old man continued, "and beaten up without question.
Afterwards, they were transferred to the garrison. It is said they
were all taken in a truck at nightfall and were never seen again."

The old man covered his mouth to stifle a cough before going on.

"The rest were not released until the next day. But many,
especially the women and children, could hardly walk from
hunger and sickness. More died from being cooped up than those
fingered by the spies."

"Not one tried to hit back?" Mando's eyes flashed. "Weren't
there many guerrillas in the towns nearby, at the foot of the
mountains?"

"One night, two guerrillas approached the garrison and shot
the sentry at the gate," answered the old man, "but they were
chased and caught. In the morning, they were brought to the
plaza and were beheaded right there before the onlookers. The
heads were staked on bamboo poles which were also posted in
the plaza. The headless bodies were hung upside down from a
tree. For a long time, the crows feasted on the rotting corpses of
the two guerrillas. That is the fate of those who try to avenge the
Japanese cruelty against the townsfolk."

That night, Mando could hardly sleep, picturing the corpses
of the two brave guerrillas who proved to the Japanese that there
are Filipinos who are not afraid to die.

---

7 bayong—a large rectangular bag of woven material used for marketing or
carrying things

Mando and his two companions followed the winding, rough, and rocky path leading to the town of Kalayaan. According to the old man, no Japanese boots had trod on Kalayaan.

There the disciplined guerrillas were firmly established. After several attempts, the enemy realized that they suffered more losses than gains every time they tried to take the place.

Next to the capital, Diliman was the strongest fort in the province. The old man told them that the garrison had several hundred soldiers who went back and forth to the adjoining towns of Buhangin and Mabato. Sometimes the enemy would visit Saga-saga, between Kalayaan and Kalumpang, which were both in the hands of the guerrillas. But they seldom went beyond Saga-saga.

Kalayaan was on the other side of the river. Behind, within whistling distance, was the edge of the forest. In fact, the entire group of guerrillas gathered in the forest; besides, they had many followers in town. They practically ran the government, for the puppet mayor had promised unconditionally to blindly obey the guerrilla leader, after he was threatened. He never broke his promise. So he remained in good health and a mayor in name.

On the other hand, the town of Kalumpang was also controlled by guerrillas belonging to a different group. The two groups didn't get along.

The Kalayaan guerrillas called the other "Kalampag Guerrilla" (noisemakers). It was said that they fought each other more often than they fought the Japanese. Between them was Saga-saga, which was often the arena to prove the manhood of the guerrillas from Kalayaan and Kalumpang.

Mando was aware that this troop quartered at Sampitan, with a large fort at Infanta, was independent of both groups. But they were not foes; rather, they would join forces when the occasion called for it. In fact, this was one of his aims – a closer union. He had brought a message to the guerrillas in Diliman and other nearby places a few months earlier. His aim was to activate the guerrillas on the plains. Unfortunately, the Japanese answered the message by taking over Diliman.

The three walked slowly, but were alert as they sighted Kalayaan. Almost at once, two armed men rushed towards them. In a loud voice, they accosted the three.

"Halt! Identify yourselves," ordered one.

The three stopped but were not alarmed. Mando briefly explained that they had come from the Sierra Madre.

"Are you pro-Jap or pro-American?" asked the man who had spoken first.

"We are pro-Filipino," Mando answered promptly. Martin and Karyo nodded.

"Hmm…You have not answered the question. Pro-Filipino. What do you mean? Some side with the Japs because they are pro-Filipino. Some side with the Americans because they are pro-Filipino. It's not clear."

"Our being pro-Filipino has nothing to do with the Japs or the Americans," explained Mando. "We are Filipino above everything else. The Filipinos and the Americans happened to join forces because they were attacked and had to defend themselves. Therefore, our stand is according to reason and justice. Never because of preference for color of the skin or shape of the nose."

Apparently satisfied, the two let Mando's group enter the town. One offered to go with them. Their leader was in town, and he was the person to see.

They were graciously received by the guerrilla chief. Mando and Magat were about the same height, but the latter's complexion was darker. He moved briskly and his eyes were as sharp as an eagle's. Mando and Magat had a detailed conference while Martin and Karyo were busy eating. Seldom did Mando have the chance to discuss important matters with a dedicated guerrilla with such principles. Martin and Karyo rarely had the chance to taste such food as was served. The three were equally satisfied with their activities.

Mando learned that Magat was also in Manila at the outbreak of the war. His guerrilla activities brought him to Kalayaan. When they were seated at the table, Magat spoke.

"Comrades, we are pleased with your pro-Filipino stand. We are one of heart. My grandparents were followers of the revolution. They fought against the Spaniards, then against the Americans. Now I am fighting the Japanese."

Magat paused; the others were listening attentively.

"The Philippines is our country," he went on. "The side of the true Filipino is the Philippines, always. On one hand, he should oppose anyone – Spaniard, American, Chinese, or Japanese – the moment these foreigners try to invade us. An invader is an invader, in any shape or manner, whether through force of arms, commerce, or religion. Let us examine closely whether their aim is to conquer and exploit us."

"And often that is their real aim," affirmed Mando.

"That is why," added Magat, "we cannot judge evil by the color of the skin. There are also serpents among our own race."

Mando related his mission the past summer as ordered by the commander at Infanta. He was to unite the guerrillas, for they had the same goals – to take down the Japanese in the land. He also related what happened at Sampitan – the result of lack of coordination among the guerrillas, those in the Sierra Madre and those on the plains.

"What is happening is disgraceful, dangerous, and a waste of lives," admitted Magat, not hiding how bad he felt. "But how can oil mix with water, sheep with wolves? Some guerrillas pretend to be enemies of the Japs, but they are worse enemies of the people."

"Treacherous guards," explained Karyo.

"Worse," corrected Magat. "Look, first they establish a reign of terror through violence and cruelty. They enter a town where there are no Japs and use an iron fist. Whatever they desire – livelihood, tools, utensils, houses, women – they snatch without a by-your-leave! Any protest will surely result in something worse. These atrocities are committed by the Japs, yes, but they are enemies, whereas the false guerrillas pretend to be defenders. Now, can you blame us that between this town and the other which they command, there should be a barrier higher than a mountain?"

When no one answered, Magat continued.

"Why did we become guerrillas when USAFFE surrendered?" asked the guerrilla head of Kalayaan. "Because we cannot condone the inhumanity of the enemy. The Japs are enemies not simply because they are Japs, but because of their actions as soon as they landed on our shores. If this is so, can we not consider enemies our countrymen, our supposed brothers, who commit crimes against their people, crimes that cry to heaven? Burglary, rape, senseless killing. From the time of Cain to the time of Hitler and Yamashita, such atrocities cry out for punishment. Now tell me," he asked again with unconcealed anger, "how to bring harmony, not to mention unity, among such groups. That would be like a conspiracy between the devil and the Archangel Gabriel."

"The guerrilla movement should have its roots among the people," said Magat, "otherwise, success is remote. Here in Kalayaan, the townsfolk and the guerrillas are one, so that whatever the guerrillas do, is supported by the town, and any action taken by the authorities receives our support. We organize groups made up of these three—town authorities, townsfolk, and guerrillas. So we have no problem about food, clothing, work, defense, attack, etcetera, that is not resolved to everyone's satisfaction and for the good of the struggle."

"I wish this were true of all places under guerrillas," said Mando.

"Here, there is no theft nor looting," Magat pointed out. "No profiteering, no tyrannical leader, no raping of women, no Japs with their bold spies. Our principle is one for all and all for one."

Magat showed them how such an enviable program was carried out. Mando remarked that if this were true over the whole country, the Japanese should have been vanquished even without the Americans. He mentioned that arms were needed, but in any fight, the will and morale of the nation are much more important than guns and bullets.

There was a room for depositing objects taken from the enemy by Magat's men – rifles, sabers, daggers, flags, uniform, shoes (for the forest and for the water), tents, rope, preserved food, medicine, books, documents, watches, pens, underwear, and more.

"We were able to get radio sets and bicycles which we are now using," Magat told them with pride.

Mando noticed a few helmets and visors for diving. To every visor was attached a rubber hose several yards long and two inches in diameter. Also attached was an oxygen tank. There were also rubber boots. Mando asked Magat if those were instruments for skin diving.

"I don't know if these are for skin diving, but I'm sure they are for diving. The Japs are expert divers, whether for fish, pearls, or wrecked ships."

"Aren't you using them?" asked Mando.

"What shall we dive for here?" joked Magat. "We just dive into that river. Take them if you need them," he graciously offered.

"We are returning to the shores of the Pacific," said Mando. "They might be useful to us or to the others."

Mando chose two visors together with the attached equipment and two pairs of rubber boots.

He dusted a visor and tried it on. Karyo attached the cylinder with the rubber shoes.

"It fits," Mando smiled.

"It's easy to adjust those," said Magat. "What is hard is diving to the bottom of the ocean."

Mando found he could breathe easily.

"I'll try this," he told himself. "How long can this last? He asked Magat.

"Up to one hour or more with the oxygen, according to the old diver living here. He says it's better than the old equipment. Simple and light."

Besides the diving gear, the three guerrillas were given clothes, food, and medicine when they left the next day.

"When do we meet again?" Magat asked.

"Perhaps after the war," answered Mando. "The days of the Japs are numbered."

"Here, they were done for a long time ago," laughed Magat.

Mando decided not to pass by the plains where they would go through Saga-saga and Kalumpang. The last was under the "Guerrillas Kalampag." They turned back instead.

VI

Christmas, 1944. But Manila, the modern city usually ostentatiously gay and noisy, was as somber as Holy Week. Bare, orphaned, and lifeless. A far cry from her former self.

Only a few people were in the streets by day. Blackout by night. Japanese sentries on street corners. One could count on one's fingers the motor vehicles passing by.

In business areas, the bazaars were unadorned. In fact, many big stores had long been closed, for there was nothing to sell and few customers. Only a few restaurants and bars at Santa Cruz and Escolta stayed open to serve the Japanese soldiers and civilians.

In a few places, the "black market" sprouted. No different from the small markets on the plazas and sidewalks. No cover nor table. Goods were held in the hands or laid on the ground. Everything was mixed up, no organization nor plan. Haggling. Cash upon reaching an agreement. All items were old—"slightly used." Food was only to relieve intense hunger.

A large area was filled with rows or groups of vendors of used items. One or two pieces. A stove, a meat grinder, a clock with broken springs, a radio with broken tubes, rundown shoes, pants mended at the knees and seats, old dresses, faded hats and ties, one or two charcoal flat irons, a few dirty cots, rusty scissors, used toothbrushes, mirrors, old umbrellas, frames with saints' pictures, a bust of Rizal, old fountain pens, law and medicine books without covers, and a thousand and one odds-and-ends. Every item was found in the "black market." Surprisingly, the quoted price was several times the original price when the item was new.

"Fixed price" was the usual scornful expression of the vendors. "You can find these nowhere else. Also, these are 'stateside,' mister."

If there seemed to be fewer people in Manila, most could be found in the black market.

In a corner could be found vegetables and fruits for sale. *Kangkong*[1] and *kamote*[2] tops were piled up together with other food for the poor, like *bataw, sigarillas,*[3] and eggplants. A small bundle of kangkong cost ten pesos; so did a handful of sigarillas. A ripe papaya cost anywhere from fifty to seventy-five pesos. Bananas were three pesos each and were scarce.

A coconut was not sold whole. It was cut up into pieces at ten pesos a piece. Roasted pieces of kastaniyog (from "castañas" and "niyog") were sold at twenty pesos a piece.

Along the row of vegetable vendors was cooked food for sale, on flat baskets or in iron pots. Boiled kamoteng-kahoy and bananas, *binatog,*[4] *suman,*[5] cassava sweet meat, but without sugar and as tasteless as the host given at communion. Also for sale were viands—like *tulya*[6] cooked with ginger and pepper. There was goat's meat *kaldereta*[7] occasionally, and *azucena*[8] every day.

---

1 kangkong—a kind of vegetable that thrives in swampy places

2 kamote—sweet potatoes

3 bataw, sigarillas—vegetables with pods

4 binatog—boiled corn kernels eaten with grated coconut and salt

5 suman—glutinous rice wrapped in leaves

6 tulya—small shells/mollusks

7 kaldereta—a kind of meat dish with sauce of tomatoes and coconut milk

8 azucena—dog meat

Many customers came purposely for these last two dishes.

The skulls of the dog and the goat were set on tin plates while the vendors shouted.

"Goat's meat kaldereta. Azucena. Newly cooked. Well-spiced. Genuine. See the skull on the plate."

The buyers scrambled for the tempting dishes. Right there and then, using their fingers, they devoured the food which they bought at twenty-five pesos a piece.

"So you love dog's meat," one nudged an acquaintance who was greedily biting his food.

"What did you say?" asked the other in Pampango. "Who cares for lechon?" And he continued chewing.

Not only the people showed extreme hunger. Flies swarmed on the exposed food.

But no one should ask for rice, beef or pork, chicken or fresh fish. These were only for the Japanese and the few Filipinos close to them. At a secret "black market," a sack of rice cost as much as twenty thousand pesos. Very few families had twenty thousand pesos, even in "Mickey Mouse" money.[9]

In one section was medicine of all kinds. Some in bottles or in small tin cans. Most were exposed on flat baskets. Various fruits, like *kalumbibit*, *bayugo*, *tuba,* and *kasuy*,[10] various roots, bark, seeds, grass, dried or fresh leaves. To be drunk, rubbed, applied as a compress or for cleaning wounds. According to the vendors, there was no illness which these medicines could not cure – from headaches to toothaches, chest pains, pimples or boils, to cholera, malaria, or smallpox.

No longer were these miracle cures for all human ailments sold by old women or bearded *herbolarios*[11] but by young men,

---

9 Mickey Mouse—money with little value issued by the Japanese in the Philippines

10 kalumbibit, etc—kinds of medicine

11 herbolarios—unschooled men who prescribe herbs, fruit, etc., as medicine

smooth-talking and light-fingered; a few were former magicians and fortune tellers who claimed to have studied medicine, massage, and palm-reading in India and Arabia.

There were also those who secretly sold real medicine. They had medicine known before the war; some medicines were newly arrived and were "made in the U.S.A." The last were brought by submarine for the soldiers and the guerrillas, but they were somehow diverted to the black market. Potent pills and tablets could be bought. Aspirin, atabrin, sulphathiazole, sulphanilamide, sulphaguanidine, and others. There was medicine for injections. But trading was conducted in whispers and in secret and, if necessary, at any cost.

The medicine dealers were unknown, for those roaming the black market were agents working on commission basis. But it was rumored that some were doctors and honorable government officials. These traders in contraband medicine grew rich overnight, while all around died the sick who could have been saved by such medicine.

On the other hand, the extreme want and poverty born of three years of occupation served as a forge that purified the soul and shaped the strength of the common man. Some learned to make shoes from old ones. Some made alcohol from coconut milk as a gasoline substitute. Tasty biscuits from cassava flour.

Cigarettes from grated tobacco leaves wrapped in ordinary paper and many other items, showing the resourcefulness and industry of the Filipino.

Now was the time to topple the centuries-old barriers that separated the people before the war. In the face of widespread want and ever-present danger, the "haves" were obliged to step down and mix with ordinary mortals. The power of money and property had lessened; occasionally, the physical strength and daring of some adventurers were more effective. They prevailed in looting, hoarded goods, amassed wealth, and dictated prices.

The poor and the impoverished rich could be seen carrying bags, rubbing elbows while buying their daily needs. They walked from their homes to the marketplace.

"This is real democracy," one onlooker said to himself.

Once a former cabinet member could not afford to buy a ripe papaya. A former judge was given a pack of cigarettes by the vendor who had been the judge's driver. The driver now manufactured cigarettes, and the judge had no means of livelihood.

"God bless you, Rubio," said the judge. Thus, the other vendors would remember his name later.

Meanwhile, the dyed-in-the-wool collaborators could be seen in cars and the newly rich put on airs as they rode in handsome carriages drawn by magnificent horses. As they sped by, people in the city threw dirty looks and muttered curses. They also caught the attention of the bearded, dirty Japanese soldiers pushing carts. Gone was their arrogance when they first occupied Manila after New Year's Day in 1942.

On such a black market and other gathering places would swoop down a group of Japanese dressed as civilians with one or two Filipinos dressed as soldiers, down to caps and boots. From the crowd, they would snatch one or two whom they sought. Should the one caught protest or ask questions, he would be mauled without mercy.

One day, Rubio, the former driver of the judge, was taken by the Japanese. Snatching the cigarettes he was carrying, a Japanese twisted his arms behind him. Another hit him with his fists, grabbed and tore his clothes, then kicked him on the legs. Only when he fell almost unconscious did the Japanese let him go.

The thick crowd moved back, forming a circle while they watched the loathsome scene. But all seemed paralyzed and were like deaf-mutes who had lost their senses. Witness to the atrocity of a few Japanese, a thousand people kept silent, could not intervene nor even protest.

When the cigarette vendor was swollen from the beating, he was left almost lifeless in the middle of the plaza. Only then did someone approach and help him. One of the vendors took him home.

The next day and the succeeding ones, Rubio the former driver and cigarette vendor did not show up. No one could tell why he was maltreated by the Japanese, supposed to be Kempeitai. According to some, he was probably suspected of helping the guerrillas. Some thought he was reported by the Filipinos who tagged along after the civilian-clad Japanese, for they were seen frequenting the black market.

When the former driver disappeared, the more mysterious the incident became. Some said he was taken from his home by the Japanese, some surmised that he was taken by his family to the province where he then joined the outlaws.

Once, an unknown man rushed into a restaurant, emptied his gun on two men drinking beer and swiftly escaped. No one recognized him. But it was learned that the slain men were Japanese spies and were the companions of the Kempeitai who mauled the driver at the black market. Someone recognized Rubio, but he wouldn't talk. When the police came, there was no one in the restaurant but the two corpses and the owner. The frightened owner was arrested.

But more frequently encountered in public, near markets and eateries were corpses not caused by the Japanese, not by the guerrillas nor by criminals, but by starvation and sickness. When found, the dead were skin and bones, eyes deep-set, cheeks sunken, but legs and feet swollen.

The public was so used to such sights that they hardly paid attention or seemed to see only a dead dog or cat. If only the authorities would pick up and bury them right away.

The seeming languor of that Christmas in 1944 was only on the surface. In fact, it was boiling and seething at the core. The Japanese knew that Judgment Day was near. This was no secret to many Filipinos. That October, the liberation forces had landed at Leyte and were pounding at the shores of Pangasinan in preparation for the landing of U.S. troops in Luzon.

Because of this, the Japanese who were at the end of their rope were preparing to carry out their final plans for obstruction, for revenge on the Filipinos, and for escape. The Filipinos were also setting up plans to carry out their own revenge and to meet the Allied Forces who would help them regain freedom.

The Filipinos were on the lookout for the fleet of modern airplanes, which, like giant eagles with stars on their wings, flew and dived gracefully. From the air, above Japanese forts and installations, they would suddenly lay bombs that exploded deafeningly and burst into flames that swiftly spread and melted everything in their path. While the Japanese were like a pack of rats, hiding and dodging, the Filipinos gleefully watched and rejoiced as if they were watching fireworks on a holiday.

The Japanese knew they had reached the end of a gamble. The Filipinos awaited a glorious day, more blessed than any Christmas or New Year.

Scarcity, violence, and terror worsened. No rice, no meat, no milk, no sugar, for most of the country. No Christmas tree, no Santa Claus, no ham, no wine, no Christmas gifts.

"Never mind, children," a mother consoled her two children who remembered it was Christmas. "In a few days, the Americans will return and your father will come down from the mountains. And we will have bread, canned goods, candy, apples, and grapes."

On the faces of the children shone the joy of innocent cherubs, hoping that the privation this Christmas would surely be followed by unequalled prosperity.

The mother and her children retired early in the dark and moonless night. Several times, the siren signaled the threatening attack of airplanes, but the three good souls slept soundly, dreaming of the happy fulfillment of "Glory to God in the highest, and peace on earth to men of goodwill."

VII

The carretela had been waiting for some time to take Pastor to town. Last night, he had arranged for Tano, the rig driver, to fetch him. He was going to Manila.

From the town, Pastor would take a truck up to Azcarraga (now Recto Avenue) near Divisoria Market. From there, he would hire a cart to carry his baggage. He would walk or help push the cart towards the wide grounds of the Monteros' on the other side of the Pasig River.

In those days, there were no more buses fit for travel. One was lucky to find space even in trucks which were packed with countless passengers and all sorts of baggage.

Once a month, Pastor went to Manila to bring rice and other farm products for the Montero family. Pastor was in charge of Don Segundo's hacienda. A ,former tenant, Pastor replaced Don Segundo's overseer who was kidnapped by outlaws. After a year, there was no serious problem at the hacienda, although Don Segundo was not as pleased with Pastor as he had been with the loyalty of his former overseer. Apparently, Pastor got along with the tenants of the hacienda and with the outlaws.

Pastor and Tano loaded the two sacks of rice and some chickens on the carretela. Pastor could lift them by himself, for at forty-one, he was strong; but Tano was helpful by nature.

Puri brought a small basket of fresh eggs, a bamboo container of carabao's milk, and a large squash. Pastor's daughter, Puri, had been her father's housekeeper since her mother's death.

Tano teased Puri, whom he had known as a child.

"Puri is getting prettier every day," the old rig driver clucked his tongue. "Who is making you pretty, ha?" And he looked her over.

"No, sir," she protested.

"Who?" insisted Tano.

"What else can make a girl pretty other than a clean and quiet life?" Puri replied.

"True," Tano turned to Pastor. "You are lucky to have such a daughter. How many young girls nowadays, even those brought up in the barrio, prize a clean and quiet life?"

Tano was not the only one fascinated with Puri. The girl was admired in the whole hacienda and was adored by the young men. She had only rudimentary schooling. Yet her beauty, her fine manners and ways, and her womanly dignity were rare for a nineteen-year-old.

When Pastor was made overseer, Don Segundo was startled upon seeing Puri. He offered to take her to Manila, promising to send her to a girls' convent school, to have her learn to play the piano, and to provide all her needs. Pastor didn't consent, and Puri also refused.

"Mother told me to look after father, sir," she had explained.

This trip, Pastor had greater hardship than before. Several times, they were detained and searched by the guerrillas, by the Japanese, by the town police. Of course, Pastor had a secret pass for the guerrillas and a printed pass of the Japanese Army, but far more meticulous were the police, especially in towns near Manila.

The Japanese were strict about guns and other deadly weapons, but not about food. The guerrillas made sure that the passenger was not a Japanese spy and that the food, if in large amounts, was not for the Japanese but for the people. But the police were worse than the Japanese until they got what they needed. It was their policy to have a share in the food brought in or taken out of Manila by ordinary citizens.

Pastor finally passed a veritable cavalry of travelers from the province to Manila during the last days of 1944. As in the past, the Montero couple greeted him, not with pleasure or thanks, but with reproach and blame.

"Why did you bring only this?" grumbled Don Segundo.

'Why are there no peanuts, *atis*,[1] or *pinipig*?[2]" Doña Julia pouted.

"See if I don't make the trip myself and get all I need from the hacienda," Montero boasted.

"It is dangerous to travel," Pastor reminded him.

"Suppose I bring a Japanese soldier?" the landlord continued bragging.

"That would be more dangerous, sir."

Doña Julia called a servant to bring in the goods brought by Pastor. Don Segundo went to his office on the first floor, followed by the farmer.

"What the devil is this?" the Don roared. "Is this my share of the harvest? Why, I don't seem to be the proprietor anymore, ha?"

"During wartime," calmly explained Pastor, "values change; customs change."

"What do you mean?" demanded the landlord, raising his brows.

"Look at what happened to our former overseer. He insisted on implementing the old policy at the hacienda or dividing expenses and the harvest. He wanted to collect all debts at once. He wished to bring all the *palay*[3] to your bodega in Manila. What happened to him and to your interests?"

Don Segundo grunted, before asking another question.

---

1 atis—sweetsop

2 pinipig—newly harvested rice that has been pounded flat

3 palay—harvested rice with its husk

"And my palay, where is it? Surely, not these two sacks, ha, Pastor?"

"Your palay is stored at the hacienda. I bring you two sacks a month, because I can't bring more. The outlaws won't allow it. They say that is enough for you. If the food is brought to Manila all at once, it might fall into the hands of the Japs or the black market, which they don't want to happen."

Don Segundo was furious and almost shouted.

"My palay is mine, and I didn't steal it. It's up to me to do as I wish. Does an owner have no more right to his property?"

"Their reason is that each one should not have more than what he needs," Pastor answered calmly still. "In war, everyone suffers, so everyone should be attended to and aided. In short, they want to place human life above property."

"Oh, I see," sneered Don Segundo. "And who will enforce that? The outlaws? Therefore, the enemies of the law are the ones making the law. The world has turned upside down."

"In their opinion, even if they are called enemies of the law, those who take advantage during the war are the enemies. They are trying to stop such opportunism."

"What are the leaders doing? Those placed by the Japanese?"

"The leaders are scared."

"And the Japanese?"

"The Japs don't want to die either."

With such an answer, Don Segundo could not pursue his questions. Then he raged, "I thought the war ended with the fall of Corregidor. It seems disorder followed. What's wrong is the meddling of the plebeians. Everything is mixed-up. Anarchy and banditry reign. This is the result. People have no more respect for the law. No fear of God. Where is this country going?"

"I feel that," Pastor spoke slowly, "the defeat of the USAFFE resulted in the revolution."

"What revolution?"

"Just like Japan, Germany, and Italy," answered Pastor, aware that he was stepping on delicate grounds. "They say the war came because they rose against wealthy nations like England and the U.S. Now, with the defeat of the USAFFE, the 'have-nots' are rising against the 'haves.'"

Don Segundo was enraged.

"Foolishness! Foolishness!" he exploded. "And where did you pick up such foolishness?"

"This is what the outlaws say when they try to get followers."

"Pastor, remember that those people are a pack of bandits. They want to grab others' property, take what others have worked hard and saved for."

Don Segundo was panting. He poured water into a glass, swallowed it in one gulp, and slumped on an easy chair while Pastor remained standing behind a chair.

Pastor's eyes were fixed on a picture on the opposite wall, a group with Don Segundo and a Japanese official. Below was a small flag of the Rising Sun. Pastor surmised that this must be the powerful military officer who was said to be a friend of the Monteros. It was rumored that Dolly was his woman and that it was he who helped Don Segundo amass wealth. Pastor stared long at the picture.

His thoughts were cut short by the landlord.

"I want to know how much palay I have in your charge," he said. "Before the war, for every hectare at fifty percent, my share was…"

"You may no longer use that as basis, sir," Pastor interrupted him, "whether in harvesting or in sharing. For almost two years, from the start of the war, the land lay idle. Many tenants moved away, and some went to the mountains. Only since I took over has there been some improvement. But the harvest is barely enough for the needs of the tenants and yourself, besides the amount demanded by the outlaws. I set aside your share. You still have about a hundred *cavans*.[4]

Pastor was saved from the impending storm when Doña Julia entered, followed by the Japanese in the picture. Like a mask, Don Segundo's sharp look and set jaw were immediately replaced by a glad and gracious smile. He stood up right away and shook hands with the officer.

"Colonel Moto, sit down. How are you? What do you want to drink?" Without waiting for an answer, he told his wife, "Julia, send for whiskey, soda, and ice."

No one noticed Pastor quietly move from the office to the yard. He had come from a far place and had been there for some time, had brought rice and other food for the Monteros, yet no one asked if he was hungry or offered him water. But the thought passed fleetingly, for he was used to the shabby treatment of the "have-nots" by the "haves" and their groveling before more important persons.

After a few minutes, Pastor saw Dolly all dressed up, going to her father's office. Then, she came out with the Colonel holding her around the waist. The two got into his car.

Pastor thought of his daughter Puri. He recalled that he used to envy the Montero girl secretly; how he used to wish his daughter would grow up like Dolly with her personality and education. Now he saw how the officer held Dolly and how closely they sat in the car, with no chaperone save her conscience. Then his eyes seemed to burn, and he thanked his lucky stars for his only child. If Puri ever acted like Dolly, Pastor resolved that he would strangle her or challenge the Colonel. But, perhaps, Dolly's parents approved.

All of a sudden, Pastor heard Don Segundo's voice calling him. The Colonel and Dolly had left.

"Our talk was cut short," said the landlord. "Do you mean to say there is no remedy for this situation at the hacienda?"

---

4 cavan—measure of rice; a sack

"If we don't agree," said Pastor," "we will lose more. We would ask for a liter and lose a ganta."

Don Segundo's ears turned red, but he realized he should not blame the overseer.

"Very well," he said, "do whatever you think best under the circumstances. But as soon as conditions improve, I'll fix that. I will not condone ingratitude. We shall restore the old setup. We shall restore it," he stressed.

He gave Pastor a small sum for the expenses and told him to bring four sacks of rice on the next trip.

When Pastor was about to go, he stopped, remembering something.

"Don Segundo," said the farmer, "where is Andoy?"

"Andoy?" repeated the rich man, as if the name was unfamiliar.

"Andoy, Ate's[5] son…"

"Ah, Andoy," said Don Segundo after a while. "Yes, the son of your sister who worked here. He's bad, a barbarian, an ingrate. He left without a word."

"He left?" Pastor was amazed.

"He just disappeared," affirmed Don Segundo. "Perhaps you knew he grew up in my care. I treated him like a son, sent him to school. Imagine, he was about to graduate when war broke out. And how did he repay me?"

"Where could he be?" asked Pastor, very much worried. He was thinking that, after the death of his only sister, Andoy was his last close relative.

"Don't bother to look for him," advised the landlord. "I heard the Kempeitai got him for joining some deviltry. If I had not been Don Segundo Montero, I might have become involved because he was my ward."

Pastor's eyes nearly popped out. In a quavering voice, he asked again, "What do you think, sir? Could he have been slain?"

---

5 ate—a title of respect for an older sister

"How should I know? And I don't want to meddle," rudely answered Don Segundo. "He dug his own grave. This is what happens to bad ones, ingrates."

Pastor left the yard with heavy feet. He wanted to blame himself for the fate of his nephew. He should have looked after the boy when his sister died, the sister who had raised him. But he had been negligent and did not even become close to Andoy. If he were alive and they should meet, they might not even recognize each other.

But what Pastor minded the most were Don Segundo's insults. Pastor could not believe that Andoy was bad. Andoy's father, Montero's houseboy and driver, and his mother, Pastor's older sister, were both models of virtue. Andoy was their only child. Pastor felt that the tree would not bear a different fruit.

VIII

Don Segundo Montero felt very sad when his friend Colonel Moto of the Japanese Imperial Army said goodbye.

A few days before, the Colonel revealed that he was preparing to leave on orders from Tokyo. Montero wanted to give a grand *despedida,*[1] but the Japanese commander was against it. As much as possible, it was best to keep it quiet. He was to perform a new mission, a military secret, he said.

And so that afternoon, the Monteros had no guest besides Colonel Moto and his aide. Both were in their clean, dashing uniforms.

Nevertheless, Doña Julia and Dolly prepared a special *merienda-cena.*[2] Although it was hard to buy food "fit for a king," the Monteros could afford the black market and didn't lack anything.

They also prepared gifts for the Colonel as a token of their friendship. Don Segundo owed much to his friend. When he went to greet the Japanese forces, a few hours before the occupation of the "Open City," it was Colonel Moto who met him. The Colonel was pleased with the landlord's gesture and assured him he would not regret giving aid to Japan.

When the Colonel was stationed in Manila, he became a close friend of Montero. Hardly a week passed without a grand

---

1   despedida— farewell party

2   merienda-cena—heavy snacks or light dinner served at about 6:00 pm

reception at Montero's home. Present were high Japanese and Filipino officials.

The friendship between the officer and the businessman was not a case of love at first sight. Rather it was simple arithmetic, where two and two make four. They both understood that their cooperation would not fail to bring them untold profit.

It was the Colonel's duty to secure funds for army expenses in the area under his jurisdiction. Montero was a businessman and could be useful. Meanwhile, the Colonel enjoyed the pleasures of the conqueror. He was single and in his prime. Fortune smiled on him. The Montero family belonged to high society. Doña Julia was still youthful, and even his almond-shaped eyes could not miss the beauty of her only child, Dolly. Through Montero, he hoped to be accepted not only as an officer but as a gentleman in high society, a society addicted to pomp and pleasure.

On the other hand, Don Segundo was entertaining similar thoughts. He was thinking of how to get close to the Japanese officer and his probable reward.

"They need funds; well, I'll take care of that," Montero decided. "They need cars, dynamos, machines, tires, rope; very well, I hold Aladdin's lamp. The Colonel likes wine and women. This is luck, yes, it is. Montero is a fool if he does not become a multimillionaire overnight." Smiling, he patted his left shoulder with his right hand.

A kind of Monte-Moto partnership was soon formed.

Before long, the Colonel became practically a member of the Montero household. In fact, he had his own room which he could use anytime. During his stay, he was served, not by servants, but by Doña Julia or Dolly.

He was often alone with Dolly, talking of topics other than the war. The Colonel enjoyed looking at Dolly; she was enamored with his bearing. He was taller than most Japanese, amiable, and obviously came from a good family.

Don Segundo became the general purchaser for Colonel Moto's office, with his own office and depot. Because of this arrangement, all bids for the Japanese forces were coursed through him. Money flowed into Montero's hands.

Such good fortune, of course, was not for free. He repaid the Colonel, not with money – for what would the latter do with Mickey Mouse money which he printed himself? – but in servility.

Besides the frequent receptions, banquets, and dances for the Japanese officers in the Montero gardens or at the Manila Hotel, Montero and Moto had their own outings almost every night. By day, Montero reaped fat profits. By night, Moto gathered perfumed flowers of pleasure.

They became regular customers of first-class hostesses of well-known nightclubs. Whenever they appeared at any amusement place, the orchestra greeted them with a special piece. The manager would greet and lead them to a reserved room. The top hostesses would enter; three waiters would serve them. Two bottles of wine would be opened, wine which was available only to them.

Sometimes, they would dance. Often, they would just drink and talk. After an hour, they would leave with the hostesses, although no entertainer was allowed to leave before the orchestra had played "Home Sweet Home" in the wee hours of the morning. But for Monte and the Colonel, such rules did not apply. The manager himself saw them to their car.

This happened everywhere. Anything they desired was given; neither the manager nor the owner could refuse, because they could order them to close down and that would be the end. It was even harder for any hostess to say no. That would be disobedience to the boss. As the saying goes, she knows on which side her bread is buttered. She was in the nightclub to make a living, not to become holy. Anyone in her place who pretended to be clean in such surroundings was a crow flapping its wings and bragging about its black feathers.

But Colonel Moto was not satisfied with the hostesses and other night birds. His secretary was alluring. He met Lilibeth through Dolly at a gathering. Lilibeth was an American mestiza; her father was American, and her mother was from Zamboanga. She was Dolly's schoolmate before the war. She was fair, shapely, and fond of comfort and pleasure.

Lilibeth had stopped schooling a few months before the war and had married an American pilot newly arrived in Manila. The pilot joined the USAFFE in Bataan. The Colonel hit two birds with one shot. First, he had captured the wife of an enemy. Second, he had a lovely secretary, a rare doll which he might have anytime. If Lilibeth was not aware of this yet, he would soon let her know. He'd take a chance on her possible refusal.

The Colonel would not remain guessing for long. He guessed right. One afternoon, he asked his secretary to stay on the pretext that he had urgent work. When the others had left, the Colonel and Lilibeth prepared some unimportant papers. Then they had supper and proceeded to a small nightclub which he didn't usually patronize. He took her home after midnight. Lilibeth had drunk too much and had to be helped by the Colonel, who had drunk just enough to keep his steps and arms steady as he held the lovely secretary.

Colonel Moto beat General Homma in Bataan in obtaining their respective "objectives." The amorous Japanese official thought Lilibeth was more desirable than any heiress or society girl who had "surrendered" to him.

One day, the office phone rang. Colonel Moto recognized Dolly's voice.

"I know why you haven't been around," she reproached him.

"I've been very busy," explained the Colonel.

"Yes, very busy with Lilibeth." Dolly's jealousy showed in her voice.

That afternoon, Lilibeth went home alone. Before dark, Colonel Moto's car could be seen speeding towards the Montero residence.

Dolly greeted him affectionately. She was perfumed and wore a sheer house dress. Colonel Moto inquired about Don Segundo and Doña Julia.

"They went up to Baguio this morning," Dolly told him. "No one was left except me and my maid. They took the other servants," she added.

"And why did you stay behind?"

"I told them we'd go together." Dolly looked straight at the Japanese officer.

"Oh?"

"Don't you want to take me to Baguio? Or can't you get away from Lilibeth?" she asked meaningfully.

Colonel Moto merely smiled, pinched Dolly's cheek, and went to his room.

"I'll just take a shower," he said.

After ten minutes, Dolly brought merienda to the Colonel's room. He had finished his shower and was wearing a colorful kimono.

"Why do you always mention Lilibeth?" he asked after eating.

"She told me about you."

"Are you jealous?" The Colonel's voice was gentle.

"What right have I?" Dolly evaded the question. "I'm not your..."

The Colonel quickly stood up, held the girl by the shoulder, and looked at her blushing face.

"Dolly," he said, "don't compare yourself to Lilibeth. I have a special regard for you. Here in my locket, on my breast, is your picture. I planned to ask you to marry me after the war."

Lovingly, he stroked her hair, her breasts. Slowly, he raised her face and pressed her lips with burning kisses.

He imprisoned her in his arms. Dolly was a willing captive. For a long time, their bodies seemed welded. Kisses and tongue-sucking, which seemed endless.

Without speaking, as if unaware of what they were doing, they moved to the bed and sat on the edge. Moto's fingers were kept busy, and he slowly pushed her down, but she suddenly drew away.

"Wait, my maid might enter," she warned. She got up and locked the door.

When she came back, the Colonel had removed his kimono and was in shorts. She saw his well-built body. He seized and crushed her with ardent desire. Dolly did not protest, for he made her feel the same eagerness. The blood in her veins was filled with craving. She was drunk without drinking wine.

Slowly, she lay down. Then she freed her lips from his kisses and asked, "Truly, am I your only love, darling?"

"You and you alone."

"Even in Tokyo?"

"Anywhere." With this, Dolly embraced him tightly. Calmly, Moto removed her dress, then her underwear. Dolly felt no shyness in baring herself before him while his eyes narrowed seeing her white skin, her swelling breasts—which were like hills not yet taken by the enemy.

When the Colonel claimed her as he would snatch a rare gem, Dolly sobbed, "You are the first…"

"I'll make you happy, Dolly."

"Is this our…our honeymoon?"

"Here and in Baguio. And all days to come."

There was silence. After an hour, when the maid knocked, the lovers were sound asleep. Dolly's head was pillowed on Moto's right arm. His left hand was on Dolly's front, which looked like a coat of arms as it caught the light. The maid wanted to ask if she should bring them supper, but there was no answer. She left, shaking her head.

"These two might die of happiness," the maid muttered.

In the morning, Colonel and Dolly joined the Montero couple in their rest house in the cold Mountain City. As Moto had promised, that night they continued their honeymoon rehearsal, a privilege which no Filipina ever enjoyed outside of marriage.

A chain of happy moments which time could not wither in their memory.

Until that afternoon when he said goodbye.

Once more he visited his room and Dolly followed. They recalled their happy moments.

"I am going, but I leave you my heart," he whispered.

"You take my love with you," said Dolly. And she hung a gold locket containing her picture around his neck.

The sun had almost set when Colonel Moto and his aide went down the steps of the house which they would never see again. Dolly was crying as she watched the Colonel go.

To Colonel Moto, who did not conceal his sorrow, it was not the sun that was setting, but the hope of his proud empire. Their defeat in the last stages of the war in the Philippines was already written on the horizon.

After a few days, the Montero family received the sad news that Colonel Moto had committed *hara-kiri*[3] at his place on Daytoa Avenue (now Roxas Boulevard).

---

3 hara-kiri—Japanese form of suicide

IX

From the town of Kalayaan, Mando's group spent the night at the house of the couple where they had stayed before. In the morning, they continued their journey.

They followed the path through the mountain to the seashore.

While resting on rocks under the shade of big trees, Mando got from his pocket a folded piece of paper, opened and read it. On this paper, he had noted the various references in the *Fili* regarding the home of Father Florentino and the place where he had thrown the iron chest containing Simoun's treasure. On the same paper, Tata Matyas had sketched map-like directions.

Tata Matyas figured it was a remote barrio outside a town in Quezon, most likely Atimonan or a place nearby; therefore, within forty kilometers from Tata Matyas' hut in Sierra Madre. This was how he explained his past search when he was fired with the desire to dive for the lost treasure.

Tata Matyas learned and told Mando about the specific place where Father Florentino lived after he retired.

Mando read Isagani's description of his town in the *Fili* and the house of his priest-uncle:

> *Surrounded by forests at the foot of the mountain and near the shore… There, far from civilization, there in*

*the midst of nature's plenty, inside the forest and at
the seashore…*

Mando went on reading until…

*From its hiding place, Father Florentino took the
famous iron chest with the great wealth of Simoun,
firmly went down the steps carrying the iron chest and
went to the ravine to gaze on the depths of the ocean.
He saw the waves of the Pacific kissing the rocks… He
was alone… Then, he threw Simoun's iron chest into
the ocean… The water swallowed the great treasure
and closed over it.*

The place was feared, and it was said that ghosts appeared
during unholy hours of the night. After Father Florentino's death,
the deserted house was neglected and went to seed till it crumbled.
After a long time, the forest completely covered its traces just as
the sea had hidden the wealth of the mysterious guest.

His companions noticed how engrossed Mando was in
the paper.

"What's that, Mando? It looks like a map, ha?" asked Martin. Mando told them what it meant and what he thought they
should do. At first the two merely laughed. Karyo said it would
be better to dive for fish so they could have something for lunch.
Martin was lazy by nature and asked how he could dive when he
couldn't swim.

After Mando's explanation, they agreed with his plans. First,
they had nothing to lose even if they didn't find the chest; but if
they succeeded, they would be the luckiest. Second, they had the
time and the equipment.

All they had to do was to ascertain the area where Father
Florentino threw the iron chest. This they could do with the help
of the map and by observing and searching. They needed food

for a few days, a banca, rope, an ax, and a few other items. It wasn't hard to find such equipment in any town near the seashore between Mauban and Atimonan, a day's walk.

The three finalized their plans. They walked towards Atimonan. In three days, they had prepared their supplies and equipment through Mando's wise management. But they kept their secret, simply introducing themselves as guerrillas on a mission. Right away, they received help to meet their needs.

Soon they started to look for a ravine found at the foot of the mountain, surrounded by forests and near the shore. They went to within five to six kilometers from the next town after leaving their banca and equipment with one of those who helped them.

At first, they seemed to be hunting for a flea among the rice stalks. Everywhere were trees, vines, stones, shore, sand. They suffered hunger, fatigue, boredom.

"Of all the jobs I have tried, this is the most exasperating," Martin grumbled. "Looking for nothing."

"I got it," Karyo shouted all of a sudden. When the others came, he showed off five iguana eggs.

They slept on wide stones after eating their ration and the boiled eggs. The moon was bright, and the night was beautiful. The slight cloud in the east was driven away by a strong gale from the sea.

"I can foresee that we won't fail," Mando declared before they lay on the rocks.

"If we should be lucky, how do we divide it?" asked Karyo.

"We are three; therefore, three partitions," promptly answered Martin. "Is that right, chief?" He turned to Mando for support.

"It could benefit not only three, but many others, should we wish it; one gem alone is enough wealth. My plan," he said gently, sizing up their reaction, "if we should find the chest, is to go to Tata Matyas to consult him."

"What for?" asked Karyo.

"What has the old man got to do with the iron chest?" objected Martin. "Aren't we the ones undergoing hardship?"

"We owe a lot to Tata Matyas," Mando explained. "It was he who thought of this, he who prepared the map and studied what should be done."

"Then let's give him a fourth share," suggested Karyo.

"Comrades, we should not think only of the partitioning," Mando explained. "More important is what we shall do with the wealth."

"What else, but divide it?" Martin retorted stubbornly. "You take care of your share and I take care of mine. Isn't that right?"

"But, of course," agreed Karyo.

"Simoun's wealth is not mine," said Mando. "Wealth kept in the ocean's womb, with a history, with a definite purpose. So, we can't just…"

Martin and Karyo showed impatience at the implication of Mando's words.

"If it won't be ours, even if we get it, count me out," Martin threatened.

"Me too," Karyo backed up Martin.

"You won't be on the losing end," Mando calmed down their fears. "Didn't I tell you one gem alone is worth a fortune?"

"I ask only for my share," Martin insisted.

"Same here," Karyo repeated.

"Well, if that is your wish, you are the majority," Mando ended their argument.

The next day, Mando found what might be part of the stone steps of Father Florentino's former home. He could no longer see the ravine, but he saw a protruding part which hardly rose above the water and was covered with tall waves. It was clear that the ravine near the stone steps of the house was swallowed up by the ocean and could no longer be reached except by swimming or by banca.

When they saw it, the three marked the place. They went back for their banca and equipment. They took the banca to the supposed site of Father Florentino's home a century before. It closely resembled the sketch on the map.

They cut down some trees, branches, and anahaw leaves and built a shed on the stone steps for shelter.

They carefully studied the best way to search. Because Martin couldn't swim, he would stay in the banca. Mando and Karyo would dive. On the first day, they would fathom the depth of the ocean in the area. They had also secured a piece of rope.

Then, they would dive to test the equipment which they got from the guerrillas' headquarters at Kalayaan and look around to check if it was the right place.

They decided to dive only in the daytime. Should anyone notice them, they could pretend to be fishing. Diving at night would arouse suspicions; besides, they had no flashlight. It would be dangerous, especially at night because of the sharks.

They found the visors and other equipment satisfactory. With the first trial, they stayed underwater for an hour. The area around the moss-grown plateau was five yards deep and the bottom was a wilderness, a jungle of corals.

On the second day, the sky was clear, and the sea was smooth as a wide mat. The fine weather seemed a sign of good fortune.

Together they carried the banca from the shore and laid it on the water.

Mando and Karyo put on rubber boots. Then Martin fixed the brass cylinder on the backs of the two with the help of canvas belts. Then the visors to which were attached the oxygen tanks.

Martin tied a long piece of rope to a horizontal piece of wood in the middle of the banca; the other end was tied to Mando's belt. Thus, if anything untoward happened, they could signal from underwater to Martin who would stay in the banca. They felt that the rope could keep them from going too far, for the length of the rope would mark their movements.

They went into the water one by one. Mando went first, carrying a spear. Karyo followed with a bolo. After about fifteen minutes, Martin was startled by a strong yank at the rope, causing the banca to tilt. He had not recovered from his surprise when Martin observed bubbles on the surface.

"Blood." Martin was alarmed.

Suddenly, Mando surfaced, supporting Karyo. At first, Martin couldn't tell who was hurt, but Mando shouted.

"Get Karyo," he said when they were near the banca. Martin supported Karyo who was raised by Mando up onto the banca.

Martin immediately rowed ashore. Running, they carried their wounded companion to their shed.

Mando quickly treated their wounded comrade, but all his efforts failed. Karyo died from loss of blood.

Mando related to Martin what happened underwater. They just reached bottom when a shark passed by, facing Karyo. Mando speared the shark and hit him in the side while Karyo hit the monster in the throat with his bolo.

Mando thought Karyo was unhurt; however, he had been wounded by the shark's teeth. After the wounded shark left, Mando noticed that Karyo staggered and then clung to him.

Sorrowfully, the two buried their slain comrade that same afternoon. Then they got the shark which had been washed ashore. They hardly spoke as they slaughtered it. The monster that had killed Karyo was the one that would save them from hunger, they thought.

X

For two days, Mando and Martin mourned. They hardly spoke, occupied with their own thoughts.

Mando grieved hard over Karyo's death, for he was a loyal comrade and a courageous fighter. He was not clever, but he had a good heart. He was ever ready to help and never shirked a task that required daring and strength. Being a peasant, he was accommodating and obedient.

Although it was an accident, Mando also blamed himself. Was he not the brains and the leader of the enterprise that took Karyo's life?

In truth, he liked and trusted Karyo more than Martin. Even if Martin was as manly, his ways, manners, and speech did not inspire confidence. He was jailed several times, he admitted. While going to jail was not enough to condemn a man, but the kind of person he had been, still Martin himself confessed, "I joined the guerrillas to save myself."

Mando felt that Martin was brave, but unreasonable, greedy, and unreliable. However, as he had said, in times of crisis, people are thrown together, so that one can't be too choosy about one's friends or foes. In buying milkfish wholesale, one accepts both big and small.

On the other hand, Martin was more regretful than grief-stricken. He wished it had been Mando who was slain. Karyo was more forgiving; Mando would make a fuss about everything. He could beat Karyo, physically or mentally; he could probably best Mando physically – although he had never tried. Mando had more brains, but in foxiness and scheming, Martin could bet that Mando couldn't beat him.

Mando was aware that his relationship with Martin from Sampitan was a necessary evil. Martin, on the other hand, thought that they were like the monkey and the turtle.

It seemed that Karyo had been their bridge or bond; but with Karyo gone, they felt the void caused by his absence.

"Tomorrow, let's continue," suggested Mando on the second day after Karyo's death.

"I have lost interest," answered Martin coldly. "I didn't know this would be very dangerous."

"Dangerous for the one underwater," Mando answered, "but you are in the banca. What should you fear?"

"Besides, I think we are just wasting our time." Ignoring Mando's remark, Martin shook his head.

"I'm sure we shall not fail," declared Mando.

For a long while, neither spoke, each one deep in his own thoughts.

"There are only two of us," Martin reminded Mando, after some time.

"The two of us can do the work of three."

"You mean, only two will divide the wealth," Martin wanted to make sure. "Is that it?"

Mando barely nodded his head.

The weather the next day was inviting. The wind was mild, and the sea was calm. The horizon was clear; as far as the eye could see, there was not a single sail.

Mando put on his diving gear. They pushed the banca to the water. Martin helped Mando fix the oxygen tank on his back.

When everything was set, Martin rowed past the bend of the former plateau.

Mando went in. One end of the rope was tied to his belt. He held a spear and from his waist hung a bolo. When his feet touched the sand, he looked around. There might be some dangerous monster. He saw none. He was fearless, but he had to be careful, especially now that he was alone.

He noticed the sea plants and the corals and thought that place was shaped like a hill, but after being swallowed by the ocean, it had been broken up by the waves. Large boulders were scattered around.

Slowly, he walked around, using the bolo to cut away the tangled undergrowth. After half an hour, he felt like yanking the rope and surfacing.

"Martin is probably right," he thought. "It's been a long time, more than half a century, maybe a century," he told himself. However, he remembered the faith of Tata Matyas. Their discovery of stone steps and this plateau, which appeared to have bent over the former ravine. He remembered Karyo's sacrifice, his hopes and plans.

"Ah, this is the place where it was thrown," he reassured himself. "So it must be here. Gold and gems do not melt at the bottom of the sea. I won't rest until I have found it."

And he went back and forth like a strange creature of a fantasy.

While Martin, reclining at one end of the banca, was getting impatient, especially with the intense heat of the sun.

Suddenly, Mando noticed something between a large stone and corals. He was attracted by the red color, different from the black stones and the whitish green corals. He nudged it with his foot, but it didn't budge. He looked closer and saw that the red was rust. It was a box with the greater portion buried in the sand, caught between the stone and the corals. His chest heaved and he felt his heart beating faster than the waves. Breathing was becoming harder. He had forgotten that he had been underwater for more than an hour. He jerked on the rope; Martin pulled him up.

"I shall rest a while, then dive again," he told Martin.

"Why?" Martin asked eagerly.

"I think this is it."

"Fortune…or false hopes?" Martin exclaimed mockingly. Mando kept his peace.

After resting, Mando dived again. The sun was at its peak, but Martin did not mind. He was almost tempted to put on Karyo's diving gear now that he had heard the good news.

An hour passed before Martin felt a pull at the ropes. It seemed heavier. Then Mando's visor appeared above the water. He quickly climbed into the banca and helped Martin in pulling the rope. He tied the rope around the iron chest after loosening it from the stone. The two easily brought it up to the banca.

The two didn't feel hungry, although it was almost two o'clock in the afternoon. They ate little, but Martin was very agitated.

"Tomorrow is ours," Mando said and went near the iron chest. "Let's open it and see if this is it."

The chest was shaped like a valise with a handle of first-class steel. Even though it was rusty from lying for a long time in the sand and salt water, it had remained intact and appeared watertight. Near the handle, still legible were engraved figures stating that the chest was made in England in the early nineteenth century. Also engraved above were large letters: SIMOUN.

The lid had to be pried open, for there was no key and the keyhole was rusty. They removed the rust until the iron shone again. Then they inserted the point of a bolo through a slit under the lid. At first, it would not budge. They kept at it and inserted a thicker part of the bolo, pounded it with a stone, and kept wedging it. They could hear the grating of the bolo as it rubbed against the iron. Suddenly, the lid gave way and opened.

They removed the glass that was sitting on top. Suddenly, exposed before them, were the fabulous jewels of the *Fili*. It seemed that such wealth could exist only in dreams, as if the genie of Aladdin's lamp had gathered them from the famous jewelry shops of Paris, London, India, Egypt, and Arabia and offered them in this part of the forest of the Sierra Madre. Truly admirable, astonishing, awesome!

The iron chest had several partitions; each part contained the same kind of gems—rings, earrings, bracelets, necklaces in one container; loose stones, diamonds, emeralds, sapphires, pearls in the second container; watches, gold medals, crosses, brooches, cufflinks, purses in the third; old gold coins and rare relics in the fourth. They seemed countless and very hard to assess.

"The war is over for us," Martin exclaimed with joy. "What more do we need?"

"We have to plan, Martin."

"I know what I'll do. It's hard only if one has no money. Now that I'm rich, I'll enjoy myself. Who and what can I not buy?"

"Go slowly, friend," advised Mando. "After deciding what to do, we need to be very careful. There is the iron chest, filled with treasure. Should the Japs or a band come upon us, we're lost. They will surely take all; we'll be lucky if they don't cut off our heads."

Only then did Martin calm down, but he insisted on dividing the treasure. He planned to return to Manila at once. Finally, he was persuaded to wait till morning, for it was almost dark.

They hid the treasure under some bushes and retired early.

At midnight, Mando was awakened by a noise. He looked around; Martin was gone. Mando left the shelter and listened.

He didn't have long to wait. Suddenly, he saw a shadow moving away, carrying the iron chest. He ran after the figure and recognized Martin.

"Martin!" called Mando. His voice rang out like a bullet.

Martin stopped at once, put down the chest, and went back. When he was near, he lashed at Mando with a bolo. In the darkness, Mando felt the sharp edge of the bolo hit his left cheek. Mando clung to Martin, and they wrestled. It seemed that Mando was losing. He could feel the blood in his face. When Mando fell back, Martin was about to hit him with the bolo, but he swiftly bent his knees and kicked Martin with all his strength. Martin was hit full on the chin and was thrown back, hitting his head on a large rock.

When Mando was able to get up, he saw Martin slumped over and blood was gushing from a head wound. Mando tried to give him first aid, but before daybreak, his assailant had died. Martin paid dearly for his greed and treachery.

XI

The past few days had been eventful for Mando: his two companions died; an immense wealth fell into his hands. And on his face was left an ugly scar.

When he was struggling with Martin, he hardly noticed his wound, although the blood flowed on his mouth, lips, and neck. But when he saw Martin lying lifeless below the rocks, he suddenly felt faint. All at once he felt the sharp pain of his wound. The bleeding stopped but not the pain.

He took the iron chest where Martin left it and brought it to their shed. Then he covered Martin's corpse with some wide leaves.

Before sunrise, he buried Martin beside the grave where they had buried Karyo only four days before. He offered a short prayer for the two.

He had no mirror, but he could feel his face swelling. His eyes and head were aching, and his tongue was numb. His throat was parched although he was quite calm. After his nap, he felt very weak. His heart beat fast as if he had a nightmare.

Mando removed the temporary shelter, placed the iron chest in the banca, covering it with some equipment. Then he pushed the banca, got in, and started rowing. The banca was moving northward. He decided to go to Tata Matyas.

He still felt bad, but he could not afford to dilly-dally. Traveling by water, he expected to make the trip in one day. It would take two and a half days on foot.

The wind favored him. The sea was calm. But darkness caught up with Mando, and he was obliged to pull ashore. He ate a little and rested. For a half hour, he stretched on the dry sand and closed his eyes. His wound was throbbing with pain.

Then he continued rowing. He was aided by the soft glow of the new moon. Luckily, that part of the water was clear. He knew it was safe to sail even without light.

The whole night, the lone rower didn't stop. The rooster was crowing and the *kalaw*[1] was singing when Mando sighted, in the pale shadow of the night, the shoulder of the hill on which leaned Tata Matyas' hut. Although he could not see the hut, he had no doubt this was the place. Only then could he breathe easily.

He pulled the banca towards the sand where it would be safe from the waves. Carrying the iron chest, he climbed the stony path towards the hut.

It was very quiet; not even the sound of crickets disturbed the silence. He stood on the stone that served as a ladder and peeped inside. He went up without a sound. He could discern Tata Matyas sleeping alone. Mando didn't rouse him. Instead he slept outside with his hand on the iron chest, which he covered with some clothes. There was no one in the house except Tata Matyas.

Although he was very tired, he couldn't sleep. When Tata Matyas got up to fetch water, he saw Mando sitting in the kitchen. The young man greeted him.

"Good morning, Tata Matyas," he said. "It's Mando, sir." He spoke in a loud voice, knowing that in the half-light it would be easier to recognize his voice.

_____

1 kalaw—a bird

"*Aba,*[2] Mando!" The old man was surprised. "What brings you at this hour? When did you arrive? Why didn't you wake me up? Are you alone?" His host plied Mando with eager questions.

He struck a match and lighted the oil lamp of half a coconut shell. He went to Mando and looked at him slowly.

"What is that bandage on your face?" he asked. "Are you wounded? Where are your companions? Where have you been? What happened?"

When the old man stepped towards the door, he almost stumbled on the iron chest.

"What is this? Why didn't you bring it in?"

"I have so much to tell you," Mando began. "Many important things."

"You have not slept, probably," the old man cut in. "Go to sleep while I prepare breakfast. I'll wake you up when it's ready."

Mando let himself be persuaded to take a nap. He was strong, but the succession of shocking events could weaken an iron physique.

Mando took the iron chest inside, covered it with a pillow and lay on the spread-out mat.

Tata Matyas let him rest. When Mando was awakened, the table was set for lunch, not breakfast.

After the meal, Tata Matyas attended to the wound on the guerrilla's face. On removing the bandage, he exclaimed, "Jesus!" followed by an "Ouch!" from the wounded man.

"If it had been any higher, you would have lost your eye. You're lucky to be alive. Who the devil did this?" He asked as he dressed the wound.

Mando related his experiences up to the time Martin attacked him.

"That will cause a big, ugly scar," said Tata Matyas. "It will change your appearance. Even your own friends won't know you."

---

2 aba—an exclamation of protest or surprise

"That would be fine," Mando consoled himself.

Tata Matyas treated the wound with his own medicine gathered from the mountains and dressed it.

The two went inside and Mando continued his story. Then he pulled the iron chest and...

"This, Tatang, is Simoun's wealth." Tata Matyas rushed to him, grasping his two arms.

"At last," he said, clasping his hands.

Mando removed the rope around the chest and opened the lid. Tata Matyas uttered an exclamation. Mando gaped. Was this a tale or a dream?

Slowly, Mando spread a wide mat, and one by one he took out the gems from the first partition.

Tata Matyas held a few gems that had caught his attention. He looked intently and repeated what Simoun once said.

"Just like a medical kit, here is both life and death, healing and poison. With a handful of these gems, people in the Philippines could be drowned in tears."

"And these could also be used for their welfare," added Mando.

"True," agreed Tata Matyas. "That should be our concern. For if there is anything more precious than wealth, it is the idea of how to use it."

Tata Matyas took out a marvelous necklace the likes of which he had not seen. It was a half-moon and made of different gold pendants shaped like *anitos*,[3] in green and blue. At the center, between two outspread wings, was a vulture's head cut from a precious gem.

"This must be the famous collar of Cleopatra found in an Egyptian pyramid after two thousand years," said Tata Matyas, gazing at the collar.

"How much would this cost now?" Mando asked.

_____

3 anitos—spirits of ancestors

"No one can tell," said the old man. "Even during Simoun's time, its price could not be assessed. Only a rich government could afford it as a museum relic."

Mando's eyes widened. It occurred to him that it might not have been Cleopatra's beauty alone that captured Julius Caesar and Mark Anthony, the foremost warriors of their time. Most likely, this collar and other riches of Egypt helped ensnare their hearts. They were the first imperialists.

"Look at these earrings. How lovely!" said Mando.

The old man took the pair of earrings and after looking closely, said, "Yes, these are the earrings of Princess Lamballe."

He looked at another earring and…

"These were given by Marie Antoinette, the consort of Louis XVI of France, to one of her ladies-in-waiting before she was guillotined."

Mando was impressed, not only by the jewels, but also by the knowledge and memory of Tata Matyas. He knew the story of every jewel.

He picked up a large ring. "I think this was one of the rings of the senators and Roman nobles said to be found among the ruins of Carthage," he told Mando. "If you offer this to our lawmakers, they would vie for it, and they can afford it."

Then he noted a large thick gold ring with a seal. He tried it on, but the ring was still loose around his combined forefinger and middle finger.

"A giant first wore this," he guessed. "This was probably Sulla's ring, and this seal was used to stamp countless death sentences."

Then Mando brought out a handful of loose stones from the second partition. They looked like tiny stars and a rainbow shining in the light for the first time since they were long hidden at the bottom of the ocean. Besides the diamonds, there were emeralds from Peru and other Latin American mines; rubies, the pride of

India; sapphires from Ceylon; turquoise from Persia; and all shapes and colors of pearls from the Far Eastern seas.

"Those are antique diamonds and other gems," said Tata Matyas. "Gifts for queens and gems for the Virgin's image during processions."

"These…" Mando shook in his right hand three diamonds, not too big, but perfectly cut.

"Ah, those are probably the gems for which the Viceroy of India offered two thousand pounds sterling," Tata Matyas surmised. "Now these should cost a hundred thousand pesos."

Mando chose two gems that looked like twin blackbirds.

"Black diamonds!" exclaimed the old man. "Very large and very hard. Priceless and without equal."

He stared at the pink and emerald green diamonds. "For this green one, the rich Chinese Quiroga offered a thousand pesos, but Simoun considered it too cheap. Quiroga wanted to give it to a white woman, a Spanish-English lady, said to be a close friend of the Captain General."

Then from among the precious gems, Tata Matyas noticed a relic, a well-wrought gold medallion sprinkled with diamonds and emeralds. On one side was a figure of a fishing boat used by the Apostle Peter which Jesus once rode in. The two men stared.

"This is Maria Clara's medallion," said Tata Matyas after a while. "This was Captain Tiago's gift to his daughter on the feast day of San Diego. But on the same day, while Maria Clara was taking a stroll with her friends, she gave it as alms to a leper who couldn't make use of it. What he needed were food and medicine. The leper couldn't sell it, for no one wanted to touch anything he touched," related the revolutionary.

"That's right," said Mando, continuing the story. "The leper gave it to Basilio for treating him, who gave it to his sweetheart Huli, daughter of Cabesang Tales."

Mando looked again at the medallion, front and back. The gold had tarnished a little. He said, "This is the famed medallion.

Once Simoun offered to buy it from Cabesang Tales at any price or to trade any of his jewels for it. Huli's father refused. But one night, Tales left this medallion with Simoun in exchange for a gun which he took when he decided to join the outlaws. His land had been grabbed by the friars."

The two agreed that among Simoun's jewels, the medallion had one of the most colorful histories. It was not among the original jewels of Simoun (for it was not said that Captain Tiago had bought it from him). However, they did not try to fathom the symbolism of the medallion which is mentioned in the two novels of Rizal, and which passed through the hands of several important characters.

The young man returned the medallion. He was about to bring out the rest, but Tata Matyas stopped him.

"We have seen enough," he said. "Now we return them all to their container." He mused awhile, then asked Mando, "What do you plan to do with this wealth?"

"Tatang," said Mando, "that is the question I am asking you. This wealth is not mine."

"As I have said, how to use it is more important than the wealth itself," the old man recalled. "Fate decided, Mando, that this should be in your hands. It is yours, and yet, not yours. So, use it for good, and not in the way that brought Simoun misfortune. What did Father Florentino say? He prayed, 'If for a holy and noble cause, you will be needed, may God permit this after a century...' And you, Mando, are the chosen one."

"I am ready," Mando answered, just like a knight errant being blessed by his king. "I said this wealth is not mine, because I won't use this for myself."

XII

For almost a year, Manila was filled with all sorts of rumors. Some were shocking; others horrifying, but most filled the hearts of the Filipinos with joy.

It was almost the end of January 1945.

A guerrilla from Northern Luzon brought some news to Manila that the liberation force brought freedom in one hand, but in the other, carried fire and sword. Every place that was freed was first wounded.

Every town had a Japanese fort and every headquarters had to be destroyed. But in destroying forts, they could not spare private houses and citizens. Bullets brought swift death, but the names of the targets were not written on them.

According to the guerrilla, the threat to the city was most serious. The Americans would not stop as long as a building stood and one enemy was hiding, no matter who got hurt. This was what the white chief reportedly warned him about.

When the guerrilla asked what would happen to the citizens who could not leave the city, the officer answered that it was their duty to leave right away. When told that some could not leave because they had no place to go, and that the others could not leave their homes and property, unlike banana plants that can be uprooted and transferred abruptly, he answered that if they loved their houses and property more than their lives, they had only themselves to blame for what might happen.

The guerrilla verified the rumors. He had seen it with his own eyes. Before the Japanese would retreat, they would turn their ire on the others by burning the houses and slaughtering the people. Countless suffered.

Naturally, on one hand was great rejoicing over the news that every day the "liberation forces" (according to American propaganda) were coming nearer. There were no more obstacles except the bridges blown up by the Japanese and the felled trees placed across the roads. The enemy no longer fought back save for the snipers hiding on top of buildings and trees.

Every liberated place was assured of safety from Japanese atrocity and from hunger. They had hardly put up their headquarters when the liberation forces started distributing food, medicine, and clothes to the shabby populace. Many were skin and bones.

How the public rejoiced! It became customary to compare the meanness of the conquerors and the kindness of the liberators.

For two days in the first week of February, the B-29's of the U.S. ceaselessly bombed the remaining installations around Manila. Like giant hawks, they would appear from behind the clouds, flying in V formation—the Victory sign—dive swiftly above the target, then all together drop bombs which reverberated upon explosion, followed by the spread of fire.

Those two days became hell for the Japanese. Neither could they fight nor escape. But there is no hell without a corresponding heaven. It was bliss for the Filipinos who watched such an effective if hasty counteroffensive.

Before sunset on February 2, the University of Santo Tomas had been won. The American and other foreign prisoners were saved.

Hardly anyone in the city slept that night. Gleefully they watched the fire towards the north caused by bombs of liberation. With anxiety they watched the flames in the south caused by the enemy.

The whole city was shocked when dynamites exploded under the bridges spanning the Pasig River. The north was completely cut off from the south.

The next day, as the greater bulk of the victorious soldiers were entering Santa Cruz and Sampaloc, the remaining Japanese forces on the other side of the river intensified their slaughter of the helpless civilians. They showed no mercy on women, the aged, or the children.

For about a week, no one could cross the Pasig. The narrow ribbon of water that peacefully ebbed and flowed between Manila and Laguna Bay, now became like the frightful river in mythology that separated the land of the living from the land of the dead. With some anxiety, the north rejoiced, while the south wept.

The ferocity and the heartlessness of the Japanese soldiers during their three years of power in the Philippines were nothing compared to their atrocities during that week when defeat was certain. Burning, rape, killing. They spared no one. Even innocent babies, holy nuns, families, groups. They used fire, bayonets, bullets, grenades. From places in the south, Intramuros, Ermita, Malate, Paco, blood flowed into the Pasig and stained its waters.

That was a long week, but it finally ended. Every last straggler was killed in his hole in the concrete buildings—the Post Office, Congress, City Hall, but only after nameless atrocities against the lives and property of people who were not involved in the war.

In the end, the whole of Manila was free, but it was a freedom dearly bought.

The capital city was left a skeleton. Ruins and charcoal, posts that looked like burnt firewood, burnt aluminum, broken glass, potholed streets, fallen posts, and cut electric wires. In some streets lay corpses—of people and beasts, of Filipinos and Japanese.

According to reports, only two cities in the world suffered such horrible destruction. Warsaw in Europe and Manila in the

Far East. Not even Paris or London, Rome or Berlin, or Tokyo, the capital cities of the five countries that started World War II, suffered as much. They were merely scratched when compared to the complete destruction of Manila after its occupation by the Japanese and, three years later, its occupation by the Americans.

The ugly rumors at the end of January had come true. The Japanese would rape the city before leaving it. The American cannons would destroy every building which harbored even one Japanese soldier who refused to raise the white flag.

How sad that together with the death of many civilians and the destruction of monuments of culture and civilization, not a few noble Filipinos died. Teachers, doctors, scientists, writers, and leaders of a society caught in the crossfire, untimely deaths that were a far greater loss than monuments and buildings and other property that could be replaced someday.

But the nation had no time to grieve in the face of life's new challenge, which could be met only by strong resolve, hard work, and greater struggle. When the guns ceased, another struggle ensued, one that was no less intense or significant: the restoration of peace. Mistakes, neglect, indifference reversed the outcome of the war. The defeated reaped the fruit of victory, or the wheels of change were blocked despite untold sacrifice.

On the other hand, victory caused not only intoxication but insanity. Some felt that victory is sweet, but revenge is sweeter.

From all sides mushroomed quarters of so many guerrilla units. Formerly hidden and moving secretly, they suddenly came forth when the Japanese sentries were replaced by the American MPs.

The whole surrounding area was searched for Japanese. Like noisy bands hunting witches, if they could not find their original quarry, they would grab any suspicious-looking person.

Once an unfortunate Japanese fell into their hands. He knelt with upraised hands like a sheep about to be slaughtered; he was very scared. But each one hit or kicked him. No one heard or pitied his plea for mercy. While the rest swooped down on the captive, a guerrilla twisted his neck; another hit his mouth with an iron pipe. His teeth fell off like kernels from a corncob. He lost consciousness. Still another guerrilla got a dagger and cut off his ear. When he regained consciousness, he was forced to chew his ear. But how could he, when he had lost his teeth and the fresh wounds on his lips and gums were still spurting blood? He was then hit several times with the iron pipe. When he was dead, the corpse was flung into a dirty canal and the ear was tossed to a dog.

Two men reported as enemy spies were captured. Without any trial, the eyes of one were gouged out and the tongue of the other cut off. Then they were roped together back-to-back and tied to an anthill. Some spat on their faces; others stoned them while most gleefully watched their slow death.

Countless guerrillas were overcome by their thirst for blood and violence. They sought to better the beastliness of the foe. On the other hand, the nation showed profuse, unending gratitude to the GI liberators.

"Hello, Joe" was everyone's happy greeting.

The newcomers captured not only the Japanese but also the heart of the nation. Some threw fresh flowers; others offered drinks and fruits. Everywhere, they were followed by a long procession of children.

And the Filipino women, who had been hard to get and cold to the Japanese, except the handful who sold themselves for Mickey Mouse money, now became gracious to all. Everyone was deeply grateful.

In countless hearts blossomed the dream of going to America and tasting the famous "American way of life" through an American husband. A few obtained such desire, but many were left at the pier waving a handkerchief at a departing ship.

This attraction of the American soldier for the women did not go unobserved. Each man enjoyed the rewards of Allied victory. Ten years before the war, the Americans in the Philippines were content to mine the mountains and have a Bicolana from a cheap cabaret for his mistress. After World War II, when they were like magnets, the Americans combined their search for gold with wife-hunting among choice society belles and heiresses.

In July, the Philippines became independent. On August 10, 1945, after the first atomic bombs were dropped on Nagasaki and Hiroshima, the Imperial Japanese Army surrendered unconditionally to the Allies. The war was over. Peace was restored.

With the ringing of the church bells and the sound of the sirens, the nation rejoiced, believing that peace had returned. The common man rejoiced, thinking that peace would usher in a new life. The guerrillas rejoiced, thinking that they would receive recognition and the back pay, which had been promised repeatedly when their sacrifice was needed.

Weeks passed, months, years. Long gone were the pealing of the bells and the noise of the sirens, the sound of trumpets and fireworks, the shouts of "Mabuhay." But still, the public could see the unhealed wounds of the war, the ruins, charcoal, and ashes, the unemployed, the homeless, the lack of money, and high prices.

The Four Horsemen of the Apocalypse had departed, but they left behind four armies, equally dangerous and devastating: the army of the wounded, the army of beggars, the army of mountain bandits, and the army of town-bandits.

XIII

Faster than fire among nipa huts in summer spread the news of Manila's liberation. It was blown by the wind in all directions. The evacuees rushed back to the city and other centers of population. All roads led to the city and other places, which had been left in haste. Now they returned. All vehicles entering the boundaries of Manila were filled with passengers and baggage.

But in the few towns surrounding Kalayaan, no one bothered to return to the capital city, for they were not evacuation centers. Fighting the hated Japanese and capturing the despised collaborators kept the guerrillas and townsfolk busy during the war.

The guerrilla headquarters under Magat was transferred to the municipal building. They lowered and burned the Japanese flag, and raised, side by side, the American and Philippine flags, for the Filipinos had not yet won independence. A provisional government was formed.

Magat invited the public to a town gathering in the plaza and informed them of the latest war news. He gave instructions. Avoid vandalism, abuses, and looting; bring captive Japanese and Makapili spies to the town hall.

"Let's give them a chance," advised the guerrilla leader. "Let's show them that we understand justice."

Magat's instructions had the force of law. All citizens suspected of Japanese leanings were brought to the municipal building and placed under strict investigation. But those who deserved it, were released at once.

One afternoon, Magat's men brought a known leader of the Makapili from a town formerly held by the Japanese. He and his companions were placed in a cell in the municipal building.

"Give them food," ordered Magat. "And don't hurt them."

He allowed the captives to rest. The next day, he sent for the Makapili leader. Magat offered him a seat facing himself.

Magat looked closely at the collaborator. He was about fifty years old, dark, with some white hair, dressed poorly and barefoot. He was a bit pale and tired, but his countenance showed no fear.

"You are the Makapili head in the town of A," Magat began.

"Yes, I am, sir," was the prompt and firm answer. Magat was taken aback, for he had expected a denial.

"Therefore, you admit, mister...."

"Andres, sir."

"Therefore, Mr. Andres," continued Magat, "you admit that you were an enemy of our country?"

"No," answered Andres steadily.

"You admitted you are a Makapili leader, didn't you?" Magat pursued.

"That is true, sir."

"How can you deny being an enemy of our country?"

"The name Makapili, sir, comes from the words 'Makabayang Pilipino' (Nationalistic Filipinos)," Andres explained. "How can nationalistic Filipinos be enemies of the country?"

"A name often serves as a cover-up for the real nature or purpose of a movement," Magat remarked. "Hitler called Fascism 'National Socialism.' The Japanese justified conquest in the name of Asia's Co-Prosperity Sphere. Slogans are a part of propaganda. Not the name, but the deeds should be judged. You

Makapilis helped the Japs during the war, and that is treason to our nation," Magat stressed his last words.

Andres smiled bitterly. "Maybe we can be accused of treason against America, but not against our country," objected the Makapili.

"What's the difference?"

"Between heaven and earth," declared Andres. "Our country is not America, but the Philippines. American power was imposed on the Filipinos."

"But America is a democracy," argued Magat.

"A democracy in its own land and for its people," answered Magat, "but a colonizer in the Philippines."

"America saved us from Spanish oppression," reminded the guerrilla leader.

"And at the same time, crushed our republic," the Makapili almost shouted. "You have read our history."

"Would you deny the good done by America?" Magat asked with some heat.

"Ah, sir," sighed Andres, "we cannot close our eyes to the truth. Let us admit that white is white, and black is black…" He paused, looked steadily at Magat, and asked sternly, "Do you believe, sir, that a big power will go to a small nation to help it?"

Magat was taken aback and had to grope for an answer. Slowly, he changed his opinion of this man, a Makapili, whom he had regarded a fool for following the Japanese, a traitor, and an enemy of his native land. With Andres' reasoning, he was obviously neither a fool nor a traitor.

Magat chose his words. "The American administration in the Philippines is a cooperative effort of two nations under a peaceful regime. It aims to establish an independent republic. Unfortunately, we were attacked by the Japanese."

"Do you think we would be attacked if the Americans weren't here?"

"The Philippines is the only bridge in Japan's goals in the southwest Pacific, just like Indonesia and Australia," explained Magat. "The Axis started the war of expansion; Germany was to occupy Europe, Italy half of Africa, and Japan the rich lands of Asia, including China and India. So, whether the Americans were here or not, the islands would have been snatched like roasted corn."

"Perhaps we would have been left alone in peace," Andres said. "It would have been better for Japan to be a friend to twenty million Filipinos rather than an enemy."

"That would not be likely," argued Magat. "Japan attacked and grabbed a portion of China even before World War II."

"Don't forget," Andres pointed out, "that China had already been cut up by the white race before Tokyo butted in. We have to admit that Japan had greater cause, in the face of what was happening. It had to get a share of the vast Chinese mainland because its small territory is not enough for its people."

Magat lit a cigarette and offered one to Andres.

The other declined. "I have no vice," he said.

"You have a rare intelligence," Magat noted. "What did you do before the war?"

"I was a barrio teacher," Andres confided. "I supplemented my little learning by reading books on history and sociology."

"Why did you become pro-Jap?"

"I am pro-Filipino, like most of the Makapilis," declared Andres. "We helped the Japanese because we wanted reform. The Japanese promised change. So did the Americans, true, but in fifty years, life in this poor country remained untouched."

"Are there not schools, hospitals, good roads?"

"In the cities, yes. But look around the provinces. Maybe you often go to the barrios. In the town is an old church and government buildings constructed during Spanish times. Two or three palatial houses of the rich families who practically own the town. In the barrio is a tiny chapel, a clump of nipa huts. No electricity nor running water. No passable road. The rural folks use footpaths. Drinking water is fetched from the river where they bathe and wash dirty clothes."

Magat listened, fascinated. Andres continued.

"It may be said that God willed this situation, which is the lot of poor barrio folk," the former Makapili said sadly, "but we suffered from unequalled oppression before the war. You are the son of a farmer, so you must have seen the brutality of the constabulary in attacking barrios while hunting for brigands. They treated all barrio folks as accomplices of the outlaws. They would ransack every house, grab and hurt the innocent, destroy furniture, steal property, pigs, and chickens. It happened so often that it became obvious that the pretext of hunting for bandits was only an excuse for looting. Who will defend the unfortunate peasants if the supposed law enforcer is the leader of atrocities and crimes?"

"Therefore, you sided with the Japs," Magat concluded, "because you were dissatisfied with life under American power."

"Because of oppression that cries to heaven," Andres said harshly. "We, the little folks, have not tasted the so-called progress and prosperity, said to be the blessings of American democracy. They are only for hacienderos and their friends. We have remained in want, sickly, in debt, unable to send our children to school. Our families die without doctors or medicine. What do we owe a government, callous and blind to the suffering of the poor? Why should we sympathize and be one with a society that drinks wine while we drink our tears? The discontent of the oppressed is not their fault. This is the work of the opportunist, the greedy, the oppressors."

Magat noted that Andres's right fist was clenched as he recited the litany of abuses against the workers. The guerrilla leader raised his hand to show it was his turn to speak.

"The nation is not made up of a bunch of the opportunists you mentioned. The nation is all of us: you, we, and others. It is the duty of every good citizen to help the motherland in times of danger, like war. The Makapilis went to the other…"

"Good you mentioned that," remarked Andres. "True, our country includes all. On one hand, the country is divided into different parties, beliefs, and philosophies. The majority are workers, the poor. They make up eighty-five percent of the whole. If democracy is the government of the nation, as we believe, what is the life of the eighty-five percent? What and who are the fifteen percent? You will agree that such a government is not a democracy but a circle of *tayu-tayo* and *atin-atin*![1] Naturally, the families and followers of those in power ceaselessly help themselves to the bounty."

The Makapili leader had pressed his hand on top of a table nearby.

"For me," he stressed, "the opportunists should not be counted as part of the nation. They are enemies. Just as microbes and parasites should not be counted as part of a man's body." When Magat kept silent, Andres went on.

"But in times of danger, and when their own interests are at stake, those in power blow the horn and enjoin all to unite to help, to make sacrifices. Those who don't follow them because of past disappointments and loss of faith are branded traitors. But remember, Mr. Magat, now that the war is over, they and the rest of the country will go back to their old paths, like flood waters. The big shots will go back to power, the small fry to their littleness, and they will barely remember those like you who suffered…"

Magat pointed out that the country, when it had settled down, would have the last word.

"There are national elections," he said. "Everyone is free to vote and run. A bad government can be overthrown and should be."

"What you say sounds good to the ears." Andres smiled bitterly. "But in our elections, have you seen a candidate who did not

---

1 tayu-tayo, atin-atin-—just us, among ourselves

spend? Have you seen a rich candidate who did not buy leaders and votes? And how many use their right to vote? Of the twenty million citizens, we would be lucky if five million go to the polls."

"Then neither the party nor the candidate is to blame," countered Magat. "The one at fault is the nation and those whom you call 'small fry.' It is said that a country gets the government it deserves."

"The greater blame belongs to the leaders who want the people to remain ignorant and timid. For otherwise…"

"Has it not occurred to you that the leaders of the Makapilis are among what you call the fifteen percent?" Magat asked.

Andres gaped, then closed his eyes and placed his hand on his forehead. He seemed cornered by the guerrilla chief.

"We are aware that many of those who helped the Japanese are opportunists," he admitted. "They love no one but themselves. Just the same, we know that in supporting a good cause, not the leaders, but the members count."

"Your unity is good, but your approach is wrong," Magat insisted. "The aim of the Japanese is evil, so helping them cannot be good."

"Our only interest is our country," Andres argued. "In every period, from the Spanish to the American regime, we have seen uprisings. At first, they were called *colorums*—fanatics, bandits, killers. Later appeared the Tanggulan, followed by the Sakdal, and during the last war, Makapili and Hukbalahap.[2] All of them are poor, oppressed, and discontented. They are just like clay molded into cooking pots, stones, flower pots, and jars. The only difference lies in the leaders who guide them or in the hands that mold them."

"That's the trouble," Magat pointed out. "They are like a flock of meek sheep."

---

2 colorums…Hukbalahap—names of groups that revolted against the government

"If the sheep falls off a cliff, it is not the fault of the flock, but of the shepherd," argued Andres. "The poor crave for reform."

"Because of this belief, you sided with Japan and fought against the guerrillas who also came from the masses. Look at my face and hands." Magat raised his hands. "I am a farmer's son and I went to school through self-study."

"What we oppose is the return to the old ways," said the Makapili leader. "All our sacrifices are in vain if we should restore the prewar system. For if America wins, as he has, we will become captives of the imperialism of the dollar. But if Japan wins, we might also be slaves, but she has promised reforms awaited and needed by eighty-five percent of our country."

"Then you aren't happy about the end of the war, because Japan lost," Magat asked slowly.

"Magat, we had nothing to do with the outbreak of the war," answered Andres. "Like any peace-loving Filipino, we desire peace."

"Even if America won?"

"We hope that victors and losers, the victors especially, will learn their lesson from the war. May they learn to rectify their errors and their sins. Let justice prevail and avoid revenge. In truth," Andres added, looking in the distance, "the importance of history is not in remembering the events but in learning from them."

"That's how it should be," agreed Magat.

After their long fruitful meeting, Magat respected Andres. No matter how he looked at it, there seemed to be little difference between their principles and beliefs about many things. What a pity this unusual man should be a Makapili and not a guerrilla. Nevertheless, he told himself, even if Andres had chosen wrong, he was still much nobler than the Kalampang guerrillas.

Magat told Andres and his companions that they would be detained in a cell in the municipal building until it was ascertained that in their being Makapilis, they had not killed or ordered killing, burned, robbed, or committed other crimes against the people.

"There are many ways of serving the country," Andres declared. "All we want is justice."

Magat was silent. Then he called an aide to bring Andres back to his cell. As the collaborator leader walked away, the guerrilla leader told himself that justice would not mean punishment for the admirable Makapili.

XIV

When the Americans came, Don Segundo once more used his technique for winning friends. If he could succeed with the unapproachable Japanese, it would be easy with the friendly Americans, he thought.

However, he could not welcome them immediately, as he had planned. The guerrillas who were hunting for collaborators were harsh and unreasonable. So he hid for a while in the home of a close friend who managed to be in the good graces of both sides.

Don Segundo's friend approached the head of a guerrilla outfit that put up headquarters the day after Manila was regained.

Some of these guerrilla leaders were former USAFFE members who became collaborators after leaving Capas. But they could not pass up a good chance. So the dedicated collaborators became instant guerrillas. And who would gainsay that they were *genuwain*?[1] Did they not fight in Bataan? Weren't they in the *Death March*?[2] Weren't they imprisoned at Capas? Their working with the Japanese was a pretext, they explained. They agreed to accept important positions, not to help, but to spy and to sabotage.

---

1 genuwain—a corruption of "genuine" that became widely used during the Japanese occupation

2 Death March—an infamous event when prisoners of war were ordered to march from Bataan to Capas. Many died from fatigue, hunger, and illness.

Gathered in this guerrilla unit were many birds of the same feather. It was not a surprise that they would be recognized and that they would recognize other guerrillas after February 1945.

Don Segundo's friend had only to ask and immediately he got credentials. When Don Segundo came out of his temporary hideout, he was arm-in-arm with a high-ranking guerrilla who called him "Monty." In the pocket of his khaki shirt were his credentials with the rank of lieutenant colonel.

This friend and the guerrilla leader brought some American officers to the Montero residence. All misgivings of the Americans were completely erased when they saw the beauteous Dolly and the alluring Lilibeth.

Dolly was in red and Lilibeth was in mourning. Lilibeth's pilot husband was reportedly killed in Bataan.

Because of the warm reception of the rich landlord-business-man and the American belief in living in the present, they easily became friends.

Monty brought out his hoarded alcohol. And the officials who were always full but also ever thirsty got engrossed in drinking.

Montero bragged about a radio hidden in a secret panel in his room. He claimed he would listen every night via shortwave to news about the war.

"That's why I knew about the trend of the fight up to the end," he bragged.

And he poured Scotch into the glasses of the Americans.

His friend then related how he and the rich merchant had aided the guerrillas secretly. Food, clothes, medicine, money. "They got no receipts," he explained, "because receipts would give them away and lead to the capture of the guerrillas. During those times, your left hand should not know what the right hand was doing."

The guerrilla leader elaborated on the stories told by Monty and his friend. He began by describing his own hardships: from the uneven combat at Bataan to the Death March, then to Capas.

He conveniently forgot his record of collaboration but related his espionage activities and sabotage of the enemy.

"We have a complete roster of our members and our angels," he said, pointing to Don Segundo and his friend. "Have you kept your credentials, Monty?" he asked.

Smiling, Montero stood up, went to his room, and returned holding a card wrapped in cellophane.

"Now, I can frame this," he boasted.

The guerrilla leader took it and after a glance, passed it on to the officer beside him. "This is the credential of a genuine guerrilla," he said.

The officer looked, nodded his head, and remarked, "This was a passport to hell when the Japs were around, wasn't it?"

"You bet your life," promptly answered the "guerrilla" leader. "But had to take the risk."

He explained that not all the members of the underground knew each other, but anyone with credentials was respected and left undisturbed. Of course, they could not admit to the group that the credentials of Don Segundo Montero were bought two weeks after the liberation forces had entered Manila.

The guerrilla leader also related how he was tricked, threatened, and forced by the Japanese to help, more than once. His obstinacy almost ended in serious consequences for his family.

"But I always outwitted them," he said, crossing his fingers. "The Japs are a bunch of fools."

Swiftly, Don Segundo shed the scales of a confirmed pro-Japanese to become a fanatical pro-American. If one would believe his boasts, it would seem that his loyalty to the U.S. was greater than that of the USAFFE itself, for he never surrendered.

"What about the ladies?" asked an aging officer. "Weren't they molested by the brutes?" The eyes of the group turned to Dolly and Lilibeth.

"We always outsmarted the damned fools," promptly answered Lilibeth.

"I salute you," the American shook hands with her.

They talked gaily of different topics. The American praised the bravery of Filipinos such as Segundo Montero. The Pinoys admired and were grateful for the nobility of the Americans. They talked of the Filipinos' impatience over General MacArthur's promise, "I shall return." Well, better late than never. A few officers present seemed to smell a dead rat because MacArthur said "I." They resented the suggestion that he would save the Philippines single-handed.

The greatest attraction for a captain and a lieutenant were the two girls, Dolly and her friend Lilibeth. Their rivalry over poor Colonel Moto had not marred their friendship.

Both had grown lovelier. The wounds inflicted by unfortunate events on their hearts left no trace on their faces and figures which were lovely and fresh. They were certainly desirable, especially to men who had just come from the battlefield.

Their smiles and lively motions proved the saying that a stain on a woman's honor could be washed away by a bath. Looking at her, no one could tell that Lilibeth had borne a child while her husband was flirting with death in Bataan. No one would guess that Dolly had carried the seed of Moto, which died in her womb.

Lieutenant Whitey was crazy over Dolly while Captain Green fell hard after his first date with Lilibeth. After a few drinks, both seemed more drunk than the others.

Whitey was an electrician in an industrial firm in Chicago when he volunteered. He was going on twenty-three and still unattached. Dolly looked him over carefully.

Whitey cut an impressive figure, almost six feet tall, with reddish hair and light-blue eyes. His accent was that of an educated American raised in the city.

He had a pleasant, friendly smile. He spent his time talking to Dolly instead of joining the others in drinking.

Captain Green was a professional soldier. He had spent twelve of his thirty-four years in the U.S. Army, the last three in the Air Force.

He was five foot seven, strong, and with a good physique. His thin hair was brown. He had a becoming short moustache.

Green told Lilibeth that he was divorced. They had separated months before the war. Before he was sent to Southeast Asia, the former Mrs. Green was already using another name. They had no children.

Whitey told Dolly that he planned to go home as soon as he could. In fact, he was waiting for orders to go home. He was planning on taking a break before going back to his old job.

"But now that I have met you," he whispered to Dolly, "my plans will probably change."

Dolly was thrilled by his words. She raised her eyes to his face as if to ask about his plans.

"I shall ask for an extension of my assignment here, because…" He pressed Dolly's hand, which Dolly did not withdraw. They remained silent, aware of the quickening of each other's pulse.

"What is your hobby?" Whitey asked after a while.

"Oh," Dolly mused, "I forgot my hobbies when the Japs were here. I really enjoy swimming and dancing. But during the war, I only went to church. Those Japs! Not one could dance."

"Then, we'll get along fine. When can we go swimming?"

"It's up to you. You might be busy."

"Where do you prefer to swim – in a pool or at the beach?"

"Anywhere."

"Beautiful!"

Captain Green and Lilibeth got along well. Their conversation was similar to Whitey and Dolly's, although Lilibeth was more boastful.

"My father and my late husband were Americans, so I'm an American citizen, but I have not been to the States."

"Do you want to go there?" Green asked.

"If my husband were alive," Lilibeth sighed, "perhaps we would've gone. But now…"

"Will no one ever take your husband's place in your heart?" At the Captain's question, Lilibeth bowed her head.

"Lilibeth?" Green waited for her answer. The young widow raised her face and looked at him steadily.

"You have not answered my question," insisted the Captain. "Can anyone replace your pilot?" he asked again.

"Only time will tell," Lilibeth pretended to dodge the question.

"Perhaps I can take his place," Green said gently. "Anyway, I'm also a pilot."

Lilibeth brushed aside her coyness. "What I want," she said without a blush, "is not a pilot nor a captain nor a general. All I want is a man who will love me as much as my late husband."

"Then you don't have to search for long."

"Oh?" Her question was a challenge.

Like duelists, they fenced with double-talk, but they understood each other. Green said he had cigarettes in the jeep's locker. Would she go with him to get them?

They went down together, and he helped her get in.

"I have never tried riding in this," said the mestiza.

The captain took two cartons of cigarettes and handed them to Lilibeth. When their hands touched, the American pressed her arm. Green drew her close and kissed her lips. She didn't protest nor draw away.

"What's on your mind?" Lilibeth asked when they finally drew apart.

"I love you, honey," Green whispered. Then he embraced and showered her with kisses. He was like a merciless gamecock that had cornered its foe. Lilibeth closed her eyes in complete abandon and moaned.

The following days, the two pairs were frequently seen passing happy hours on the beaches near Baclaran in the morning and later, in the nightclubs. They would swim or go boating, drink and dance the whole night.

One morning, Whitey and Dolly left Manila in a jeep. The Lieutenant asked permission from Doña Julia to take Dolly to a whole day gathering at Nichols Field. He also invited Doña Julia, but she declined. She knew that a chaperone was not included in the plans of young American men.

Actually, the two were not going to Nichols. They had agreed the day before to go to a place where they could be alone.

"Even for a day," begged Whitey. Dolly nodded and smiled.

They passed Las Piñas, turned left at the crossroad in Zapote, straight along the long savannah to Biñan, stopped at a refreshment parlor in Calamba. They went to Pansol, but seeing the place full, they proceeded to Los Baños.

Los Baños was one of the first towns in southern Luzon recovered by the liberation forces. A group of Americans and other foreigners were imprisoned here during the occupation. The town's good swimming places were hardly damaged. After the war, two or three rest houses were built and served as hotels for vacationists.

Whitey took a secluded room with a private swimming pool. It was ten in the morning and very hot. From the window, they could see the bronze-colored bay on the left and the green Mount Makiling on the right.

"Now we're here, and the world is ours," said Whitey as he drew Dolly towards the sofa. In one part of the room was a wide bed, which seemed to beckon.

Dolly sat on her lover's lap, and he kissed her.

"Happy, darling?" Whitey asked as he stroked her breasts.

Dolly said she was happy but tired from the one-and-a-half-hour trip. "Let's swim in the pool," she said.

They changed. Whitey removed his khaki shirt and pants, leaving nothing but his "fatigue" shorts. His chest was hairy.

Dolly had a pink robe over her bikini. Her swelling breasts over-flowed her bra.

The private pool was below their room and could be reached by a secret ladder. It was five by three meters, and the water was waist-deep. The water was warm and clear; one could see the bottom covered with tiny white stones.

Whitey went in first and helped Dolly down the stone steps. They tested the water, got themselves wet, and swam slowly. Then he dived and grabbed her thigh. Dolly wriggled free, dashed water at Whitey, and he did the same. As they gaily laughed, they embraced tightly like a pair of wrestlers.

"You're crushing me," Dolly complained. Without letting her go, Whitey kissed her. Suddenly, Dolly's bra was removed and over her breasts were the hands of the American. Dolly shivered.

"Please don't, please don't," she pleaded, but soon her protests ceased. Whitey proved that he was not only a good pilot but was also used to the submarine.

Not long after, they were a veritable Adam and Eve, like twin fish playing, now chasing each other, now entwining their legs and arms, while around them, the bubbles floated.

It was high noon when they climbed out of the pool to their room. After changing, they went down to the dining room, and lunched on rice and seafood; a salad of young coconut meat, avocado, and tomatoes; and sweet *macapuno*[3] for dessert.

There were some guests at the other tables, but all were en-grossed in themselves. Their purpose in coming here was obvious.

After lunch, Dolly suggested that they go.

"It's a little too early and the road is an oven," objected Whitey. "Let's have a little nap."

"If you say so," she agreed.

As they lay together, Dolly reminded him that they might get home late.

---

3 macapuno—a glutinous type of coconut used for sweets

"Why worry when we're together?"

Dolly didn't answer. Her lips were sealed by her lover.

"I'll sleep like a dead log," he said, pressing her hand over the mattress. He closed his eyes, but his hands were busy. Twice, they repeated their sweet encounter in the warm water of the swimming pool. Now, it was more satisfying as their bodies melted together. The two fell asleep, drunk with love.

XV

After several months, Dolly and Doña Julia suddenly went to Hong Kong. Before leaving Manila, there was a great change in Dolly's appearance and disposition. She had lost weight and had blue rings under her eyes. Contrary to her natural inclination, she avoided gatherings. She tired of her favorite dishes and craved unripe fruit. She lost interest in swimming and dancing; instead she spent the day in bed.

It was Doña Julia who first noticed her daughter's unusual behavior. When she asked, Dolly was evasive.

"Nothing, Mama, nothing."

"Tell me the truth, *hija*," she coaxed gently. "I won't be angry, because I wish to help you."

"Ah, I am fed up." Dolly made a move to go but Doña Julia held her back.

"Hija, don't keep secrets from me," she advised. "I'm your mother, a woman like you."

"I'm tired of living." Tears welled in Dolly's eyes.

Through her mother's coaxing, Dolly admitted what Doña Julia had guessed.

"This has happened to many girls your age," she consoled her daughter, who flung herself into her mother's arms. She did not reproach Dolly. No one would notice any change in her voice when she spoke again.

"Before I got married, I, too, had a similar experience."

Dolly raised her head and their eyes met. Dolly's eyes were wondering, while Doña Julia's were slightly closed. She spoke as if she were at a confessional.

"Yes," she added, "your father was not my boyfriend. I was engaged to another," Doña Julia stated. She swallowed hard before going on.

"We had gone the whole way," she admitted. "But his parents sent him away to finish his studies."

"And Papa?"

"Your father was courting me, but I didn't care for him. Then, your father would bring goods to the province and exchange them with goods to be sold in Manila. My father liked him and made me marry him."

"Therefore, Mama, you didn't love Papa?"

"Not at first. But time heals all wounds. Your father is good. I learned to love him. If I hadn't, would you have been born?" Doña Julia stressed her last words.

"And your first boyfriend?"

"He finished his studies, got married, and is now a provincial governor."

"Is it Governor Doblado, Papa's friend?"

"None other," admitted Doña Julia. "He is a governor but your father is a millionaire."

They were silent for some time.

"Does Papa know?"

"He knows that Osky was my boyfriend. But he does not know that we had gone that far," confided Doña Julia. "And why should he know? In the first place, that was not during his time. Second, I don't want him to think less of me."

"That is your good fortune," Dolly said softly.

"You see," answered Doña Julia, "you have to believe in luck. I told you my story so you can see how fate works. What is not meant to be, won't be. Moto was not fated for you. Neither was Whitey. Why make yourself crazy over it? Are they the only men? You are young, beautiful, and rich. You won't lack suitors. You cannot lack suitors."

Dolly felt relieved. She feared the ire of her parents, although they were more to blame, especially Don Segundo. But seeing that her mother was not angry and was even consoling her, she felt better.

"Look at Minnie," said Doña Julia. Minnie was a prominent society figure and was never absent from gatherings at Malacañan, Manila Hotel, and other plush places. "She's old enough to be your mother," she added, "but she acts as if she were your age. And really, she doesn't seem to age. Actually, she has shed her skin several times. Before the war, she was the mistress of an American; afterwards, she got attached to a Spaniard; then, she lived with a Japanese officer during the war. Now, she has an American lover and a sugar daddy at the same time. See how much more popular she is now and still beautiful, always in the papers, on trips, in society."

And Doña Julia mentioned other well-known names.

"I don't envy such women, Ma," Dolly protested.

"I don't say you envy or imitate them," explained her mother. "I'm citing their example only to show that you should not think this is the end of the world."

This woman talk happened two months after Whitey left for Iwo Jima. This sudden departure was his army head officer's answer to his request for an extension of his stay in Manila. Hurriedly, he bade Dolly goodbye. He was afraid to be sent to Tokyo for a long stint, because the U.S. forces had so much to do as a result of Japan's surrender. Everyone from MacArthur down to the last soldier was to stay long in the Empire of the Rising Sun.

Whitey promised to return to Manila but couldn't say when.

He vowed he would not forget his promise to marry Dolly but could not say when either; he was a soldier. It was not for him to decide, Whitey explained.

Dolly grieved. What could she do but wait? But her condition could not wait. Then her mother noticed. No doubt her father would too. Right now, he was always busy with his business and was seldom at home between breakfast and supper.

Even before her talk with her mother, Dolly told herself that this was not her first disappointment. Colonel Moto was still a fresh memory, but he was dead. Besides, even then, she considered that affair merely a way to pass the boring period.

But with Whitey, Dolly did not plan to take a chance or while away the hours. Whatever losses she suffered with Moto, she planned to recoup with Lieutenant Whitey, with interest. Moto was Japanese. What Filipina would be serious about a non-Christian, even with his prominent position? Whitey was American, a member of the liberation army who came to Manila at a time when every American was deemed an angel descended straight from seventh heaven. Followed by public adulation, even though his conversation was limited to wine, canned goods, and comics.

Dolly gambled for high stakes, confident of a sure win. Only a few women of her race could have the good fortune of being desired by a white man with a high rank and a bright future. However…

Doña Julia and Dolly didn't let anyone know the real reason for their Hong Kong trip. It was a vacation. Doña Julia was not afraid of Don Segundo because she could throw his guilt in his face. But Doña Julia did not want to upset her husband with women's affairs. If this should be revealed, Don Segundo would possibly explode like cogon set on fire.

And neither did Doña Julia tell Dolly at first what she had planned. But in their talks, she gradually prepared her daughter to accept her plan.

They occupied adjoining rooms in an expensive hotel. Back then, only a few Manila residents made regular trips to Hong

Kong. The Philippine peso was stable, and the dollar was not too costly. Smuggled coins and jewels had not yet made their way onto Hong Kong's black market. Neither had the greedy wives of high government officials. For a few days, the two women toured well-known places in Hong Kong and Kowloon, ate at popular eateries, bought clothes and souvenirs, crossed the ferry to Macao, returned by train to the New Territories.

Once, Dolly was too sick to get up. Doña Julia made inquiries and obtained the address of a Portuguese doctor, a known specialist for women. His name was even known in Manila!

The next day, the two went to his clinic. The Doctor examined Dolly and confirmed that she was pregnant.

He said that something could still be done. He could perform an effective and safe operation and guaranteed secrecy. His clinic did not keep records of such uses of his expertise.

Doña Julia bit her lips when she learned the fee, but she had to accede because of Dolly's predicament. She promised to return as soon as possible.

At first, Dolly protested. She raged and cried. She had sinned in the eyes of men; she did not wish to sin in the eyes of God. Doña Julia argued that it was no sin, for this was a mere seed, incomplete and shapeless, more likely to whither than to grow, and should it live, it would probably be stunted because of her feelings. Doña Julia reminded her of the ensuing scandal, the stain on the family honor, the shame and handicaps for her future. On the other hand, an abortion would be easy; nothing would change, she would keep her figure; she would appear unblemished, and she would continue to be wooed. Not even Don Segundo would know.

Dolly was finally persuaded. Whitey did not know of her condition. Besides, she was neither the first nor the last angel to burn her wings. Why should she bear the burden of their sin alone? What right had she to bring a fatherless baby into the world?

For two days, Dolly stayed in the clinic. On the third day, Doña Julia took her back to the hotel.

"You look the same as before," said the Doctor when they said goodbye.

Her mother helped Dolly in front of a large mirror in their dressing room.

"Look at yourself, you haven't changed a bit."

Dolly smiled bitterly and shook her head. "Mama," she said, "what you don't see in my face is imprinted on my soul." She felt very weak.

"You'll get over it, now that you are your old self." Doña Julia comforted her. "Believe me, time is the best healer."

Within a week, Dolly's ringing laughter was heard at a Hong Kong social.

XVI

The so-called liberation became like a noisy town fiesta in honor of a patron saint. Bands of musicians, fireworks, feasting in every house, rich or poor. But after the feast, what? Litter, disorder, debts, fatigue, ill feelings, and headaches.

There were more than four hundred little feasts in the Philippines. The rejoicing over liberation was added to such feasts.

The "bowlegs" were wiped out; the GI's returned. The drunken soldiers in the bases and streets did not lessen.

On the surface, peace had returned, for the noise of cannons and guns had stopped. But after the initial surge of order and contentment, the noise and turmoil had passed on to the minds and hearts of the people. The struggle continued unabated, not with weapons, but in civil rights and in making a living. And the opponents were no longer Americans and Filipinos against the Japanese, but the powerful against the weak, the real guerrillas against the fake, the capitalists against the laborers, the landlord against the tenant, the vendor against the buyer, the suffering people against the high cost of prime commodities.

After the war, the first step naturally was to restore conditions to normal. It was easy to erase the dividing line between the loyal and the disloyal, even though such a dividing line was written in blood. Once more would surface the old markers and signs of rights, of property, of the words "legitimate" and "legal."

Without warning, the landlords immediately got back their lands, which they had abandoned and left idle in times of trouble. They evicted and threatened those who had patiently tilled these lands and kept them from being swallowed up by the forests or the river. The owners made use of the so-called civilian guards, most of whom were Japanese collaborators. The guards were given arms and money to ensure the recovery and protection of the owners' property.

Naturally, these measures became the fuse of new disorder and strife. The farmers were mostly dedicated guerrillas, so that bad blood between them and the collaborators was inevitable. The latter were itching for revenge against the guerrillas who were tougher than the real soldiers. Both believed in "a tooth for a tooth."

Seemingly, the government was neutral, but because the rich had risen back to power, the balance was heavy on their side. Just as it was before the war, the weak were oppressed once more.

The pseudo-guerrillas were recognized and rewarded, while the real ones remained only on the rosters of their units, or were even removed, for failure to give bribes.

Naturally, their frustration worked like poison in their minds and hearts. They felt that the new dispensation did not aim to mete out justice to all, but to favor those whom they wished to.

During the first year of liberation, workers and employees were paid pre-war wages. All knew that the cost of living had multiplied four times. Prices spiralled, while funds were short. However, the scarcity of goods was not the chief cause of high prices, but the greed of the middleman who wanted to make a killing.

To protect themselves, the laborers began to form unions. Meanwhile, the farmers' groups were spreading. The laborer had not forgotten the lessons of the war. He felt that he should not always remain fodder for the cannon during times of peace.

He decided to demand his due, the rightful share of his labor.

He knew he would not get this if he was satisfied with grovelling. The union was his strength; if he learned to use it, it would bring justice. It would not turn the miserly master generous, but he would have to listen. In his hands rested his own emancipation.

From all sides could be heard protests and complaints against the greed of those who controlled the economy. Town meetings lambasted the sharks, mostly foreigners, who had come to the Philippines with nothing but a shirt and a pair of trousers. Unbelievably, at the end of a war that cost millions of Filipino lives, those foreigners became owners of factories and warehouses and made decisions regarding food and other prime commodities. What made them so influential with the government? Why were they always heeded by the leaders? Why were they able to go on sucking the nation's blood? And why was the nation like the Arab who was kicked out of his tent by the camel whom he had charitably sheltered from the cold wind?

Meanwhile, the country realized that politicians were not angels. Rather, they were a flock of birds of prey, not content to snatch and kill the living, but would feed on the corpses without mercy or horror. "What are we in power for?" was a common expression. While in power, why not feather one's nest?

Rizal's remark was once more proven: that what was long was extended and the short further shortened. Those at the top cared only about enriching themselves through graft and corruption.

Two contrasting views could be seen inside and outside Manila. On this side were the jobless and thousands of families in *barung-barongs*.[1] Children thin and dirty, mostly orphans of the prisoners of Fort Santiago or the casualties of Bataan. Women sick and emaciated, many of whom were mothers of these children.

Armies of guerrillas waiting for backpay for their services or any kind of job. Armies of the wounded with no hospital to admit

---

1 barung-barong—shanty

them nor medicine. The school-age youth with no school buildings to accommodate them without a politician's recommendation.

Infants with large heads and deformed bodies due to malnutrition. Because the lots meant for puericulture centers were occupied by plush gasoline stations. No milk for the children of the poor; plenty of gasoline for the cars of the rich.

On the other side, another picture could be seen.

As if by magic stood the grand palaces of steel; marble and crystal on lots, each of which could hold a hundred shanties of the starving poor. In every yard, surrounded by sturdy walls could be seen admirable gardens, a garage wide enough for half a dozen cars, a swimming pool as elegant as the private baths of the Roman nobles in the days of the Caesars.

In the modern palaces, the lucky residents basked happily day and night. Ten days a week. From the time they rose till they gave up the next day, hardly a break between breakfast, lunch, merienda, supper; dancing, mah-jongg, poker, bingo, and all sorts of gatherings for all sorts of reasons. Birthday, wedding, baptism, confirmation, wedding anniversary, despedida, *bienvenida*,[2] graduation, house blessing, fashion show, garden show, benefits of all kinds, contests to choose Miss Philippines, *Miss Pilipit,* or *Miss Pilit*,[3] often without any excuse except the desire to show off and for pleasure. They comprised the elite in the government, in business, in society.

The creatures in those two opposite scenes—in the barung-barong and in the palaces—seemed to have nothing in common. There was a great gap between them—blood, situation, and citizenship. But that is only on the surface.

Actually, many in the palaces were high government officials, capitalists, proprietors, businessmen, and their ilk. Needless to say,

---

2 bienvenida—welcome party

3 Miss Pilipit, or Miss Pilit—Miss Twisted or Miss Forced; a pun on Miss Philippines

in the barung-barong lived the humble employee, the laborer, the jobless. The former reached the top by stepping on those below. They enjoyed wealth and ease by denying the latter their just share.

Needless to say, there was no love nor understanding joining these two worlds created by post-war conditions—conditions which had existed for centuries. Abuse and insult, envy and hate. Like heaven and earth, they are linked together but are always apart.

One desires to keep the status quo; the other is impatient for drastic change.

When the public learned of the move for Philippine Independence on August 13, 1945, instead of July 4, 1946, a large gathering was held to support the move. Their resolution stated "Independence is the only solution to our problems. We should learn to swim—swim by ourselves and overcome life's waves."

But the leading politicians, the capitalists like Segundo Montero, vigorously opposed the move. They claimed that staying under the wings of America was the only guarantee of a stable future.

They asked: "Would we have been freed from the iron heel of Japan without America's power? Could we stay in the vast Pacific in the face of the great onslaught of communist Russia and Red China? How could the Philippines survive now that cities, ports, streets, buildings, railways, and communications are wrecked? Now that her fields are laid waste, her animals and farming gone? How can she get back on her feet again without leaning on U.S. support?

And they answered their own questions. "We need the care and protection of America. We have to build our cities and towns; repair roads, bridges, and ports; rebuild wrecked buildings; accept reparations—aid, money, and American expertise. We need new trucks and gasoline. We need new machinery, planes, tanks, guns, bullets, and know-how in modern warfare." Following their logic, we should not even desire to cut off Uncle Sam's apron strings.

"If we should have a plebiscite now," Don Segundo said loudly at a gathering, "the country will vote against independence," and he added, "unless the country is crazy."

"What the country needs is not independence but food," remarked a reporter. "The only meaning of freedom these days is freedom to starve."

"Hear! Hear!" agreed a few.

Independence would mean inevitable change, risk, sacrifice. Certain disappointment before victory, losing one's way before finding the right path. Those who were getting much didn't want this. Why should the fortunate still look for other fortunes? Why lie on the floor when there is a bed?

Thus, for some time after the war, the meaning and spirit of real liberation, the settled feeling of peace, and the joy of victory were denied to the majority. Everything was unsettled and in disarray.

Many asked if their sacrifice was not useless—the loss of lives, the bloodshed, the loss of youth. There was no answer.

Many more asked if the Filipinos—the molave and the stone who refused to surrender but fought with great courage—were among the victors. There was no clear answer either.

XVII

When Mando descended the Sierra Madre, he did not proceed to Manila. He went to Kalayaan to see Magat, the guerrilla chief. Although they had not yet met again, that one meeting had tied the bond between them.

Magat did not recognize Mando because of the large scar on his left cheek. But he had the same physique, although he had lost weight, the same eyes, mouth, and voice. The same grip and warmth of his handshake.

Magat searched Mando's face. "What happened to you, brod?" he asked with great concern.

Smiling, Mando embraced his friend and said, "Not all wounds are marks of misfortune."

Mando told Magat briefly of his experiences since their last meeting. He did not relate how Karyo and Martin died, only that they were slain and he barely escaped. He made up a story of an encounter with the Japanese a few days after leaving Kalayaan. Fortunately, he killed his Japanese opponent and escaped from the others who chased him. The wound on his face was from a bayonet. He related how he was nursed by an old man in a secluded place at the foot of the Sierra Madre.

He had gone afterwards to some places near the shore and met some evacuees from Manila. Mando mentioned Dr. Sabio, one of his former professors in college and a renowned Filipino scientist.

It was there that Mando heard the news about the surrender of the Japanese in the Manila area.

Magat told him of his own plans to return to Manila. "I have finished my mission here," said the guerrilla head of Kalayaan.

Mando inquired about Magat's plan. He confessed that there was nothing definite, but he would surely look for work.

"What was your job?"

"Copyreader and proofreader," answered Magat, laughing softly. "A lowly position, but I learned a lot. Imagine reading the whole day. Different topics. And I learned to write. Before the war, I was able to publish several articles in weeklies and I would have been promoted to style editor."

"Then," said Mando, "probably it won't be hard to change from proofreader to editor."

"Editor of what?"

"Of a newspaper."

Magat looked at Mando, wondering if he was joking, but Mando was serious.

"Some of my friends whom I met at the evacuation place are planning to start a newspaper in Manila. They also have proposals for education. They offered me the management of the newspaper, but I have no time. They asked me to look for trustworthy men who can help."

"I lack know-how," Magat said humbly. "That is a big leap from my former job. And that was in a printing press, not a real newspaper."

"That's the same thing," Mando reassured him. "What we need is not so much knowledge of topics as character, courage, honesty. Dr. Sabio and I agree that a newspaperman is different from a literary writer. Many can write well, but they are timid and easily scared by power or can be bought. And scared of the truth."

"If it were only leading guerrillas…" said Magat.

"Managing a newspaper and leading a fight are not too different," explained Mando. "I also lack experience. But the real mission of a newspaper is to reveal the truth, without fear or favor; therefore, what is needed is a newspaperman who can't be bullied or bought. As to experience, isn't that a part of daily work? Did you and I experience mountain life before we became guerrillas?"

"That's true."

"Get ready, then," said Mando. "We'll discuss this again in Manila."

"I will agree on one condition," Magat said, smiling.

"What?"

"That if I won't do as editor, you'll demote me to proofreader."

With a hearty laugh, the two shook hands.

"Why don't you come with me to Manila?" Mando invited.

Magat answered that he had to attend to some things in Kalayaan. They agreed to meet later.

Mando returned to the capital city after a three-year absence. Just as he could not be recognized by former acquaintances, so did he fail to recognize Manila under the heap of ruins and charcoal.

Mando spent a few days looking over various places north and south of the Pasig River. What he saw was far worse than the news that reached them in the mountains.

One morning, he went to the old Montero home in Singalong. Mando was amazed to see a large concrete house. With its surrounding walls and tall trees, it looked like a green isle in the midst of the black ruins left by fire and bullets. He thought, Don Segundo was not only clever but lucky as well. Almost all buildings nearby were razed, but the Montero house was left standing, hardly touched by fire or dented by steel. It looked like a proud boxer with his right hand raised above its sprawled opponent.

"*Weeds don't die*,[1]" he told himself.

As he wondered at this strange happening, he saw cars coming and going through the gate. Some were American military men and some looked like businessmen or gamblers who had won the grand prize in a lottery.

"The *operation of the saw*,[2]" he told himself.

For half an hour, Mando observed the vicinity unnoticed. He left after finding out what he wanted to know—that Don Segundo and his family were alive, that they still lived there, that the Don was richer than ever, that he was still close to those in power.

After a month, Mando got a printing press in Azcarraga. A two-story building with a press on the ground floor and the offices and copy room upstairs.

Mando rented a house in the suburbs. One day, he returned to the Sierra Madre and coaxed Tata Matyas to live with him in the city. At first, the old man refused, saying it would be hard at his age to change his way of life. Mando argued that he needed to consult the old man about his plan. Should they not work together to put to use the wealth and power, which came to him through Tata Matyas? No other living person knew Mando's secret, and the old revolutionary had no one but Mando. He had touched the right chord in Tata Matyas' heart and the old man finally agreed.

So Tata Matyas and a young orphan boy, their former courier at the seashore, came to live with Mando in a Manila suburb.

By then, Magat was in Manila. He brought Andres, the former Makapili leader. After a rigid investigation, it was proven that Andres did not commit any crime, for his aid to the Japanese was in cultural matters. Having committed no abuses, his hands were not stained with blood, nor was his name under a cloud.

---

1 Weeds don't die—Philippine proverb; rough equivalent of "Only the good die young"

2 operation of the saw—double-dealing, suggested by the forward-backward movement of a saw

Magat persuaded Andres to come, believing him to be a man of principle and ability. He wanted Andres to help in the work offered by Mando.

Mando had no objections. He had confidence in his friend's judgment and was satisfied with his brief talk with the former Makapili.

"I have no experience in this work," confessed Andres. "I plan to go back to teaching."

"Sometimes we give too much importance to experience," said Mando. "I think it is enough to have the ability and the desire to learn. Some of our experiences are modified by what we learn."

Magat knew a young man named Iman who had stopped schooling a year before graduation. He was very happy to accept the job offered by Magat.

Iman brought along Santillan, a newspaperman who served in a daily, which folded up during the Japanese occupation. He had gone home to the province, raised poultry and planted sweet potatoes and didn't use his pen. He would fetch his wife if he could have a permanent job in Manila. He was grateful for the chance to go back to newspaper work.

"Santi, why didn't you write during the Japanese times?" asked Magat.

"I preferred to live by selling eggs and sweet potatoes," he answered, "than to use my pen to weave lies. I have a son whom I'd like to become a writer someday."

"Once we start our paper, you won't have to sell eggs and sweet potatoes. Count on it," promised Magat.

"Thank you, sir. I'll tell my wife."

Mando invited the staff to dinner. The newsmen under Magat, the printers, and the employees were present. Mando left the talking to Magat.

"You already know that we shall publish a newspaper," Magat began. "Some progressives backing up our friend Mando will provide the capital. We shall put in our skills and effort. It will belong to us all. We shall receive a just pay, share in the profit, if any, but not in the losses. Probably, we will suffer losses at the start."

All laughed when he mentioned losses. They knew that in the history of journalism, none made a profit at once and countless more threw away money like water poured down a rat hole.

Magat continued.

"Our newspaper will be named *Kampilan* and will be published in Pilipino. We want to address the nation, and we should not use another language. The *Kampilan* will stand for truth, reason, and justice. This is our slogan and our pledge—truth, reason, justice."

"We shall have foes and friends. For sure, there will be more foes than friends." (More laughter.) "The time will come when those who tell the truth will be branded subversives, and there will also be times when defending reason and justice will be tantamount to rebellion. We shall not be scared or bullied."

"We will accept ads, but the advertisers will not be our masters. We will not become tools of any political party nor of the heads who run the government. Our only guide will be our honest view of truth and reason. We shall defend the freedom of every individual from group pressure and the dictatorship of the establishment. The beauty of democracy is not only the right of the majority to govern, but also the equal right of the minority to dissent. This is our principle; this is also our policy. If anyone is opposed, let us understand each other before our first issue."

No one raised his hand. Everyone agreed; everyone was ready. They happily raised a toast to the *Kampilan*.

Mando told Magat that he would ask him to run the newspaper. After a few weeks, Mando would travel abroad and be away for some years. He would go to Europe and then to the U.S. Nevertheless, he would get in touch by cable or overseas telephone.

Mando asked Magat not to divulge that the corporation had asked him to look for a good rotary press to replace the old one. Should they buy the adjoining lots, their present site would be good for a large building. There would be space for two or three newspapers and a radio and TV station.

"So we will fight big." Magat was awed by Mando's plans.

"How can we win the case for the nation, I mean truth and justice for the nation," Mando explained, "if we lack the courage and sincerity which we ask from our helpers?" He added, "Our weapons should be as efficient as the enemy's. Was this not our problem in the Sierra Madre?"

"I thought the war was over," Magat said with satisfaction, and he winked.

"It's just beginning," Mando laughed.

The following week, the newsboys were hawking the maiden issue of the *Kampilan*. A newspaper of eight pages, almost bare of ads, few pictures, no comics page, no news about socials and personal tidbits, but full of news and information not found in commercial newspapers and mouthpieces of vested interests.

When Mando gave Tata Matyas the first issue of the *Kampilan*, the old man almost snatched the copy, which still smelled of printer's ink. His face showed his eagerness as he read the headline news about prominent men involved in graft and corruption. Then he read the front-page editorial lashing at the threat to deny freedom of speech and assembly to groups that refuse to kneel before the administration.

"If Father Florentino could read this," Tata Matyas said enthusiastically, "he would feel that his prayers regarding Simoun's treasure were not in vain."

XVIII

Everywhere, intense heat pervaded the air. In the countryside and in the city. The heat was not only because of the season but also because of current problems, especially the cost of living.

In the fields, the situation was explosive in the face of the growing discontent of the farmers. The city laborers were also restless because of increasing unemployment. Those who had work lived from hand to mouth.

Soon after the war, Don Segundo Montero carried out his threat. He would restore everything in the hacienda to the old setup. He called for Pastor to carry out his orders. Start collecting old debts, deduct them from the shares of those *balasubas.*[1]

Pastor hesitated, pointing out that the tenants were even asking for better conditions. Expenses should be borne solely by the landlord, for this is part of capital and the harvest should be divided equally. Pastor also informed him of the tenants' claim that they had no more debts, for the amounts in Don Segundo's list were merely interest.

Montero raised his thick eyebrows. His nostrils flared like a bear who smelled gunpowder. The landlord got up from his seat. Pastor, who was standing before him, stepped back.

---

1 balasubas—derogatory word for those who refuse to pay their debts

"I said I will not put up with their shamelessness," he shouted. "I kept silent during the war. But now reason should prevail."

"They feel they are not getting a fair deal," explained Pastor.

"Because they wear their conscience in their ass," Montero exploded. He added an ultimatum: "Those who don't like my terms should leave. I would sooner have my land become a jungle than harbor those snakes."

Pastor said he could not carry out Don Segundo's wishes. He didn't want trouble if he could help it. Besides, he also believed the farmers deserved some relief.

Don Segundo turned on Pastor.

"On whose side are you?" he demanded fiercely.

"Mine or theirs? Well, if you can't do what I ask, it's up to you. You have one month."

Pastor left, feeling that the one-month period ended that same day. He was neither angry nor sad because of the effect on his own situation. He was more anxious about the possible effect on the peace at the hacienda.

He returned to the province at once. Puri was waiting.

"How was your trip, Tatang?" she greeted him.

"Not too good," he answered without enthusiasm.

While Puri was setting the table, Pastor told her what Don Segundo asked him to do. Puri told him that some tenants had come for an important purpose.

"When they learned that you were called by Don Segundo, they said they'd come back tonight."

"Who were they?"

"They were five, including Mang Tumas and Danoy."

Puri had just finished the dishes when they heard someone at the gate. Pastor met them.

"Come in, come in."

Inside, Pastor asked them to sit down and asked if they had finished supper.

"Yes, we have, *pareng,*[2]" Mang Tumas thanked him. He was the oldest of the group, a little older than Pastor. Danoy was the youngest. All were tenants of Don Segundo.

"We heard you went to Manila, pareng," said Mang Tumas as Puri entered. She had come in to greet the guests.

"Yes, pareng, Don Segundo called for me. Even if you had not come, I would have gone to see you."

Pastor informed them of the landlord's decision. Before they could speak, he added, "If he will wait for me to carry out his wishes, he'll wait till Judgment Day." Pastor's voice was firm.

"And if he tries to do it himself, he might hasten his Judgment Day," said Danoy.

"Let's not do it standing, if we can do it sitting down," advised one tenant.

"Whoever thought of that saying is not a friend of the downtrodden," objected Danoy. "That is the same as 'those who tread softly don't get hurt much' and 'count up to ten before raising your hand in anger.'"

Pastor ended the argument by informing them that Don Segundo had given him a month to carry out the orders and find out who did not agree.

"Even now we can tell you not even one agrees," Mang Tumas declared.

"That's what I thought," said Pastor. "But besides your refusal, what terms do you want? I know more or less about expenses and the harvest. But you have not told me what you have agreed on lately."

"Pareng," said Mang Tumas, "never have we considered you an outsider. You are a farmer like us, and perhaps our parents have the same story. This hacienda was a wilderness. Our ancestors cleared and cleaned it, our parents tilled and planted on it. And

---

2 pareng—a corruption of compadre, denoting relationship between the godfather and the parent of the godchild; used loosely to show camaraderie

we inherited this serfdom. Meanwhile, the owners of this land, from the friars down to Don Segundo, have profited endlessly. Only those who sweated blood remain poor. Now, is it too much to wish to be free from this oppression?"

"Then…" Pastor surmised.

"What we want, pareng, is not just land, but justice. It just happens that in the life of a farmer, land is the symbol of justice. You know that we have formed a union. Its aim is to ask the government to buy this hacienda and other agricultural lands and divide these among the farmers at cost. We will pay by installment with the harvest as collateral. If we have our own farmland, the fruit of our toil won't be snatched by those who live by extortion. Is it clear, pareng?"

"And if the government has no money?" asked Pastor.

"The government cannot lack funds," declared Mang Tumas. "In fact, it often throws away money on useless things. And the land need not be paid in cash. First, the land should be assessed. This will be the basis in computing annual earnings. And this amount will be paid to the landowner until the full amount is paid."

"In this case," Pastor observed, "you will still be tenants of the government, instead of the haciendero."

"At the start, until the land becomes ours," agreed Mang Tumas.

"Is that not the 'same dog with a new collar?'" asked the overseer.

"There is no similarity," the old man disagreed. "An individual owner like Don Segundo has no interest but profit. His concern for a tenant is just like a rig driver's for his horse. On the other hand, the government is concerned with the public welfare, the contentment of the majority. Even if the program that will bring that about will mean losing money."

"Your reasoning and proposal are good," agreed Pastor. "What I don't see is its fulfillment. First, Don Segundo will be sure to oppose it, unless he gets the price he wants. Second, the government is different from the heads of government. I mean, the voice of Don Segundo will have greater weight with the officials."

"We'll see," challenged Mang Tumas. "The sound of silver won't always be master. In a confrontation, silver can't win over iron."

"Pareng Tumas…"

"I don't mean anything wrong, pareng. If the little ones join hands, their voice will be louder than several Segundo Monteros."

Such heated air from the fields spread and was felt by laborers in the city.

Later, representatives gathered in different factories, business firms and offices and decided to form a federation. They published a resolution on just wages, hours of work and the relationship between capital and government, on the cost of living, houses, clothes, medicine, and other needs of every family. They complained about the miserable conditions of the jobless.

Iman of the newspaper *Kampilan* interviewed the union leader, Rubio. In his thirties, Rubio was well-built and well-dressed. He moved fast and spoke even faster. He could be mistaken for a member of the Lions or Jaycees, but Rubio was a real laborer; his hands and chest were thick; his skull, even thicker. Iman learned that Rubio never knew his parents. At seven years-old, he was selling newspapers and magazines in the streets of Manila. He lived with a supposed uncle who depended on Rubio's earnings.

Rubio grew up amid life's hard knocks. After his uncle's death, he worked as an office janitor at a low pay, with free meals and a chance to go to night school. After high school, he became an agent for a drug firm, but he became sick and had no money for medicine. For a long time, he roamed the streets, jobless. Then he became an "extra" in the movies, but his wages were not enough to pay the tailor for the suit he used. He joined different unions and different creeds until he became the bodyguard of a politician; the experience made him hate politics and politicians.

Iman laughed very hard listening to Rubio's experiences while they had coffee in a small restaurant.

"Oh, yes, I became a driver for a judge for a short time," Rubio continued. "This small-time judge was kind and honorable, and poor. During the war, I made and sold cigarettes. One day, I saw the judge without money even for the price of a cigarette. I gave him a few packs."

Rubio confided in Iman but asked him not to publish his being beaten by the Kempeitai as he was selling cigarettes at a market. His body was almost torn apart.

"Two spies reported me. I didn't know for what offense," said Rubio. "I was crippled by the Kempeitai; my face was swollen from their fists. But not one of the thousand onlookers could speak out. After a few days, I killed the two spies, went into hiding, and soon fled to the hills."

Rubio left his sickly wife in a safe place, but when he returned, she could not be found. Even the house where she stayed was not there.

Such colorful experiences completely opened Rubio's eyes especially when he joined the outlaws during the war. He realized that, alone, the common man is like a stone that is kicked around or swept by the tide. But when the stones are put together and joined by a meaningful cause, they become a post supporting large buildings or an impregnable fort.

"Like the jobless," he said. "For their own sakes and for the organization, it's a crime for them not to have a chance. They were educated, and trained; they have developed their skills, physically and mentally. Now they are like unused tools. The voice of two million will not be lost in the middle of the desert."

Iman agreed.

The laborite also explained why the cause of labor was right and should succeed.

"The fruit of the land is for all," he continued. "That is according to the Bible. But has this ever been realized? Is not the

Filipino worker up to this time still oppressed in the economy, in society, and in citizenship? Is there a laborer's wife who plays mah-jongg by day and stays in a club at night or who is not tied down to washing and ironing? Are children of laborers brought in a Cadillac to colleges and universities? Are there families of laborers living in palaces in Forbes Park? Do they spend monthly vacations in Baguio or go back and forth to Hong Kong and Tokyo or frequent New York and Paris?"

Rubio paused. Then jutting out his lower lip, he declared, "So, if in spite of these facts, the cause of the laborer loses, it won't be for lack of merit, but because of the outmoded rules of society and the cross-eyed vision of the judges."

One day, with Iman's help, the farmer's federation and the worker's union joined forces. Rubio, Mang Tumas, Danoy, and others of the same persuasion had a long conference. They realized that they had the same problem and the same foe. The problem was to fight social injustice and the tyrant who raised and tended and gave orders to this monster.

Some farmers recalled that during the war, their paths often crossed, for Rubio was a die-hard guerrilla.

Soon, the farmers and laborers both presented their petitions. The landlords, the businessmen, and the government were all shocked.

XIX

Mando's preparations for his trip went without a hitch. He informed only a few, including Magat, Tata Matyas, and Dr. Sabio.

As his right hand in the *Kampilan*, Magat was told that Mando would be gone for some time. In addition to his other plans, Mando was asked by the corporation to buy a modern rotary press. He assured Magat that the needs of the newspaper were taken care of. He had deposited a sum in the name of the paper. Magat could deposit and withdraw from these funds.

Tata Matyas knew the real reason for Mando's trip. They had discussed this fully for several nights.

They agreed that the jewels should be turned to cash as soon as possible. Storing it indefinitely would be like leaving it buried underwater. Some things cannot wait. To carry this out, funds were needed, and the best markets for old jewelry were outside the country.

Mando realized that, like a diamond, he needed more expert cutting. Indeed, he gained a solid foundation from his college education, wide readings, and war experience, but he still felt inadequate. Much more was needed, just as wood for a pillar should be cut only at the right time. He could make up for his shortcomings by traveling, by observing people, countries, events. If all of these could be gathered in one receptacle, they would give

Mando the experience, ability, and wisdom, which could count for more than all the wealth of Simoun.

Like ice, any amount of wealth could melt in the hands of one who doesn't know how to use it. The best plan will come to a bad end despite the noble aim of its proponents, unless they have know-how, vision, and good judgement.

"What you wish for is necessary," agreed Tata Matyas. "Of course, the problems are here and we know the illness and the cure. But, as I have said, it is best to consult doctors with more experience and to search for more effective medicine. Is this your feeling?"

"Yes, Tata Matyas," Mando answered. "We both realize that the wealth entrusted to our hands is not a privilege, but a great responsibility. That it is not for our personal welfare, but for the majority. How should we use this weapon? What should we do? How? These questions demand honest, intelligent answers. The right answers shall be our guide. Is that right, Tatang?"

"I am pleased with your analysis," the old man smiled. "Yesterday is the foundation of today, and today is the pillar of tomorrow. The spirit of our heroes who fell in the night should light the way for those who love their country in these times. The fruit of your efforts will strengthen those who will follow."

Mando consulted Dr. Sabio about their common plans like Freedom University, Hacienda Montero, and others. Mando had great esteem for his former teacher Dr. Sabio, for he was not only a lawyer, professor, sociologist, and *Filipinista*,[1] but he also continued to study and research on ancient history and current events in the Philippines and outside. Still, the professor had no knowledge of the source of Mando's wealth. He thought Mando was the heir of Tata Matyas.

Dr. Sabio had traveled to many lands. He had wide knowledge of solutions to land problems in the new republics in East-

---

1 Filipinista—a Filipino nationalist

ern Europe and the successful management of cooperatives in Scandinavia. While they were at the evacuation place, Dr. Sabio convinced Mando of the importance of knowledge. It was then that they discussed the establishment of Freedom University.

Mando remembered this conversation.

"What was the aim of Rizal and other noble heroes?" Dr. Sabio had asked. "To free our country from darkness. Our ancestors were enslaved by foreigners, not so much by physical force, but by blinding them. Do you remember Rizal's letter to the women of Malolos, which he wrote at the request of Marcelo H. del Pilar? At the same time, Bonifacio and Jacinto were trying to spread the Katipunan and they had a newspaper, which would transmit their message to the citizens. Ignorance is the mother of cowardice and slavery. Rizal most desired to open the eyes of the Filipinos, to see the truth, so that they would struggle to be free. As he said, 'There are no masters where there are no slaves.'"

"We can see that in this war," confirmed Mando. "Some grovel before the Japs, but the country remains free."

"Still, the most serious illness of our country is ignorance," declared Dr. Sabio, after agreeing with Mando's remark. "The Filipino believed that the foreigners who came here were liberators, although they robbed him; believed that life in this world is not the real life, for there is a heaven without end. Believing that he would enjoy that glory if he died suffering, which he equated with holiness, the Filipino endured more hardships than Job. He bought everything peddled by the cheats who placed chains around his neck and blindfolded his eyes and brains."

Mando commented, "Painful truths discussed by Rizal in his books."

"You sound like a Rizalist, Mando," Dr. Sabio complimented him.

"Like you and the other nationalists, I love our country."

"Good. Then you are aware of the bitter truth described by our courageous martyrs." As if reading passages from the *Fili* on Mando's face, he said, "Throughout centuries of slavery, the Filipino who before held high his brows and enjoyed freedom was now shorn of his identity and his culture and became a miserable nonentity. The Filipino forgot his old legends, his alphabet, songs, poems, laws, and customs. He memorized doctrines, prayers, and beliefs from far-off places, which he didn't even understand. He imitated foreign manners, ways, and wants which didn't fit his situation. He humbled himself completely and became contemptible in his own sight until he became ashamed of anything native, while he worshipped and adopted anything foreign."

Dr. Sabio stopped and looked into the distance. Mando remained silent, thinking of what he heard.

"We cannot hope to change and prosper," Dr. Sabio continued, "while these diseases are not attacked at their source. Expose the sick on the steps of the temple. The evil of those in power, the rottenness of their Filipino tools and the ignorance of the country as a whole, were all exposed by Rizal. He didn't stop at writing books and pamphlets. He took practical steps— organized Filipinos in Europe, established La Liga Filipina in Manila to bind patriotic intellectuals. When he was captured and exiled to Dapitan, the Liga became the flame of Bonifacio's Katipunan. Even in exile, he opened a school, taught, and set a good example. Neither place nor situation was an obstacle to Rizal in his work for the country's good. He provided a good example at every opportunity."

Mando admitted his great admiration for Rizal, but he felt that every hero belonged to his own time, and that the times and the situation created its own hero.

"It is true, Dr. Sabio," said Mando, "the wisdom and vision of Rizal can be used as a guiding light of the nation. But, certain conditions demand certain decisions and actions. This is true in war, as in rehabilitation and a new life. A passive attitude of the intellectual is sometimes an obstacle to the implementation of a program. This is where Bonifacio differs from them—in decisiveness and determination, in the lack of hesitation. Therefore,

Doctor, what our country needs after the war is a leadership that is not only given to thinking but to action."

"A combination of wisdom and action," agreed Dr. Sabio. "In short, a Rizal and a Bonifacio combined."

"Yes, sir, that's it," said Mando. "Of the millions of Filipinos, there has to be someone with the same qualities. Although, sad to say, in our so-called democracy and in the elections you have seen—for I was only a student and a houseboy then—it's not always the best man who wins."

"That's so, for in an election, the ones who vote are the majority," answered Dr. Sabio. "And among the many, only a few have principles. Many are guided by personal interest, by emotions, or by greed."

The two continued to discuss various problems. They agreed on Mando's need to travel. His itinerary was approved by the wise professor.

"May you return whole in body and mind," was Dr. Sabio's parting reminder.

"I solemnly promise," Mando answered, smiling.

"Good," Dr. Sabio said and gave Mando some instructions. He also prepared letters of introduction to his friends in different universities and cultural societies.

He explained the program of Freedom University.

"A new university is superfluous if it will become a diploma mill," he said, "or enrich the capitalists. We shall make it a forge to mold the nationalistic youth who will become useful in various fields. From them will come worthy leaders in the government, in society, in economics, in natural science, and in political science."

"In other words, you won't make education a business."

"Certainly not," was the professor's firm reply. "For half a century, we invested money, time, and the lives of the youth on the old educational system of America. What happened? The pro-liferation of unemployed professionals. Do you know that many teachers are peddling on sidewalks because there are no teaching jobs? How many lawyers are willing to be ordinary policemen and dentists, to work as messengers? How many took the civil service exams a year after the war in order to become clerks? Forty thousand! Is this the future of the youth? Oh, Mando, it would be many times better to have a nation of farmers and fishermen than a nation of clerks and messengers."

Mando told his adopted father about his talk with Dr. Sabio.

"It's only right that you should consult him before you go," said Tata Matyas. "It would be better if he could go with you."

"I have reasons for going alone," answered Mando. "Just think, Tatang. There are secrets known only to the two of us."

"That's true," agreed the old man. He added, "You will travel in other lands for the sake of your work here. When you return, remember how Ibarra, the hero of the *Noli*, returned after finishing his studies, full of hope and noble aims. But he was obliged to leave as a fugitive and traveled as one persecuted. When he came home again, he was already a Simoun who had no aim but revenge against those who killed his hopes."

Tata Matyas picked up a copy of the *Fili* from his side. Handing it to Mando, he asked him to read aloud Simoun's confession to Father Florentino before his death.

Mando read up to the part where Simoun expressed doubts about a God of Justice who had denied him help. Father Florentino answered, "Never will one who helped oppress a country be honored for its salvation. Hate will bear nothing but horror. Sin is a crime. Salvation means courage and sacrifice. And sacrifice is love…"

Mando closed the book and handed it to Tata Matyas.

"I expect you to return from your trip neither a Crisostomo Ibarra nor a Simoun," said the old man.

"I'm sure I shall return with the money from the jewels." And in a low voice he said, "And also with knowledge which money cannot buy."

"You will return as the fulfillment of Rizal's hope in the youth.

You won't be like the poet Isagani who was content with hope, nor the pitiful Basilio who aspired to nothing but a life of ease as a doctor, who closed his eyes to the evils around. Especially not an Attorney Pasta, a tool and accomplice of our country's foes who became rich from such schemes. Now, our so-called high society is full of Attorney Pastas." The old man sadly shook his head. "Oh, you will not return unfit for earth or heaven, a foreigner in his own land."

"A brown American," Mando laughed. Then he said seriously, "The Mando Plaridels and Matias Dipasupils become foreigners in their own land only when foreign masters and their Attorney Pastas and other hired tools prevail. But the country will not be fooled all the time." Then he added, "We shall not allow this, Tata Matyas. No! And it won't be long—two or three years. On my return, we shall do things, which would justify to Father Florentino our taking of the jewels from the bottom of the sea. And even Rizal would be proud."

Glancing at Tata Matyas, Mando noticed that the old man could hardly keep his eyes open.

XX

After breakfast, Mando and Magat left in a jeep for Hacienda Montero in Central Luzon.

The two agreed to look into the situation at the hacienda. They heard that after the war, the gulf widened between the owners and the tenants in large agricultural lands, especially at Hacienda Montero. The chief cause was the insistence of the landlord on going back to the pre-war policy on farming and leasing, and the tenants' demands for reforms.

Dr. Sabio had planned to join them, but he had to first attend to some business in Cabanatuan. Hacienda Montero was a forty-five minute ride from Cabanatuan, so he would join them later, perhaps after lunch. The learned professor had a wide background on the history of lands in Luzon and had made an intensive study of agrarian relations. Nonetheless, he wished to have a clearer picture of current conditions at Hacienda Montero. Freedom University planned to buy or manage said lands in Central Luzon.

The two friends discussed various angles and aspects of the agrarian problems. They were aware of the common claims of both sides.

"Everything has changed except our treatment by the haciendero," the farmers complain.

"The law is in force again," the landlords claim. "We should obey the law."

They also discussed the role of the *Kampilan* in the face of these complications. Mando observed that while it is true that newspapers should publish both sides of an issue, it is a greater duty to discuss and reveal the truth. This is the stand of those without fear or compromise.

"This is a period of excessive propaganda, an aftermath of war," Mando warned. "Let's not depend on the press release nor be carried away by radio chatter. Let us learn to sift the truth from propaganda."

For example, he cited a costly government office whose main job is spreading concocted news. He also mentioned a loudmouthed official who based decisions on newspaper and radio announcements and wasted his time in amusement places.

Mando told Magat of his wish to observe various parts of the Philippines, if only he didn't have to take this trip abroad. "This bad practice should be changed," he said. "We should first know our country and people before we travel to other lands."

"This inclination comes from our training," explained Magat. "As a conquered country, the first thing we learn is to look up to our master. We were made to believe that they came for our welfare. We were also made to believe that they bring and sell what is good for us. Their language, their commerce, their way of life, even their vices. The Filipino became a good ape, an expert in imitation. But the trouble was, we imitated the bad. Our women don't care to wear our native attire and prefer sheer material that hugs the body. The youth are drawn to leisure instead of work. The children don't want rice but bread; they don't care for native sweets but candy, not bananas but apples. That's what the teacher taught: 'An apple'...and did not clarify that the Americans eat apples because they don't have bananas. 'We have no bananas today.'"

Mando chuckled over Magat's colorful description.

"The slave mentality is deeply rooted in our countrymen," said Magat. "We have leaders who have made several trips abroad but have not visited Batanes nor the South. Everyone finishing medicine or law who has influence and funds flies away to America for 'specialization' That would be okay if their real aim were knowledge. But what hurts is the implication that their learning here is inadequate and poor."

"That is one of the things I discussed with Dr. Sabio at the evacuation site," Mando said. "He plans to make the first aim of Freedom University the awareness of life's truths. According to him, most universities aim to prepare a student for a definite profession and that is all. So that they fall into what George Santayana calls 'the barbarians of specialization.' Dr. Sabio's program has three bases: scientific—that is, to discard superstition and reactionary thinking; nationalistic—to place the welfare of the country and people first. For example, in teaching Philippine history we shall not say that Magellan discovered the islands, but that he was the first white man to come here. And finally, it will be for all, not for the rich few. More scholarships will be offered to the talented, but its doors will be closed to those with silver in their pockets but nothing in their heads."

"That will be a hard blow to the diploma mills."

"Definitely. Just imagine, the diploma mills bring in more profit than factories. It will also expose some exclusive colleges for the children of the elite."

Mando also spoke of Dr. Sabio's plans to teach high school students practical things. "Two food items of the Filipinos are rice and sugar. Yet, how many city folks know how rice is produced, the tilling of fields, sowing of seeds, transplanting the seedlings, harvesting, threshing, and milling? The same with sugar, from sugarcane that is planted, tended, cut in the fields, crushed by machines, boiled in vats, filtered, and refined before it is mixed with coffee or ginger tea and with various foods."

The jeep stopped at the foot of a temporary wooden bridge, the only way across a river. The old stone bridge which was blown by dynamite during the war had not been repaired. There were rows of trucks, jeeps, and some cars on both sides.

"Just like those vehicles," Magat pointed out. "They seem to be signs of progress; perhaps so. But while we have no factories for motor vehicles, no supply of gasoline of our own, these are a burden to the economy. Even before the war, we were the foremost Asian country importing cars and gasoline from America."

"A necessary evil," answered Mando lightly.

"I think what we need are more railroads for electric trains. Electricity can be supplied by our hydraulic plants the moment we harness the power of our rivers and falls. Such means of transportation is cheap and easy and needs no frequent replacing of parts. Motor vehicles, especially heavy trucks, are like demons destroying roads and wasting money. In Manila and suburbs, the streetcar should be restored and owned by the government or Filipino capitalists."

"That's a good idea, especially the street car," agreed Mando. "Publish an article on that in the *Kampilan*. It's high time we awakened Filipino leaders to industry and the use of our natural resources. We don't lack capital; it is just timid. We prefer usury or pawnshops, with a sure income rather than investing in fishing. We would rather build a cinema than a factory."

"If the Japanese had stayed long," Magat surmised, "many of our natural resources would surely be dug up."

"The Americans will do the same. That's why they insist on parity in mining and agriculture."

"The problem is," Magat said, "if foreigners dig up our mines, our wealth falls into their hands. We will in time be like Hawaii, Panama, and other banana republics. They have progressive industries, but the natives are still poor."

As their jeep passed the length of the bumpy road between Bulacan and Nueva Ecija, Mando said that it was not as dangerous to travel here as it was during the Japanese times. Then, there was horrifying news of robbery, kidnapping, and killing along the provincial roads.

"They have gone down from the towns. There, it's hard to tell the wolves from the sheep," joked Mando.

Magat doubted that there was no danger. "There will always be danger until the discontent of many is gone," Magat said. "Are we not on our way to the hacienda where there is unrest?"

"Banditry is different," blurted out Mando. Magat would not let that pass and slowed down.

"Different?" repeated Magat, stepping lightly on the gas. "You might say they are probably the offspring of one mother. Cabesang Tales was an honorable and industrious citizen named Telesforo Juan de Dios before he was robbed of his land. In the end, he became the fearsome bandit Matanglawin."

Mando understood his friend, but he kept silent. Magat's mention of Cabesang Tales reminded him of Simoun. Didn't he have Maria Clara's medallion, the storied jewel which she gave as alms to a leper, who gave it to Basilio for treating him and which Basilio gave Huli, Cabesang Tales' daughter, as token of his love? In the end, when Cabesang Tales stole Simoun's gun, the old man left the medallion as payment, although, only the night before, he had refused an offer of five hundred pesos or a trade for any piece from the jewelry chest of the Captain General's mysterious friend.

They were entering the hacienda when Mando was startled from his thoughts.

"This looks like it," he told Magat.

"This is it," agreed Magat, pointing to a wooden sign, which said "Hacienda Montero."

Mando remembered that during the war, some time in 1943, he went to some barrios near Hacienda Montero while on a mission. The places were not new to him, for he was born there. Even while serving the Monteros, he sometimes came along. He saw the poor condition of the hacienda and the clump of farmers' dwellings.

He inquired about his uncle and cousin. After learning that they were alive and well, he stifled his intense desire to see his late mother's only brother. This was against orders. The mission was a secret. He had to assess the enemy's situation at the hacienda and that of the townspeople and make a report right away. So Mando left the barrio the next day.

If he had given into his desire, he would have met his only cousin, who was growing into a lovely girl.

The hacienda covered almost two adjacent barrios in Central Luzon. The first town was made up of a clump of nipa huts clustered around a yard with an average-size house and a bodega. Here lived Pastor the overseer and his daughter Puri.

Mando and Magat noticed that only a small portion was cultivated. The rest was idle and full of talahib.

The silence was odd. Magat thought it was like the silence that reigned during the war before both sides started firing.

Mando wondered if he should tell his friend the other purpose of this trip. For him, this was more important. He wanted to see his uncle, Tata Pastor. He knew his uncle was a tenant. Mando had left Manila when Pastor was made overseer after the preceding one was kidnapped by outlaws.

Mando recalled that the last time he saw his uncle was during the wake for his mother. He was a teenager called Andoy. With Tata Pastor were his wife and daughter. His uncle wanted to take him to the province, but Don Segundo would not let him go. He said that in recognition of Andoy's parents' long service, he would send Andoy to school. In truth, Andoy was useful to the Monteros. He was Doña Julia's houseboy and the obedient menial in charge of Dolly's room.

Pastor gave in, thinking that his nephew would have a brighter future in that house where his parents had worked. In the fields, he would be a farmer all his life.

Mando couldn't remember seeing his uncle again. Even when Tata Pastor's wife Nana Hilda died, he didn't go, for Don Segundo didn't tell him of her death. When Pastor became overseer and brought rice and other food to Manila, Mando was a guerrilla in the Sierra Madre.

So, when Pastor inquired about his nephew, Don Segundo answered that he left suddenly and that he had been taken by the Kempeitai. He was supposed to be involved in some "deviltry." Of course, the Don didn't say that he had reported Andoy to the Japanese and that Andoy had escaped.

In the end, Mando decided not to tell Magat about his uncle, inasmuch as Magat didn't know other secrets of his past.

Magat stopped the jeep at the gate. They got off, approached the house and called out a greeting. With the second call, a young girl looked out of the window. Her thick hair hung loose as if she had just bathed. Magat secretly nudged Mando.

"Good morning," said the two men.

"Good morning to you," she answered.

"We would like to ask where we can find the overseer," asked Mando courteously.

"He lives here," said the girl. "Please wait." She came down and asked them in.

"Is he home?" Mando asked.

"If it's Tatang you want, he left for a while, but he's coming soon. Please sit down."

The two men sat on a long wooden bench. The living room was made of mixed materials and had no expensive furniture. There was a table at the center, two long benches near the opposite walls and three old chairs.

Mando and Magat barely noticed the surroundings. Like the eyes of a wild bird attracted by light, their eyes hardly left the girl. She was wearing a plain house dress, which seemed to enhance her beauty.

To Magat, she was a rare orchid hidden under the leaves of a vine in a forest. Mando thought of the immaculate pearls in the chest of Simoun.

"Such beauty, like a country flower," thought Magat as he looked at the dreamy eyes and the dimples on her light olive cheeks.

Mando remembered Dolly Montero. Even though he never liked her, Mando could not deny that she was very attractive, like a gaudy color or a heady fragrance. Like the sparkling champagne in a crystal goblet which one is tempted to take in one gulp. But this young girl was different, very alluring in her purity and modesty, not intoxicating but enchanting, just like a star peeping through the clouds.

Mando stood up and introduced himself and Magat. "I am Mando Plaridel and this is my friend Magat. We are newspapermen from Manila."

"Magat Dalisay, ma'am," added the guerrilla.

"I'm the daughter of Pastor, the overseer. I'm called Puri."

Mando started in surprise when he heard the names.

"If this is Pastor's daughter, she must be my cousin," he told himself. Once more he marveled at his cousin's beauty.

XXI

Magat was not at all impatient waiting for the overseer. So what if he was delayed, he told himself; he was enjoying himself looking at and talking to Puri.

Mando would have dragged the minutes along so Mang Pastor would come home at once. He was eager to know if this Pastor and this Puri were his uncle and cousin. They had not met for a long time, and he wanted to be sure.

Mando hesitated about what he should do, now that his original plan was changed after seeing Puri. On his way to the hacienda, he thought only of Tata Pastor. Now he felt that his first concern was Puri. Should he make himself known or should he keep his identity secret? What would result from immediate recognition but the usual joy of reunion among long-separated relatives? On the other hand, his secret might be exposed to the Monteros and others who considered him an enemy. Mando was still in doubt when Pastor arrived.

The two guests stood up respectfully and Puri told her father who they were. Mando tried to see in Pastor's face some resemblance to his mother.

"Sit down, sit down," Pastor welcomed them after learning their purpose. "Take these chairs." And he brought the old chairs nearer.

"This is fine," Magat declined and sat again on the bench. Mando did the same.

Pastor whispered to his daughter who then went to the kitchen. The father took one of the chairs.

Magat continued the short explanation by Puri. He said their aim was to learn firsthand of the happenings at the hacienda and to expose the oppression of the farmers.

"The problem of the workers is the problem of the nation," said Magat, "whether in the factory in the city or on the farm in the province. The worker sacrificed the most during the war. What is his reward during times of peace?"

Pastor nodded his head several times. Mando looked at Pastor. He could see signs that this man and his late mother were related.

"Good," said Pastor, "the tenants will be glad their case has caught attention in the city. The owner of this hacienda lives in the city. Perhaps you know him."

"He is well-known, sir," agreed Mando. "Is he not Segundo Montero?"

"None other." Pastor added a slight correction, "Don Segundo Montero."

"As I have said," Magat continued, "the case of the worker is important. Social justice is concerned with the workers and the well-being of the nation."

"You nailed it," Pastor said.

"That is the mission of good newspapers, sir," added Magat. "Other Manila newspapers reported that the disorder in the hacienda was started by troublemakers. That is also Montero's charge. We want to know the truth, so we came. For our paper, truth comes first."

"Perhaps I should not say this because I am the overseer," Pastor spoke gently. "You should hear the leaders of the farm. But, as you said, truth comes first. We cannot deny the oppression of the farmers, sir."

"That is your opinion," said Magat. "Have you not said this to the proprietor?"

"Ay, it's just like talking to the deaf," Pastor sighed. "How many times have I told him? Every time I go to Manila. And what do I get? Scolding and blame. The last time he threatened that if his orders were not carried out, he would get another overseer. It's up to him."

Pastor related how the strict overseer during the first months of the Japanese times had insisted on a one-sided arrangement. He stated bluntly that the harvest had to be increased because the Japanese needed it. "One night the outlaws came and the ferocious overseer vanished. I don't wish to be like him. I have a daughter…"

Mando and Magat glanced at Puri, who was standing in the doorway. The girl smiled.

Pastor went on.

"Might should end; right should prevail."

"Have the people sought the help of the government?" asked Mando.

"They are fed up," Pastor said. "First they went to the governor who told them to be patient. Seeing that they were stubborn, he promised to talk to Don Segundo. Up to now, no results."

"That is unfair," said Magat.

"Because the governor and Don Segundo are like that," Pastor entwined his two forefingers to show what he meant. "So…"

"So, the tenants have lost their patience," Magat concluded.

Pastor nodded.

Puri came in and whispered to her father.

"Well, friends," Pastor stood up. "Let's have lunch first."

Mando and Magat exchanged glances. They didn't realize it was noon.

"Aba, no thank you. we have to go," Mando declined.

"Thank you, sir, but we should not put you to any trouble," said Magat.

"No trouble." Pastor held Mando by the arm and moved towards the dining room. "But do you eat *sinigang*?[1]"

"You don't have to ask," Magat said. "We were both in the mountains during the war."

"Oh, guerrillas?"

"If that is still honorable, sir," Magat answered with restraint.

"Then consider this house yours," said Pastor.

The old man sat at the end of the table with the two on opposite sides. Puri stood by, ready to wait on them.

"Join us, daughter," Pastor said.

"Yes, please," urged Magat.

The girl first served them steaming rice, a cup each of sinigang with a slice of milkfish and sauce in saucers. At the center was a plate of *tapa*.[2] Puri also set glasses of water.

"I'm sorry we have no ice in the barrio," she said, smiling. Then she sat at the other end.

"Who is not from the barrio?" Magat remarked.

"If you are guerrillas," Pastor said, "perhaps you met my nephew, Andoy." He looked at his two visitors.

"Andoy?" Magat repeated. Trying to remember, he puckered his lips and stared at the tiny holes in the nipa roof.

Mando drank water. He felt very hot.

"He is about your age," Pastor continued. "When I last saw that boy, he was in his teens. The only child of my elder sister who took care of me. He was living in Manila with the owner of the hacienda. But he disappeared. There was news that he was taken by the Kempeitai. Some say he went to the mountains. We never saw each other again." Pastor sighed. "Poor boy."

He stopped. His sorrow over his nephew's fate was obvious.

"No, I have not met anyone named Andoy," Magat said. "How about you, Mando?" He turned to his friend.

---

1 sinigang—a dish with sour broth

2 tapa—dried beef

Mando pretended to reflect, felt his scar, then exclaimed, "Andoy! How could I forget Andoy? But we used to call him Andy. Tall and thin, but strong. Before the war, he was studying in college and lived with the family of Monte...Montero, that's it. That must be the same Don Segundo Montero."

"Is he alive?" asked Pastor eagerly.

"Alive and well when we last met," Mando assured him. "He left for Infanta before the Japanese attacked Sampitan in 1944. Those were dangerous times. So, when we parted, he left a box with me and asked me if I should go near the plains—for I was then assigned on secret missions here—to inquire about his uncle named...Castor. Oh, yes, Pastor. He had a daughter who should be a young woman by now... He asked me to give him that box."

"That's him," Pastor decided. "Do you recall your *Kuya*[3] Andoy, Puri?" he asked. She nodded, her lips slightly parted.

"I have the box," Mando said.

"What could it contain?" Pastor wondered.

"He didn't say, sir, and I have not opened it. I'll bring it soon," he promised.

"Maybe I should go to your place," Pastor offered. "It's too much trouble..."

"Don't worry," Mando said. "The truth is I have been remiss. I should have looked for you right away..." He looked at Puri's comely face. She looked away.

Magat stared at Mando, puzzled. What is this story about Andoy and a box? But he knew that Mando had secrets, which he knew only because Mando had told him, such as the scar that was not there when they first met.

---

3 Kuya—a title of respect for an older brother or male cousin

XXII

After lunch, Mang Tumas and Danoy came, the eldest and youngest leaders of the farmers.

"We were passing by when we saw the jeep," Mang Tumas said. "We thought there might be news about our petition."

"It's lucky you passed by," Pastor welcomed them. He introduced the two leaders to the guests from Manila.

"They want to have information about the real happenings and situation," he added.

"We really came to see you," affirmed the *Kampilan* editor.

Mang Tumas and Danoy were interested to learn that Mando and Magat were the publisher and editor of the paper, which was read by many in the agricultural regions. When they were seated around the table, Mang Tumas related the story of the present conflict at the hacienda. Danoy supplemented his explanation.

"We inherited this problem from our parents and Mr. Montero, from the former owners," said Mang Tumas.

"An old issue which was left hanging for many years, but with an easy solution if we want it—just one word: justice."

Magat pointed out that justice is often seen according to the color of the viewer's glasses.

"Real justice is not changed by the color of one's glasses," insisted Mang Tumas. "What is the basis of our petition?"

From his pocket, he got an old wallet and took out an envelope yellow with age. He brought out a newspaper clipping with hardly legible letters. It was a news item with a picture of Manuel Quezon, the first president of the Commonwealth.

"This is the basis of our petition." He handed the clipping to Mando.

"The late President Quezon was also a landowner; he had lands in Arayat," related Mang Tumas. "A few years before the war, he gathered his tenants and he voluntarily gave this charter. A bible of harmonious relationship on the farms. So I always carry it."

Mando handed the item to Magat who calmly read it.

"Please read it out loud," asked Mang Tumas. Magat read the following paragraphs:

> *Friends: The term Kasama (tenant), which is the Tagalog word for the tiller of the land, means sharer, and this title which we inherited from our ancestors gives the true spirit and meaning of the relationship between landowner and farmer.*
>
> *For in fact and in law, they are sharers. The landowner puts in his capital, which is the land; the tenant tills this and they share the harvest.*
>
> *At first, the tenant was not just a sharer, but he and his family were regarded as relatives.*
>
> *This is a human and profitable relation. However, as time passed, because of avarice and greed, the landlords took advantage of the tenant. The tenant was cheated of the fruit of his labor through various means; the most common was the high interest for his debts.*

Pastor commented, "Quezon had a deep understanding of history."

"He knew how to look back on the past," remarked Mang Tumas.

Magat continued his reading:

For many years we owned this land, but we did nothing. One reason why my wife and I wanted to own land was because we wanted to show by deed what we preached regarding the relation of the landlord to his tenant. Example is always better than words.

We will be real sharers; we shall give you work animals. You will pay for them on yearly installment, but those who are industrious in tilling the soul and caring for the carabaos will get back the amount they paid.

First, we shall erase your old debts. Those who have debts to the former owners have no accounts with us, although in the sale, these debts are included and transferred to us.

Any debts you might have with us in the future, like advance payment for your food, clothes, palay, and money, if repaid in palay will be according to current market prices. We shall not lend you for gambling needs.

Mando's laughter was contagious. "That is the pitfall of the poor—gambling," he said.

"The government should be blamed for the spread of gambling," declared Magat. "All big-time gambling is licensed: sweepstakes, horseracing, jai alai, cock-fighting."

"And *jueteng*,[1]" added Pastor.

"It is tolerated by officials who accept bribes," answered Magat. After a short exchange of opinion, he continued reading:

We shall give every family half a hectare of land which you can plant with vegetables or bananas or use for poultry and pig raising. We shall make improvements to increase the harvest, but you will not spend a centavo.

If you have any complaints, bring them to either Mrs. Quezon or me. And if we don't give you justice, you

---

1 jueteng—a game of chance

> *go to court. For like all citizens, we are under the power*
> *of the court if we commit injustice or break the law.*
>
> *Be industrious and work well. Consider the fields*
> *you till your own, for you can depend on this land as*
> *long as you wish and while you fulfill your responsi-*
> *bilities according to our agreement.*
>
> *Here you are free to become Communists, So-*
> *cialists, Popular Front, or anything. Even though I'm*
> *a Nationalist, you don't have to join my party or vote*
> *for its candidate.*
>
> *I shall do the best for you. Besides giving you what*
> *is according to law, I shall give you special rewards if*
> *you are industrious and selfless.*
>
> *But remember that no one who does not strive*
> *will get anything from me. No one has a right to live*
> *on another's sweat.*

"Hear that," Mang Tumas repeated, stressing each word, "'No one has a right to live on another's sweat.' Is that not lacking among the Segundo Monteros?"

"But he is a capitalist," Mando mocked.

"So, the product of our toil belongs to the capitalist?" challenged Mang Tumas.

"According to law, the landowner has a right…"

"To live on another's toil?" Mang Tumas sneered.

"To make a profit, too."

"Let's finish this," Magat read the last part.

> *We shall be real partners and sharers. What is good for*
> *you is good for me, and what is good for me is good*
> *for you. By means of this understanding, we shall be*
> *not merely partners but friends.*

"Truly, Quezon had no peer in his time," praised Pastor.

"If Quezon the landlord could do that before the war," Mang Tumas declared, "why can't other landlords do it now? It needs only a little consideration."

"There lies the difficulty—consideration," remarked Magat.

"Or fear," warned Danoy.

"What I like best is freedom in politics, that anyone is free to be a Nationalist or Communist," said Danoy.

At this point, they heard someone call out. Puri went to see who it was and returned at once.

"It's Dr. Sabio," she told them. "He is looking for you, Mr. Plaridel."

The professor followed Puri. Pastor and Mando stood up.

"Come in, Doctor," Pastor welcomed him.

"Doctor, I knew you'd come," Mando greeted him happily. He introduced him to the group as president of Freedom University, a learned and sincere sympathizer of tenants, who planned to buy Hacienda Montero, etc.

"What for?" quickly asked Mang Tumas regarding the plan to buy the hacienda.

"For the sake of farmers and the country," Mando answered promptly.

"We shall discuss that," added Dr. Sabio.

When everyone was seated, Magat told Dr. Sabio about their talk on the late President Quezon's agreement with his tenants in Arayat. Mando took the clipping from Magat and handed it to Dr. Sabio.

"I'm familiar with this," said the professor, glancing at the old clipping. "This is an example of a good haciendero," he added. "During his time and in the face of the anomalous system and practices of most landowners, Quezon's terms were good and just."

"They are really good," cut in Mang Tumas, who was so used to unfair treatment.

"But during these times, they are no longer ideal," objected Dr. Sabio. "Quezon's justice was based on paternalism. In spite of all his kindness as a father of a family, he was still the landowner and the tenant only shared in the hacienda. His capital was the land, which he bought for a fixed amount, while the investment of the tenants was their strength, their lives. But in the end, he got equal share with each tenant. If he had one hundred tenants, he would receive one hundred shares, while the tenant had nothing but a part of his labor."

"Nevertheless," Dr. Sabio added, "President Quezon himself said that in the struggle over right to life and right to property, the right to life should prevail. That was the basis of his program of social justice, although even now, in our courts, the right of property always wins."

The farmers were amazed at the logic of the president of Freedom University. He was really learned; they were convinced and ready to listen.

"The ideal or desirable land system at this time," continued Dr. Sabio, "is for the tiller of the land to be the owner, or he should have a greater share of the harvest. Not based on one or separate parcels, as is the common practice in our agricultural provinces, but by means of cooperatives. A cooperative is a kind of association owned by all who live and work on farms. The organization spends, but the harvest is for all the members, with equal shares and no landowner to monopolize it. The storehouse is the property of the association, which is made up of all the former tenants, not just one haciendero or his family."

"That has long been our dream," said Mang Tumas, "but we don't know how to carry it out. First, we don't have any right over the land; second, where would we get the capital?"

"That will be the role of Freedom University," replied Dr. Sabio. "The university will put in the capital. It will collect its capital, but little by little, and the tenants will hardly feel it. The cooperative will manage the hacienda."

The farmer leaders were for Dr. Sabio's plan and were ready to help carry it out.

"That is the only right solution," said Dr. Sabio, "not only in agriculture, but in large industries. Change the old system. Reap and produce to take care of everyone's needs, instead of to enrich a few."

"I think that is socialism," surmised Danoy.

"Yes, more or less," agreed the professor. "Socialism means ownership by the state of all means of production and of production itself, to be used for the good of the country. In the present situation, society is divided into two classes with conflicting interests. The first class lives and becomes rich from owning the means of production, like land, mines, factories, electricity, transportation, raw materials. This is the capitalist class. The second is the laboring class, which is used by the capitalists to serve them. In other words, the capitalist class buys labor at a cheap price; that is, the first buys the second, not for the whole of production, but only for the time he works. The profit is pocketed by the capitalist."

He added, "On the other hand, the laborer lives by his sweat. There are different types of laborers, but most use their arms or their brains. The condition of the intellectual laborer is a little better; they are also workers. They produce garments, houses, medicine, cars, radio, television, refrigerators, office papers, and more. But because this pay is not enough, they are always in need. Often, they can't buy or enjoy their products. For under capitalism, it's not the ones who work themselves to the bone who earn much and profit, but those who own more and don't sweat and live in luxury and ease."

"Just look at the Montero family," Pastor sighed.

"All the Segundo Monteros," corrected Dr. Sabio.

The learned educator cited some examples of the sudden wealth of the Segundo Monteros. He described the outright exploitation in factories and business firms, where laborers and employees work from ten to twelve hours, which is illegal, and are paid beggars' wages. The capitalists know that four to five hours of work of each laborer is enough to finish work equal to his pay; therefore, his production during the extra five to six hours is free and is the sole profit of the capitalist. If he has a hundred laborers, the capitalist gains no less than five hundred hours a day; therefore, he receives, for free, the production of one hundred laborers for five hundred hours.

Dr. Sabio explained that the small salary becomes even less, for the money has already been spent on basic needs.

"Money in itself has no value," said Dr. Sabio. "But it is important because it is used for buying the needs of the family. While prices of goods are high, as they are now, the value of money becomes less. Under socialism…"

Mang Tumas cut in, "But it is often said that socialism is a dream which cannot be realized, a…" Mang Tumas groped for the right word.

"Utopia," said Mando.

"Utopia?" asked Dr. Sabio with reproach. "Because they don't want change; they fear change. The leeches and fleas who live by sucking others' blood die when there is no more blood. The same with those who become rich and fat by exploiting their fellow men."

Uninterrupted, the professor went on. "Of course, we should not hope that socialism will cure all social problems and people's hardships. But without a doubt, it will lessen the intense suffering of many—unemployment, hunger, sickness, ignorance, super-stition, and crime. For excessive opportunism will be curtailed. Food, clothes, medicine, and other prime commodities will be for the people's use, not to make millions for the few.

"A five-to-ten year economic program will be implemented to regulate the production of many prime commodities. Thus, it will put a stop to anarchy, monopoly and cannibalism in industry in this system called free enterprise, where production is based on what will net more profit and not on what is more needed and useful to the public. For example, rice, fish, and meat, which are the food of the Filipinos. Why do we always have a shortage of these? In a socialist system, the needs of the citizenry will be given priority, instead of the selfish interest of the small clique of industrialists and businessmen. The real profit will not be the money hoarded in the moneybags of the greedy or the additional tools of production, but the comfort and prosperity of the consumer."

"Therefore, socialism is good," said the three farmer leaders.

Dr. Sabio had hardly caught his breath when Mang Tumas made another request.

"Please explain communism. We are often called communists and we don't know why. Is it communism to join a fraternity? To protect against the *cacique*?[2] To strike against a bad landowner? Is it communism to protest against the cruelty of the soldiers and the civilian guards? To vote contrary to the order of the haciendero and against their candidates? Dr. Sabio, we are often caught, jailed, or beaten up for these things, for they claim these are doings of communists and reds."

Dr. Sabio frowned, shook his head, and answered slowly. "Unfortunately, communism is misunderstood, not only by you, but by the soldiers and civilian guards hired by those in power. Ignorance is widespread and dangerous," the professor stressed the last. "What you are doing is not communism and you are not communists. These are rights guaranteed by our constitution and the laws of the land. These are inherent freedoms of people in a democracy, in a government said to be established for the good of the country. But you are threatened and force is used so you won't fight for your rights, so you can't obtain justice. They want labor to remain cowardly and ignorant."

"Then, what is communism?" persisted Mang Tumas.

Dr. Sabio looked around before speaking. "Well, the answer is probably known to our friends Mando and Magat. It should be made known to all labor leaders and laborers. The word communism is older than Christ, for in ancient Greece, there was a

---

2 cacique—Spanish word for a local political boss

class of communists who forbade private property. Just think, private property was illegal. But the modern Marxist communist is different. It was propounded by the philosopher Karl Marx in his book *Das Kapital*. Marx was a German who spent most of his life in England; his close collaborator, Frederick Engels, grew up in Manchester, so *Das Kapital* and their combined work the *Communist Manifesto* are based on social conditions in England before the Industrial Revolution. Thus, communism is not a Russian ideology; rather, the Union of Soviet Socialist Republics was a result of said ideology. Marx traced to its roots the source of capitalism, which is nothing but the accumulated profit from exploitation of labor. Marx complained that many learned men give too much importance to the world; for him, it is the world that should be changed. What resulted was a new kind of communism which is called scientific Marxism or revolutionary communism."

Dr. Sabio paused and asked, "Do you follow me?"

"It's very clear, Doctor," said Mang Tumas. Pastor and Danoy nodded.

"As I have said," continued the professor, "communism is revolutionary while socialism is somewhat evolutionary. The aim of the first is to wrest power from the society or the state by means of class struggle or by revolution. When it gains power, it will establish the dictatorship of the proletariat or the laboring class, based on the principle that being the majority, they create and produce all goods. Rich and poor classes will be abolished, capitalists and measly wages, in order to establish what you often hear—a classless society, whose goal is the equality of all."

The professor cleared his throat and looked at Mang Tumas.

"Before, this state was called a utopia or a dream, as you noted a while ago. But now, it is a reality. There is the Soviet Union, and we have heard of the People's Republic of China. Like twin world powers, they compare with the U.S. But it is misleading to compare the present strength of these two camps. For America, the most prosperous of the capitalist states, is at its peak, while the Soviet Union is just starting, crippled by two world wars. Hardly half a century has passed since the revolution against the Tsar's empire in 1917."

"What then is the difference between socialism and capitalism?" asked Pastor.

"Socialism has many forms. With the loss of people's belief in kings and when science proved that these kings are not sons of heaven, the republic appeared and a number raised the banner of socialism. There are still kings in Scandinavia, but their framework of government is socialist. Quite a few are called Christian Socialists. Socialism has also risen in Britain and is now prevailing in Indonesia, India, and some new African states after they got rid of colonialism and imperialism. But Britain and India have not gone far from utopian socialism. Their steps are slow and careful because the conservatives are still powerful. Some means of production have been bought and are run by the government, but most are the losing enterprises. The transfer of power is through democratic process, by election or expropriation. There is no plan to have a dictatorship of the proletariat."

"Sir, why are the Soviet Union and New China also called socialist states?" Danoy asked.

"Because both follow Marxist socialism or scientific socialism. Both are moving towards communism, which depends on revolution, the downfall of capitalism not only in one country, but everywhere. That is why, although there are similarities in policies on ownership of means of production, socialism and communism differ in methods and goals. Because of this, they are often close rivals, like India and China. At any rate, they have similar aims—to expect the citizen to give his best to the state and to receive from the state according to his need."

"Doctor, you mentioned revolution. Is that what we often hear—a peaceful or bloodless revolution?" Danoy asked in a puzzled tone.

"The term peaceful or bloodless revolution comes from re-
formers, who are also for the status quo. They think that illness
can be cured by palliatives. Give a dog more rations and it won't
bark. Loosen the prisoner's chains and he won't grab a knife.
Fools! How can bloodshed be avoided in a revolution, when the
very defenders of the status quo—the heads of the Establishment,
the capitalists, the landlords, the financiers and monopolists, those
aristocrats and parasites and their tools, the army, the police and
other armed forces—are the first to use force, the first to kill? Just
look at the strikes, the demonstrations, and picket lines; those
in power show excessive violence. Would they be calm during
a real revolution? A revolution has to be bloody, not because of
those who seek justice, but because of the cruelty, ferocity, and
cowardice of the enemies of change, of freedom and democracy."

"Therefore, sir, a peaceful revolution is an empty phrase?"

"A phrase of the turncoat politicians who are for both sides,
of priests who fear the hatred of the nation, but who don't fear
God, of the greedy who want to stop the march of time."

Mang Tumas, Danoy, and Pastor looked at each other and
reflected on Dr. Sabio's words, each one wondering whether the
professor was advocating revolution or merely stating an observation. Danoy broke the silence with an eager question.

"Then, Professor, do you feel that, because of the unfortunate
events after the war, one of which is the land problem, we can
not avoid this feared bloody revolution?"

Dr. Sabio hesitated, but after calm reflection, answered quietly.

"There are two inevitable laws, my friends," he said. "These
are evolution and revolution. Both mean change. Evolution is slow,
gradual, often unnoticed. Revolution is harsh and swift, sudden,
a big leap. A socialist revolution, which is surely what you have
in mind, is a definite change and a revolt of a class against the
opposing class. The aim of the revolution is to change, replace,
destroy the old framework and establish a more progressive and
satisfactory one. But to succeed, first it needs the complete frus-

tration and hopelessness of the majority in the existing conditions; and second, the weakness and ineffectiveness of the power to be replaced. This is called 'revolutionary situation.' When this situation is ascertained, then the hard blow of the struggle will take place. More or less, this was the situation in the Philippines when Bonifacio started the Revolution of 1896."

When Dr. Sabio paused, Pastor spoke.

"Let us go back to socialism. In your opinion, what is a good system of government for the Filipinos? Would socialism be right for us?"

Everyone's attention was on the president of Freedom University.

"A good question, and timely. But you, Pastor, Mang Tumas, and Danoy, should be the ones to answer it. For a long time, you have worked on the land under a landlord and you have much experience in the oppression of workers in their relations with the haciendero. It is the same with workers in factories, shops, mines, centrals, business firms. Long hours of work and meager wages. All profits go to the capitalists. I have explained that in socialism, all means of production are state-owned; the state is the whole nation and its government. In politics or installing heads of the country, there is also a big difference in comparison to the 'tayu-tayo-ism,' which is the termite in a democracy. In our democracy, all important government positions are monopolized by the powerful—Malacañan, Congress, the judiciary, and the army. Because money is powerful, as are mass media, which are all sorts of propaganda and other bourgeoisie influences."

He sighed and glanced at the others, who all seemed to agree.

"On one hand," Dr. Sabio stressed, "any system of government is not a definite cure or a panacea. Every country has its problems, different from others. We should always consider the conditions, customs, habits, education, culture, religion, population, especially the economy of the country and the people. At any rate, we can be sure that the kind of socialism which meets the conditions of our country will be a greater blessing than the promises of a democratic capitalism which is only for a small group. We can't deny that the unity of the Filipinos during the revolution against Spain and during the war against the United States has been torn apart between two opposing classes—the haves and the have-nots, those who count and those who don't."

They were so engrossed in the lecture that they didn't notice that it was almost dusk, until Puri came in with refreshments.

"I'm sure this can't compare with your discussion," she remarked as she served the guests.

"We shall have another talk," Mando said, ending the meeting.

"We learned a lot," Mang Tumas thanked Dr. Sabio.

After some more exchange of views, the three guests from Manila started to leave.

"We shall publish your side in the *Kampilan*," said Magat.

"Our side," corrected Pastor.

"Yes, our side," repeated Magat.

Mando went to Puri and thanked her. He held her hand for a long time as he said goodbye.

"I shall return soon," he said, "and bring your cousin's gift."

"It's up to you." Her lips were like twin rose petals as she smiled. Her gentle eyes revealed that she would be waiting.

XXIII

After a few days, Mando returned to the hacienda alone. He drove the jeep into the yard.

Before he got off, Pastor graciously met him.

"Good morning," greeted the overseer. "What has brought you?"

"I brought your nephew's package."

"Oh." And Pastor asked him to come in. He looked up the stairway and called his daughter.

"Puri," he said, "we have a guest." He turned to Mando. "I told you not to trouble yourself."

"It's no bother. Anyway, I have the jeep."

Upstairs, Puri knew who the guest was. She heard the sound of the jeep and looked out the window. She hurriedly fixed herself, changed her dress and powdered her face a little.

"Puri," again called her father.

"I'm coming, Tatang." And she went down. She shook hands with Mando.

"You are alone," she remarked.

"I didn't come for news; my trip is personal," answered Mando, smiling.

"He brought Andoy's package," Pastor told her.

On the table was a small box wrapped in newspapers. Mando got it and handed it to Pastor who turned it over to Puri. She held it, looked at it, and then returned it to her father.

"Why don't you open it?" Mando suggested. "I've had it for years."

Carefully, Pastor removed the wrapping, as if afraid to tear it. It was an ordinary old cardboard box. Pastor removed the cover. Inside was a small package wrapped in foil, the kind used for cigarettes. A folded note was attached to it by a rubber band. Pastor opened the note and read.

August 1944

Dear Tata Pastor,

> *Nanang told me before she died to regard you as my parent. Events have kept me from seeing you for a long time.*
> *Now I am with the guerrillas in the Sierra Madre. Only God knows the fate of one who defends his country.*
> *In my sleep I see Nanang and she says your name.*
> *I leave with my comrade Mando this small token for you and my cousin, who must be grown-up by now. He often goes to the plains, so I asked him to look for you. May this at least show that I think of you as Nanang had wished.*

Your nephew kisses your hand,
Andoy

After Pastor read the letter aloud, tears welled in his eyes. Puri was crying.

"Where could he be? Is he still alive?" he asked anxiously. Mando was silent.

Then Pastor opened the package. He and Puri were amazed. The package contained money—plenty of money. Twenty and ten peso bills with "Victory" stamped on them. As Pastor was counting, a small object fell on the floor. It was a ring. He picked it up.

Holding it with his thumb and forefinger, he showed it to Mando and Puri.

"A diamond ring," exclaimed Pastor.

He handed it to his daughter. Puri's eyes widened.

"Wear it," suggested Mando.

Puri appeared shy, so Mando took the ring and put it on her left middle finger. Puri wanted to draw back her hand but Mando held it firmly.

"There," he exclaimed, "it fits."

Feeling very uneasy, Puri immediately removed the ring, and blushing, she protested, "I don't want to wear it. People might think I have a sweetheart." She pouted timidly.

"Don't you?" asked Mando.

"No." The girl blushed harder.

Puri seemed embarrassed, but Mando was obviously pleased. After removing the ring, she handed it back to her father.

"Use it or keep it," said Pastor. "It is for you."

"It fits," added Mando.

Pastor finished counting the bills. A thousand. He glanced at the ring in Puri's hand.

"Where did Andoy get this money and that ring?" The joy in his eyes dimmed. "Weren't the guerrillas poor, with hardly any food?" he asked.

"Not after the submarines came," Mando explained. "The paper bills marked 'Victory' were brought by the Americans and given as advance payment to the guerrillas. The ring was given by a family whom Andoy saved from the cruelty of Japanese soldiers."

"I see." And Pastor's eyes brightened again. A slight smile appeared on Puri's lips.

"I wonder how much this ring cost," said Pastor.

"I heard Andoy say it cost ₱3,000."

"Good Lord! That's a fortune," explained Pastor.

"Then I really can't wear it, if it's that dear," said Puri.

"Why not?" asked Mando.

"People in the barrio might think I'm showing off. You know how people talk."

"As long as it's not stolen, there's nothing to fear," Pastor said.

"In Manila, the newly rich wear very large diamonds. Good if they became rich through good means." Mando was thinking of some who bought Simoun's jewels.

"Even then," Puri still refused. "A barrio girl's hand should not be covered in jewels, but should be used for work."

"The hands of one who works have more right to wear jewels," Mando remarked.

"And to hold money," Pastor added.

Finally, Puri agreed to keep the ring, because it was her cousin's gift, her cousin whose fate they were anxious about.

"What could have happened to that boy?" Pastor was worried. "Have you had any news since you parted?" Pastor asked Mando.

"None. I have a hunch that he is still alive," Mando answered. "He could have joined the U.S. Army during liberation. I would not be surprised if Andoy were among the guerrillas sent to America."

"May God bless that boy."

Mando told them of his plan to travel, perhaps the following week. "It's for the newspaper," he explained to Pastor.

"That is a long time," said Pastor when he learned Mando would be gone for two or three years.

"Travel is easy these days," said Mando. "One can reach any place in thirty-six hours. Wherever I am, I can come home at once if necessary. About the farmers' petition on the hacienda, even if I'm far away…"

"Many are feeling bad," Pastor admitted. "I'm not sure I'll stay as overseer. I'm offered a parcel of land at the barrio's edge. I might buy it with Andoy's money. Puri and I can stay there."

"That's a good plan. Besides the move of the farmer's federation, a Filipino corporation wants to buy the hacienda, the same corporation that owns Freedom University in Manila. Oh, yes, you have met Dr. Sabio. They plan to make a big laboratory of the hacienda, to improve the harvest and the condition of the farmers."

"Yes, I recall Dr. Sabio's plans," said Pastor.

"So, if the hacienda can be bought from Montero, they will implement a modern program. The former tenants will remain under favorable terms. Meanwhile, they will assign land and agriculture experts, and students to help the farmers. In short, as the students learn agriculture and sociology, they help improve the living conditions of the farmers. For, in the final analysis, more than agricultural land, the farmers need a just share of the fruits of their toil. Is that not so, sir?"

"Only the blind won't see that truth. Because the tenants of Don Segundo are fed up, many want to go to Mindanao if they can get homesteads. Or to try their fortune on the plantations in Hawaii or California. Wherever they can live in comfort, that's the place for them."

"Even Mindanao is owned by big landowners, mostly high government officials," said Mando. "During the past fifty years, many homesteaders went there, sweated blood clearing the forest and the mountains until they died from hardship and sickness. Later, their children learned that the land they and their parents cultivated for years was recorded in the name of persons with high positions. In the end, many were slain or jailed, for they refused to leave the land when they were being driven away by the law."

"Why does God allow such evil?" Pastor fumed.

"About the plan to go to Hawaii or California," Mando explained, "they should know that there is no shortage of labor there. The U.S. adjoins Mexico where they can get workers besides their fifteen million Negroes, in addition to the Chinese, Japanese, Cubans, Puerto Ricans, and other so-called inferior races. But the Filipino receives the lowest pay and poorest conditions of all the foreigners, which are still better than prevailing conditions in the Philippines. I think the Filipino farmer should not go to other lands, for wherever he goes, he will be enslaved by exploiters. He should stay here where he has invested much and fight for his rights."

"By nature, the Filipino farmer is accommodating and peaceful," Pastor said. "He wants to avoid quarrels whenever possible. But he is no coward. There is no farmer's house without a bolo for chopping wood. At times, this bolo is used to split the skull of the wicked."

When a shareholder came to see Pastor, Puri came in from the kitchen to be with Mando while her father was busy.

"Please stay for lunch, sir," Puri asked Mando. "Thank you for your trouble coming here, although you are busy."

"It's a pleasure. Here, I can breathe fresh air."

Puri glanced at her father and his guest at the doorway. She and Mando were seated at the table facing each other.

"During my travels, I shall write to you whenever I can, if it won't bother you."

"It might be a bother to you," retorted Puri, "to be wasting time on a nobody from the barrio. When you're there, it won't be likely that you will remember us."

"I won't say you think low of me," Mando reproached her, "for you have a noble heart. But if I did not forget your cousin's request after three years, although I had not met you, how can I forget you when I'm gone, now that I have promised it?"

"Because there are many pleasures there," Puri explained, "beautiful scenery, shows, lovely women."

"I will travel, not for pleasure or amusement," Mando assured her. "And regarding beautiful women, no one can hold a candle to you."

Puri stood up and was about to leave, but Mando held her hand. Pastor and his guest had their backs turned.

"Promise me," asked Mando, "that when I return, you will be the same Puri."

"Why should I promise?" she pretended not to understand.

"Because…" Just then, Mando heard Pastor call his name. The guest had gone.

So Mando said goodbye and would not be prevailed upon to stay for lunch.

"I shall write often," he addressed the two, but his eyes were on Puri.

"God be with you in your travels," Pastor said. "Let us know in case you meet my nephew."

"Count on it…" He said "Adios" and waved as his jeep left the yard.

XXIV

Mando Plaridel was traveling outside the Philippines for the first time. He ascended the steps to the airplane without looking back. There was no announcement about his leaving, so no one except Magat and Andres saw him off. He would travel alone. He brought some letters from Dr. Sabio. The professor had stayed long in Europe and America before World War II. Before takeoff, Mando fastened the leather seat belt across his chest as instructed. Just once, he peeped through the small, thick glass window and saw a group of people waving to the passengers. Magat and Andres stood apart from the crowd.

In two days, Mando would arrive on the other side of the world. The plane would make several stopovers on the Eastern Europe route. He would get off at Madrid.

Mando brought most of Simoun's jewels. The rest he left with Tata Matyas.

Mando had secret partitions made at the bottom of two large portable suitcases where he hid the jewels.

Even if the suitcases were examined, these would not be noticed, unless they were slashed. But this was not done, unless the traveler was under suspicion.

Mando had a twofold purpose for the trip: first, to sell the jewels at the best price; second, to study and observe. Mando wanted to enrich his knowledge and experience.

He realized he was young and had a lot to learn. He had a vast and ambitious program which fate placed in his hands. It was his duty to prepare for it; first he had to prepare himself. He had a lot of money, but money was only one of his tools. If he lacked preparation, strength, and vision, the money might even bring him ruin.

Among other things, he wanted to learn more about organizing a modern newspaper; low-cost printing, efficient and fast distribution. Also cheaper printing of worthwhile books, which Mando planned on his return.

He also wanted to observe new methods of husbandry and animal raising. How to shorten the time so there could be earlier gains.

He would learn about cooperatives. How the farmers could get and enjoy the fruit of their toil without being exploited. What he wanted was pragmatic, practical learning, and prevailing practices, not untried theories. He believed theory should be based on specific experience, not on opinions or surmises. Otherwise, a theory will remain only in the mind.

Some months before he left, Mando had quietly sold some jewels. From these, he had funds for his trip and the press.

He made inquiries about those who amassed wealth during the Japanese times and liberation. Those bloated ones hurriedly bought lands, houses, jewels almost wholesale.

One of those approached by Mando's agent was Doña Julia. Her mouth watered each time she looked at or touched the veritable garden of jewels. But her throat would go dry when she heard the prices. She bought for ₱10,000 only one ring with a gem as big as a cat's eye glaring in the dark.

A well-known society woman, one of those mentioned by Doña Julia to Dolly, wanted three diamonds, perfectly cut, but not too big. She could not let them go, just as she could not let go of a sugar baron, her lover. Especially when she learned that the Maharaja of India had offered twelve thousand pounds sterling. At the equivalent of even four dollars a pound, the rate of exchange after World War II, that would amount to ninety thousand Philippine pesos.

The woman was apparently fascinated by the identity of the first customer. She asked for a few days, for her sugar daddy was not in Manila. The next week, she learned that a famous foreign actress, a friend of a shipping magnate, was looking at the gems. The sugar daddy's mistress grew hot all over and told the agent to get them at once. She bought them for fifty thousand pesos.

Mando agreed to the price because of his immediate need.

A cabinet member bought a ring for seven thousand pesos.

"For his wife?" Mando asked his agent.

"For his secretary."

"So, the cabinet member is rich, hmm?"

"It's his wife who is rich, but she looks like a Japanese tank. Naturally, she doesn't know that the seven thousand is to buy a solitaire for his private secretary."

There was also a matron noted for her love of art, and her little experience as an actress—the wife of a millionaire collector of relics. She bought a ring of a former general of Alexander the Great. She paid ten thousand pesos for the ring, which was for a handsome army officer who had conquered her.

The matron and the gallant officer became close during several relief operations in rural areas after devastating floods and typhoons, according to the stories. The operations for charity became romantic operations. Both risked their names and positions and met in various places in Baguio, Tagaytay, Hong Kong. It created quite a scandal.

"The matron offers an excuse that her husband is a queer and not circumcised," said a gossip.

"Then, how come they have three children? Or is it four?"

"Aba, even queers have instruments—and how do we know who the real fathers are?"

"But, the officer is also married."

"You mean, he has a collection; a complete collection."

"Oh, these women. The moment the itch starts…"

"They'll die for their desires. But, *chica*, a woman goes wrong because of the man. If he knows how to hold the reins, the horse won't buck."

"Then, it's up to the jockey on the horse, ha?"

"On the rider and on the horse. They should match."

The two gossips laughed, noting where the talk about the ring had led.

Two other buyers were mentioned. The first was a senator who chose a bracelet with rubies alternating with emeralds. He gave it to a popular society matron. This woman, noted for her beauty in her prime, was the daughter of a low-ranking employee. She married a wealthy businessman, a semi-invalid, so that, like D.H. Lawrence's Lady Chatterly, she was thirsty while surrounded by water. And she fell for the Senator who was a real man. The bracelet bought by the Senator was only a token. The matron reciprocated with gifts double the price, also taken from Mando's jewels.

But the most unusual sale was that of a circle of five society matrons who bought wholesale a set consisting of a gold ring with five small diamonds, a man's bracelet, cuff links, a tiepin with five rubies. This does not seem extraordinary unless one knows the reason and the recipient.

The five matrons, in a reversal of the usual situation, took care of a gigolo. A young mestizo, tall and robust, with firm muscles and steady arms and knees. He had not finished his studies but could speak fluent Spanish and English. He did nothing but keep his physique in good condition. Also his mind and enthusiasm seven days a week.

He was supported by the five matrons whose ages ranged from forty to fifty. They paid for his apartment, bought him a secondhand car and in addition to household expenses, he received a net amount of five hundred pesos monthly.

His role was to sleep with and to give pleasure once a week in his apartment to each member of the circle. One was scheduled for a day from Monday to Friday with a special benefit on Saturdays, when each took turns. His Sundays were free; Sunday was for his real girlfriend, a sexy mestiza, none other than Lilibeth, Dolly's former friend who had an affair with Captain Green after liberation.

Like a jockey, he rode six different horses, seven days and nights, so he knew various ways of horse riding. Some were hot and eager, ready to gallop two miles, nonstop; some for a short time, but giving all their strength and fire like a dynamo. While he gave pleasure to the five in a replica of the Marquis de Sade's harem, he was made happy by his own client, Lilibeth, the whole day and night every Sunday in his apartment.

The husbands of the five were all rich and well-known, but just as man does not live by bread alone, woman is not made happy by money alone. Sex is needed now and then by a healthy woman, just as a plant needs water and sunlight.

Of the five, one or two had insatiable sexual appetites, and would seek other bed partners. If the mestizo were to be interviewed, he would have much to contribute about the likes, ways, and hunger of the daughters of Eve, just like Dr. Kinsey's survey.

This seemed natural to them, unnoticed by their husbands and social circles. In fact, they were always present at social gatherings like the frequent despedidas and bienvenidas. They always looked happy in group pictures which appeared in the society pages of the commercial newspapers.

"If the jewels on the persons of lovely women and handsome men could tell their stories," said Mando, "there would be a reenactment of Jehovah's anger against Sodom and Gomorrah."

"The stories of one thousand and one nights are nothing compared to this," answered the able agent.

Mando was able to sell other pieces to a number of big shots for about half a million pesos. While the poor majority complained about money, it was obvious that one reason for poverty was the control of wealth by a few.

XXV

Dolly's ordeal was soon over. The seed in her womb was secretly taken out and put away in a hospital room in Hong Kong. As her mother had said, this was a common occurrence to many well-known society girls in Manila and some Visayan cities, maidens only in name.

"You can count the virgins on your fingers," said Doña Julia, whose ears were keen on such gossip.

Dolly was whole again. After her "vacation," she wanted to return to Manila. Her health did not suffer and she felt good. Her looks suffered not even a scratch.

But Doña Julia would not allow it and persuaded Dolly to go to Europe and tour famous cities, then to stay in Paris to study fashion or interior decoration. Then to go home when their mansion was finished.

Dolly acceded; Doña Julia supposed that her heart had not yet healed as much as her figure, which had regained its freshness. Besides, her studying in Europe would erase any suspicion from their friends because of their sudden trip to Hong Kong.

So Dolly proceeded to Europe and Doña Julia returned alone to Manila. On her return, she told Don Segundo that Dolly would study in Paris. Dolly had written the same to her father.

"Why didn't you go with your daughter to Paris?" asked Don Segundo, who had no inkling of what happened in Hong Kong.

Doña Julia answered, kissing Don Segundo's cheek, that she was also thinking of her "papa" who was alone in Manila.

Those days, Montero was busy remodeling his palace in Singalong. He contracted a young architect, the Chinese mestizo Pong Tua-son, son of the businessman Son Tua, well-known in the Chinese community and to the authorities in Greater Manila.

Rumors said that Son Tua had arrived at a southern port wearing a pigtail. He came from Sungsong in a large crate of goods and was able to embark with the help of a port guard who was bribed by a Chinese old-timer. Son Tua served this Chinese until he became a young man. When his Chinese "owner" died, Son Tua came to Manila.

Son Tua had his start buying old furniture and was known as a junkman. After some years, he opened his own textile store.

He married a young, childless widow who had inherited some property from her first husband.

Son Tua quickly extended the widow's assets, sold the textile store, and started a gambling and opium den. In this business, he became close to high government officials in Manila and adjoining provinces.

The role he played during the war was not very clear, but it was rumored that he played ball with both the Americans and the Japanese. After the war, he was a millionaire, just like Don Segundo Montero.

Pong Tua-son was one of the many children of Son Tua and the widow. Pong easily made a name for himself, for his fees were lower than others, and he could easily get materials. The children reversed their father's name to Tua-son. Their rise in society was as fast as an escalator.

One of the Tua-son girls married a rising army officer, Major Bayoneta, who became a collaborator after coming from Capas and became a general two years after liberation. Another daughter married a prosecutor. As for Pong, it was said that in Dolly's presence, he always had sheep's eyes.

Don Segundo asked Pong to give his all in building his mansion on his old lot in Singalong. "The most beautiful house in the Philippines. That is what I want," Montero told Pong as he looked over the old house, which was still in good condition.

"As you wish, Don Segundo," said Pong. "More bonito than the Malacañan Palace."

Monty clucked with pleasure, and he declared that he would invite the papal representative to officiate at the house blessing unless the Philippines had their own cardinal. He would ask the President to be a sponsor so that they would become compadres.

"And your room, we'll make it more grand than the President's. And air conditioned."

"Of course."

"A bed worth ₱10,000?" asked the architect.

"Agreed," said Monty, "but regarding the bed, better ask Señora Montero. Ever since our wedding, she has always chosen the bed."

Pong nodded his head. "Well, the room of Doña Julia will be more elegant than the First Lady's."

"Excellent, Pong, excellent."

"And Señorita Dolly's room. I shall make use of all I know in architecture," promised Pong Tua-son.

Son Tua, Pong's father, had mentioned his son's interest in Dolly. Monty jokingly answered, "The wooer brings sweets."

"Now, what will you do with Señorita Dolly's room?" asked Don Segundo.

"I was thinking of a room similar to Princess Margaret's in Buckingham Palace. Dolly is more beautiful than Princess Margaret."

"Of course," the father accepted the compliment. "Have you seen the princess' room?" he asked.

"I have seen pictures, including the dresser, bed, and bath-room. We'll copy it, but it will be more special."

Don Segundo had no doubt that he had found the best architect.

In two weeks, Pong finished the plans. A three-story house with a wide garden, a large garage, and a wide swimming pool. The servants' quarters were behind the garage.

The ground floor would have a large hall, a private office for Don Segundo, a bathroom, and a dressing room.

On the second floor would be the rooms of the family with a bathroom in every room. There would be guest rooms.

The third floor, which would be high and airy, would be for entertainment. It would have a small bar and dinette, a poker and mah-jongg den, a radio and TV set, and a library. Here, Don Segundo would confer on business, politics, etc. An elevator would connect the floors.

Not satisfied with the old one-hectare lot, Don Segundo did not rest till he got the adjacent lots. He found out that being owned by foreigners, they were taken by the Japanese during the occupation. After the war, they were transferred to the administration of enemy property. Using influence and bribes, Montero had these adjacent lots transferred to him. The widened grounds were right for a three-story building.

In those days, there were no obstacles to the wishes of a Montero and to the vision of an architect as long as, in Pong Tua-son's words, "there are enough funds."

Meanwhile, within shouting distance from the Montero garden, a thousand families who had lost their roofs because of the occupation and the liberation became squatters in schoolhouses and private buildings that had escaped the bullets and fire.

Many gathered burned roofing and blackened wood. Hurriedly, they set up lean-tos and barung-barongs on vacant lots, in a race against the rain and other dangers from the sky.

Groups of dirty children roamed the streets by day, like stray dogs. But at night, after satisfying their hunger on whatever they could pick up or steal, they would curl up together under a ruined building or a demolished bridge. They would try to snatch a few hours' rest until awakened by the wheels of a passing truck or driven away by a policeman.

More fortunate than these children are their parents who died during the war, for they are sleeping soundly in unmarked graves.

XXVI

Considering that it was Saturday, Governor Oscar Doblado rose early. It was only nine in the morning and he had come from the bathroom and was having breakfast. He had heard high mass and received communion at San Agustin church an hour earlier.

He was alone. In his left hand was the morning paper, a cup of coffee in his right hand.

His wife Doña Ninay was in her room on the second floor of this house in Quezon City. Food was brought up to her. Doña Ninay went down only occasionally, leaning on her personal maid. Since she had become bedridden and half-paralyzed, she preferred to stay alone in her room, read Spanish novels, and amuse herself watching TV. Once a day, Oscar would come up to see her.

The governor rose early, although he had stayed up the night before. He had invited some friends to a "concierto" or poker at his house. He went to mass first, for luck at the poker table.

"Come before noon," he called up his friends. "We shall have lechon, *lapu-lapu*[1] with white sauce."

After breakfast, Oscar told his cook that he had ordered food from a restaurant. There was enough wine at the bar.

Being governor of the province where the Hacienda Montero was located, Doblado commuted between his mansion in Quezon

---

1 lapu-lapu—a kind of fish

City and his office at the capital. His car could make it in one and a half hours. He would start after breakfast, and at ten o'clock, he would receive guests at his office.

Receiving visitors and signing papers would take up all his time in the morning. Once a week, he would meet the provincial board.

When Governor Doblado left his office at noon, he would not return that day. Anyone who inquired was told "the governor is out on inspection."

In a house of durable materials on an average-size lot surrounded by a concrete fence in a town adjacent to the capital, the governor would relax. There, he would have lunch and rest until it was time to go home to Quezon City.

This house was owned by a youngish, good-looking woman said to be a relative of the governor's wife. Being an orphan, she was sent to school by Doña Ninay. For companions, she had only two children, a seven-year-old girl and a four-year-old boy, supposed to be the niece and nephew of this woman, Aling Tindeng. Nevertheless, some gossips gathered around the *sari-sari store*[2] across from Aling Tindeng's house said that she was the governor's mistress and that the two children were the offspring of the affair.

If the governor's wife in Quezon City was aware of this, she showed no signs. Perhaps, she left everything in God's hands, especially now that she could hardly leave her room after a near fatal stroke.

Born to wealthy parents, Oscar Doblado had been a wastrel even as a student. He learned vice before he gained knowledge. He graduated without any distinction; rather, he was among the "lucky" ones. His diploma was framed and used as decoration in his parents' home. His first appearance in court was not as a

---

2 sari-sari store—convenience store

lawyer, but because of a brawl in a gambling club, and another lawyer defended him.

Before his father died, Oscar married the wealthy Ninay. Choosing a door open to the likes of him, he entered politics. Favored by his lucky stars at last, he became governor in the first postwar elections.

In their twenty-year marriage, his sickly wife bore no child. She used to say jokingly that she actually had a child, for Osky was equal to six teenagers.

Governor Doblado didn't invite many to his poker "concert." Four to six was a good number, but each one brought capital no less than ₱20,000.00.

They would play continuously after lunch till midnight. And the "*tong*[3]" was more than sufficient for all of Osky's expenses. He would make from six to ten thousand.

From lunch to merienda to supper, they had the excellent services of a well-known restaurant. Like condemned men before hanging, poker players could ask for any food, wine, or smokes.

Even before any guest came, a roasted pig still steaming on a large platter was already on the table on one side of the room. There were some bottles of various wines: scotch, brandy, port, sherry, burgundy, ice cubes in a deep crystal container, olives, pickles, peanuts, and empty glasses and cups. A houseboy stood beside the table, waiting for orders.

First to arrive were Bishop Dumas and Judge Pilato. The Bishop was older than the judge and wore a black habit; the judge was in *barong-Tagalog*.[4]

"We're early, Governor, aren't we?" the Bishop said cheerfully when Oscar went to greet them.

---

3 tong—a gambling den's percentage of the winnings

4 barong-Tagalog—a native Filipino long-sleeved shirt for men—usually made of embroidered material, and worn for special occasions

"Just right, Monsignor; Monty called and said he would fetch Senator Botin."

They had hardly sat down when Oscar offered drinks. "Have a drink first. What's yours, Judge?"

"Scotch and soda."

"You, Monsignor?"

"Don't bother. I'll pour my own." Taking a bottle of brandy, he poured some into a goblet and drank it straight.

"Excellent," he said, savoring the liquor on his tongue. "Nothing can compare to aged brandy."

They nibbled the crispy skin of the lechon.

Before they could finish their wine, they heard the loud mouth of Montero and saw the large face of Senator Botin. There was no need for introductions, for they often met at such gatherings. They shook hands.

"I better have lunch served," suggested Governor Doblado. "You must be hungry."

"Who cares for food?" said Monty looking at the lechon and the wine. "This is enough."

"Those are only snacks. Wait till you see the real meal," said Osky. "I won't invite you unless it's special. Have a drink first, Senator."

"Martini, if there's any."

Osky asked the servant for a martini and poured some into a cup for Senator Botin.

Monty poured his own drink into a glass.

"Sherry for me; doctor's advice," he said. "Sherry comes from fruit juice while whiskey is fifty percent alcohol. I prefer whiskey and didn't learn to drink any other, but señores, whoever wishes to live long should obey his doctor."

"Do you have high blood pressure?" asked the judge.

"My heart is overworked," answered the haciendero.

"That fatigue is not due to whiskey," said Oscar with a meaningful look.

"I'm tired of muscatel," said Bishop Dumas. "That's what the altar boy hands me every mass. So, outside the church, my stomach craves another—straight brandy which is not as strong as scotch."

"So that is why you can take more brandy than muscatel," teased Senator Botin.

"Hey, Monty," said Judge Pilato, "is that your palace being built in Singalong?"

"At your service, Judge," said Monty.

"I thought it was another temple of the Church of Christ," joked Pilato, glancing at the Bishop, who ignored him.

"It's getting to be a problem," complained Monty; "the cost of materials is too much."

"For one as rich as you," said Pilato, "sky's the limit. And you're lucky. If you were in Australia, you couldn't build a mansion. How many are you in your family ?"

"Three," said Monty.

"Only three—ah, you can't have a mansion. There is a definite size allowed according to the family. After the war, the Australian government implemented a housing program—homes for the homeless. No one can hoard more materials than he needs. You can get materials for a house for just three persons, because if only those with money can buy all the materials they want, the others won't be provided with houses."

"That's why I prefer to stay here rather than Australia or elsewhere," said Montero. "Here, people are free. As long as you have the money, you can do what you want."

"When is the inauguration?" asked Oscar.

"It's not even finished and lacks many things. But maybe we shall have it when Dolores comes back," said Montero. "Julia won't allow it while her princess is away."

"Is your daughter in Paris, Monty?" asked the Bishop.

"Yes, Monsignor, she is studying at Sorbonne." The father was not sure what the college was but said Sorbonne.

"Sorbonne." The Bishop thought awhile. "Ah, Sorbonne is good. It is a Catholic institution. One of the first colleges in Sorbonne established by Cardinal Richelieu is one of the best schools of theology in Europe. Paris is a city of temptations, but those studying at Sorbonne are safe from worldliness." After saying this, Bishop Dumas gulped down the remaining contents of his goblet.

"Lunch is ready. Let's go to the dining room," invited Osky. He led the Bishop ahead of the other guests.

When he came to the head of the table, Bishop Dumas looked back at Senator Botin and graciously offered his seat.

"You stay here," he said.

"You do, Bishop," declined the lawmaker.

"If we follow protocol..." said the Bishop.

"The more you have the right," finished the Senator and added, smiling, "I am only a legislator of our government, while you are a prince of Rome."

"If all legislators were like you, Senator," the Bishop kidded in return, "there would be no conflict between the state and the church.

"This is my position—Render unto Caesar what is Caesar's, and unto God what is God's."

Osky settled the discussion and sat the Bishop at the head of the table. Senator Botin at his right, Judge Pilato at his left, and Montero and Osky sat across from each other.

"Are there no others, Governor?" Bishop Dumas looked at Doblado before scooping his spoon into the soup plate.

"General Bayoneta promised to come, but he was delayed," said Osky.

"Why do you have us raided by the General?" Montero asked in mock protest.

"Have you heard of any gambling of the elite raids ?" retorted the governor. "Anyway, you know, Senator Botin, Monty, that his wife is the daughter of the Chinese millionaire Son Tua, I mean, Tua-son."

"That's why I cannot imagine how he can be an enemy of vice. Would you believe his father-in-law worked to place him in his present position?"

"He is the enemy of jueteng," insisted Osky. "I should know…"

"Because his father-in-law does not deal in jueteng," said the Senator.

"But he is not the enemy of gentlemen's games like monte, poker, chemin de fer. These are safe from him. And he plays for high stakes."

"Of course, because he does not have to say mass at dawn to earn money." Bishop Dumas smiled.

"What would you do if you could carry the campaign against vice," said Osky, "and be the son-in-law of the financial broker of the majority party? Aba, it's clear profit, coming and going, like a saw."

"I believe what an authority says about such things," Senator Botin said meaningfully, and everyone laughed.

Then a servant approached Oscar and whispered that there was another guest. Oscar went to the door and returned with General Bayoneta. Oscar introduced the new arrival, who bowed and told them to go on eating. The servant handed him a bottle of scotch and a glass with ice.

"General," greeted Judge Pilato, "we thought you would raid our poker game, but we have not even started."

"I'll wipe you out in a legal way," threatened the General. "Governor knows me," he added.

"What kept you?" asked Oscar.

"There was a conference on exterminating rats in Mindanao. Reports say they destroy not only plants but also property." Bayoneta gulped down his whiskey. He was seated by the host at the other end of the table, opposite the Bishop.

"Why exterminate only the rats in Mindanao?" asked Monty. "Are there not many big rats in all corners of the government?"

"When you went near the sherry, Monty," the Senator retorted, "the more easily you became drunk. Remember the saying 'He who spits at the sky...'"

"I mentioned no names, Senator," Monty interposed. "So I think not of 'spitting at the sky' but of the children's game of 'Run, he who's got the gold.'"

"The General is not eating," observed the Bishop.

"I have finished, Monsignor. Lunch was part of the conference."

"Then, let's go." The Bishop stood up. "Thank you, Governor, for the delicious feast."

The others also stood up.

XXVII

From the dining room, Governor Doblado led the guests to another air-conditioned room on the same floor. It was his den.

The floor was carpeted. There were sofas, some lounging chairs, and a low, small *kamagong*[1] table. At the center was a round table made from one piece of thick wood covered with green velvet, which could easily accommodate ten persons.

An oil copy of the famous painting *September Morn* hung on the wall. On top of a wide kamagong cabinet was an ivory bust of Psyche. There was also an electric clock on top of the cabinet.

In the afternoon, the room was bright because of the crystal paneling. At night, it was effectively lit by fluorescent lamps in four corners or by the lamps standing on pedestals.

Oscar had bottles of wine, glasses, and cups brought with ice cubes. He opened a box of Coronas.

"Let me pour you some brandy, Monsignor," Oscar offered.

"Thanks," said the Bishop, "I don't drink during a game, but I prefer Coronas."

"As for me," bragged Monty, "the more I drink, the more I enjoy the game. Unfortunately, *señores*, now I can only drink sherry and in limited amounts."

---

1 kamagong—a kind of reddish-brown hardwood

"There are reasons both for drinking and not drinking while playing," Judge Pilato joined in. "Those who don't drink want to have greater concentration. Those who drink need the wine to give them courage."

"I drink because I want to, not for courage," Monty objected. "I bet, not on the strength of the wine, but on my cards. If I hold five aces, wild, you can have all the saints of the Roman Church."

"Let us not drag sacred things into gambling," protested the Bishop.

"With me, it's different," said General Bayoneta, "I'll tell you my poker secret." And he looked around as if he would reveal a planned coup d'état. "When the cards are weak, that's when I push the chips and 'top me.'"

"Therefore, General," Senator Botin joined in, "your method is like the old military tactic. Whenever you are losing, that's when your noisy propaganda says you're winning."

The group chuckled at the comparison, but General Bayoneta retorted, "If my tactics are poor, you know what to do when I say, 'Top me.'"

"I'll remember that," laughed the Senator.

A new set of cards was taken by Oscar from the cabinet. He broke the blue seal and gave the Bishop the cards wrapped in cellophane. Oscar also took out the box of chips which had a pen and a list.

Bishop Dumas removed all the cellophane, rifled through the pack, then separated the twos, threes, fours, and fives. Also the jokers. He meticulously shuffled the remaining cards.

"The old rules," Oscar informed all, as he piled the chips of four colors.

"Strictly cash, isn't it?" said Monty.

"If you wish," was Oscar's tactful reply.

"Among friends, that is the proper thing," Monty agreed. "We're different, of course, but at a poker table, señores, the unexpected often takes place. Maybe you haven't heard of the president who gave the invitations but played without capital. Now, who can refuse a president? You also know of the bank director who left a debt before the war. The war is over and he has not redeemed his I.O.U., although the house has paid for it. A banker, just think of that."

"It is said," Oscar confirmed Monty's story, "that the place to know a real gentleman is at the gambling table."

"Very well, how much are the stakes?" asked Senator Botin, looking bored.

"Small stakes only, Senator," said the host-cashier, "a thousand pesos each, but you can get as many as you like."

"Hombre, is a thousand small?" objected Botin. "The salary of a member of Congress is only six hundred pesos a month."

"What is salary compared to allowance and sideline?" Monty bellowed.

The Senator threw Monty a dirty look but said nothing.

"Give me three for a start," he told the governor and took out six five-hundred-peso bills for his chips.

"Fresh from the Central Bank," Oscar kidded him and waved the neat bills for all to see.

"Hey, I'm no ten-percenter," protested Botin.

The host-cashier counted out twenty white chips worth ten pesos each, eight red chips at one hundred pesos each, two blue at five hundred each, and one yellow worth one thousand.

"Is that enough, Senator?" asked Oscar. "It seems slight."

"Simple living," the Senator winked. "If only we had something from reparations or got a share in barter."

Oscar took the three thousand, placed it in the box and entered in his list: Senator B, 3.

Senator Botin got his chips, counted them, and arranged them in three piles before him.

"Judge?" The cashier turned to Judge Pilato.

"Three also."

Cash and chips swiftly changed hands. The cashier entered: Judge, 3.

Bishop Dumas asked for five; Montero and Bayoneta, six each. Oscar added to the list: Bishop, 5; Monty, 6; General, 6; total 23.

They sat around the table. From Bishop Dumas going left: Judge Pilato, Senator Botin, Montero, and General Bayoneta.

"Won't you play, Osky?" the Bishop asked the governor.

"The five of you may start."

"Six can play."

"I'll attend to our merienda first," he excused himself.

"And the tong," added Monty. (This was Osky's cut of the pot for hosting the game.)

"Very well, *hermanos*, let's start," said Bishop Dumas. He appeared to bless the pack of cards with his right hand.

"Amen," whispered Senator Botin.

The Bishop gave each a card. Judge Pilato showed an ace; so he was the first dealer.

The Judge shuffled the cards again and threw a white chip to the center, saying, "Stud, simple."

The four followed the dealer and each placed a white chip.

Judge Pilato dealt each player one card facedown from Senator Botin to himself. He followed with one card each, faceup. The card of Senator Botin was a seven, Monty a queen, General Bayoneta a ten, the Bishop Dumas, a knight, and Judge Pilato, the dealer, an eight.

"Queen," called the dealer.

"Size of the pot." Monty placed five white chips in the middle, together with the rest.

"Call," answered Bayoneta, meaning he would pit his cards with a ten on top against Monty's cards with his queen. The General placed a red chip and got his change of five white.

"Good for me," Judge Pilato retreated, turned his eight on top of his other cards, and didn't add to the pot. Thus he showed he would not pit his cards against those who said "call."

"Deal," warned Pilato and gave Montero a third open card. "King," said the dealer.

He threw a third before the General and said, "Knight."

The Bishop got an ace.

"Bet the ace," said the dealer.

"Let's sweeten the pot with two hundred pesos." Smiling, Bishop Dumas threw two red chips on the pile at the center.

"And whom will the king fear?" countered Montero, who also placed two red chips.

"And who will overcome the General riding a horse?" said Bayoneta. His red chips were added to the pile.

"Deal," said Pilato and gave each of the three an open card.

Montero got an ace, the General a king, the Bishop a knight. Each had four cards: three open, and one face down. Before Montero could be seen a queen, a king, an ace, and one more card. The General had a ten, a knight, a king, and one hidden. The Bishop had a knave, an ace, a knave, and one more.

It appeared that based on the open cards, Bishop Dumas was ahead, for he had a pair and an ace. Montero and Bayoneta had no open pair, besides being crippled by the king and the ace.

Without raising his eyes or showing any change in his facial expression, the Bishop threw a yellow chip to the center. He looked like a priest who remained calm while listening to the confession of a married woman having an affair.

Montero said nothing. He turned down all his cards, as a sign of surrender.

General Bayoneta held a yellow chip, but he didn't let it go. He stared at the Bishop as one would stare at a captive to make him admit the charges against him. He remained in this stance for more than a minute while the Bishop quietly looked at the yellow chip, which stood out at the center of the whites, reds, and blues.

"Very well," said the General. "Call." And he placed the yellow chip on top of the one placed by the Bishop.

From behind, Governor Doblado picked up with two fingers a blue chip for the tong. This was the "customs" duty for a heated game.

"Deal," said the dealer and gave a last card each to the Bishop and the General.

"*Pinta,²*" promptly said the Bishop and caught the last card meant for him.

Also facedown, Judge Pilato dealt General Bayoneta a card. The two poker players peeped at their last cards, but one could not tell whether they were good or bad. Not from the movements of their eyelashes nor their lips nor from their breathing. Both wore poker faces.

Without a word, the Bishop showed a ten, and the General, a horse. Therefore, of the two sets of four open cards, there was a pair of horses, a king, and a ten for the General, while the Bishop had a pair of knights, an ace, and a ten.

"I told you, a horse ridden by a general is rare," jeered Bayoneta. "See now, there are two."

"I was put to shame by the knight." Bishop Dumas shook his head.

"In honor of the two horses, top me," exclaimed the General and pushed all his chips forward.

The Bishop looked at him. All stared but didn't make a sound. Senator Botin, Montero, and the dealer Judge Pilato were all silenced by the first deal.

Then the Bishop looked at his cards, at the cards of Bayoneta, then at his face. He counted with his eyes the pile of chips pushed by the General and the chips before him.

"I can't top you, General, for you have more chips," the Bishop said calmly.

"Then," answered Bayoneta, "I top you."

---

2 pinta—to take a peek at playing cards

"You were right, Governor," said the Bishop without answering the challenge to bet all. He meant that Bayoneta was really a heavy gambler.

"I revealed my secret earlier, didn't I, Senator?" the General reminded him about his betting move when his cards were weak.

"I won't be carried by propaganda," Bishop Dumas sneered, "even with the radio, I don't listen to the commercials."

"Well, you have the last word, Monsignor."

"How much is this?" the Bishop asked himself and slowly counted his chips with two fingers. "Three thousand two hundred ninety," he said.

"Aba, the General wants to get such a big amount. This is not easily earned by an old priest. How many masses, weddings, baptisms, confirmations, burials?"

"You have time to retreat," advised Bayoneta. Then as if against his will, he removed some of his chips, to leave only the equivalent of the Bishop's. "How much did you say, Monsignor? Three thousand two hundred ninety?"

"Right," answered the Bishop quickly, at the same time pushing his chips toward the center. "Call."

Absolute silence reigned around the table. The General was first to speak.

"Two pairs," he announced triumphantly as if accepting the surrender of Datu Kamlon. Quickly, he showed the hidden card, which was a ten. So he had a pair of knights and a pair of tens back to back.

Bayoneta thought he had won, so when the Bishop was silent, he was about to draw the chips, but he stopped when he heard the voice of Monsignor.

"No good," he objected. He showed his hidden card, which was also a knave; so he had three knaves—a trio. A trio is higher than two pairs.

The General was shocked, but the Bishop paid no more attention to his reaction, for both hands were gathering the chips.

One more blue was fished out by two fingers of Doblado.

"What was found in water, to water will return," Senator Botin whispered to Judge Pilato, but was careful not to be overheard by the General, who was perspiring profusely.

In that single encounter, Bishop Dumas won five thousand and the General lost four thousand six hundred. Oscar got a tong of one hundred fifty.

"Between a good poker player and a good bishop, I choose the poker player," said Senator Botin.

"But of course," agreed Judge Pilato, "more than a senator."

"Even in poker," Bishop Dumas said quietly, "prayer is heeded by God."

"Or by Satan," groaned General Bayoneta.

XXVIII

"Señores, the game is fun, but the merienda waiting for us is more delicious," the host Governor Doblado asked the gentlemen poker players to take a break. A senator, a bishop, a general, a judge, and a landlord-businessman—this power elite could risk a fortune that could save thousands of the poor from hunger in one round of poker .

The five guests had spent three hours in the four kingdoms in the air-conditioned room. Bishop Dumas continued raking in while General Bayoneta was losing. All in all, the military chief had coughed up twenty thousand, and the same amount of chips had gone to the monsignor. Senator Botin and Monty had each lost three thousand; Judge Pilato had recovered his capital.

In one round, General Bayoneta asked for a new deck of cards. This was their third change. The scotch bottle on his left was less than half full.

Actually, the five poker players were about the same in skill and not one of them would hesitate to face Professor Hoyle, the famous author of the poker bible, if said expert would show enough capital. More than a cheat, the one person most avoided in this game was the one who played without money. The cheat could be beaten, but what could you win from one without money?

Just like any other game of luck, in poker, one's skill was only half the game. If the player did not receive a good hand, he would keep placing ante in the pot and not be able to "call." And if he should stick to the game without a fighting chance, it would be like throwing a live cat to a hungry crocodile. So, as in a horse race, he would be included only at the start.

Bluffing can be profitable occasionally, if the opponent is uncertain. But if his cards are good, the bluff is nothing but a blow against a strong wall.

More or less, this was the experience of General Bayoneta that afternoon. No player escapes superstition during a game. Often he counts on this; he hopes that his bad luck will be replaced by a lucky streak and the tide will turn against the opposition. Thus the General would change his seat, his glass of whiskey, press his heel on the face of an animal in the carpet's design. Once he asked for a new deck when it was his turn to deal. But he seemed dogged by bad luck. No matter what he did, two thirds of his thirty thousand still took flight.

"General, it seems that the peace and order situation is getting serious in many places," observed Montero. "What's going on?

General Bayoneta straightened his shoulders, thinking that this was one topic where he could answer without losing any of his chips. Nevertheless, he was careful in expressing his views.

"In this group," Bayoneta told Montero, "I should not answer this alone. Here are Senator Botin and the governor. Maybe they know more than I do about the causes of the loss of peace and order. Judge Pilato and the monsignor surely have their own view of the problem. I'm only a soldier and my primary duty is to enforce the law; in a word, to prosecute the enemy of the law."

"Perhaps, we all agree that the root cause of what's happening now is the last war," Governor Doblado declared. "The war destroyed the nation's economy, which can't be easily restored. Trailing this are unemployment, poverty, hunger. An empty stomach is a bad counselor. Robbery, for example; there are many robberies, not because of inborn evil in the robbers, but often, because of their desire to live. I know. In my province alone, not a few are jailed for this. It's worse in the city. They look for jobs but can't find work. They beg but no one gives alms. What will they do? Risk helping themselves to the property of those who have more than their needs…"

"During the war and even after, man forgot God," Bishop Dumas spoke slowly, then shook his head. "That is the first sign. Both the haves and the have-nots forgot; the wealthy became greedy and decided to keep for himself all the bounty entrusted to him, while the latter came to believe that society is to blame for his poverty, and because of this, he has the right to get other's property. When a man forgets God, he becomes Satan's follower."

"Aba, I don't neglect my duties," butted in Montero defensively. "Magno, you know about my donation to the church. My wife heads the Catholic women and my daughter always helps in fundraising for the Red Cross. Aba, what more is expected of me?"

"I wasn't referring to you," Dumas said. "You're not the only rich man in the country." Governor Doblado tried to get Montero's goat.

"*Hoy*, Señor Millionaire," said Oscar, "don't boast like the Pharisee that gives alms one day and exploits for one year."

"Osky, you're dragging your own tail," Montero retorted meaningfully.

Judge Pilato removed the ashes of his cigar before speaking.

"Even the courts are often blamed for the situation," he said. "If the sentence is light, we are condoning crime. If heavy, we're cruel. If an important person wins, the judge was bribed. If nobody is sentenced, the poor have no chance. But we judge the case, not the person. We did not make the laws. The judge does not sentence according to his wishes, but according to the law." Judge Pilato puffed his cigar before continuing.

"Look, a father steals money to buy rice. If caught, he has to be jailed. But a powerful person steals a hundred thousand, but he cannot be charged because there is no evidence nor witness... Now..."

"That's what I mean," the General agreed. "In performing our duty, we set aside our personal feelings. If in bringing about peace and order, the soldier must use force, don't blame him for doing his duty."

"Who was the sage who said that when a person is ashamed of his actions, he uses duty as a pretext?" Senator Botin said pointedly, making the General look at him sharply.

"If a soldier is afraid to do his duty, he should look for another profession. He should be a politician," Bayoneta retorted.

"Why?" the Senator asked angrily. "Doesn't a politician know how to perform his duty?"

"I mean to say, Senator, that when he pleases the public or his district, the politician thinks everything is all right. On the other hand, fulfilling his mission is the sole aim of the soldier. No matter who gets hurt. The politician is swayed by public opinion, the soldier is not..."

"Do you mean that the army does not believe in democracy?" charged Senator Botin.

"That is far-fetched, Senator. I mean, the army is not politics."

"I think there's a big gap between government policy and your methods. In a republic, all agencies of the government, the army included, should follow the democratic system. Isn't your policy too harsh? That remedy is worse than the disease. Are you aware that the barrios complain of the ferocity of the army? They say that every time we start a peace-and-order campaign, the peaceful folks suffer more than the outlaws. You want to stop the fire, but you are pouring oil."

A sour smile played on the General's lips. His jaw was set as he fenced off the lawmaker's thrust.

"There are some diseases like cancer which require an operation. The army is often caught between the sword and the wall. Shall he allow the enemies of the law to prevail, or should he restore the prestige of the government? Deny it if you will, but at this stage, the army is the pillar of democracy. Those who don't heed the church and don't fear the courts are forced to listen to the gun."

"A social problem can never be solved by the sword," insisted the Senator.

A guest arrived just in time to catch the General's last remarks and the Senator's firm answer. Governor Doblado introduced Dr. Sabio, who was already known to some as the head of Freedom University and an expert on political science.

"You will enjoy this discussion, Doctor," said Osky, "but have merienda first."

"Just coffee," said the new arrival.

"We were discussing the alarming peace-and-order situation," the governor told Dr. Sabio. "Thefts, burglaries, killings, disorder everywhere. These are obviously the result of poverty and crimes caused by the war."

Dr. Sabio first sipped his coffee.

"I caught the last remarks of General Bayoneta and Senator Botin. Don't blame the war. These problems could have been aggravated by the war, but not caused by it. How can the creature precede the creator? The social problem is similar to the question: which came first—the chicken or the egg? We have to admit that ten to twenty years before the war, a governor was killed by his political opponent, a landlord was slain by a sharecropper, a doctor was killed by the husband of a patient. Long before the war, there were big strikes. The colorum rose in Pangasinan, the tanggulan in Bulacan and Manila, the sakdalistas in southern Luzon, the fighting between the Constabulary and the Moros in Mindanao. Therefore, these happenings are not recent phenomena. The root causes undeniably existed before the war."

Dr. Sabio finished his coffee. No one objected; he was like a professor lecturing to a class.

"What do I call root causes? A man's taking advantage of another through position, money, or brains. Taking economic advantage in many forms and schemes. This is the source of a man's discontent. And it spreads. We know that a spark easily causes fire."

"I said earlier that both the haves and the have-nots are to blame," the Bishop said.

"That's true, Monsignor, if you refer to the worsening of the situation," agreed Dr. Sabio. "But at the start, only one was to blame: the opportunist, the deceitful schemer. You will agree with me, Monsignor, that God knew and He, Himself, sowed in Paradise the seeds of sin."

"God gave man the intelligence to know good from evil, and the freedom to choose," answered the Bishop.

The rest were silent. Dr. Sabio went on.

"Now, what do we see? Each man for himself. Those on the top step on those below; the latter struggle to free themselves from their miserable lives. The favored ones, even those with their duty to the country, attend to nothing but their own welfare. They have hardly warmed their backs in their positions when they build palaces, buy two cars, and amass money for their vices. I'm not against fair profit and just reward, but I think those in the government have no right to live very differently from the ordinary citizens whom they lead."

"Even if he spends his own money?" asked Senator Botin.

"Even then, Senator. A leader should give a good example to the public. If the nation is in dire need, it is immoral for a leader and his family to wallow in luxury and ease. If a citizen walks in muddy streets, it is indecent for a leader to recline in his Cadillac. Don't you think so?

"As long as my conscience is clear," retorted the Senator, "I have nothing to fear. Why, does one have no right to live the way he wants?"

"You see," the General reproached him, "now you say 'while your conscience is clear'; earlier, you objected when I said 'as long as I do my duty, never mind who gets hurt.'"

"What do you suggest, Doctor?" asked Judge Pilato.

"Better education, especially for those below, not just learning in professions or occupations," explained the professor, "but a deep understanding of morality, one's obligation to his fellow man and to society. In short, training on being men and citizens."

"Religion!" Bishop Dumas boomed. "More religion is what the nation needs. Those who were reared in these times are steeped in materialism. What do you think, Doctor? Isn't religion needed in school?" The Bishop had an idea that this was not the policy at Freedom University but he asked the question anyway.

Dr. Sabio gave the Bishop a respectful look and answered calmly and slowly. "Knowledge and fear of God are the first things learned by man. Because of lack of faith in himself and in the face of countless wonders in nature, man worshipped the Power that created these mysteries and everything his limited mind couldn't understand. But nature was conquered by science. Man learned that he is like any other being on earth and that even earth is not the center of the universe, but only one of the planets revolving around the sun. Hardly a thing is left unchallenged and unreached by man's mind. Thus, what happened was to be expected. Man developed a greater concern for everyday life than for his dream of the next life. So, the power of religion diminished. But the ethics and morality taught by religion, the humanitarian basis of all creeds and all prophets from Moses to Buddha and from Christ to Mohammed, are still the golden rule of all churches, philosophies, and secular institutions. I refer to the commandments 'Love others as you love yourself' and 'Don't do unto others what you would not have others do unto you.'

"The moment mankind forgets to behave thus, what difference is there between man and beast? So that Voltaire, an agnostic, said, 'If there is no God, man should create one.' Monsignor, it may be that compulsory religious instruction is against the separation of church and state, but we agree, I think, that morality is what the country needs at this time."

"Although I don't fully subscribe to your theory," said the Bishop, "I don't completely object. Even science is limited just as man's knowledge is limited. Only God is omniscient. What science lacks should be supplemented by faith. Or we could follow St. Thomas Aquinas who said, 'There is only one Truth.' So that truth of science and truth of faith should coincide."

Then the Bishop turned to the professor and asked suddenly, "Doctor, may I know your religion?"

All eyes turned to Dr. Sabio at the thrust of Bishop Dumas. But the professor was not rattled and answered quickly.

"Religion is the secret of every man's conscience," he said. "But if you wish to know, my religion is truth."

"God is truth. He is the Way; He is Life."

"With apologies to St. Thomas Aquinas, that is where science differs from religion," Dr. Sabio disagreed.

"Therefore, you are an agnostic?"

"I look for proof in everything."

"And without proof, you don't believe?"

"That, sir, is the law of truth."

"And who made such a law?"

"Nature."

"And who made nature?"

"Nature itself."

The Bishop gave a soft, skeptical laugh. He told himself he had found an enjoyable opponent, though hard to convince. He said pleasantly, "I would be delighted, Dr. Sabio, if we could have a long discussion sometime."

"Thank you, Monsignor. When I find time, I shall pay you a visit, sir." He added, "I hope that someday, those who rely on faith and those who rely on truth can have worthwhile discussions. They could agree to disagree."

The host, Governor Doblado, looked at his wristwatch, hinting that it was time to go back to the round table.

"Maybe we should settle things at the poker table," suggested General Bayoneta, who was getting bored. He was losing a lot. "You play, don't you, Doctor?"

"Rarely, and for small stakes," answered Dr. Sabio.

"The Doctor came for another purpose," explained Governor Doblado. "He wanted to discuss his university's plans about a hacienda in my province."

At the word "hacienda," Montero looked at Oscar. "What hacienda?" he asked.

"He owns Hacienda Montero," said Oscar by way of introduction.

"Then he is the one I should see," said Dr. Sabio, "but some other time."

"We shall see," was Montero's only reply.

Dr. Sabio said goodbye. After he left, the poker players went back to the air-conditioned room.

XXIX

The phone was ringing at the *Kampilan* news editor's desk. Andres picked up the receiver.

"Hello, yes, Santi? Two children killed by their mother. She stabbed herself... Serious... Why? How's that?... From extreme poverty... No food... No one to help... Husband in jail... What? Welfareville refused help... Yes, I've got the names and ages... Good... Get other details... Living in an *entresuelo*[1]... The children's bodies at the morgue... Mother in the hospital. Call back... Okay."

Andres was looking over the likely items for the front page when Magat came in from the editorial room. He had a copy of the afternoon paper.

"Andy, anything new on the Blue Ribbon exposé?" asked Magat. "That's a big scandal."

"I asked Iman to interview those involved. He will get statements from the two department secretaries and the matron. I also sent a reporter to the chief investigator to find out if there is concrete evidence."

The two cabinet members exposed by the Blue Ribbon Committee were charged with receiving bribes in some big deals. It was said that one received a fishpond and the other a house and

---

1 entresuelo—mezzanine

lot in Baguio. The matron, the wife of a government official, was said to be the financier of some members of the Kitchen Cabinet who make frequent trips to Hong Kong, Tokyo, Bangkok, and Singapore. They smuggle out dollars and bring in contraband goods, which give them huge profits.

Andy told Magat Santi's news about the desperate mother.

"Any good news about the strike at the pier?"

"What do you mean by good?" Andy looked up at Magat who remained standing. "Bloodshed? Yes. The police attacked the picketers; two strikers were wounded. The cops will be charged with physical injuries and the strikers with resisting the law enforcers."

"Good," said Magat. Andres, who was not used to the ways in a newspaper's copy room, was puzzled.

"Why do we say 'good' when something bad happens? Like the mauling of the strikers by the police."

"The event is bad, but the news is good," Magat explained. "The reader likes to read about the unusual and unexpected, the sensational. So, it's not news when a dog bites a man; it's news when a man bites a dog. What's been done about the reported school crisis?"

"What else but the old remedy? Appropriate more funds, look for more buildings to be rented, hire new teachers," Andres answered.

"Where will they get the funds?"

"There's a plan to double the matriculation fee of the students and to hold twenty lotteries every year. The money earned will be added to educational funds."

"Therefore, the twenty-four sweepstakes and lotteries we have will now become forty-four," Magat pointed out.

"Twenty-four for charity, twenty for education," explained Andres.

"Is there no means other than gambling to finance good proposals?"

"Any proposal of the present officials will have the same result; the country will be fried in its own fat."

"What about the tenants' petition for the government to buy the hacienda?"

"They have presented this to the office concerned; they have not received any answer but 'wait'…it will be studied…that is the policy of the government, but the problem is money…however…"

"The problem, Andy, is not lack of money, but lack of action, of implementation." Magat seemed to be diagnosing a patient's illness. "There are many good brains in the government, many good ideas, plans, programs. But they end there. When it comes to implementation, it hesitates, retreats, and is scared by obstacles. The proposal is left hanging, sleeping, forgotten until they are jolted by the grave outcome of such negligence."

"The government is like a spider which spins a web and sleeps at the center, just waiting for the fly or moth that makes the mistake of entering," Andres answered with a laugh.

"That's a good comparison," Magat agreed. "So it is imprisoned in its own web. We shall fight against its apathy and indolence," vowed the editor. "We shall unmask the hypocrites, expose the wolves in sheep's clothing, wake up the sleeping. On the other hand, we shall boost and praise the deserving. As Jefferson said, a good newspaper is preferable to a bad government. In critical times, the newspaper is an effective fortress of truth and reason."

"Napoleon admitted that he was more afraid to fight a newspaper than a thousand bayonets. Sometimes a powerful editorial can shock more than a bomb."

"True," agreed Magat, "but don't forget, Andy, that our goal, both in the news and the editorial, is not only to expose and destroy. We want to help in building, in creating, in propagating. That is the difference between guns and ideas. A weapon only destroys and kills; an idea destroys and builds, kills and gives life."

The phone rang. Andres answered it.

"Yes, Santi? Oh, the mother of the two children died. Is that all? …Okay."

Then a messenger came and handed Andres a picture with a typewritten news item attached.

"Oh, a pre-war Miss Philippines," he said after glancing at the press release. "Now she's married to Gordo, the banker. She will hold a dance at the Manila Hotel and has invited a thousand guests on her birthday." Andres looked at the postscript. "Don't fail to include this latest picture and send a photographer to the affair."

The two editors burst into laughter.

"Maybe I should use this picture on the front page," he said mockingly. "Let's use the headline 'Feast for 1,000' and beside it, the picture of the mother who killed her two children, then killed herself afterwards. We'll headline it 'Three Killed by Hunger,' what do you think?"

"You're the news editor, pal," Magat laughed.

Iman strode into the copy room and went to Andres' desk.

"What have you got?" Andres greeted him.

"The two secretaries will sue the Blue Ribbon chairman for libel," answered the reporter. "According to them, their respective wives bought the property which were said to be given as bribes. They have photostat copies of the deeds of the sale. Secretary A has the title to the fishpond and Secretary B, the lot and bungalow in Baguio."

"Naturally," said Andres. "And Madame XX?"

"She refused to talk, as instructed by her lawyer."

"Naturally," said Andres again.

They were commenting on Iman's report when the phone rang again. It was Madame XX's lawyer.

"You'll answer for libel if you mention my client's name," he threatened.

"Then," answered Andres, "we shall report your phone call and your threat of libel if…"

"Don't even mention…"

"Mister," Andres' voice was hard, "the *Kampilan* is a free newspaper and has no master. No one tells us what we should print or not..."

"It's up to you." And the conversation was cut short by the "well-mannered" lawyer.

Magat invited Andres to the editor's office.

"Come," said Magat, "and let's discuss my editorial."

When they were seated and Magat had lit a cigarette, he handed Andres three typewritten sheets.

"There, see if it's not too much or too little."

After reading the title and the first paragraph, he looked intently at Magat.

"Fifty years ago, or on October 30, 1908," Magat related, "the newspaper *El Renacimiento* published an editorial entitled 'Aves de Rapina.'"

"The courageous Filipino newspaper was sued by an American high official because the editorial created a big scandal involving the American. The owner and editor of the newspaper lost the case, his property confiscated. In the end, the *Renacimiento* folded up. But its editorial was a shout of protest that was not stifled, and every time there is oppression, exploitation, and injustice, that editorial resounds again."

"I have heard of that editorial," answered Andres. "But this is the first time I've read it."

"It's half a century old, but the situation pointed out is not any different from what we see today. Perhaps a thicker swarm of birds of prey."

"Without a doubt," said Andres, and he went on reading.

"Birds of Prey"

On this earth, some are born to eat and devour, others to be eaten and swallowed... Their relationship depends on the greed and strength of the first until he is given satisfaction at the other's expense.

There are some people who don't only want to be like the merciless Eagle, but have also some marks of a vulture, an owl, and a large vampire which sucks human blood.

To climb the mountains of Benguet to classify and measure the skulls of the Igorots in order to study and enlighten this race while having the sight of birds of prey at the same time spying on the location of large gold deposits kept by the Igorots in the vastness of the lonely hills, to claim these afterwards, thanks to legal procedures which are changed regularly, but always for his own benefit.

To allow, against law and health, the forbidden slaughter of diseased cows to profit from the decayed meat which he himself forbids by virtue of his position.

To introduce himself at every opportunity as a scientist with lines on his forehead and devote his life to the wonders of the science laboratory, although his only scientific undertakings are the classification of insects and the importing of fish eggs, as if the fish in this country lacked nutrients and flavor, so that they have to be replaced with fish from other places.

To scheme, with the help of secret agents and partners, to sell to the city at fantastic prices worthless lands which the city dads cannot refuse for fear of incurring the ire of the man behind the scheme; and they cannot refuse, because it is also for their own gain.

To patronize concessions of hotels on unclaimed land, hoping to make large profits from the people's lifeblood.

These are the marks of this person who is also an Eagle that spies and devours, a vulture that fattens on the dead and on decayed flesh, an owl that pretends to possess all knowledge in his temperamental head, and a vampire that mercilessly sucks the blood of its victim until it has dried up.

These birds of prey always triumph. Their flight and their designs cannot be stopped.

Who will stand in their way?

Some share in the loot. Others cannot protest because of their weak voices. And still others die from the frightening destruction of their own strength and welfare.

And suddenly appears the horrifying, deathless phrase: "Mane, Thecel, Phares."

****

Gone is the loathsome creature who used the disguise of the eagle, the accursed vulture, the owl, and the vampire, but he left his descendants and the descendants of his agents and partners. They can be found not only in the mountains but on the plains, fields, lakes, seas, towns, and cities; in large buildings, in high positions, in important causes. Their sharp beaks, teeth, and claws are still used for devouring and sucking the blood of their victims.

But one day, and that day must come, no longer will it be the mysterious hand of fate to write on the wall the warning of disaster, like that read by Belshazzar, but the hand of the oppressed and the exploited will render justice.

This is not a prophecy, but a certainty which cannot be delayed, but is inevitable.

***

"This is the editorial," Andres said admiringly, when he finished.

"A thrust of the *Kampilan*," said Magat as he lit another cigarette.

XXX

The past few days, the newspapers reported that Congress was about to pass a bill Filipinizing retail trade, including sari-sari stores. Crowds flocked to Congress during the last days of the discussion of the bill.

The session was scheduled for nine in the morning. It was already eleven and many seats in the Senate were empty.

Meanwhile, on both sides of the hall, the gallery was jam-packed. In the front row were small businessmen who wanted to witness the fate of their proposal. Although the papers predicted the passage of the bill, they were anxious because there were persistent rumors that several million pesos were being passed around by foreigners who opposed the bill. The campaign for and against the bill started before the war.

There was a big crowd of kibitzers inside the hall and outside. The jobless who hoped to see their representative or senator, law students, the idle who enjoyed watching the sideshow in Congress.

"Some senators are better comedians than Pugo and Tugo," said one.

"But imagine how much the country spends on them," answered another.

Some women in the front rows were fanning themselves or fixing their lipstick. Their paint and getup made them look like

Indians on the warpath. Sometimes, they would wave their fans at a senator who happened to glance back. One kibitzer whispered to another that these women were bait of the lobbyists. The other couldn't get his meaning.

To the left facing the chairman's table on a platform was the press section, looking like a deserted fort.

In contrast, the Congress employees and helpers, the secretaries, stenographer, and messenger had been in their places for some time. From their expression and glances at the gallery and their words, one could see their imagined self-importance.

"The way those monkeys behave, you'd think they were senators," said a student with annoyance. "Some day, when we occupy those seats, the first thing I'll do is to kick out that one, if he is still around." And he pointed out a security guard who irked him.

The platform with a large table and throne-like chairs was still waiting for the senate president. All around the entrances on both sides of the hall flitted the guards. They bowed before the high officials but cast sharp glances at the common people as if these were suspected bomb throwers.

The kibitzers had dissected the personalities of each of the few who had arrived. Two oppositionists were speaking noisily and gesticulating. Another kibitzer explained that the division between the majority and the minority was very vague. The two often exchanged members.

"The practice is to join the party where there are more benefits. This is the politics of the stomach."

"Like Senator Batalla." And he pointed with his lips towards one of two men noisily talking on one side of the hall.

"That one does nothing but contradict any popular bill, good or bad. But once, he gave himself away. He kept attacking a bill; it turned out that he was the author."

Each time the front door opened and disgorged a gentleman with unusual attire or bearing, the whispering would grow louder and the gossip would mix with the smoke of cigars and cigarettes. They would whisper loudly about who the newcomer was and discuss his public and private affairs both as a legislator and as an individual.

"There's Senator Discurso," said the first kibitzer to his seatmate who hardly spoke and pointed to someone rushing in, a short, stout man with a wide mouth and large eyes.

"That one is fond of making speeches, even out of order," said the kibitzer. "It's hard to stop him unless his false teeth fall out."

A man entered with faltering steps. He seemed to be deep in thought. He twisted a cane with one hand, and on the left lapel of his woolen coat was a gaudy rose. Eyes followed him until he put down his cane on his table and sat back on his swivel chair. Then he raised an arm to acknowledge the greeting of the newspapermen.

"That's Senator Estrellado," whispered the kibitzer. "He is always well-dressed and elegant. You'd think he would do something worthwhile, but he does nothing but wear out his seat. He never joins a discussion or says 'yes' or 'no.' Nevertheless, he is a winner in elections."

"Really? How does he do that?"

"By overspending," said the gossip. "Some newsmen and photographers are on his payroll, so his statements and pictures always appear in the papers. Every time the reporters choose outstanding legislators, he is always on the list. Even if he did nothing the whole session. Naturally, what counts is the giving of 'envelopes.'"

"So, that's it, ha?"

"Aba, partner, money talks. Many are carried away by propaganda on the radio and in the papers. With money, it's easy to make a crow white and a heron black." And he snapped his fingers softly.

"You can't believe there are many straight ones among those legislators."

"So it seems."

Two more senators came together. Senator Botin, whom we have met before, was in a sharkskin suit; the other was in barong-Tagalog. The latter looked young and energetic despite his white hair.

"Those two are very good," said the gossipy kibitzer. "The one in the coat, Senator Botin, is good at gambling. The one in the barong is Senator Maliwanag. He has the most brilliant mind in Congress."

The other laughed at the amusing comparison.

"Maliwanag is good," continued the gossip. "Because of this, he is often alone. He seems to be in the middle of the wilderness. In gatherings like this, one should not be intelligent or patriotic. An acrobat or a poker player is better. Senator Botin can get more than Maliwanag for he is a wily gambler and an expert bluffer."

After eleven-thirty by the big Senate clock, the senate head went up onto the platform, took the mallet, and pounded it.

"The session is open," he declared, and sat on his large chair, rested his head on the back, and puffed his cigar.

The floor leader rose and moved that they omit the roll call and the minutes of the preceding session. There was no objection. He presented the first bill on the agenda. The opposition leader quickly stood up and questioned the quorum.

"Ask for a quorum in voting on a bill," reminded the floor leader angrily. "If you always take note of the quorum, no session will take place."

"In *dat keys*," shouted the oppositionist, "*dis siyempul* anomaly is *di responsibility ob di madyuriti*. According to *di* rules *ob di* house…"

"Let's set aside rules first," the floor leader shouted back. "We need to finish, so don't waste time on rules."

The veins on the neck of the opposition leader bulged as he screamed in Cebuano English.

"Mr. President, your honor," he said, stuttering, "*Di* members *ob di madjuriti* are *olwis* absent in *awir* sessions. We were sent *hiyer* by Uncle Sam, no, I mean, by Juan de la Cruz, to work, *en* work religiously. But many *ob* you abandoned your duties. You simply *istil di* money *ob di pipol*. What do members *ob di madjurity* do? Waste time on money in junkets *en* junkets. It's *imposibol to heb* a quorum because one *hap ob di Senit* is elsewhere outside *ob di* Filipino territory. At least five senators in United *Estets*, one is in *Espin*, one in England, in France, in Argentina, and three in Tokyo, making deals in *reperesyons*. *Wid dem* are *dyr waibs, tsildren en* company, at *di* expense *ob awir guberment en pipol*. Your Honor, *dis abuses* are a national *iskandal en* calamity. *Di iliktorit* will *siyurli panis* your party in *di* co   ming *iliktions*."

The attack by the opposition was rewarded with loud applause from the gallery. The majority floor leader objected, claiming that the opposition was out of order.

"We have an agenda, Mr. President," he pointed out.

"Go on," the chairman said.

"The bill Filipinizing retail trade is up for decision today," declared the floor leader. "The committee has recommended its approval."

"Mr. President, I believe that our nation is a democracy. Each one has the right to exercise freedom of judgment and opinion. I am against the Filipinization of retail trade because I am a friend of equal rights and opportunity before the law. Many Chinese owned shops prosper not because they are Chinese but because they are skilled managers, more hardworking and diligent and more frugal in their business. They are not to blame. On the contrary, we should be grateful to the Chinese for giving Filipinos a valuable lesson. I am afraid that the moment the businesses are transferred to the hands of our compatriots, they will exploit our countrymen. We have enough proof of this. What is also happening is that the fish that are abundant in our rivers and seas are more expensive than the meats imported from Canberra and Buenos Aires. Likewise, the prices of bananas from our land are higher than apples and oranges from the United States. *Que barbaridad*!"

"La intention del bill de Felipe-nisacion es para despohar y escluir a los estranjeros del negosyo de sari-sari, no es berdad?" interrupted Senator Discurso.

"Mas y menos."

"Entonses, es una intencion injusta e indigna, pero gagawin instrumento nga lang ang isang ley," said Discurso vehemently.

"It's a nation's duty to itself to pass laws to protect its interests," the floor leader informed him.

"Sinyor Presidente," Discurso shouted, *"quiero hablar en contra de la proyecto."*

"Senator Discurso," the chairman said, "wait for your turn; Senator Maliwanag has the floor."

Calmly the floor leader asked Discurso not to oppose the administration, for he was a member of the majority. The Senator's face turned red at this reminder, so he screamed in *chabacano.*[1]

"Mr. President, I believe that our nation is a democracy. Everyone has the right to exercise freedom of judgment and opinion. I am against the Filipinization of retail trade because I am a friend of equal rights and opportunity before the law. Many Chinese-owned shops prosper not because the owners are Chinese but because they are skilled managers, more hardworking and diligent and more frugal in their business. They are not to blame. On the contrary, we should be grateful to the Chinese for giving Filipinos a valuable lesson. I am afraid that the moment the businesses are transferred to the hands of our compatriots, they will exploit our countrymen. We have enough proof of this. What is also happening is that the fish that are abundant in our rivers and seas are more expensive than the meats imported from Canberra and Buenos Aires. Likewise, the prices of bananas from our land are higher than apples and oranges from the United States. *Que barbaridad!"*

---

1 chabacano—pidgin Spanish

Que barbaridad was not a part of his speech, but was an outburst when his dentures leaped off his gums. Luckily, he caught them with his hand before they fell out of his mouth. He stared openmouthed as laughter resounded from the crowded gallery. The crowd was quickly silenced by the chairman's mallet and his instructions to the bouncer to warn those who made noise. But even the senators were laughing hard.

"Serves him right," said a kibitzer who favored the bill. "The Chinese must have given him a large sum."

When order was restored, Senator Maliwanag stood up. He was recognized by the chairman.

"I shall explain why we should approve the bill giving retail trade to our countrymen," said the handsome senator in eloquent Tagalog.

"Talk in English," asked Senator Batalla.

"*En Castellano*," said Discurso.

"Gentlemen of the Legislature," continued Senator Maliwanag, unperturbed by the requests. "I thought that every member of this body knows what is known to every ordinary citizen—that the Philippines is free and independent. But because it has not been very long, colonial mentality has not yet disappeared."

The whispering in the gallery expressed approval.

"One of these signs we saw when I started to speak. In any legislature of a free and independent country, when a member uses his native language, other members don't ask him to speak a foreign language. In a legislature of a free and independent country, the wretch who behaves in this manner will be brought by the bouncer out of the assembly hall. He will either be charged with disturbance or have his head examined. Here, this merely arouses laughter instead of reproach and shame."

Sudden applause from the gallery.

"I prefer English," insisted Batalla from his seat.

"*Hangal!*" said Senator Maliwanag.

"Who is a fool?" And the one who didn't approve of Tagalog stood up.

"If you understand *hangal*, then you understand Tagalog," said Maliwanag. "But if you don't, sorry."

Laughter resounded among the kibitzers. The Senator continued.

"The Philippines is the land God gave to the Filipinos. But look at the unhappy events. Here the Filipinos are poor and the foreigners prosper. Who owns the mines? Foreigners. Who owns the banks? Foreigners. Who owns the foremost industries and business firms? Foreigners. Who owns electrical services? Foreigners. Who owns communications services? Foreigners. To whom belong almost all prosperous factories and businesses? Foreigners. Go to Stanta Cruz, Binondo, Quiapo and see the painful irony. The big bazaars, groceries, and stores all belong to foreigners while our countrymen sell wares in a box or a basket on the sidewalk. And they are chased by the police and dragged like animals to wagons."

"One question." Senator Botin rose. Maliwanag nodded.

"Will the Filipinization of retail trade correct this lopsided economy?" asked Batalla. "Is that not just a balm on a wound?"

"That is a good question," remarked Maliwanag. "The falling of retail trade into the hands of foreigners is not an illness but a symptom of a serious illness. Just like unemployment, poverty, and widespread discontent are the offspring of one mother; separate wounds from one source. Applying a poultice to a painful wound brings only temporary relief to the patient. This doesn't mean, however, that the treatment will stop there. If an operation is needed, that operation will be performed."

"Can you specify the illness that brought about our sufferings?" Senator Botin asked again.

"Perhaps it's no longer a secret," Maliwanag promptly answered. "I refer to colonialism. During the four centuries of foreign domination, the Philippines was used to chop wood and fetch water and was asked to attend, not to her needs, but to the needs of the master. The Philippines was assigned to the production of raw material and importation of finished products. She sold cheap and bought dear. It was inevitable that this situation would breed poverty, unemployment, and discontent. Nationalism is the cure. So I ask for unanimous approval of this bill." This was Maliwanag's ardent plea.

"Approve! Approve!" shouted the gallery as one.

But the Senator had hardly returned to his seat to drink water when he heard Batalla calling attention to the lack of quorum.

"To pass an important bill without a quorum is equivalent to falsification," he shouted.

There was no quorum, but because their stomachs were growling, the table adjourned without action on the Filipinization bill.

"The foreigners will rejoice again," groaned a Filipino owner of a sari-sari store.

XXXI

A man with an impressive bearing, five feet ten inches tall, took twin rooms with a private bath at the plush Hotel Ritz in Paris. He was dressed in gray English wool. He wore black leather shoes, a white shirt, and a purple tie with silver dots. Under his right arm was a portfolio; his left held a Homburg hat bought in Rome.

When he approached the receiving desk, he spoke fluent English. The first thing noticed by the employee were his white teeth and the large scar on his cheek. The employee wondered what kind of sharp weapon could have caused such a scar. He wore light green eyeglasses.

Opposite the suite number in the guest book, he quickly signed his name.

MANDO PLARIDEL

"Mando Plaridel," read the clerk. "Mexican?" he asked tentatively, handing the guest the key to the suite.

"No," he answered, "Filipino."

The clerk didn't catch the answer but said nothing. He thought that this man was a native of a Spanish province or the Near East. He relied on an old policy of the owner of the Ritz, who began as a waiter and ended up a millionaire. He had taught his men to see all without looking, to hear all without listening, and to learn all without asking.

The clerk recognized the common characteristics of the Chinese and Japanese who had pale, yellowish faces and al-mond-shaped eyes. This man had reddish-brown skin and black, round eyes.

Mando took the elevator to his room on the third floor fol-lowed by a bell boy carrying his luggage.

Mando had just arrived that afternoon from the city of London. He took a BOAC airplane from Croydon airport in England. As he comfortably read the English paper and drank martini, the plane smoothly crossed the Canal de la Mancha, and gently landed at Le Bourget Airport in Paris in an hour.

The questions of the customs agents were respectful and brief. In less than half an hour, he obtained the okay of the examiners of the passengers' luggage. No meticulous search, no inquisitive questions. The employees accepted the declarations of the guests. The French show their visitors that they are delighted to have the tourists. There is a ring of delight in their greeting "Welcome to Paris."

After exchanging dollars for French money at the airport, Mando took a Citroën taxi to the Ritz Hotel.

After arranging his suitcases in the dressing room, Mando took off his traveling clothes and went to the bathroom.

After a bath and a change of clothes, he took the phone and asked for a waiter. It was about seven in the evening. He ordered drinks and supper. In Paris and other cities on the continent, a drink is not cold water but hot wine. Two or three kinds of wine were served with the food.

While waiting for his order, Mando took out his diary and sat on the sofa. He wrote down the date and time of his arrival in the French capital. He turned the pages of the diary.

After supper, Mando wondered if he should go out and begin his acquaintance with the enchanting city. Paris was beautiful by day, but she was an enchantress by night.

Mando could breathe the delicate breeze from the window of his room. He looked at the sky, which hung like a huge canopy shading the lovely city. The darkness was overcome by the bright lights, which were like long necklaces that glittered along the twelve boulevards, which met and joined at the lovely Place de l'Étoile. Mando saw at once that the brightest boulevard was the Champs-Élysées, where his taxi had driven that afternoon from the airport. The driver had stopped for a while beside the Arc de Triomphe. In halting English, he explained that this was built by Napoleon in commemoration of France's victory in war. Only after Mando showed that he understood did the taxi move again.

To Mando at the window, the famed Eiffel Tower, with its height of nine hundred thirty-four feet, looked like a giant standing at the Champ de Mars. At the tip, a red light like the eye of a giant bird.

Mando's attention was attracted to the waters of the Seine River, which were like the silver scales of a long serpent reflecting the lights. Not far was the silhouette of the Trocadéro Palace. He turned his eyes beyond the shady trees of Champs Élysées; west of the Tuileries was the Place de la Concorde, formerly called Place de la Guillotina. The new look and décor of the riotous square did not bear even a trace of the disorder, panic, and horror of the execution of King Louis XVI and his queen, Marie Antoinette, at the hands of the revolutionists. After a few years, the leaders of the revolution were the ones trapped by unending intrigue and revenge. Mando felt the breeze, but it was not the lament of Madame Roland, the beauty who helped and was slain by the revolution and who, before the guillotine severed her head, defiantly exclaimed, "Oh liberty, how many crimes are committed in thy name?"

Mando returned to his seat and drank martini. Silently, he ate supper brought by the waiter, then drank strong coffee. He lit a cigarette and poured another martini.

He told the waiter that he would call for him if needed. He looked up some names in the directory and listed these on a sheet of paper.

Mando decided not to go out that night. Instead, he changed into pajamas. He reclined on the bed, holding his diary.

He relived the events from the time he quietly left Manila almost a year before.

XXXII

Mando had gone to most of the important cities of Europe. He saw and learned a lot. He had a wider vision, which would be hard to measure and describe. There was an obvious change in his appearance, dress, and movements.

According to his diary, he stayed in Saigon, South Vietnam. He flew to Bangkok, Thailand, stopped at Rangoon in Burma, Karachi in Pakistan, and Cairo, Egypt. He crossed the Mediterranean to Ankara, Turkey, and to Milan, Italy, then proceeded to Madrid, Spain.

At some Asian cities, he was tempted to stay and tour ancient places he had read about in geography and history. But Mando stifled such desire and told himself later, because his real goals were the famous cities in Europe. He did not put off the real purpose of his travel.

Although he only stayed a short while in these places, Mando obtained worthwhile information about their conditions, people, cities, government, progress or lack of it, strengths, and weaknesses.

He thought it best to stay longer in Madrid and there learn about mother Spain at close range. He often traveled from Madrid to Barcelona. These two cities were the intellectual, commercial, and social centers of the former kingdom that had given the

Philippines the name of its ruler. Some ancient parts of these cities reminded him of Intramuros and San Nicolas in Manila.

He met some Filipinos who enjoyed living there and had no plans of going home to the Philippines. Likewise, there were Spaniards in Manila, Iloilo, Zamboanga, and other places in the archipelago who didn't want to return to Spain. Mando thought that people were like plants that live where they take root and agree with the climate.

Mando often visited the former palace at the Congress of Representatives and the famed University of Madrid. At the palace, the credentials of the visitor were closely examined. It was ordered by the generalissimo, who had been almost assassinated several times by the nationalist foes of dictatorship.

Mando looked for the former printing press of the newspaper *La Solidaridad* published by del Pilar, Jaena, and Rizal as the voice of Filipinos in Europe. The house had been replaced by a modern building and had not even a humble marker.

He spent many days at the National Library. In this foremost museum, he examined books and looked at relics of the Spanish occupation of the Philippines. He copied some important data, which he could use to correct some wrong accounts of the history of the archipelago.

Mando discovered that Spanish citizens were very friendly to Filipino tourists. Their women had sweet smiles, their vino de Pasto, amontillado, and amoroso gave heat, and their sardines and tomato-pepper sauce were spicy. At first, he could not understand why they had this special fondness for Filipinos. The Filipino seemed a long-separated and long-missed relative on a visit.

Based on his observations, Mando thought that all advanced countries were almost the same: peaceful and generous, quiet and kindhearted. But often, the representatives sent to conquered lands were unworthy, who exploited and committed abuses. He felt that if the Spanish officials and friars had been like these ordinary citizens of Madrid and Barcelona in their dealings with Filipinos, perhaps the ties that bound the Philippines and mother Spain would not have been broken bloodily. Nevertheless, Mando felt it was best that way, for a steel chain and a gold necklace have the same effect if used by the master to choke a slave. Once, Mando asked a Filipino who had been living in Spain a long time about it. This was his explanation:

"Spain is a good and honorable country," he said, "but its ministers are to blame. Colonizers often send undesirable elements to the colonies. That is the first reason. Secondly, the Spaniards changed their impression of Filipinos when they revolted in 1896; they realized that the Filipinos are not a tribe of slaves."

In Madrid, Mando visited some old churches, which were the same style and size as the churches built by the Spaniards in the Philippines. He watched the popular bullfights. He noticed the contradiction between the state religion and the state amusement of Spain. The first preaches holiness, but the second displays cruelty. He guessed that it was the same reason that education was in the gentle hands of the religious orders and the government was controlled by the iron hand of autocracy. Occasionally, they were reversed or fused.

After some months, he proceeded from Spain to Italy. He stayed in Rome.

Rome is one of the oldest cities in the world. According to legend, it was built by the twins Romulus and Remus who had been found and reared by a wolf. One of the fast-selling souvenirs in Rome is that of two infants nursed by a large wolf, their foster mother.

The center of religious and political power of the Roman Catholic Church is in Rome—the Vatican, an independent state, separate from Rome and Italy, a sovereign power, although it has less than fifty hectares. Here reside the pope and one thousand residents, most of whom are heads, employees, guards, and servants of the Roman Catholic Church. The Vatican is surrounded by high walls.

On the other hand, the city of Rome has a population of two million. Mando was surprised that the holy city of the Vatican also had the greatest number of communists outside the Soviet Union.

The first thing Mando noticed at the airport was the abundance of crucifixes and statuettes of Venus de Milo. Both were naked. Christ was bare of all vanity and worldliness at the moment of his supreme sacrifice at Calvary, while Venus de Milo showed the unadorned, natural beauty of woman.

Rome was a city of contrasts. The ruins of a coliseum built before Christ and the modern building of a United Nations Agency.

Just like in Manila, government offices in Rome, banks, and other establishments are closed on Saturdays and Sundays. However, theaters, stores, restaurants, and bars are open. But on Sunday there is complete abstinence—no business for department stores, bars, and bazaars. On the other hand, the three hundred Catholic churches are open and there is a brisk sale of religious objects like crucifixes, rosaries, veils, medals, sacred pictures (*stampita*), prayer books, images, candles, and all kinds of stamps depicting activities of the pope and the holy church, countless relics and souvenirs prized by pilgrims and Catholic tourists.

Tourism is the chief industry of Rome and other famous Italian cities. Besides Italy's noble ruins of more than two thousand years, its art, opera, architecture, sculpture, and other cultural forms are the foremost in Europe.

Mando joined a tour of Rome and its suburbs. The usual tour, which takes the passenger to historical places, lasts three hours. But tours that include Naples, Capri, Pompeii, Sorrento, Amalfi, and other places last several days. So the traveler's budget includes food, hotel, and other conveniences.

Mando stayed in a hotel near the Basilica of St. Mary Major, one of the four patriarchal temples of Rome. The other three are St. Peter's Basilica, the world's largest and most famous; the Basilica of St. John Lateran; and the Basilica of St. Paul. According to legend, in August 352 A.D., the image of the Virgin Mary appeared to Pope Liberius and told him to build a church where snow fell that night.

During one outing, Mando went around the large Basilica of St. John Lateran, where he saw the huge statues of the twelve apostles and the mausoleum of the painter Raphael and he signed in the old book of guests who came from all parts of the world.

He also visited the Basilica of St. Paul. In front was a statue of St. Paul holding a sword, showing that he was not only a ferocious Roman guard against the first Christians but also a martyr beheaded for being a devout follower of Jesus.

But the grandest, most powerful and impressive was the Basilica of St. Peter in the heart of the Vatican. Every day, thousands of people go to this holy mecca of Christendom to fulfill a vow or desire, to hear mass at its very heart, to see the pope, or to stand rapt viewing the matchless creations of art and marks of civilization. Almost all religions, Christian and non-Christian, Muslim, freethinkers and atheists, are fascinated watching the ceremonies of the most widespread religion and the monuments of culture and history.

Alighting at St. Peter's square, one faces the tall obelisk brought home by Caligula from Heliopolis during his Egyptian campaign. The cathedral and the pope's palace are on one side. At the wide door of the cathedral stands a tall Swiss guard as rigid as a statue, wearing a colorful uniform and holding a spear. On each side of the stairway are the monuments of St. Peter and St. Paul. There are five doors to the portico. On the left is the statue of Charlemagne, and on the right, Constantine, who built the first basilica, said to be built on the exact burial place of St. Peter. Mando noticed the bronze statue of St. Peter, who was seated. Its feet were worn out from endless kisses.

After the rites celebrated by cardinals and bishops at the main altar, pilgrims and other onlookers flowed out of the cathedral into the middle of the square. All eyes were on the window on the third floor of the palace. Then a white banner was unfurled from the second window. In a few seconds appeared the pope with his hand raised to bless the crowd below. It was high noon, but the sun was mild.

On other excursions, Mando saw the remaining ivory columns of the Roman Forum, the old meeting place of the citizens, and the Curia, the former conference hall of the senators. At the Curia was enacted the tragedy of Julius Caesar, who was killed by his adopted son Brutus and by the other conspirators. Fearing that Caesar would be crowned, they meant to save democracy. But this very crime or heroism paved the way for the rise of a series of Roman emperors called Caesar. This was followed by autocrats of other kingdoms. Thus appeared the kaiser of Germany and the tsar of Russia.

Mando also went to see the arches and monuments made by famed sculptors, like the arches of Constantine and Titus, the monuments of Marcus Aurelius in older times and of King Emmanuel of a new Italy; also those of Galileo, Garibaldi, and Cavour. Surprisingly, on one side of the shore of the Tiber River still stood intact a tall column. According to the guide, it was built by Benito Mussolini in honor of his closest friend—himself. In fact, the concierge at the hotel where Mando was staying loudly proclaimed that Mussolini was the greatest Italian after Julius Caesar. This reminded Mando that there were still many fascists despite the numerous socialists in Rome.

One of the most interesting excursions brought him to the rows of catacombs or underground graves after the bus had passed several kilometers of the Appian Way. There were nine different catacombs. They visited the one belonging to Domatillus. They went down the winding passages lined by niches. They went down the stone steps around a platform, went down many stops again and reached a chapel. They were received by an old priest whose deep-set eyes and pointed nose made him look like a mummy risen from a niche. The priest related the history of the catacombs. There used to be four floors, but these were buried under the ruins and had been unearthed for only eighty years. During the early days of Christianity, thousands were killed by the Roman pagans. He mentioned the names of martyrs and saints buried there. Then they went to other sacred rooms of an old cemetery. The paths were of hard earth and the darkness was emphasized by the dim light.

As Mando stood in a corner looking at the niches, empty except for the dust of those buried for twenty centuries, he thought how easy it was to kill and dissolve a person's body, but not his spirit, his beliefs and principles. It has been proven every time. The first Christians were persecuted, condemned, imprisoned, assaulted, nailed to the cross, and killed. They didn't surrender and didn't fear death. When they were gone, then flourished, spread, and triumphed the truths for which they died. Truths about freedom and the equality of men. Thus the cruel group of executioners were the first to bow and wave the flag of the new faith.

On their way back from the catacombs, they stopped by the Quo Vadis chapel along the Appian Way. Here St. Peter and Jesus Christ were supposed to have met. At that time, the persecution of the Christians was at its fiercest and Christ had died on the cross outside Jerusalem. St. Peter was fleeing from Rome when he met the Nazarene.

St. Peter was startled and asked his teacher in wonder, "Domine, quo vadis? (Lord, where are you going?)" Christ quickly answered, "To Rome, to be crucified once more." St. Peter felt ashamed as he did when he denied his master at the garden of Gethsemane and the cock crowed. So the foremost apostle turned his footsteps and hurried back to Rome to face his death.

Mando concluded that the real greatness of Rome or Greece and Athens was not due to their feared legions, which were finally vanquished at the time. They bequeathed richness in civilization and culture like Greek literature and Latin laws to history and to succeeding ages.

Mando was fascinated by the mystery and truth of the Vatican—the official residence of the Holy Father and the seat of power of the Roman Catholic Church. Just one square mile and with less than a thousand residents, but its voice is heard and heeded by five million followers all over the earth.

Many times Mando would meditate as he sat on a pew in the large St. Peter's Cathedral. He visited the honored Basilica of the Vatican, which was grander than King Solomon's palace. He visited the tombs of St. Peter and his successors, from Linus to Pius XI. He saw not one of the thirty-eight antipopes, who claimed to be the true pontiffs from the second century till 1440.

More than the statues of those who established different orders of the church, Mando admired the mural and paintings of Raphael.

Mando researched at the Vatican Library. There he saw manuscripts older than the Christian religion. These were the first copies of the Bible made of papyrus and handwritten in Hebrew, Greek, and Latin.

Mando was startled to see the so-called Index and "Propaganda Fide," a blacklist of forbidden books and reading material. Mando didn't read the whole list, which ran into thousands of authors and works covering all topics under the sun.

He had sinned many times, he found out, by reading the works of Voltaire, Victor Hugo, the Dumas father and son, Zola, Rabelais, Stendhal, Flaubert, Anatole France, George Sand, D.H. Lawrence, and other famous authors. Several times he read the plays of Maeterlinck and Bernard Shaw, which he enjoyed. He had no idea he was endangering the salvation of his soul in the next world. Looking at the Index, he recalled *Paradise Lost* by Milton and *Faust* by Goethe, world masterpieces. In the English epic, Satan was the protagonist when the king of the devils rebelled against God. In the German poem, the chief character was Dr. Faustus who sold his soul to Mephistopheles in return for a woman, pomp, and power.

Mando recalled his student days. Every Lent, he would read the *Life of Jesus* by Ernest Renan. This was banned, he learned. He could not imagine this for Renan had studied for the priesthood before he became interested in writing history and biography. Also works on astronomy by Copernicus, Kepler, and Galileo, from which he drank in his intense thirst for knowledge. Didn't these writings change obsolete beliefs about the place, shape, size, elements, purpose, and meaning of the planets, sun, moon, and stars?

Mando doubted if he could still gain pardon for long-past pleasures from the philosophy of the sages, Spinoza, Bacon, Hobbes, Bergson, Swedenborg, and Kant; Darwin, Adam Smith, Proudhon, and Hegel; Marx, Engels, and Lenin. Why should he wonder that the novels and other works of Rizal should be opposed by faithful followers of the church, although they honored the martyr of the brown race?

Mando closed his eyes for a while. Then he approached an old employee of the library and courteously asked about the question bothering him.

"Bad reading material is more dangerous than swords," the employee said bluntly. "St. Paul showed what should be done with bad books. He burned them. The popes succeeding St. Peter did likewise. For the holy church cannot err, and in guiding all Catholics, it is her duty to keep all their reading material clean."

Then he took another list and handed it to Mando.

"This is the blue list," he said. "There is no lack of good things to read. You can see that on this list." And he left.

Mando looked at the blue list with its recommended books with the nihil obstat of the church censor and with the imprimatur of the bishop of the diocese where it was published.

It mentioned the Catholic Bible, especially the New Testament; the prayer book of Father Lasance; the *Imitation of Christ* by St. Thomas A. Kempis; the writings of St. Thomas Aquinas, St. Ignatius de Loyola, and St. Alphonse de Liguori; some works of G.K. Chesterton and Graham Greene; all the books of Cardinal Spellman and Monsignor Sheean; *Lives of the Saints* by Butler; and the encyclicals of different popes, especially *Rerum Novarum* and *Matrimonio Cristiano* of Pope Leo XIII and *Cuadragesimo Anno* of Pope Pius XI.

Mando left the Vatican Library and crossed the square to the cathedral. Entering the door, he dropped a hundred liras into the box for alms near the front.

When he left the cathedral, Mando was still thinking of what the old library employee said about the burning of bad books. He recalled that Hitler and Mussolini became known for book burning, and that the Japanese in the Philippines often made bonfires of mountains of books, which they said were not worth reading.

Mando reassured himself by thinking that it was better to burn books than roast in hellfire.

He continued comparing the pictures etched in his memory with the entries in his diary.

He recalled his trip to Switzerland, a small country nestled among the Alps. As a boy, Mando had read the story of William Tell, the archer-hero of the Swiss. Mando discovered that this country still possessed the same undiminished heroism and courage.

Mando was impressed by the small republic, which was less than one seventh of the Philippines and with only five million people. It remained free, economically and politically stable. It remained neutral, peaceful, and safe during World War II. It didn't have to pour money for armaments although surrounded by warlike countries like Germany, France, and Italy.

Mando's tourist guide explained that the Swiss weren't too concerned with politics, but with industry, agriculture, and other productive activities.

"The president serves only a year, without reelection," said the guide. "He is elected by the legislature from among the members of the council whose two houses are both elected by the people."

While Mando and his guide were talking at a corner in the city of Berne, a middle-aged man on a bicycle passed by.

"Look at that man," the guide told Mando. "He is a watch maker who became vice president. After his term, he went back to watch making."

The guide explained with pride that watch making is an important profession in Switzerland and that Swiss watches are the best in the world.

"Such an important person goes around on a bicycle," Mando wondered.

"Here, one does not enrich himself in a government position."

Mando raised his eyebrows but made no comment.

He observed that the Swiss were as industrious as ants. The only ones who wandered about seeking pleasure were the tourists. The Swiss made much from tourism. At the stations, trains brought products from different parts of this wonderful country, from giant locomotives to small ring watches and especially cheese, butter, and canned milk, which were unequalled in quality.

Mando passed by Geneva, the city by a lake, where international conferences had been held since it became the seat of the League of Nations after the First World War. At present, there were many standing committees and commissions of the United Nations stationed in Geneva. Representatives from different nations gathered here.

Before he left for other places, Mando deposited several million francs and some of Simoun's jewels in a reputable Swiss bank.

After coming from Geneva, Mando spent some weeks at Benelux (Belgium, Netherlands, and Luxembourg). These three states were a good example of how to remain independent and prosperous. Even if the first two were ruled by kings and the last by a duke, their constitutions guaranteed religious and political freedom. Neither the king nor the government can impose state beliefs, especially regarding the thoughts and conscience of the individual.

Mando was in London when England turned Socialist. He couldn't imagine why the party of Churchill fell, when this premier during the war, along with Franklin Roosevelt of the United States, counted as the foremost leader of democracy.

An English writer whom Mando had met on his trip greeted him upon his arrival in London. He explained the political system in Britain.

"Not all war heroes make good leaders during the period of reconstruction," said the Englishman. He mentioned the great generals, from Alexander the Great to George Washington, who weren't good administrators. And he added that every leader has his own time, and every period has its leader.

The English writer boasted that England not only developed its culture but also brought civilization to the jungles of America, Africa, and Australia.

"You are a colonizing country," remarked Mando. "You bring civilization and take out gold. Spain did the same earlier, but it brought religion which was also paid for in gold."

His English friend respected Mando's opinion, but insisted on what he said about civilization. Although Mando knew its history, he listened patiently to the story of the birth of the English constitution when King John signed the Magna Carta in 1215 on the fields of Runnymede, recognizing the rights of the nobles. Mando agreed that the Magna Carta became the model for the Bill of Rights of the United States, which was in turn, the model for the citizens' rights in the Philippine Constitution. He also mentioned the Industrial Revolution, which took place in England in the middle of the eighteenth century. Since then, the belief that work is heaven's curse was supposed to have disappeared, for with the miracle of the machine, man was freed from the yoke of hardship until he obtained a new dignity and standard.

On the other hand, Mando reminded him that the Industrial Revolution nourished capitalism and was the foundation of the Machine Age, where the means of production were more import-ant than people's lives. "Man became a slave of the machine," said Mando.

Mando was brought by his friend to different places. They entered the Buckingham gardens. His friend explained that the queen in this palace is only a symbol. The real power is at White-hall, the center of the government elected by the people, which then happened to be socialist.

They visited large printing presses on Fleet Street; Mando observed the different parts and activities of a modern newspaper. He learned that thousands read the English newspapers, like the *London Times*, *Daily Mail*, *News of the World*, and others.

"Here, democracy is not just a flower of the tongue," Mando's friend said with pride.

And they went to Hyde Park, the famous park in London, and listened to speeches of different groups on the wide square. One criticized the queen, another hit the prime minister. One gathering was about communism.

"They are free to float all kinds of ideas," said Mando's pal. "They don't even need to ask for a permit from anyone. No policeman will bother them."

Meanwhile, Mando saw that the leaders learned to practice self-discipline. They were not used to placing themselves above the law. One afternoon, Mando was brought by his writer friend to the house of a member of Parliament. It was a poor flat compared to the mansion of the typical Filipino legislator. After receiving them in his library, the M.P. lit the fireplace. He was going to boil water for tea.

"Is there no electricity?" asked the writer.

"Because of austerity," answered the host, "it's forbidden to use electricity before six in the evening."

Mando looked at the clock on top of the table. It was five-thirty. Half an hour more. Mando's eyes glistened with admiration for the English legislator. Then a sigh escaped him when he thought of what a Filipino lawmaker would do if he needed to make coffee in the face of such a ban in Manila. Would he still light a fire or just switch on the electricity? Mando was sure of the answer.

As they drank tea, they discussed various things. Mando asked, "The war has long ended, yet why do you still use coupons for buying and selling?"

"To avoid the black market, to prevent hoarding by the rich, so that goods will be available to the ordinary consumer. We can do this because production is adequate. Supply and demand are balanced."

"Why are American cigarettes so expensive—two dollars a pack?"

"Sometimes even more," answered the official, "because we want to protect our own production. We have cigarettes, which are not inferior to the imported ones. If we don't charge high taxes on those made in the U.S.A., we'd be killing our own industry. We have our own, therefore those from other countries are luxuries and should be expensive."

Mando saw very clearly why Filipino producers don't prosper and why, in Manila stores, imported products sell fast.

Like any tourist, Mando didn't tire of going to historical places and buildings in the two parts of London divided by the Thames River. He climbed the London Tower, strolled in Mayfair Park, visited Westminster Abbey, and watched a meeting of Parliament. He bought a few things and souvenirs at Piccadilly Circus and Trafalgar Square. He also bought some books at Haymarket on Chancery Lane.

Whenever he had time, Mando always went to the incomparable British Museum, which housed a very big library. Every time he went, Mando felt like he was entering a holy temple.

The first time he went there, he was with his friend who informed Mando that it had more than five million books and two million manuscripts. If the bookshelves were placed side by side, they would reach sixty miles, the distance from Manila to San Miguel de Mayumo.

The complete collection of English poems from Chaucer's *The Canterbury Tales* to the last collection of Dylan Thomas were all there. Attracting the most attention were the plays and poems of Shakespeare with copies of translations in all languages.

As Mando read a yellowed book of the history of the socialist movement in England on an old table in the reading room, Mando seemed to discern the shadows of Garibaldi, Marx, Lenin, Rizal, Sun Yat-sen, Gandhi, and other revolutionaries who had spent long hours in this room.

Mando was mesmerized by the English genius in industry and commerce. Only an island slightly bigger than the Philippines, England produced almost all of man's needs, from pins to giant ships, from candy to giant hydraulic plants, and everywhere it sent its ships and airplanes. While the Philippines could not even produce mediocre toilet paper.

After reading the last pages with the entries of his travels, Mando took out from his portfolio a tiny notebook and studied it closely. It was an important list of Simoun's jewels which had been sold, to whom and from where, and the selling price. When Mando summed up, the sales reached a few million dollars. Less than half the jewels had been sold. He had made no transaction in Paris and his contact in the United States was getting impatient.

He deposited the money in the banks, bought bonds, and invested in stable industries. For all his financial moves, he consulted an internationally known Swiss corporation. In Madrid, he deposited several hundred thousand dollars in the national bank, almost a million in the international bank at Geneva, and more than two million in the London bank. Half a million was used to buy stocks in the railroad industry in Switzerland, and he bought bonds in Berlin, West Germany. He had enough traveler's checks in Swiss and American dollars, two of the most stable currencies in the world.

He had five million dollars to his credit at that time.

More than fifteen million Philippine pesos, he told himself.

He reassured himself that this was not a dream but a fact.

And barely half of Simoun's jewels had been disposed of.

Mando noticed that it was almost midnight. He became engrossed in his diary and in his thoughts. He got up and smoked.

When he stood again by the window, the red light at the top of the Eiffel Tower seemed to wink at him. It was very late, but just like a beautiful enchanted princess, Paris was just starting its giddy nightlife.

XXXIII

Mando remained an early riser. Ever since he worked at the Monteros' before the war, he would rise at dawn. And more so as a guerrilla in the Sierra Madre.

But the next morning at the Ritz Hotel, he hadn't even brushed his teeth when the telephone rang. It was Helen, a Spanish-Irish mestiza who was born in Intramuros, Manila, but was in Europe during the war. Helen had lost both parents and became a cosmopolite traveling on the continent. She lived on her earnings as an agent for anything saleable, from a fort in Gibraltar to the crown of King Farouk. When she was younger, it was said that she was used to receiving offers for her smooth and alluring body for a night at the Grand Hotel or a week at the Riviera, instead of her wares.

Mando met Helen in Geneva on business. There the Spanish-Irish Filipina adventuress helped Mando sell his jewels at a good price. He gave Helen five percent of any cash sales, and her commission was not small. To a young king in the Near East, she sold a set of jewels worth a million dollars. This was a gift to a Hollywood star with whom he was infatuated. The king and the star met at a vacation place in Switzerland, and Helen guessed right away what spell could attract both the king's gold, which came from his petroleum mines, and the heart of the actress. In that transaction, Helen earned fifty thousand dollars.

In his notebook, this was one of the biggest sales. In Madrid, he sold to a famous Spanish millionaire from Manila who was vacationing in Spain some jewels which he bought without haggling at the original quoted price of half a million. Mando heard that these were given at the wedding of a daughter of the caudillo, and in exchange, he received a gold medal and a citation for his deeds in honor of Spain in the former colony.

Cleopatra's collar was bought by a bank of the Rothschilds in England at six hundred thousand pounds sterling—about two million dollars. The bank official expected to profit by no less than fifty percent for its investment in the storied collar, which it sold to a multimillionaire collector in Chicago.

Before the bank of the Rothschilds bought the famous collar, Mando's agent first offered it to the English government.

"Such a collar and similar jewelry are only for aristocrats," said the spokesman of the Socialist government. "We won't waste a single penny on anything not needed by the country, but any amount for food, housing, and coal." If it were not for his moral responsibility, Mando would have given the collar as a gift to the Socialist government in London. He felt then that the gap between the new government and the old conservative regime was like that between heaven and earth. After a time, he was startled to learn that the opposing parties were both made up of politicians. They were two faces of the same lead coin.

Mando invited Helen to breakfast. When the woman-agent arrived, they went down to the restaurant of the hotel. According to Helen, she had just arrived in Paris and immediately sought out Mando. She was staying at the Normandy Hotel.

"A New York playboy is here," said Helen as they were having coffee. She mentioned an American heir who had been married and divorced several times. Each adventure in love was international news.

"Prospect?" Mando asked.

"I heard that he keeps following a ballet dancer, a Viennese, now the favorite of Paris," said Helen. "He is said to be throwing away a fortune in flowers and perfume alone."

"Very well, see what the playboy will like."

"What the ballet dancer will," corrected Helen.

After breakfast, they returned to Mando's suite and he showed her a list of the jewels. Then he brought out a case of different gems, which Helen had not seen before. Rings and earrings, necklaces, bracelets, pendants, pins, combs, and other pieces of all shapes, colors, and styles. Some were shaped like butterflies, dragonflies, bees, centipedes, fish, elephants, tigers, serpents, flowers, stars, statues, human heads. Some were made of gold, yellow or white, and sprinkled with diamonds, pearls, emeralds, rubies, turquoise, garnets, sapphires, opals, and stones with the colors of the rainbow. Helen chose a few and asked the price.

"I'll proceed to the ballerina's hotel," said Helen. "It's said she does not rise before eleven." She looked at her watch. It was past ten. "Very well," she said, "I'll be seeing you."

"Come back this afternoon," Mando said. "I'd like to see Paris. Be my chaperone."

"Okay, monsieur." Helen waved her hand, and she left.

Helen returned at suppertime. She informed Mando that she had set up the deal amounting to three hundred thousand dollars.

"It's in the bag," she said proudly. The ballet dancer could not let go of the jewels. Helen had asked for an appointment with the playboy heir. "If you have the head, business is easy."

"First you need something to sell," answered Mando.

"Of course," said the *corredora*.[1] "Only a racketeer sells nothing."

"In Manila, business-influence peddling is different. Nothing to sell, no capital except their saliva."

---

1 corredora—agent, usually of jewelry

"The influence peddler, wherever he may be—Manila, Paris, or Washington—is a racketeer," said Helen. "Most of them are politicians in power."

"You're really a wise gal, Helen," said Mando in admiration.

"I've been around." Helen winked her blue eyes.

"Hats off to you."

Mando asked the telephone operator to send up some drinks.

"I'll just change," Mando told Helen.

When they went down, their car was waiting. They went to a small restaurant on the bank of the Seine River. Despite Sun Yat-sen's claim that the Chinese were the best cooks in the world, the French were considered the experts, especially by gourmets. They said that the Chinese discovered more dishes, but the French were more choosy; they have rare sauces and don't cloy with too much lard or seasoning.

Helen asked for stewed rabbit and Mando for *agatsonas*[2] sautéed in champagne.

After dinner, Mando asked what Helen wanted to see—the Opera or the Folies Bergère.

"For you, let's go to the Folies Bergère," suggested Helen. "There are operas in all the big cities, but there is only one Folies Bergère of Paris. It was imitated by the Ziegfeld Follies in New York, but an imitation is an imitation."

They had to pay extra for tickets, for the ticket booth was closed. Tourists from all over the world filled the famed burlesque theater every night.

That night, impresario Paul Derval was presenting *C'est de la Folie* with two acts and thirty scenes. The whole show was about two hours.

According to the printed program, which was sold at three hundred francs, the women's costumes were exclusive creations of a famous male couturier, and it warned that they could not be

_____

2 agatsonas—a kind of bird

copied without his permission. But in the eyes of the audience, the women were more alluring without clothes, from the star Nita Raya to the group of chorus girls.

The best-liked scene where the audience hardly blinked was the one entitled "L'Enfer des Femmes" which depicted hell aflame. At the side stood a well-built Lucifer who looked more like a Mister Universe. Then like a swarm of moths appeared beautiful women, young, fair, shapely, with nothing to distract the eyes except the flowers in their hair and the rings on their fingers.

Such was the delight of the audience that two American sailors seated behind Mando and Helen decided there and then to look for hell.

"Buddy, sure there's heaven in that place," a sailor said to his companion. The two agreed to search for the place immediately.

Mando whispered to Helen that this kind of show was not allowed by the authorities in Manila and would be opposed by the good matrons who were the guardians of morality.

"But this is art," protested Helen.

"In Manila, it would be called indecent, obscene."

"Indecency and obscenity are in the eyes of the beholder. When did a beautiful body become indecent? Then we should destroy statues and paintings from Venus de Milo, *Adam* by Michelangelo, and *The Naked Maja* by Goya."

"Manila is a Catholic city."

"So is Paris," answered Helen. "But she sees art in a nude, not ugliness and indecency. Otherwise, she wouldn't be Paris."

From the Folies Bergère, Mando and Helen went to Bal Tabarin, a popular nightclub in Pigalle. The place was full, but they were assured of a place when Mando gave the floor manager a fat tip.

At this time, the United Nations Assembly was having sessions at the Palais de Chaillot in Paris. Helen told Mando that most of the guests at the reserved tables were delegates from different countries. Mando could recognize some Filipino delegates with their white women friends.

"Look at those people at the long table," Helen told Mando. "Seated together are representatives of democracies and totalitarian countries. Having so much fun drinking champagne and eating caviar."

"But when we read their statements in the papers, a third world war seems about to break out," observed Mando.

"That is diplomacy," answered Helen, "a war of words. Better a battle of tongues than a battle of cannons."

"But of course," agreed Mando. "That's the Cold War."

Mando and Helen danced. After the cancan dance, which was the special attraction, Helen asked to go, for the next morning she would meet the playboy customer.

As they were leaving, Mando noticed a woman at a table. She was at the center of a group of guests.

Mando stopped and looked. "Her face is familiar," he thought.

He tried to remember, but the music was loud and Helen was saying something. They went out, and Mando took Helen to Normandy Hotel. He then returned to Bal Tabarin.

The woman and her companions were still there. He looked at her and tried to remember. He was surprised to hear himself exclaim.

"It's Dolly Montero!"

XXXIV

For a long while, Mando was rooted to the spot. As he gazed at the brown woman, who was like a muse in the midst of the white women, and searched for further proof that this beauty was truly Dolly Montero, memories of the past flashed through his head from the days before the war until the victory of the Japanese in the islands.

Mando recalled that even when his parents were still alive, he was already working for the Monteros as a servant. His duty was to clean Dolly's room and to run errands.

Mando was witness to the heartlessness of the family, their harshness in giving orders, and their lack of appreciation for good service. Often, Don Segundo would hit Andoy's father for every shortcoming. Often Doña Julia would hurl abuses at his mother when some clothes were torn while being washed or ironed. He also bore the insults or knocks on the head by Dolly when he neglected to clean her room or couldn't find what he was told to look for.

He felt hurt because of his family's plight. It was easy to take the hardship, for they were used to work, but not the abuse and the insults.

But he and his parents wanted him to finish his schooling; otherwise they would not have endured the cruelty of the Monteros.

Mando recalled the time when he was obliged to lay down his cross of servility. His very soul was bruised by the abusive words of Don Segundo when Mando was slapped by the Japanese at the headquarters. All because he failed to salute. Instead of sympathizing and helping him explain, Don Segundo insulted and threatened Mando.

He also recalled the grave cause of his leaving the Monteros and joining the outlaws. One day, Dolly found in a notebook of Andoy's (Mando's name) a typewritten radio news report about the war outside the Philippines. Dolly gave this to Don Segundo who angrily confronted Andoy, hitting him and threatening to stop his schooling. He also threatened to report Andoy to the Kempeitai, who were being befriended by the Monteros.

At that time, a certain Colonel Moto was a frequent visitor at the house in Singalong. Dolly often went with the Colonel to gatherings. She was effective bait for the couple so they could profit more under the new state of affairs.

That night, as Mando stood on one side of the renowned Parisian nightclub, and as he gazed at the woman who caught his eye, these memories rushed through him. He was glad he was no longer Andoy who was used to abuse, no longer a student-servant who cowered before the sharp voice of the master. He was now Mando Plaridel, a man with no master but himself, tested in the fire of war and by a thousand dangers. He possessed a new personality with complete self-confidence, free, aware, alert, and intelligent; he had a strong physique and a stout heart; in his hands was entrusted wealth greater than the Monteros'. Mando knew this; now he could look anyone straight in the eye.

He wanted nothing from Dolly. True, she had grown lovelier, but in Paris and other cities, he had seen lovelier women. He had no wish to know this girl whom he used to serve, either to teach her a lesson, to seek revenge, or for any other reason. But despite his decision, he couldn't move nor draw his eyes from that gay and alluring brown face that stood out among the other beauties.

Mando tried to get away from his memories. He went to the dimly lit bar and asked for a drink.

There were only a few guests at the bar.

His throat had hardly warmed from the whiskey when she entered accompanied by a white man. They sat near Mando but didn't pay him any attention. The man asked for straight whiskey and the woman, champagne.

Mando could hear their loud voices. The man had a French accent.

"Dolly, *chérie,*" said the man, so Mando was sure that she was really Dolly Montero, "you are free, now that classes are over."

Dolly pouted before answering, "I told you I don't plan to leave Paris during vacation. This is my only chance to go shopping. You know that I'll soon leave for Manila."

"But just a week, Dolly chérie," insisted the man. "Ah, you have not seen the beach of Cannes, a paradise visited by famous stars and fashion models. We'll just stay a week there, chérie; this is the ideal climate—spring. We'll go boating and swimming by day and dancing and drinking at night. A carnival of joy, chérie."

"Don't insist, Pierre," Dolly pleaded. "Invite Yvonne or Odette and enjoy yourselves."

"You are avoiding me," the man said harshly. "Is there someone else? The American?"

"No, no one," she answered coldly.

The man stood up and tried to kiss Dolly. She turned her face away. Pierre persisted, obviously drunk. Dolly stood up and started to leave, but Pierre stood in her way and tried to embrace her. She tried to free herself, pleading...

"No, please..."

This scene did not bother the other guests. They were used to this and thought the two were sweethearts who had drunk too much. But to Mando, the incident could not be ignored. Here was a man molesting a woman; the man was a foreigner and the woman was a Filipina.

Mando could not remain seated. He approached the two.

"Mister," he addressed the man who would not loosen his grip on Dolly's arm.

"Mister" looked back and pushed Mando.

"This is none of your business," he shouted and dragged Dolly away.

"Please, please," Dolly begged Mando for help.

So Mando was obliged to intervene, but the man socked him and barely missed his glasses. Mando returned with a left jab on the chin. The man let Dolly go and he fell like timber on the carpet. Mando quickly took the girl out before any scandal ensued.

"Please take me home," Dolly asked her rescuer.

In the taxi, Dolly asked to be brought to her dormitory. Mando remained silent.

"Sir, are you a Mexican?" Dolly asked.

Mando turned to the girl on his left, smiled, and courteously answered in Tagalog.

"I'm a Filipino. And you?"

"We are countrymen. I'm from Manila. Dolly Montero."

"I'm Mando Plaridel." He offered his hand. The name didn't ring a bell with Dolly.

"I was lucky you were at the bar. Pierre is American-French, who grew up in Paris. Impulsive and a bad drinker."

"Why do you have such friends?"

"In Paris, choosing friends is just like buying goods—attractive in the display window. In Parisian society, you can't tell the prince from the pauper, the heiress from the taxi dancer. But in Manila…"

"Ah, in Manila, one's true color cannot be denied," said Mando. "There, the beggar can't pose as a prince, the dancehall girl can't be mistaken for an heiress; as a crow can't be mistaken for a dove," he added meaningfully.

Dolly made no comment, thinking that Mando was just making a general remark.

"But perhaps you have been away from the Philippines for a long time," she surmised. "From your appearance…"

"For a long time," said Mando. She supposed he had been in Europe much longer than she had.

Mando told her that he had been to different cities, traveling for a newspaper in Manila. Dolly explained that she had finished a course in Paris and would return soon to the Philippines. She wasn't sure if she would go to the United States; perhaps she would just pass by on her trip home.

At the door of her dormitory, Dolly thanked Mando profusely. She would not let him go until he promised to have lunch with her the next day. She chose a restaurant on Champs-Élysées.

Although it was almost dawn when Mando returned to his hotel, he couldn't sleep, thinking of the strange coincidence. Who would have thought that he, a servant before the war, would now be regarded as a gentleman living in a grand Parisian hotel? And who could have guessed that the haughty and mean daughter of his master would be indebted to him and not recognize him? Truly, one reaps what he sows. Had fate decided that Dolly should reap the abuses she had sown? Would Mando avenge his oppression at the hands of Dolly and the Monteros? With these thoughts, he fell asleep.

The next day, he was awakened by a call from Helen who said she was coming. When she came, Mando was in the lobby and had just sent a cable to Manila.

"Let's go to your room," she suggested. "If I give you these three hundred thousand dollars, hombre, the Paris gendarmes will rob you," kidded the lively Irish-Spanish-Filipina.

"You sold it fast, huh?"

"And not in French money."

Every dollar then was worth three hundred forty francs and could easily buy five hundred on the black market. During Mando's stay in Paris, the francs were spent like the Mickey Mouse money in Manila during the Japanese times. It was hard to exchange francs, whether Belgian francs or Swiss, especially for the English pound or the American dollar.

After Helen had given Mando the money for the jewels bought by the playboy heir for his ballet dancer and had received her commission, she expected Mando to take her to lunch.

"Sorry, Helen, but I have a date. In fact, I'm late now," he said, glancing at his watch.

Helen laughed, "I knew that after twenty-four hours, this poor chaperone would be excess baggage."

When Mando arrived at the restaurant, Dolly was there. She was even more beautiful in her light-blue dress.

"Did I keep you waiting, Miss Montero?" Mando asked as he sat beside her.

"Call me Dolly, and I'll call you Mando," she suggested. "I've been waiting since you left me at the dormitory," she joked and looked straight at him.

Only then did she notice the scar on his left cheek, but she merely glanced at it and fixed her laughing eyes on his dark eyes. She didn't ask how Mando got his scar.

Dolly related her experiences in Paris while she studied at a finishing school. She also mentioned her life in Manila, her experiences during the war, and the liberation. Of course, she neglected the chapters about Colonel Moto and Lieutenant Whitey, her stay in a private hospital in Hong Kong and…

She asked Mando to talk of his adventures in the exciting cities where he stayed, his sweethearts, his preferences among the Spaniards, Italians, Belgians, English, and Parisiennes.

"I have no sweetheart," said Mando. "Before you court a girl, you have to love her first," he explained. "I have met many beautiful white women, but not one made my heart beat faster."

Dolly put down her fork and fixed her eyes on Mando's face.

"I salute you, Mando," she said. "But, it's a surprise, if not a miracle, that during your long stay in Europe, you've had no girlfriend."

Mando thought for a while and admitted that he did have a friend in Brussels.

"She is Flemish," Mando recalled. "Young, perhaps, twenty years, but aged early with sorrow. With red hair and blue eyes. I was window shopping around the famed Bon Marche in the foremost square of Brussels when I heard a cool voice. 'Don't you want entertainment?' she invited. When I turned, I saw in her beautiful face a mixture of shyness, fear, and need. 'How much?' I asked. 'Not as dear as the goods you're looking at,' she sneered. I was then looking at some pipes from London. I could see that she was hungry, so I brought her to a restaurant. She drank two glasses of beer and ate enough for two. Then she said contentedly, 'I'm ready to do whatever you wish,' and clung to my arm. The night was cool and inviting, but I didn't take her to my hotel. Instead, I hailed a taxi and brought her home. She lived in a hole of a cellar with her two small children. 'I'm a war widow. I have to keep them alive,' she sighed. 'No other way.' While I was in Brussels, that unfortunate woman didn't have to roam the streets at night. With a little charity, she could rest early together with her children."

Dolly was touched.

"Now, I don't only salute you," she said with admiration. "I want to kiss your hands. I feel like a Magdalene before Jesus." She threw Mando a meaningful look.

From the restaurant, they went to different famous places in Paris, which Dolly said he had to see. They went to the Louvre, the largest and most famous museum in the world. Mando was eager, and Dolly didn't tire of looking at the art masterpieces and statues and paintings, murals, and frames, marble, bronze, drawings, sketches without compare, Venus de Milo, Helen of Troy, Pallas of Velletri, Heras of Samos, Athena, *Mona Lisa*, *Maria de' Medici*. There were the works of Michelangelo, Cellini, Donatello, da Vinci, Raphael, El Greco, Murillo, Goya, Lautrec, Rembrandt, Titian, Tintoretto, Corregio, and many more that cost a fortune. They visited Les Invalides where lay the remains of Napoleon Bonaparte and other great men. Before dusk, they sat on a seat in the Notre Dame Cathedral where Dolly silently prayed the Angelus.

They spent a half hour in the quietness of the park of Bois de Boulogne and watched the lighting of countless lamps along the boulevard before Mando took Dolly to her dormitory.

"Come back for me in two hours," Dolly said.

"Aren't you tired?"

"In Paris, a contented heart doesn't know fatigue," Dolly said happily. "I'll expect you. We'll have supper, then go to a nightclub, where no one will bother us."

On his way back to his hotel, Mando thought this was a dream—the difference between his relation with Dolly in Manila from 1940 to 1942 and their present relation in Paris. Then he was a miserable tool hardly noticed by Dolly; now he was the idol of the haughty darling of the Monteros.

"Only lightning…" Mando cut his own musings and lit his cigarette.

XXXV

Mando and Dolly were both handsome in their evening clothes. The weather was fine, neither cold nor hot. At that hour, Paris was like a lovely but coquettish sweetheart that promised joy to all her suitors. All were caught by her fascination, whether strolling under the trees along the boulevard or riding in cars along the Champs-Élysées.

Dolly was elegant in her Christian Dior gown, but it was neither her dress nor her jewels that first caught Mando's attention. The fragrance which she gently sprayed on her hair and body was intoxicating. At first he could not decide if it was Lucien Lelong, Caron, or Guerlain.

Dolly's necklace, earrings, and ring were quite uncommon. But to Mando's eyes, which were used to seeing the unique gems in his collection, they seemed like glass.

When Dolly came down, Mando greeted her in admiration, "Who would notice the *Mona Lisa* at the Louvre?"

Dolly pretended to be displeased and reproached Mando for comparing her to a five-century-old painting.

"Forgive me," said Mando. "I meant that even Leonardo da Vinci's original can't compare to you."

"Thanks," smiled Dolly, "but tell me which you like most, my hair, my dress, or my perfume?"

"All," he complimented her. "But you, above all; even if you crumple your hair, even without perfume, or in a cheap dress."

In high spirits, they got into the car, and Mando told the driver where to take them. The car stopped a while at a flower shop. Mando got out and bought an orchid corsage. Dolly asked him to pin it above her left breast. She broke off an orchid and placed it on the left lapel of his coat.

"Just say where we're going," said Mando, "I'm a novice in Paris."

"Very well. What do you want—French food, American, or Spanish?"

"Is there anyone who eats American food but the Yankees? Hot dog or pork chop?"

Dolly laughed and recalled the fishy canned sardines and tasteless sausage, which she always ate during the first days of liberation. She felt nauseated thinking of them.

They went to a small restaurant on the banks of the Seine, a place called the Forbidden Fruit. The small restaurants of Paris were unlike the "fly-eateries" of Manila. They were small but lacked nothing in elegance, luxury, and service, including an orchestra and a floor show.

When their car stopped, they were welcomed courteously by the porter dressed in a uniform similar to that of a hearse driver in Manila. He opened the car door and led the two guests to the restaurant. Mando gave him a tip.

Bowing, the head waiter welcomed them and ushered them to a reserved table. Two waiters immediately approached. Mando asked for scotch and Dolly asked for sherry.

When they were seated, a girl brought a basket of fresh flowers. Mando gave a bouquet to Dolly. Then a cigarette girl approached Mando and he bought a pack of American cigarettes. The flower girl and the cigarette girl were both scantily dressed and looked like live dolls.

As Mando and Dolly had their drinks, the first violinist glided towards them, playing "Hearts and Flowers," and stood before Dolly.

Mando gave them several hundred francs.

When the orchestra played, Dolly asked Mando to dance. The waltz was sweet and the lights were dimmed. The partners became dancing shadows crisscrossing in the spotlight, which moved around the hall.

Like a petal attached to the wings of a butterfly, Dolly's shapely body was caught in Mando's right arm; she was as light as cotton. She rested her head on his shoulder and he could smell the fragrance of her hair.

Dolly was inviting; Mando was controlling himself.

To the amorous Dolly whose heart was as playful as her eyes, the events were not surprising. Mando came into her life when she was in trouble, when the rash Pierre tried to force his attentions on her. Mando saved her from being molested. She did not know him then, but her heart began to beat faster.

When she met him the next day and had looked at him closely and after they had talked on different topics, her fascination was complete. She saw his build and his height, which was unusual for a Filipino; she deduced his intelligence and wit from his questions and answers. And she saw that he was a gentleman, from his manners and his regard for women.

Dolly made comparisons. She quickly decided that Mando was superior to any man she had known. Mando was different from Colonel Moto, who was like a coiled snake. Different from Lieutenant Whitey, who was an opportunist and conceited. Much more different than the disrespectful and irresponsible Pierre, who thought of nothing but a good time.

Dolly trusted Mando more than anyone else. In his arms, she felt like a bird content in the safety of her nest. As they danced, she would lightly press Mando's left hand and she would deliberately brush her cheek against his lips.

On the other hand, Mando felt like a house divided. He was aware of Dolly's invitation, perhaps as a sign of gratitude or of a daring and flirtatious heart. But Mando was hesitant. He could not decide whether to enter the open door or close it and turn his back.

Only a few days ago, he had told himself he wanted nothing from Dolly, he didn't care even to get acquainted as Mando Plaridel. Many women in Paris were far lovelier, and in Paris, money was king, and Mando was richer than a king.

But despite his first impulse to avoid her, and because of the unforeseen events, Dolly was here imprisoned in his arms and he could smell the perfume in her hair, which was like countless snares to catch his heart. He no longer hated her. The image of a young girl who shouted and ordered him about was now a pale shadow. That person could not have emerged into this lovely girl smiling happily, with feet that seemed to fly and a body smooth as silk, whose every word showed a special affection.

Mando thought that even if the sharp edge of Martin's treachery had left a permanent scar on his left cheek, the pain of oppression he endured from the Monteros should have been healed by time. There is no misfortune without a corresponding blessing, just as there is no dark cloud that has no silver lining. Because of the Monteros' cruely, he had to leave. And how had this affected his life? If Don Segundo, Doña Julia, and Dolly had been kind, he would not have thought of leaving. So he would still be their servant or a clerk.

But because of what happened, he was on top of the world and he was gazing at Dolly. Should he wish to, he could make her pay dearly.

The music ended and the two went back to their table. The waiter opened a bottle of champagne.

"Pierre called this afternoon and apologized," Dolly said. "Imagine, he had the nerve to ask for a date."

"Making up is fun," Mando said, baiting her. "As delicious as this champagne." He sipped from his cup.

"You know my answer?" bragged Dolly. "'I forgive you,' I said. 'But I don't want to see you again,' I told him."

"But why? Is there another one, the 'Americain'?" Mando mimicked Pierre.

They burst into laughter. Dolly moved her face closer to him and said lovingly, "Hoy, not 'Americain,' but Filipino," she said, stressing the "F." "Let's celebrate," she added.

She raised her cup and they drank.

After Mando had paid and given the two waiters and their captain a fat tip, they left the Forbidden Fruit.

They proceeded to La Puerta del Sol, a nightclub with a Spanish motif. They drank, danced, and watched a floor show a la Madrileña. From La Puerta, they went to the Crazy Horse. They didn't stay long because it was crowded and there were three boisterous Americans whose eyes were like those of a rotten fish. One was cursing angrily, insulting the French whom he said were at the mercy of the Germans during the war. He claimed that they owed their lives to the American marines who landed on Normandy in May 1945. Otherwise…

"Crazy," said one, as he stared at the neon light of Crazy Horse.

They went to the Naturalists, which featured "natural" beauty. Here, they ate a special omelette while a starved-looking French artist made a crayon sketch of Dolly and Mando. By the time they finished eating, the sketch was finished. They admired the close likeness and the artist kept saying, "Merci, Monsieur" upon receiving two thousand francs, which was equivalent to four American dollars on the black market.

It was dawn when Mando and Dolly left the last empty champagne bottle at the Moulin Rouge. As they watched the special burlesque number, they were both intoxicated. As they went out, Dolly could hardly walk. Mando had to help her in and out of the car. In the car, she reclined in his arms like a baby.

Earlier that night, Dolly had told Mando about a dormitory regulation against coming home after twelve, even with a permit.

Under no circumstances should they go home drunk.

"If we should stay after twelve and if I should get drunk," she reminded Mando, "don't bring me back. Take me anywhere. I'll make up the alibi the next day."

So they went to his suite at the Ritz Hotel. In Paris, a guest's room is his castle. Mando woke up a waiter friend and asked for hot tea. He asked Dolly to drink a cup and wiped her face with the contents of the other cup. Then he fixed Dolly on a separate bed. After he changed his clothes, he lay on a couch in his receiving room.

But Mando could not sleep, for Dolly was moaning. Several times he had to go to her, and the last time, she threw up the drinks of the previous night. He led her to the bathroom. Then he brought out a robe, for her dress was soiled.

Mando didn't feel good either. His head was spinning and he could hardly lift his feet. This was how he felt when he was wounded by Martin. He was not used to drinking heavily. A few cups of champagne were enough. And he seldom went beyond three glasses. But that night, he let himself be carried away. Dolly also let herself go. They wanted to make merry and both forgot themselves. Awareness and pleasure are seldom good partners in an amusement hall.

When Dolly returned from the bathroom, she saw Mando stretched on the bed. Feeling as weak as a vegetable, she dropped onto the bed. Her head was on Mando's chest. They both slept soundly as if they had smoked opium.

The hot rays of the sun were piercing the curtain of the open windows when Mando opened his eyes. The first sight that he saw was the girl embracing him, sleeping as if she didn't want to wake up. On the floor was the robe; Dolly's breasts were exposed, like the Holy Eucharist abandoned by its guard.

He thought he had been dreaming at dawn. But Dolly's appearance and his own showed that what happened between them was not a dream.

Mando brushed back Dolly's rumpled hair and kissed her. Her lips smelled of the acid of the champagne and the fragrance of Guerlain, and he went back to his disrupted dream.

XXXVI

It must be true that good fortune, just like misfortune, does not come singly. Just like a guest that brings along others who were not invited.

Mando was selling his jewels and acquiring knowledge according to schedule. On top of this, he obtained some unexpected rewards. With hardly any investment, and unexpectedly, the rare gem of Dolly's beauty fell into his hands. Since the wine had given way to their early intimacy a few weeks past, the alluring Manila belle seemed to crave him. Dolly was infatuated with Mando, but it would be hard to say that this was true love. Undeniably, she esteemed Mando more than any other lover. Like a new gown that she wanted to wear constantly, she sought Mando.

For an inexperienced girl, Dolly's feelings could be true love. But she was fickle and capricious. She would not rest until she got anything that caught her eye or her heart. So, no one could be sure, not even Dolly herself, whether what she felt was lasting love. Only time could tell.

As for Mando, his heart beat fast and his blood was aflame when he was alone with Dolly, which was often, for Dolly was persistent and impulsive. She had refused Pierre's invitation for a week at the beach, but it was she who persuaded Mando to stay for fourteen days at a private cottage. Nevertheless, Mando felt nothing but desire, which was natural for a healthy, lonely male in his prime.

In drinking from the cup of pleasure, neither the past nor the future matters. For Dolly, it was best to close the door of memory on the dark past. She would not spoil the present with worries about the uncertain future. True to her accustomed ways and her nature, she enjoyed the honeymoon of the happy night and never minded whether the sun would shine or not the next morning.

Mando had less need to look back, for his past was the constant companion of his present. In his schedule, Dolly became a part during his stay in Paris, but she was not in his plans after Paris. Although he seldom took any step unrelated to his general plan and Dolly was a gem of great value, still she was among the things he left to time or chance. Unlike his cousin Puri.

Ah, Puri, a simple maiden outstanding in her simplicity, like a meadow flower which scented even the wind, although hidden within the folds of a leaf. What if Puri were in Paris instead of Dolly? But such musing comes only fleetingly, like the streak of a comet in the darkness of the sky.

Mando didn't spend all his time in Paris on Dolly, nor in selling the jewels. As he attended to his pleasure and his business, he did not neglect other important goals.

After seeing historical places, the old palaces which were being used by the present republic, the museum, the cathedral, the parks, and other relics of the past and the present progress, he observed the life of the people, especially the common man.

As can be found anywhere, the common man in Paris, and especially in the rural areas, is industrious, loyal, and quiet. More fond of work than pleasure seeking, he knows how to have fun, but he attends to more worthwhile things. The French father and husband is loving and few look for happiness elsewhere.

But above all, the French citizen loves freedom—of thought, of speech, and of assembly. Only the boulevardiers add freedom in love. So in France almost all parties, organizations, churches, and movements are found. All beliefs and doctrines enjoy equal respect of the law. The laborers, the intellectuals, even the anarchists and communists enjoy constitutional rights to establish and to form unions and to spread their principles.

Strikes are ordinary happenings in disputes between capital and labor. During strikes, the police are neutral, not picket breakers nor capitalist tools.

Even the free thinkers, the agnostics, and the atheists have their own organizations and movements. No one accuses them of being dangerous enemies of the law and society, just because they openly attack fanaticism and belief in one creator. The voice of the minority is not drowned out by unreasonable persecution, although ninety-seven percent of the French are devout Catholics.

Mando witnessed a massive strike outside Paris when all workers in all factories of weapons and bullets stopped working, three years after World War II. The workers opposed the government policy, arguing that the country needed bread and butter, not guns and bullets.

Both sides stood firm, but the government gave in a little and pursued its program. It assured adequacy of food and vowed to avoid provoking war and to move cautiously in the Cold War.

Mando observed the efficiency of the parliamentary system where the legislature, which was made up of representatives of the country, decided important issues. It was not just a signer of laws; rather, it felt the pulse of the nation at all times. So that in deciding any national issue, if the decision of the administration was nullified by Parliament, the leaders immediately resigned to give others a chance. The advanced democracies in Europe consider the presidential system passé, too slow, and democratic only in name. Even if the party of the president loses in other elections and even if the country curses the mistakes and abuses of the administration, he and his assistants cannot be replaced if the president does not wish to be, until the next national elections or, if the country is lucky, until he is snatched by death before his time.

One day, Mando's impatient U.S. agent arrived in Paris. Mando spent the whole day and night with Mike planning how to bring the jewels to America. According to Mike, although the giant Statue of Liberty stands on Staten Island in New York, nothing could freely enter without paying the corresponding tax. If taxes would be levied on the remaining jewels to be sold in the U.S., Mando might have to withdraw all his deposits in Spain, Switzerland, and England and turn them over to the United States.

"Leave it to me, we can solve this problem," Mike promised.

When Mando asked how, Mike's expression suggested a valuable secret, like the first hydrogen bomb in the third world war. But all the American whispered was that he had a friend, an important member of the United Nations from a banana republic in Latin America.

"We shall invite him and you know...the unfailing prescription."

"Dollar," guessed Mando.

"Wine and women," replied Mike.

"If that's all, I'll give you a blank check; you write the price."

According to Mike, said delegate was returning to Lake Success in New York after the U.N. session in Paris. He had a diplomatic passport, so his baggage and belongings were not opened at the port.

Mando recalled the wife of a Filipino ambassador whose baggage filled two trucks when she left Manila. There were supposed to be reports, papers, books, and other documents in the large crates. Actually, they were costly furnishings like rugs, chandeliers, silver dining sets, paintings, textiles, perfumes, wine, and so many other items. How easy it is then for a diplomat to carry an ordinary valise like a portable typewriter.

Mike and Mando completed their plan. They would befriend the emissary of the banana republic. Butter him up, so to speak. And they would ask him to bring the valise to New York. Of course, they would not tell him what it contained. Mando would keep the key. He would take the boat, while Mike and Mando would go by plane.

"See how easy?" Mike bragged when they had planned all the details.

Mando felt a twinge of conscience. Nevertheless, he thought of the importance of his purpose and plans in Manila for the welfare of his country. Thus his anxiety disappeared. His mind and his conscience were reconciled.

The next night, the two men met Colonel Mosca, Mike's diplomat friend. Mando offered him dinner, but they didn't bring Dolly nor Helen. Instead, Mando invited three luscious artists of the Carousel through their manager. He would reward the three artists with a month's pay; the manager was pleased with a traveler's check.

After supper, they spent several hours nightclub hopping. Carousel was the only nightclub they didn't visit. Later, they agreed to go their separate ways. This was precisely as Mando expected.

"*Hasta la vista*," said the Colonel as he and his companion took a separate car.

Mando immediately brought his companion home without reducing the fee agreed upon. The beautiful artist was surprised but pleased.

The next day, they met again for lunch. The Colonel practically promised the earth and sky. He had been so pleased the previous night.

"You ask me a favor, amigo," he offered. Mando saw his chance regarding the valise.

"The Filipino and the South American are the same in their ways and temperament," said the soldier-diplomat. "Both gallant and lady-killers. They inherited these from Mother Spain."

Mando answered with a smile, "But there is one thing where we differ. We don't have your fondness for revolutions. For a slight thing, you revolt against a bad government."

"And what is stopping you, amigo?" Mosca asked swiftly, but he took back his question. "Let's set politics aside. I want you to know that that was some feast last night. A dish I won't tire of. If it were possible, I'd like an encore every night."

"Your partner is the cancan star at the Carousel," Mando informed him.

"I found out," said Mosca, "that she does the cancan better in bed." And he rubbed his lips together.

"And how was yours, Mike?"

"Like Goya's *The Naked Maja* in the flesh," Mike clucked his tongue. "If she was discovered by a Hollywood scout, she would surely be a star in a super production."

The representative of the banana republic nodded, twirled his moustache, and spoke as if he were giving an interview.

"We should take our hats off to the French for their three specialties," he declared. "They are number one in making wine, perfume, and beautiful women."

"Maybe wine and perfume help a lot in making beautiful women," Mike suggested.

"Of course, in our land, you will also like the señoritas. I'd like you to go there someday, amigo," he told Mando. "Ah, our señoritas are also hot tamales. But beside the Parisienne, they are like rice wine before champagne."

"Why, they can't beat the American gal, especially in the shapeliness of the legs," boasted Mike, who was a Texan.

"The American is a good sport, with beautiful legs, but doesn't offer much," said Mosca, who spoke like a Rubirosa. Or an Achmed Sukarno. "What I mean is that the American is cold, like a package from a refrigerator. I had a steady in Washington, a receptionist at that. Every time we went on location, if she wasn't chewing gum, she was reading the comics."

Colonel Mosca himself burst into laughter, followed by Mando and Mike.

"Amigo, tell us about you and your partner," he asked Mando.

"She looks like a real spring chicken."

"She looks tender as a pullet, but she's an old hen," said Mando. "Besides, I was not in the mood. When you left, I took her back to her apartment."

"You should have asked her to join me," the Latin diplomat said regretfully. "Then I would have shot two birds with one stone."

"That's easy," said Mando. "Here's her phone number." He wrote her number on a napkin, which he gave to the Colonel.

The next few days were the last meetings of the U.N. Meanwhile, Mando finished his work in Paris. He prepared for his trip to New York.

Colonel Mosca took the second trip from the Paris station, accompanied by Mando and Mike. The Colonel was bound for Cherbourg from where he would take the boat for the U.S.

Mando gave him a gold Swiss watch.

As they exited the railroad station, Mando's fingers were playing with a small key inside his pants pocket.

On the eve of his departure, he and Dolly also had a despedida. Only the two of them the whole night. They shortened their visits to the nightclubs and lengthened their private rendezvous. The lights in Mando's suite at the Ritz Hotel were on all night.

XXXVII

For a long time, Mando and Dolly had lived under the same roof in Manila, but on this night of utmost intimacy, they were almost strangers. Other than a sketchy narration of his past, Mando was not known to Dolly. She was unaware that what she saw was the mask of a tourist, the disguise of a cosmopolite. Her former servant Andoy was hidden by the veil of time. The roots of peasant folks were hidden by the handsome covering of a cultured gentleman.

Likewise, it could be said that Mando didn't know Dolly, the real Dolores Montero, although she surrendered to him her whole body and her beauty. Was Dolly in love or just amusing herself? Was she whiling away her loneliness in a city famed for its worldliness? Was she contaminated by the cravings of her companions in the dormitory, some of whom were white flowers in the midst of sin, and some were rags painstakingly put together?

And Mando, how did he really feel about Dolly? Did true love bloom in Mando for the girl who had been the object of envy, attraction, and admiration, but whom he secretly despised and avoided because of the great gap between them? Or did he desire to enslave her completely, to possess her, to enjoy her fragrance and pluck her honor, without marrying her? Did he wish to take advantage, to give satisfaction to his vengeance?

These thoughts crossed Mando's mind during these moments with Dolly on the wide bed of the Ritz Hotel suite. But he got no reassuring answer. It was the same with Dolly. She was not sure if Mando was to be the last man in her life.

On the other hand, they were both spellbound. They were sucked up by a force, which they could neither fight nor evade. This was their last night in Paris. It could be their last night anywhere, forever. The lights were dim, their bed was soft and comfortable, the night breeze was balmy, and in the room floated a scent that seemed to blur their minds but sharpened their senses.

Mando turned to Dolly. She was in a sheer and transparent negligee. She had no other covering. Peeping through were her breasts, which were like twin Spanish melons ripened on the tree. Her smooth white legs were spread out and Mando's hand would rub them or she would entwine them around his firm legs. Several times, Mando had seen the statue of the Venus de Milo at the Louvre. Dolly, at that moment, was a brown Venus but of flesh and bones.

"Are you thirsty, Dol?" Mando asked after a while. He stood up. His right hand rested on Dolly's breasts, and he would alternately rub and press the twin Spanish melons.

"I thirst for your love, darling," she answered with a languid look and pulled his arm. He embraced her gently and kissed her lips. Dolly wound her arms around his shoulder until their bodies fused. Their kisses became fiery tongue sucking.

"How happy I am," whispered Dolly when her lips were free. "And you, darling?"

"I'm not dead, Dol," whispered Mando.

Mando rose again, took Dolly, and placed her on his lap. The belt of her negligee came loose, revealing the beauty of the Montero heiress. Mando rubbed with his eyes and hands its hidden treasures. Dolly made no protest; rather the touch of Mando's hand seemed to give her greater satisfaction.

"I'm yours," she gaily offered.

"Until when?"

"As long as you wish."

"But I'm going away."

"Do you have to hurry? Why don't you wait for me, and we'll go home together. Just a few months... Then we'd have months of this. Don't you want this, darling?"

"I'm behind schedule in my mission," answered Mando. "My client in the U.S. is getting impatient."

"Your mission is more important, is that it?"

"Come on. It just happens that I have to attend to it first."

They stopped talking for a while. Dolly got up from Mando's lap and sat beside him. They leaned back on the pillows. Like Delilah, she played with her fingers on the key to Samson's strength; her fingers toyed with Mando's manhood.

"I have a hunch that after Paris..." Dolly looked at Mando.

"Our Paris will not end..." said her lover. "In Manila, in Baguio..." And he kissed her cheek. "Let's have a drink." Dolly nodded.

Mando got up after fixing his pajamas. He poured a martini into a cup. Dolly also got up and they sat together in an easy chair. Both took the cold martini. Not just one cup, but two, three and...

"Next to your love, this gives me the most pleasure," said Dolly, who seemed affected by the wine.

"I have to leave you in Paris," Mando reminded her.

"That is the sorrow of my life."

"When I'm gone...you might be consoled by other friends," he teased.

Dolly pouted and pulled his ear.

"Who... Pierre?" she laughed.

"The 'Americain'..."

"Life is so busy, very busy, with Mr. Plaridel," the tipsy girl laughed.

"Aren't you hungry, Dol?" he asked after a while.

"I have no hunger except for you, oh, darling," Dolly suddenly embraced him and buried her face in his chest.

That was neither the first nor the second incident. What they had started had become customary and what was customary became a habit. If it didn't bear fruit, it was because Dolly had learned to take care. She was given a lecture by a specialist in Hong Kong before she enrolled in Paris. And in her handbag, every time she had a date with Mando, and even before they met, she carried a bottle of pills. The pills were not yet a headache to the Vatican.

It was midnight. After they finished the bottle of martini, she went to the bathroom. Mando had a hot shower. Dolly had a towel bath and bathed her hair and body with Guerlain.

"I get more drunk with your fragrance than with the strongest wine," said Mando.

"That's the way it should be," said Dolly.

They were a real Adam and Eve when they returned to bed. When they were embracing and their chests were pressed together and their legs entwined, Mando said:

"As the master of ceremonies of the Folies Bergère said, 'This number is the last night in Paris.'"

"'This is a night in paradise,'" Dolly corrected.

"Oh, yes."

"Don't you want the lights out?"

"It's hard to find happiness, darling, so let's not let it escape in the dark."

Their lips were sealed in an unending kiss. And their bodies and souls became one.

Morning still saw the bright lights in Mando's suite at the Ritz Hotel.

XXXVIII

Athletic Club, New York City.

Mando was having merienda with Mike and Colonel Mosca five days after they parted in Paris.

Everything went smoothly as scheduled. Colonel Mosca left Paris ahead, but Mando and Mike were the ones who met the diplomat when he got off the boat at a New York port.

Mosca handed the valise of "souvenirs" to Mando. When Mando opened it at his hotel, the jewels were intact.

That afternoon, Colonel Mosca was happy and even more handsome. His wavy black hair was shiny and his moustache was like the horns of a black beetle. Mando noticed a gleaming pin on the tie of the elegant Colonel. He didn't have this in Paris. Mando was sure it was not among the jewels he had sent through the Colonel.

When Mando took notice of the pin, Mosca said he had good news, something related to the pin.

Mando wondered if the Colonel would sell his banana republic to Wall Street. He was wrong, but the news was truly sensational.

Colonel Mosca would marry an American widow with multimillions.

Mike stood up and raised his hands.

"Mando," he exclaimed, as if he had been robbed of his last dollar, "our business is penny-ante compared to the Latin genius. Millions in a single transaction, and, imagine, with no capital."

"Hey! Mister, don't insult a friend," retorted Mosca. "Look at me, my bearing. What widow would regret giving up her millions?"

They had met in the dining hall of the *Ile de France* on the first day it sailed the Atlantic. He was introduced by a friend, an attaché of the State Department. They talked about beautiful places in Latin America. The widow said she would travel there the following year. "If you need an escort who knows Latin America as intimately as his fingers, I'm at your service," the Colonel offered with all gallantry.

Such gallantry was like Ali Baba's "open sesame." The widow put on her glasses and looked him over from his glossy hair to his shiny shoes and back again. Mosca stood erect like a soldier about to be conferred a decoration by his queen. She smiled and made room for him to sit beside her.

"But you're a married man, aren't you?" she asked directly.

"Divorced."

"Aha."

That night he was the sole dancing partner of the wealthy American in the ship's ballroom.

"You Latins are real experts at dancing," complimented the merry widow.

"Even better in love," Mosca replied.

"Porfirio Rubirosa or Don Juan?" the widow asked jokingly.

"Both," he boasted. "But, Señora, call me by my real name—Carlos."

"Carlitos."

From the ballroom, they went up to the deck. When she complained of the cold wind, Mosca took off his jacket and wrapped it around her.

The next night, Colonel Mosca was sure of the biggest catch in the Atlantic.

"She took this pin from her dress and pinned it on my necktie. That is the whole story."

"But you didn't mention how she looks," Mike said.

"Well, I won't say she's as beautiful as the three artists of the Carousel," Mosca admitted. "Forty-five, two hundred pounds, and fourteen million dollars."

"Heavyweight in every way," Mike said. He figured Mosca was only thirty-eight.

"She is a little older, but younger than her years. Don't look for youth and beauty, for her beauty is in her bank book. Her late husband was a stockholder in several oil and steel corporations, and she inherited everything."

"You're lucky, Colonel, congratulations," Mando said.

"When's the wedding?" asked Mike.

"In a week."

It occurred to Mike that they should sell the jewels to the diplomat within the week, so he asked to meet her.

"When you're married, you can run for president of your republic. You'll have plenty of friends. It's in the bag."

"Any position you like," added Mando. "In a capitalist democracy, an election is a real auction."

Mosca looked at his friends and answered, "Comrades, what for? When I'm married, goodbye politics. I don't know how it is in the Philippines, Mando. But in our country, a politician aims for a position to enrich himself. When he has amassed wealth, he resigns or is driven out by a coup d'état or a revolution. He seeks refuge in America or Europe, buys a villa and enjoys life. My future wife is a multimillionaire. Why would I need to be president? Why should I rob a poor republic?"

"Then what are your plans?" asked Mando.

"Plans?" The word seemed new to Mosca. "Amigo, a man with money doesn't have many plans. To make merry, to amuse himself, to enjoy life. My future wife wants me to resign and help her manage her interests. What more can you ask of life?" And he twirled his moustache.

Before the wedding, the American multimillionaire bought from Mike a set of jewels worth four hundred thousand dollars. Included was a ring with three choice gems—ruby, diamond, and sapphire—in the colors of the flag, costing fifty thousand. It was the widow's gift to her fiancé.

Mando was captivated by America, her hugeness and progress. He sought the secret of her greatness and discerned that it was not a secret, but a truth in modern history. Without a doubt, America is the most powerful country today. Although only one and a half centuries before, she was a poor English colony, a vast wilderness. Now, her railways and cemented roads stretch from the Atlantic shores in the East to the Pacific beaches in the West, from the Canadian border in the North to the Mexican border in the South. Her trains, ships, cars, and airplanes, her skyscrapers, all kinds of plants and factories, her mines, from black gold (carbon) to liquid gold (oil), her industries and agriculture, her arms for defense and offense are greater than any other wonders known to history. To Mando, there was but one key to their wonderful success—work. Industry in work, love for work, respect for work.

Mando saw and respected countries that worked day and night. They did not rest in the cities and farms, in the mountains and in the desert, on sea and on land, in the air and in the heart of the ocean, also under the earth; in laboratories, in hospitals, in schools, in all places and on all occasions. No stopping, no tiring from work, from discovery, from searching, from creating, from making old and new; food, clothes, houses, wealth, all the needs of men. This world is too crowded and, in a few years, they will surely conquer other planets.

And this is due to American manpower, to the American laborer, to the ordinary U.S. citizen. Mando was filled with boundless admiration as he rode the elevator to the top of the one hundred and two stories of the Empire State Building, or as he rode the subway hurtling through a tunnel under the Hudson River, or as he watched television at the famous Columbia Broadcasting at Radio City, or as he looked at the display windows along Fifth Avenue and gazed at the countless goods made by American industry.

"There is nothing that can't be bought in America and nothing that she can't afford to buy," thought Mando.

As if in answer to his thoughts, Mike came one day and told him of an offer of five million for all his jewels from a noted jewelry store on Broadway.

"That's a good offer," said Mando. "Wholesale."

"There is a collector offering one million for antiques made before Christ."

"Then separate those, for a representative of the store is coming today."

Mando sold the jewels for five million, leaving only a few loose stones for his personal use. The store's representative said he was prepared to buy good jewels no matter how many and at any price. Mando remembered the jewels he had left with Tata Matyas. They could bring in about two and a half million dollars.

According to the Broadway store's representative, they also accepted pawning; in fact they were keeping a dozen crowns of Europe as collateral for loans. Some had been forfeited, for the owners had no hope of returning to their thrones. Some former rulers had become employees and mechanics in the U.S.

The sale of the jewels was over, and Mando thought of finishing his other business. He had been away for more than two years. In every city where he stayed, he received a letter from Magat informing him of their newspaper and important news from the Philippines. Unemployment and disputes in the fields were worsening. Once, Magat visited Hacienda Montero where the situation was critical in the face of the stubbornness of Don Segundo and the tenants. Pastor had been removed as overseer and was living with his daughter on a small farm outside the hacienda. The two were all right. Pastor had joined the farmers' movement because of his anger with Don Segundo. Puri was sending her regards and said she received Mando's postcards. Tata Matyas was well and was a devoted reader and critic of the *Kampilan*.

Magat also asked if Mando had bought a rotary to replace their old press. "Even if you are enjoying yourself, please tell us when you're coming home," Magat said in his postscript.

Actually, it wasn't pleasure that delayed Mando's return. He did not waste time. Except for the nights of pleasure in Paris, he devoted his time to his duties. Mando had tested his willpower. He overcame numerous temptations in the cities of Europe and America. He realized why many Filipino students forgot their books in America. Thousands of Filipino laborers who had emigrated to earn a living could not save and would not return home like a misguided Ulysses. Government emissaries neglected their missions and attended only to the good times.

Mando's good sense never deserted him. He deposited six million dollars in two New York banks and bought shares in a few stable industries. The money in Spain and part of the money in England were transferred to the United States. Upon the advice of the multimillionairess, the new Señora de Mosca, he invested two million dollars in steel and oil where the money would earn more than from a bank.

Full of wonder at the limitless wealth of America, Mando went uptown one morning. He walked from the Commodore Hotel instead of taking the streetcar which connected Grand Central and Times Square, the heart of New York.

He happened to pass by the Bowery, which was within shouting distance from Fifth Avenue. Mando was shocked to be continually approached by men in rags, unkempt air, unshaven and unwashed. All were pale and thin. Everyone had his palm outstretched...

"Spare a dime for a cup of coffee. I have not eaten breakfast."

Mando was amazed that in New York City, with its Wall Street where the richest banks and corporations on earth could be found, there were numerous beggars. Mando gave away more than a dollar in alms.

With a few quick steps, he was on Fifth Avenue. He encountered matrons, untouchable in their grandeur, shopping at plush department stores.

XXXIX

Mando saw both sides of silver and lead coins. Most pictures had two faces—smooth on the surface and rough inside.

Mando admired the greatness of America but its weakness brought him sorrow. Like the poverty exposed to him at the Bowery. Like the signs he read in many places: off limits to dogs and colored persons.

After some months in New York, Mando took a train to Washington, D.C., the nation's capital. He planned to travel slowly from the East to the West of the United States and to visit centers of education, science and research, law, art, industry, and commerce, transportation, unionism, and national movements.

While New York was the show window of American financial power because of her great industries, Washington was the glass window of culture and civilization, of government, of democracy. In New York could be seen and bought all the nation's products, cars fresh from the Detroit factory and goods made of Pittsburgh steel, canned meat and food packed in crystal from Chicago, movies made in Hollywood, fruits and vegetables from Florida and California, beer from St. Louis, clothes, shoes, stockings, lipstick made in New York, Philadelphia, and other cities on the Atlantic Coast, books on all topics, technology, biography, history, religion. While in Washington, D.C., the Capitol Building, its incomparable library, the White House with its famous rooms and garden, the museum and galleries of the Smithsonian Institute where one could see all creations of nature and man, animals, plants, minerals, stone, machines, art, etc., the monuments and memorials of Washington, Jefferson, Lincoln, Lafayette, the Peace Monument where rested the heroes who died in battle, headquarters of different foundations, organizations of various movements, charity, culture, art, churches, and cathedrals of almost all faiths, almost as many as the number of nationalities.

Mando listened to the lively sessions of the two Congressional houses on Capitol Hill. Imprinted in his memory were the resounding speeches of some members about their pride in the land of freedom, the equality of men and nations, their inalienable right to the pursuit of happiness.

He visited the Jefferson and Lincoln Memorials. He kept repeating what he studied in his boyhood about their deathless principle regarding men's freedom and equality. He went around Arlington Cemetery on the other side of the Potomac River, including the former villa of General Robert E. Lee, commander-in-chief of the Confederates in the Civil War, and Mount Vernon, the personal estate of President Washington. These scenes heightened Mando's impression of the glory of America.

But one day, in Washington, in the heart of American democracy, Mando's eyes were opened. He saw that few things didn't have "heads" and "tails."

Mando attended a meeting of former soldiers who served in other lands during the last war. The purpose of the meeting was to make a stand on equal treatment for all American citizens—white, red, yellow, or brown.

The organizers complained that while America was made up of all races, the whites were favored above the colored races. This was the situation before the war; it continued through the war and became worse with the return of peace.

This was witnessed in the army, in factories and business firms, unions, schools, vehicles, and public amusements. The blacks were segregated. Many schools, hotels, restaurants, vehicles, shows, and other institutions were "off-limits" to any colored person. In not a few Southern states, where the blacks outnumbered the whites, they could not vote freely. If they weren't slain, they were tarred and feathered if they voted for a candidate not backed up by the powerful whites. Mando saw this bitter truth.

They pointed out that of the millions of army men, a black very rarely rose in rank. It was usual for blacks to be carriers, waiters, dishwashers, drivers of heavy trucks and bulldozers, climbers of telegraph poles, diggers of tunnels and trenches, hunters in the forests, and waders in the rivers. The porters, servants, watchmen, and laundrymen were black.

Mando sat on one side of the theater where the meeting was held. He noticed the announcement at the bottom mentioning six hotels and restaurants in Washington, D.C., some bars and movie houses where the delegates could go. Only these places were not off-limits to the Negroes, while the others were Dixiecratic and were closed to all colored people. Mando was thinking of this problem when someone tapped his shoulder and sat beside him. It was a tall, lean Negro.

"Hello, there. Remember me?"

Mando recognized him. How could he forget Steve? This black man was one of the first scouts who reached the mountains of Luzon before the Allied liberation forces. All who knew Steve honored his courage, his good heart which offered everything to everyone, his willingness to help with his hands and shoulders, always supporting others in any hard task.

"How do?" Mando gripped the arm of the former soldier.

"Leading a dog's life," Steve said with a dry smile and pain in his eyes.

Mando asked why. Steve was a real hero and should have no cause to complain after his country won the war.

"True," said Steve. "I was given a medal. But can a medal hide the color of my skin? The same day I was awarded the medal by the Secretary of War along with those cited for America's victory over the enemies of democracy—that same day, I went to a hotel for a good meal. I was stopped by a porter who courteously said, 'Sorry, buddy, but your color is no passport to this establishment.' The porter was following instructions. What could I do? I was wounded in the war and nearly died, but when I returned to the land for which I made that sacrifice, with the medal still dangling from my chest, I could not eat in peace in a decent hotel in this impossible capital city of democracy."

Steve related that he bought two bottles of whiskey, went to the park, and got drunk. He was arrested by a policeman and charged with vagrancy and disturbing peace and order. That night, the bed bugs in the police cell kept him awake.

According to Steve, he had no job and it wasn't his fault. His job before the war was given to another. Besides, he no longer had his old stamina nor his skill from before he was wounded in battle. Now he was surviving on a small pension.

"To think that I'm not yet thirty," Steve sighed.

No, he wasn't married. His sweetheart, a mulatto, was gone when he returned. Now, what woman would be crazy enough to share his poverty?

Mando invited Steve to one of the restaurants listed in the program. During lunch, he asked his friend to come to the Philippines where he would give him a suitable job.

When they parted, Mando felt what was happening in Washington and in other places in the U.S. was painful and ugly. Racial prejudice was its Achilles heel and bad propaganda for America's good name. For every three citizens in Washington, D.C., one was black; therefore, in the very capital, one-third of the American citizens did not enjoy justice and equality. It was bandied about that Uncle Sam went to war twice for justice and democracy on behalf of the oppressed countries. Mando could not reconcile this boast with the problem of Steve and the millions with his color and fate.

"A great contradiction," thought Mando. He felt that soon the blacks would rise and the whites would regret their arrogance.

Mando met a Filipino old-timer. He had come from the sugar cane and pineapple plantations of Hawaii, moved to the asparagus orchards in California, and proceeded to the salmon fisheries in Oregon and Alaska. He witnessed the oppression of laborers who had emigrated to America during "peacetime"—Filipinos, Mexicans, Chinese, and Japanese. He endured the term "brown monkey," ban against marrying or fraternizing with white women, and was resigned to the lowliest work for little pay.

But this Filipino bore all of this in his desire to earn, save, and study somehow. Thank God for his strength, for he finished a course in university. America's affection for the Philippines during the war and the first years of peace had quickly vanished. The old loathing for colored races returned. It really seemed hard to mix oil and water.

This Filipino thought his problem might be resolved by becoming an American citizen. This way he could claim the rights of a real American. He expected this to open doors to a good job, to socializing at gatherings, and to marriage. It would no longer be forbidden to marry a blonde.

So he became an American citizen. He was happy and proud.

One day, he invited a friend, a Cuban mestizo, to a snack at a club. He was then in Washington, D.C. The Cuban was not an American citizen, but was fair complexioned because of his Spanish father. At the door of the club, the Americanized Filipino received a hard blow to his ego. He was not admitted because he was brown, but his companion was. The porter didn't pay attention to his credentials, which he waved to show that he was "American."

He admitted sadly that what mattered was not the document or the identity tag, but the color of one's skin.

"A Filipino is a Filipino and can't ever become an American," Mando said after hearing the story of his countryman who tried to change his race by the stroke of a pen.

"Even in the Philippines," Mando continued, "not a few of our countrymen think it's good to become foreigners. They change their language, clothes, and manner. Even at home, they speak to their children only in English, are ashamed to wear their native attire, don't care to see their own plays and movies, don't want to eat rice, and claim their stomachs are upset when they smoke local cigarettes. But they only become the laughingstocks in the eyes of those whom they ape."

The Filipino was dumbfounded. Then he asked for advice.

"But what should I do? A man without a country. I spent half of my life in Hawaii and the United States. Even if I should go back now, it would be hard…"

Mando looked with pity at the Filipino, then calmly said, "What should you fear in going home to the Philippines? That you would find many things unfamiliar? Didn't you encounter greater hardship and obstacles when you came here? Look back on your first year, the manual labor, the prejudice of the whites. Did you experience this in your own country before you left? It is not wrong to go to a foreign land to improve. But when you have prospered, you should come back to your origin and use what you gained. No foreign land can ever replace the land of your birth."

Tears welled in the eyes of the other man.

"Thank you for your advice," he said. "I shall think over what you have said. I have a profession and some savings. If I should return, it would not be in shame like many who bring nothing but disgrace to the Philippines."

"The Philippines was destroyed by war," said Mando. "Every good citizen can do something to help."

Mando and his countryman met several times. At last, the latter realized that his being a Filipino was an indelible stamp of nature which he could not turn his back on. The last time he visited Mando, he brought other Filipinos.

"They also want to go home," he told Mando. "They won't be a burden to our country. They have some savings which they plan to invest in an industry."

"*Mabuhay* to all of you," Mando said, greatly pleased. He shook hands warmly with each of his countrymen.

XL

Three letters were sent by Mando almost at the same time—for Magat, for Tata Matyas, and for Puri.

Mando and Magat often exchanged letters. He had also written to Dr. Sabio. Mando's latest letter came from Washington.

Dear Magat,

> *As I have told you, a book would not be enough for what I have seen and learned in the countries I have visited. I hope that you will have the same chance to travel.*

> *Now I shall be content to discuss some food for thought for our countrymen, including those who consider themselves well-informed because of our relationship with America.*

> *The United States became free from England through the revolt of the thirteen states on July 4, 1776. They informed the world through the Declaration of Independence written by Thomas Jefferson, that 'all men are created equal, that they are endowed by their Creator with certain inalienable Rights, that among these are life, liberty, and the pursuit of happiness.'*

> *At that time, this new country had only three million people and they did not know the vast forests,*

plains, mountains, and rivers beyond the Mississippi. But in one and a half centuries, they performed miracles, and the land where people fled to in order to escape persecution by their kings and from poverty in Europe is now the world's leader in wealth and progress. The three million became one hundred seventy million and the former forests and deserts became industrial cities, of plenty, of modern homes. These miracles were not due to nature or to God, but to man, to the brains and the industry of the American people. They started with nothing but their wits and honor. In the past, hardly any foreign country wanted to help or lend her aid, while her natural resources were not yet drawn from the womb of the earth and from the bottom of the seas. Nevertheless, they triumphed, for they resolved to work and to succeed.

This was true for the overall progress of the United States. However, for the sake of accuracy, the Negroes from Guinea and Africa and the prisoners from Europe helped immeasurably in clearing the forests and leveling the mountains, in opening roads and plowing the plantations. In the final analysis, the wealth of America came from her land and only its produce was finished and improved by industry. Therefore, the black and dirty hands of the first laborers sowed the seeds that blossomed into a new civilization.

The Philippines became independent of America on July 4, 1946. It had thirty million citizens, its natural resources were rich and hardly touched by machine, an archipelago much bigger than its population. But the country is impoverished and does not profit as it should, because she does not want to work hard. She depends on others, on God's will. God does not help a man or nation that won't help itself.

In all branches of the government, there are foreign advisers, who tell us what to do. From the president to the army general, to the head of education. Naturally, their first advice is that the nation cannot stand without the help of foreigners, foreign capital, foreign experts, foreign management. Like children without minds of their own, those in charge of our administration followed such advice, until the nation became like a plant without roots, hanging in the air, and became a caricature of a country, neither occidental nor oriental. While she is made a puppet by the West which she apes, she is ridiculed by the orientals whom she wishes to snub. Only a Filipino whose sensibility is not in the heart but in his pockets will not be disgusted by this situation.

There are many good things which the Philippines can copy from America. Unfortunately, as Rizal feared, the first things picked up are the bad examples, the vices, and weaknesses. Many Filipinos try to live like Americans in language, clothes, manner, and customs, although that's impossible. They oblige the youth to forsake their own music, songs, dances. They boast that they can copy the rough ways of the foreigners, that they don't want to watch anything but foreign games, services, and other amusements nor read anything but that written by foreigners or written abroad. Where will the youth go with such inclination and upbringing?

In our land, it is often said that even before the war, the Filipino has had the highest standard of living in Asia. The basis is that the Philippines buys from the United States the greatest number of cars, cigarettes, preserved food, magazines, women's apparel, electrical appliances, radios, movies, and other things not used by other countries in this part of the world. Even if such comforts are not enjoyed by the whole country but only by some. And is this the right measure to determine the so-called high standard of living?

I think many Filipinos have a wrong concept of standard of living and cost of living. In our desire to have and use things which are not necessary, we pay dearly; our taste becomes expensive. Our standard of living does not improve, but we become poorer in the long run.

Look at the cars. For every imported car, the Philippines continues to spend for gasoline and oil, tires, and replacement motor parts. Not one of these is made in the Philippines. Thus, so much money is thrown away every year to maintain these flashy cars. The car is a sign of progress, but the Philippines should not remain an importer. Like Japan, Australia, and other neighboring countries, she should make her own cars.

In Manila, students, employees, and laborers smoke only American cigarettes. Do you know how much our country spends just on cigarettes? We are the world's biggest buyers. This is the saddest part. While the Manila cigar is said to be the best, we don't buy any. This is why the distributors of American cigarettes get rich, our own factories close down, and our tobacco growers starve.

I go back to the standard of living. Here in the United States, if a laborer works for ten hours, he earns enough for a week's expenses; there in the Philippines, on the other hand, one has to work a month to earn a week's expenses. Here, goods are cheap because they are produced locally, while there, goods are expensive because they are imported; besides, the buyer shoulders the cost of transportation, taxes, ads, and the profit of the businessman.

An American worker who earns ten dollars a day spends thirty cents for a pack of cigarettes. A Filipino who earns four pesos a day or less spends a peso for American cigarettes. Think of the difference and see if you don't grit your teeth or shed tears.

I don't say that the Filipino worker should earn as much as his American cousin. Of course, this would be only right, at some future time, for how is a white man superior to a brown man? It is only right that the worker should afford his daily needs. Why should a man work if the fruit of his labor is not enough for the basic needs of his family—like food, clothes, and a home? But how can this be expected of a country that imports its needs and whose businessmen are foreigners greedy for profit? They have become used to squeezing blood from a turnip. The leaders think only of their own welfare. So they allow the Philippines to be impoverished due to foreign exploitation. If the country grows thin from hardship, the leaders and their kin are bloated like leeches bursting from sucking the blood of their victims.

And this they do whenever they have the chance. I have seen the first rule of nepotism in our diplomatic offices. Wives, children, in-laws, nephews, and relatives of the emissary are appointed, although they are here to have fun, to study, or to have a vacation. I know the wife of an important diplomat who does nothing but visit well-known dress shops and beauty parlors, and well-known places of amusement and relaxation, but would never visit the slums, hospitals, orphanages, schools, factories, libraries, or worthwhile theaters.

Many of our emissaries live like the maharajahs wherever they go. I heard the reproach of an American official in Washington that we keep sending missions to get loans or aid, but our delegates vie with princes from the oil countries in the Near East. They live in royal hotels, their feet don't touch the ground, and they don't attend to their duties here but instead have a good time.

One of our diplomats is despised by his countrymen because he cares for nothing but self-publicity, so that while he is known in many places, especially in private schools for his lectures, giving interviews and issuing statements together with his pictures, most Americans have no idea about the Philippines, whether it is in South Africa, or whether its people have tails or live in trees, or whether it is an island of Guam, the U.S. Navy base in the Pacific. He is the most ardent spokesman of American interests, especially in carrying out their aims in the Philippines. If Philippine elections were to be directly influenced by Wall Street, the American Chamber of Commerce, the Rotary Club, the CIA, and the American Legion, you could bet that he would be the next president of the Philippines. And where would he bring the country? But don't they interfere and meddle not only in elections?

I have observed that here and in Europe, many of our diplomats should be sent home for good, or if possible, we should have them live in the barrio from time to time. Their indefinite stay in other lands is not good for them or for the country. One bad effect is that they care less about the welfare of the Philippines than of the country where they are assigned. They forget that the life, welfare, policy, and conditions of their own country are different from the country where they have been sent. I met a Filipino ambassador who seemed like a hired agent of the country where he had been staying for years.

Besides, it seems a mistake to follow the example of big powers like the United States, the Soviet Union, Britain, France, and others of similar rank, to send and spend for ambassadors, plenipotentiaries, ministers, consuls, and their respective employees, aides, chauffeurs, and families according to the whims of our politicians, and to give positions to their kin and followers. There are only a few countries with whom we trade. While it is desirable to increase them, it is stupidity to imitate the big powers but do nothing else. Our provincial roads, our town schools are very inadequate. Is it not proper that we should first spend on this instead of wasting money on diplomatic offices everywhere, with no duty except to meet and serve our junketing leaders and Filipino tourists? There are many member nations of the United Nations who don't send representatives to some cities, but assign one of their citizens living there, or ask to be represented by a friendly nation. This is the policy of many Latin American countries, and many are more economically stable than the Philippines.

Don't think that there is no graft and corruption here. There is, my friend, and I'm inclined to think that this is one of our imports from the United States. There is theft in the government and outside. I bet these diseases cannot be absent from a society which measures everything in terms of money. As in our country, the big thieves are seldom caught. It should be the reverse, for stealing is a habit to the mighty, while it is a necessity to the poor. What will you do to a person who steals because he has to, and one who has more than he needs but steals just the same?

I have not lost hope for the future of the Philippines. Our struggles during the Japanese times and the gradual awakening of the country after the war are signs that our failures and mistakes are merely lessons in growth and progress. A mouse won't grow without falling on the ground. Every child learning to walk stumbles and hurts himself. The country makes mistakes because of its leaders, but the leader is easily replaced and removed, while the country goes on. She can be betrayed, but not sold out completely by traitors. In the long run, she will meet her destiny and salvation. Did we not experience this during the Japanese times?

On the whole, in the face of what I have seen, I am sad that I am a Filipino. My heart bleeds because after we were freed from one foreign power, most of our so-called leaders took the path of the slaves. Because it's the only way they can exploit the nation and remain in power: with the help of the former master. You might miss your deadline because of this long letter.

Always,
Mando

P.S. We have a new press, not the best, but good enough for our needs. It is not the machine but we, you, and your helpers, who make the newspaper. Don't be impatient; I'll be home soon, even before this machine.

The following letter was addressed to Tata Matyas:

Tatang, my trip has been good. According to plan. I'm glad you are well. I'm coming home soon.

Puri carefully folded and kept her letter together with other things sent by Mando. This was the note:

My Dearest Puri,

During my entire trip, I have failed to meet a girl who could compare with you and your virtues. And I am glad I failed. Don't think that I am flattering you.

Regards to Tata Pastor,
Mando

With Mando's long letter to Magat, he enclosed a clipping from a liberal paper in New York City. The article was written by a Filipino student in response to an American businessman who attacked the "ingratitude" of the Philippines in protesting against the Bell Trade Act.

Wall Street Binds the Philippines

Manila, the capital city of the Philippines, remains a heap of ruins three years after liberation. But the people, the ordinary citizens, have undergone a metamorphosis in mind and soul in a short time.

Even during the dark days of enemy occupation, the Filipino laborer knew that labor should use one language, that he had to overcome the handicaps of country and race. Because, everywhere, labor is a struggle, and should move forward to its destination: the liberation of all from the chains of cruelty, fascism, and imperialism.

The Filipinos have long suffered. They bore the burden of imperialism for many centuries. They were abused and exploited by the conquerors and the Spanish friars for three hundred seventy-five years. During the last war, for three years under the Japanese, they were sucked to the bone, when the whole country of twenty million people was made into a giant prison camp.

The Filipinos are noted for bravery and love of freedom. During the long midnight of colonization, a revolution would break out every five years. During World War II, they stood in Bataan in an epic struggle against oppression and slavery. But more courageous and more glorious was the fight of the people themselves (as moths against fire). When the United States forces surrendered in Corregidor, the people continued on in the wake. From the fields, villages, meadows, mountains, slums, and swamps sprang the nation's army, an army without weapons or bullets, but armed by a soul that would not be conquered.

This army of the people won the war for democracy, not only in the Philippines, but everywhere—in Europe, Africa, Asia, the South Pacific, America. Nevertheless, fascism is not yet crushed. It still lives, despite the death of Hitler, Mussolini, and Tōjō. It is still in power in the Philippines.

Under the guise of altruism, the Yankee monopolists plotted to strengthen their grip on the Philippines in politics, economy, and the military. The return of independence on July 4, 1946 became a mockery and a cruel joke. The prostrate country was threatened and blackmailed to pawn its heritage in exchange for a can of sardines and surplus junk of the U.S. Army. The Filipinos had to amend their constitution to give parity or equal rights to the Americans and American big business, and their sovereignty was left uncertain by allowing the islands to be placed under more than twenty military bases controlling land, sea, and air, for ninety-nine years. In these bases, the Filipinos have no authority.

The government became chicken feed by order of the financial tsars of Wall Street and the Pentagon. Seats in Congress were removed from the elected representatives of laborers and farmers. Strikes and pickets were forbidden. Labor leaders were persecuted and some were killed by agents of the administration; company unions and scabs were coddled. Political freedom of the progressive elements was curtailed, while all help was given to spread the influence of the church, the Falangists, and other enemies of democracy.

The National Federation of Farmers, with its half a million members, was banned. The Hukbalahap, the terror of the Japanese during the war, was outlawed. The Congress of Labor Organizations, with its one hundred industrial unions and a stable base of democratic unionism, is continually discredited and persecuted. These abuses and oppression have forced the nation to protest and condemn the fascistic ways of the party in power, so that the fear spread that the poor classes might be obliged to adopt the stance of "a tooth for a tooth."

In spite of the excessive publicity about the American way of life, no one enjoys it except a small group of favored ones led by the politicians, landlords, and puppets of Wall Street and other supporters of the status quo. Only they have palaces surrounded by walls, flashy cars, air-conditioned offices. On the other hand, the Filipino worker, with five to six dependents, earns four pesos a day, worth about one American dollar. For one ganta of rice a day, he spends two pesos, or half of his day's earnings.

Seventy-five out of one hundred farm workers have no land of their own. They are tenants or sharecroppers. They serve under an antiquated system based on the economic needs of the United States; so they are forced to produce sugar, tobacco, abaca, copra, and timber, and to dig mines to support American industry. America buys these products by quotas and returns them finished from large factories without paying taxes at the Philippine customs. And yet the country is always short of rice and corn, its staple food.

The Philippines was promised reparations by Japan. Instead, the Supreme Commander of the Allied Powers, MacArthur, stationed in Tokyo, ordered the Philippines to send iron to Hirohito's reactivated factories. Then the materials were sold in Manila as kitchen utensils, silverware, bicycles, hardware, and all kinds of toys.

You say you saved the Philippines from the hands of conquerors on two occasions—once from Spain, the second from Japan. Perhaps. The Philippines was free in 1898 when Admiral Dewey arrived in Manila Bay and, with a few cannon shots, sank three rotten Spanish ships. You freed us, but stayed for half a century, and aren't you there even now? In 1941, the Japanese attacked us because the U.S. flag flew over Malacañan. That was not our war, but we were forced to fight and to sacrifice. You returned in 1945, after three years of untold sacrifice by the Filipino nation, and when the enemy was helpless and almost wiped out by the brave Filipino guerrillas. So the Japanese turned savagely on the people during liberation, and didn't spare even women and children.

In the Philippines, you will not find an American shivering from the cold and begging for a cup of coffee that you see all over the Bowery in New York City. The ex-soldier and other adventurers go there, and after some years, they are managers of corporations or capitalists of mines. As in Hawaii in the beginning, the richest mines were the pockets of the Pinoy heiresses who, because of their studies in Europe and America, were inclined to radish-complexioned husbands.

Actually, the United States' generosity to Juan de la Cruz was not a one-way traffic. It was mutual, a profitable exchange enforced by Uncle Sam. For it was hard for the well-informed Filipino to believe the lie that a country should occupy another land for the good of the conquered and not for its own welfare. Such deceit is obsolete. It has always been the sales pitch of conquerors since Caesar and Napoleon.

America gained a noble friend in the Far East in two world wars. But the eyes of the Filipino people are opening to the bitter truth that they are neither regarded nor treated as friends and equals. The Filipino "mucho amigo" is GI Joe's flattery for the gullible brown man. Perhaps they will not allow themselves to be used again as fodder for the cannon in times of danger and later as beasts to pull the carts.

Never again, never again, in this generation of Filipinos, the hope for their noble heroes.

XLI

The women writers of the society page ran out of words to describe the reception at the Monteros' for their housewarming and welcome for Dolly, the product of a finishing school in Paris.

For some time, the "royal" building had been standing on its two-hectare lot. But Doña Julia decided to postpone the inauguration until Dolly's return from Europe.

When the mansion was finished, the architect Pong Tua-son offered a small dinner for some newspapermen and photographers. Doña Julia showed the guests the wide garden, the swimming pool, and the three floors of the house. The lovely rooms were built in different styles and had different furnishings and paintings. The mansion built at the center of the garden was a combination of old and modern architecture, classic-modern, because the Monteros wanted to give the impression that they belonged to the "old families" who could trace their roots to the first Spaniards who settled along the shores of Maalat. However, they also wanted to prove that they were not behind the times. These wishes were given shape by the Chinese-mestizo architect in his Gothic-Renaissance framework and modern décor and conveniences. In short, with the help of an unlimited budget, he combined beauty, utility, and durability.

The first who saw it were lavish in their praise. The walls of the living room were made of dark paneling. The ceiling was gold and the floor was covered with a thick red carpet from Persia. There was an arrangement of a few sofas and a set of antique chairs and a small table of dark mahogany. Decorating some corners were large porcelain jars. Hanging on the walls were three or four paintings of old masters. From the center of the ceiling hung a blazing chandelier like the gaudy collar of a rich widow. At the end of the hall stood a large grand piano.

The rooms were just as grand. Señorita Dolly's room was called the Princess' Room. According to the architect-suitor, this could compare with the room of Princess Margaret in a real palace in London. Dolly herself did the main décor of her room when she arrived. Naturally, she wanted to try what she had learned in interior decoration at the finishing school in Paris, where she enrolled in addition to her studies at the Sorbonne, besides her observation in the cities she visited on her way home.

The three rooms and the living room were the main gems, but the whole mansion was a showplace of Philippine architecture. All four rooms were air-conditioned. Each bed had a small radio at the foot and a lamp at the head.

A few days before the affair, the grounds were decorated and looked like a small carnival. The carpet grass was mowed, the trees and the vines on the walls were trimmed, and the two-hectare grounds were cleaned. The servants, together with their relatives, were called to help. Doña Julia was obliged to bring out old clothes and to have some bills changed to reward the industrious helpers.

When everything was spotless, they hung hundreds of Japanese and native lanterns from the low branches of the champaca, calachuchi, and agoho trees.

No less than three bars were set up, one near the swimming pool, one in the front yard, and one at the back, wherever the male guests would gather.

The whole garden was filled with round tables for twelve; three long tables were heaped with delicious dishes prepared by two well-known caterers. Each guest could help himself or ask the waiters to serve any food to suit his taste—Chinese, French, or Filipino dishes, including lechon.

Before dark, two choice orchestras started to play from their platforms, one under the trees across the swimming pool, one at the side of the terrace. The multi-colored marble floor made a satisfactory dance floor.

That night, Manila's "four hundred" arrived. Cars crowded around the estate. The road was temporarily closed by the police, and only those going to the Monteros' were allowed to enter.

Policemen on duty could be seen chatting with the uniformed chauffeurs. They wondered whether they would be given rations outside or allowed to enter and choose their food and drinks. The policemen had to drive away the dirty, curious children who came from the squatter area not far from this palace.

Before seven that night, almost everyone who counted in high society—in government, finance, politics, and industry—had arrived. There were also some distinguished foreigners. Bishop Dumas, who was asked to officiate, came early. The Archbishop was abroad and the papal nuncio was called to the Vatican. Beside the Bishop, like an aide, was General Bayoneta in a gala uniform with a medal on his chest. No one could remember if the medal was for helping the Japanese before Bataan surrendered or for serving the Americans after Manila was won back.

Meanwhile, the Montero couple were getting uneasy over the delay of the President. He had the habit of coming late even on national occasions. The couple had been waiting for an hour at the main entrance and could not attend to their other guests. The Bishop and the General joined a group in the garden. Among them were Senator Botin, Governor Doblado, Judge Pilato, and other associates. The waiters came carrying trays with drinks and hors d'oeuvres.

"We have a quorum," observed Senator Botin.

"For poker, yes, but not for a Senate session," commented the governor.

"What's the news, General?" Judge Pilato greeted Bayoneta. "Peaceful."

"If it is peaceful, why does the army demand a large budget?" Botin retorted sharply.

"Because a small budget is the fuse of trouble," explained Bayoneta. "Especially among the army men who don't receive a raise and the increased boldness of the outlaws."

They were startled by a long siren followed by the sound of motorcycles.

"The President," said the General and hurried to meet him. Right behind was Governor Doblado. The President shook hands with Montero and Doña Julia. The First Lady and Mrs. Montero rubbed their cheeks against each other.

"Come in *compadre*, *comadre*," loudly declared Montero as he led the honored guests to the living room. Montero immediately claimed the right to call the First Couple comadre and compadre because they would be sponsors at the house blessing.

When the President entered, the guests stood up and sat down only when he graciously gestured. Those who were known to the President and his wife immediately came and paid their respects.

After a while, Dolly entered with Don Segundo leading her by the hand, followed by Doña Julia.

"Compadre, comadre," said Don Segundo, "here is my daughter Dolores. She just arrived from her studies at Sorbonne."

"Monte, so you have a Miss Philippines," said the President.

The First Lady asked what Dolly studied in Paris. Upon learning that she was an expert in interior decoration, she invited the girl to the palace at the first opportunity.

"The palace needs a new look," the First Lady said, smiling. The President nodded, but after looking around at the numerous women guests in the wide hall, he added, laughing, "But it seems to me that the whole New Look is here." The First Lady looked to see what he meant—the clothes, jewelry, manner, and hairstyles of the women, both married and unmarried.

The First Lady and a few others were in *ternos*,[1] but most wore dresses of costly material fashioned according to the imagination of the designer—a battle among the chemise, sack, and trapeze, although these styles were just being tried out by Christian Dior, St. Laurent, and other designers of Paris and New York.

Flocks of aging but coquettish matrons were strutting like hens sighting a rooster; young matrons acting like hens who had discovered a snake in their nests, and girls with pointed breasts, wide hips, and wriggling bodies restlessly sitting or standing. Only they could recognize their real selves.

Someone greeted the mother-daughter pair Betty and Betsy Labajita who looked like sisters. It was no secret that Betty, the mother, was widowed, and Betsy, the youngest of her three children, was sired by her latest catch, Labajita. Both were dressed gaudily, coiffured like Audrey Hepburn, and had the same bag and shoes. Betty would laugh aloud when they were called the "Labajita twins."

Also noticeable was Balbinitá Cuatrovientos, a former hostess who married a Spanish *pelotari*.[2] The pelotari became a businessman after saving enough from his fixed games. Balbinitá was a veritable dragonfly flitting to and fro in the ballroom, perhaps because of her former occupation. She spoke in a mixture of English-Chabacano. She was bragging that a daily massage and a tepid bath sprinkled with cologne was good for her figure and complexion.

In one group, Blancanieve Cienfuegos was relating a secret for keeping slim. No one could tell she had just come from the

---

1 terno—traditional Filipino dress with butterfly sleeves

2 pelotari—a player of Jai Alai

maternity ward. "Of course, I always deliver by Caesarian," she said. "Let the nursemaid feed them."

Meanwhile, in another group, Maggie Siemprejoven was lecturing on an effective hair dye. "Even after three weeks, the dye does not fade and looks natural," said Maggie, and she smoothed her hair and lowered her eyelashes. Most of those listening were wives of cabinet members and senators whose first concern was how to turn back the hands of the clock and the pages of the calendar.

A group of women made up of Mercy Mahabaguin, Conchita Pantoche, and Doña Julia invited the First Lady to a benefit for the city's poor.

The women were like goldfish in an aquarium. In fact, most of them flocked to such gatherings, not to please the host or see the house, and especially not to eat, for many had problems with their digestion, but to show off their colorful attire, their gaudy jewelry, their imported bags and shoes, and other trinkets dear to the hearts of society women. Every gathering they attended became a fashion show with new and unusual clothes at fabulous prices.

In the midst of all these, Dolly still stood out. Her dress was unique. It was created expressly for Dolly by the upcoming St. Laurent who had a shop at Place de la Opera in Paris. It was made of cloth that seemed to be woven of silk and fine glass, silver with a touch of sky blue, revealing her chemise and her shapely figure. It had a low sweetheart neckline that dipped to her cleavage, sleeveless but for a narrow strap of pearls showing her white arms. Her beauty was enhanced by that dress with a simple ornament for accent—a ruby collar and a large red rose in her hair.

Everyone complimented Dolly. Architect Tua-son was like a tame Pekingese who kept following her.

Dolly had become lovelier since she left Manila two years before. Her stay in Europe and the culture of Paris added to her innate sheen and polish. Her experience in the loveliest city of the world added to her color, sweetness, and allure. She was no longer a young girl, but a complete woman at her peak, no longer a bud smiling at the kiss of light, but a full-blown flower, exuding an intoxicating fragrance. If the President became a widower and decided to remarry, or if Bishop Dumas were freed from celibacy, the two men past their prime would likely be tempted by Dolly.

But Dolly was obviously not content in the midst of such gaiety and adoration. One could see her listlessness, her forced smile, and her pale cheeks.

She would stop to listen to the sound of every car coming or the name of every guest announced at the door.

The house-blessing rites were over; most had eaten and many were dancing.

Dolly was waiting for a guest. Mando Plaridel. She talked to Mando on the phone that afternoon and made him promise not to fail her. But it was nine in the evening and he was not yet there.

Only Dolly was bored and lonely amidst such joyous hours of pomp, plenty, and pleasure. Dancing with some guests like architect Tua-son, Governor Doblado, General Bayoneta made her more bored and impatient for Mando's arrival.

All were engrossed in watching a native dance on the terrace, including Bishop Dumas, who suggested that this be presented on stage instead of indecent vaudeville and burlesque where the female performers were practically naked.

"Art and morals are not enemies," said Bishop Dumas. "In fact, at first the dance was a religious ceremony. But the devil makes everything his tool, so that later, he used the dance the same way he quotes God's words from the Bible."

"Even for commerce and propaganda," answered Senator Botin, "our native dances should be presented in our theaters. First, our artists would earn and we would not have to import dancers from America and Japan; second, we would show the skill and the beauty of our native art."

"It's unfortunate," added Judge Pilato, "that the foreigners are the first to appreciate our native dances in barrio-fiesta style gatherings and in expositions abroad. But here, the wealthy are crazy over ballet and the plebeians over jazz."

The *Pandanggo sa Ilaw*[3] was rewarded with loud applause, but for Dolly that applause was a welcome for Mando, who was at the entrance of the living room. No one noticed his arrival except Dolly, who hardly watched the show on the terrace.

"Am I not too late?" asked Mando, apologizing for his tardiness.

"I'll die waiting for you," Dolly reproached him, but gone was her listlessness; her loneliness and paleness were replaced by roses on her cheeks.

Dolly introduced Mando to her father, the President, and some guests. After the floor show, all eyes were on Mando and Dolly as they danced.

To those who didn't notice the scar on Mando's left cheek and who saw only his bearing and elegance, he seemed like a foreigner.

"This is the first time I've seen or heard the name of that man," the President remarked to Don Segundo.

"He stayed long in Europe," replied the host. "He met Dolly in Paris."

"What does he do?"

"Dolly didn't say, but he is rich and bright. Which reminds me, it seems he is behind the newspaper the *Kampilan*."

"Oh, the radical paper," exclaimed the President.

This was the same topic of the others—Governor Doblado, General Bayoneta, and others who couldn't understand why the women considered Dolly's friend charming and attractive. Architect Tua-son went to the bar to drown his sorrows.

---

3 Pandanggo sa Ilaw—Candle Dance, a folk dance

XLII

Mando was pleased that no one recognized him or even suspected his identity. He knew a number of those present. They would surely remember him if given some reminders. Foremost were Don Segundo and Doña Julia; Governor Doblado who had been a constant visitor before the war; General Bayoneta who was a mere lieutenant or captain and aide to a high Japanese official during the last days of the Japanese in Manila.

Mando was not surprised that he was completely forgotten. Not only because of his change in appearance but because Andoy, his former self, was never important enough to them to be remembered, a servant whose disappearance would hardly be noticed or like a useless tool that could easily be replaced, of value only when used, but otherwise, who would remember?

When he came down from the Sierra Madre soon after the war, Mando had changed much. He had a long scar on his left cheek, which Tata Matyas compared to a medal. Had he belonged to a gang in Manila, he would surely have been called "Scarface." He had grown taller and stood straight as a rod. His firm muscles strained beneath his clothes. He had grown older; gone was the youthfulness from his face and bearing. His dearth of knowledge was replaced by perseverance, experience, marks of struggle.

Even the observant Magat didn't recognize him when they met again after liberation. Finally, he asked, "What happened?" And he himself peered at his face in the mirror, shook his head, muttering with mixed feelings: "This is no longer Andoy… This is Mando."

And now, he had returned from a long journey in different lands and nations, after being honed by the modern things he had observed and experienced, filled with knowledge he had striven to gain. Who would even associate him with the thin Montero houseboy, the timid and silent Andoy in khaki pants and faded polo shirt? Indeed, who would suspect that he was also this elegant man with the magnetic personality whose manners were those of a nobleman before his men, a leader among his followers?

Dolly who used to shout and knock him on the head for every mistake, this haughty mistress had no inkling that the houseboy whose disappearance she had hardly noticed, was the same man she met and became infatuated with in Paris. She had not noticed any resemblance even in their intimate moments in Mando's suite at the Ritz Hotel and other places of rendezvous. Despite the ugly scar, his attractive personality caught the attention of the President, who had asked Montero who he was.

But it was not Mando alone who had changed in appearance and outlook. Not just personal relations. Many things had changed, for what does not change with time? That house which was obviously a rich man's house was now an imposing mansion for a millionaire. Even the surroundings were different. Gone was the small pre-war hut of Andoy and his parents where now stood a large garage. Gone were the stones beside it and the low faucet where his mother used to wash clothes all day. But here remained Don Segundo and Doña Julia who had not aged. Doña Julia seemed to be winning her fight with the advancing years. And here was Dolly, the rising moon, now in her full glory.

Mando's thoughts were cut short when Dolly lovingly nestled against her partner.

"Don't tell me you're thinking of our nights in Paris," she said. Mando laughed but said nothing.

"Don't you want to see my room?"

"Later, Dolly." Mando was evasive. "You have many guests."

"Okay. Next time you come."

When the orchestra stopped playing, Dolly invited Mando to the garden which was lit with lanterns and multicolored lights.

"I'm hungry," she complained. "Imagine, I've had nothing since this afternoon. But hunger is nothing compared to waiting for you." She threw him a look of reproach.

Mando had not had supper either, for he got so engrossed in a meeting. They went to a long table laden with food. They got two plates, took some salad, *relleno,*[1] and bread. Then they sat at a table away from the crowd.

Only a few were dining. Many were dancing, some groups were chatting, and some men were drinking. All were making merry.

"Now that we are in Manila," Dolly reproached Mando, "you seem to have no time for me."

"Not really, Dolly. The truth is, I was away on a long trip and left much work which I have to attend to right away."

"In the daytime, yes, but how about at night? Since you arrived, we have not gone out."

"I often work late in the office. Make allowance for my shortcomings. Believe me, this does not mean I'm cooling off."

"Very well. I expect you'll find time for the picnic prepared by Papa's overseer."

"Picnic? Where?"

"At our hacienda. The overseer, a former army captain, came to invite us to the picnic in my honor. You'll come, won't you?"

"We'll see," he answered lightly, but his thoughts were on Puri, Tata Pastor, Hacienda Montero, and the tenants. "The new overseer wants to show off," he told himself.

---

1 relleno—stuffed chicken

"I won't take no for an answer," Dolly insisted, noticing Mando's hesitation.

Before Mando could answer, Don Segundo came to tell them that the President was about to leave but decided to stay for coffee. Don Segundo invited Mando to join them.

Tua-son was behind Don Segundo so that when Mando stood up, he immediately sat beside Dolly.

The President was in Don Segundo's private office on the ground floor with Senator Botin. Both were seated on easy chairs. Don Segundo and Mando sat on the opposite sofa.

"I was going to ask Monsignor, but he has left," said Montero.

"Why is it that for weddings of the rich, the Archbishop or the Bishop officiates?" observed Botin. "I have not heard them wed the poor." The Senator knew the answer but threw out his loaded question anyway.

"As in other professions, the Archbishop and the Bishop have their price," explained Montero, making the President and Mando smile.

"Aren't there doctors who will treat none but the rich? And lawyers who will appear in court only if paid their fees in advance?"

Two waiters brought the coffee. Montero poured.

"I read your paper," the President addressed Mando.

"I'm glad, sir," the publisher said courteously. "What is your impression, sir?"

"I have a feeling you are anti-administration," remarked the President.

"And politicians," added Senator Botin.

"And also against landlords and capitalists," added Montero.

Mando cleared his throat and bit his lip before answering the three. "No newspaper can exist if all it does is make enemies," he declared. "A newspaper's mission—the *Kampilan's*—is to find out and report the truth. If, in doing this, some are hurt, it's not because they are the targets of the paper. In supporting a policy, believe me, Honorable President, gentlemen, that we have never been moved by personal aims and feelings."

"It's your duty to support the government," declared the President, "because the government represents the nation. The government has no aim but the welfare of the nation."

Then he took the cup and drank half of the strong, steaming coffee. When the President brought out a cigarette, Don Segundo quickly got the matches on the table and lit it.

"Tell me, is there anyone more concerned about the nation than its government?" the President asked, looking steadily at Mando.

"At first glance, so it seems," Mando said, "but in practice, it could be the opposite. If you'll pardon me for saying so."

"You're making an accusation," quickly answered the President.

"I'm only citing actual happenings," answered the head of the *Kampilan*. "I shall explain, if you'll allow me."

The President leaned back on the lounging chair, while Senator Botin lit a cigar. Montero drank his coffee.

"I admit that your institution is good, your heart is pure, and your hands are clean," continued Mando. "But on what issue did you win the election? That you will secure more aid from America. A mistake from the start."

"Our country was destroyed and our economy in ruins," interrupted the President. "It is America's responsibility to aid us, for we were involved because of her. What can we do…"

"Pardon me, Your Excellency," quickly answered Mando. "I was not against asking for aid or reparation, which is America's responsibility. What I mean is that we should not be satisfied with aid and charity. Many other American allies were laid waste by the war. They, too, should receive aid, payment, if you wish. But, above all, we should depend on ourselves, our ability, our natural resources, our brains, and our physical strength."

Mando paused to give the others time to ponder his words. Then he continued.

"I am still waiting, sir—if you'll pardon me, but I wish to be frank," he said steadily. "I am still waiting for a leader who will tell our country that we shall stand on our own feet, that we shall not be clinging vines, but straight and firm like the molave atop the mountain, or amidst the lashing of the wind and the hurricane. Either we remain conquered or we become independent. Frequent asking for doles like a beggar lessens one's worth. Who does not admire the ant that toils unceasingly, stores food, builds its houses, and dies fighting, even against men, if it is harmed?"

The President lit another cigarette and serenely answered, "You are clearly an idealist. I began in politics with a vision just like yours. A new Quixote. I thought I could conquer the windmills. Attacks and optimism are good to hear from the opposition when they want to wrest power. But the moment you assume office and you are swamped with the problems of the nation, countless problems, one after another, then you will see that doing is different than preaching. Who does not know that the country's number one problem is want and poverty? Who doesn't know that the results of this are unemployment, discontent, disorder? Who doesn't know that we import more than we export, so that the poor cannot afford necessities because most are imported? Many remedies have been suggested by experts—foreigners and Filipinos—and many have been tried. You saw the frustrations of my predecessors. I don't say that I have failed but it is sad to admit that we are going in circles, ending where we started."

The President took a deep breath, as if said circle was a small ball removed from his throat.

"That, sir, is a vicious circle," Mando continued the analogy. "I said our policy was wrong from the start; therefore, also our plans and procedures. We should be independent and free not only in name. Let us cut off all strings; let us open a new path if necessary and stick to it. We should have our own goals in our economy, education and defense, agriculture and industry, in our foreign relations and trade. Let's do what's best for the Philippines, cast aside superstition and hearsay. Let us be like the river, ever flowing to the sea. Even in the wilderness we can hear its sound."

"You have an exceptional idea," conceded the President later on. "But my friend, don't forget that theory is different from practice. I told you that I, too, was a dreamer. Now that I'm in the position, I realize that the problems of the nation can't be solved by the President right away."

"Not even by two or three presidents, sir, if they don't learn to do right," agreed Mando. "Nevertheless, I believe where there's a will, there's a way. If the theory is right and it fails, the procedure must be wrong. The plan of the house may be good, but the architect is bad."

"What do you think of the plan and execution of the house?" Don Segundo managed to butt in.

"Excellent!" Senator Botin spoke before Mando could reply.

"Let us be honest with the people," Mando continued after seconding the Senator's praise. "Let them know the truth, the weaknesses, the sacrifice demanded of all. And may the leaders show the right example. The mistake of the politicians, if you'll pardon me, is to promise what they can't do."

"How would you win an election?" asked Senator Botin.

"That is the trouble. The politicians think that winning an election is enough. They do everything to win, by hook or by crook. Success should be measured by the satisfaction of the whole nation in their administration."

The President disagreed. "Pleasing the whole nation is a dream," he said.

"That is why the goal to be desired is the contentment of the people," Mando replied. "For if a thing is easily obtained, where would be the beauty and nobility of a dream?"

After more than an hour exchanging views, the President stood up and shook hands with Mando.

"Give me a chance," he said. "I'm not afraid of criticism. But perhaps, it would be good for all if you would help me instead of mudslinging."

Mando nodded but made no comment. He felt that he couldn't sacrifice the truth even for the President.

There were still many guests in the hall and on the terrace, but they started to go, after the President and the First Lady had left. Mando didn't stay long after Dolly walked with him to his car in a corner of the grounds.

As Mando opened the front door of the car, Dolly held his arm and lovingly asked:

"Mister, aren't you going to kiss me?"

XLIII

Many frowned or raised their eyebrows at the sudden wealth of some Filipinos after "liberation." Their progress was not hard to trace, however. They used the war to enrich themselves, often through illegal means.

Like Horatio Alger were Segundo Montero and his Chinese friend Son Tua, now Tua-son, who started from scratch. Their origins still showed. True, both were well-off before the war. Montero owned the hacienda and some business enterprises. Son Tua owned gambling and opium dens. Legitimate businessmen could not amass millions in such a short time. There was no doubt that the two were now multimillionaires.

Montero himself said after the war that he would be like the saw, biting both ways, coming and going. He practiced this with the Japanese and the Americans. Son Tua moved like a chess player, feeding pawns to corner a king. The Chinese millionaire had a limited Tagalog vocabulary, but he knew *padulas, parating,* and *pabagsak.*[1]

It was unnecessary to look at a crystal ball to know the secret of their sudden wealth. Manila had many such "geniuses."

One night, before nine, two guests arrived at the Montero mansion in a low-numbered car. Montero met Governor Oscar

---

1 padulas…—various terms meaning bribe

Doblado and General Magno Bayoneta. They had sent word of their coming.

They took the elevator to the third floor which was for conferences. The Chinese millionaire was there, reclining on the lounge chair with his back to the door. He didn't notice the new arrivals until General Bayoneta kissed his hand.

"Have you been here long, sir?" asked the General, who had married one of Son Tua's daughters.

Governor Doblado heartily greeted the Chinese millionaire.

Montero got drinks from the bar, the waiter not being allowed at such conferences.

"Well, let's drink first." Montero poured the newly opened scotch into two glasses. He poured brandy for himself. Son Tua never drank.

"No, thank you, Monte," the Chinese man declined.

After warming their throats, they sat facing each other. Son Tua remained seated on his lounge chair.

"This is a meeting of our corporation," began Montero, slowly. Casting an affectionate glance at the Chinese, he went on. "Our friend Son Tua and I have decided to expand operations. The dollar, opium, and jewelry trades are good. Also the blue seal, rice, and canned goods, as shown by your dividends. But, now, the greatest demand is for arms. So, we shall concentrate on arms."

Montero first cleared his throat. "For every gun we buy at forty pesos wholesale, we shall gain as much as three hundred, and in cold cash."

The governor and the General exchanged glances, for other contraband goods hardly netted two hundred percent. This was seven hundred percent!

"But arms are a great risk," objected Doblado. "Diamonds and opium are easy to hide, especially by a woman. Rice is easy to sell. But Thompsons, Garands, machine guns...aba!"

"How about the General? And you, Governor?" challenged Montero, looking at Bayoneta as if asking for support. The General smiled. Son Tua nodded.

"You take care of 'protection,'" Montero answered his own question. "The same tactics: meet and convey. That's why, after deducting capital and expenses, the profit is divided into four."

"What is the plan for the weapons?" Doblado asked quietly.

"Very simple," answered Montero. "Just like drinking." And he finished his brandy. "Arms are in great demand in many places. The rebellion in Indonesia, the opposing camps in Indochina, the landlords in Thailand, in…"

"While trade in arms is that great, an agreement to reduce armaments is remote," Doblado pointed out.

"Also the end of the war, especially civil war," Bayoneta surmised. "If the army is increased, there will be fewer unemployed."

"Business first, before the army," Son Tua reminded his son-in-law.

"As usual, Son Tua and I provide the capital," said Montero. "And you two take care of operations and protection."

"And the men?" asked Doblado

"Get trustworthy ones. We have tested ones, haven't we?"

General Bayoneta explained that they had to choose the best sources at a low price. He mentioned some military bases with new and surplus arms in the warehouses, a few transports sailing to and from Manila, and installations outside the Philippines.

"As soon as you contact the officers in charge, it is as easy as buying matches at the sari-sari store," Bayoneta concluded.

"The General is right," agreed Montero. "But this should not be known by the buyer's agents nor by rival corporations," he warned. "Try to monopolize the transactions."

"Just let them try to do anything behind my back and we'll see where they land," threatened Bayoneta, clenching his right fist. "They can do that only if we allow it."

"Good!" Montero said. "As usual, Osky, you keep the arms until they are to be delivered. The warehouse has to be in your province where you're the king. General, you take care of the delivery. Is everything clear?"

"About the helpers, transactions, couriers, yes."

"Just list down the expenses," said Montero. "Have I ever complained about my obligations? Son Tua and I understand. We have to spend more for public and private relations, representation, contact, etcetera, etcetera. The etcetera cost even more," he complained.

"Customs everywhere, right?" commented Doblado.

"Too many checkpoints," added Son Tua. "Same as paying customs."

"More, sometimes," corrected Montero. "If you pay taxes, you pay only taxes. Pay the fixed amount and that's it. But here, there's no limit. As Son Tua said, too many checkpoints."

"Going around the law is not only expensive, but risky," reminded Bayoneta.

"Depends on the person," the General's father-in-law disagreed.

"Why have many been forced to do this?" asked Montero. "It's the government's fault. Isn't it, Son Tua?" Son Tua nodded his head with its thin white hair.

"Is it not the government that's killing the initiative and activities of business?" Montero asked. "I have pointed this out to Senators Botin and Maliwanag. I have mentioned this to the President, my compadre. Taxes upon taxes and intricate controls, plus so much red tape. You are not only overburdened, but your hands are tied."

"Control can be avoided, Montero, if there is 'put,' (bribe)" Doblado hinted.

"Why not? In this country, money is king. But we businessmen want to help the government if possible. Therefore, if one is forced into this kind of business, it's because we are protesting against its bad policy. It wants to strangle legitimate business; we should not be blamed if we try to survive through illegal business."

"What happens to customs fees?" asked Son Tua.

"They squander them in pleasure," quickly answered Montero. "If they would only spend it for the country..."

Montero got a small memorandum book from a drawer at the bar and showed it to the three.

"Look at this month's expenses. If our business were legal, this money should go to the government treasury."

Doblado and Bayoneta looked at the list.

"This is Latin," said the governor. "This looks like MacArthur's cable that angered Truman—'top secret.'"

"Of course, it's for me alone," explained Montero. "Even if others should get it, in case of an investigation, no one would understand. But I need it to keep track of expenses. Or else how will I know how much I have advanced for expenses?"

At this remark, Son Tua cleared his throat.

"See who can guess the meaning of this," bragged Montero and read the first entry: "Chief, four."

"I'm used to cables, but that's new," said Bayoneta.

"See," laughed Montero. "Well, this is the chief of police that received four thousand for a service."

"There are many chiefs," observed the governor.

"Off the record, please." And Montero whispered his name.

"That one asks extra from me," said Son Tua. "Very greedy."

"Don't give anymore, Papa, unless it's me," the General kidded him. Everyone laughed.

"Here's another: Secretary," Montero read.

"Big potato, ha?" guessed Doblado.

"Seven thousand for a secretary."

"Surely not the secretary of a counselor?" Bayoneta remarked. Everyone laughed again.

Montero continued reading the list.

"Two Ham. Two."

"Sounds like algebra," chuckled Doblado. "How do you read it, General?"

"I can't make head or tail of it," admitted Bayoneta.

"Wait, wait," said Doblado. "Two hams at one thousand each. What expensive hams. Right, Monty?"

"I thought you were weak in algebra," answered Montero. "These are two heads of bases that helped a fat deal. They asked for a blowout. So I asked for two white call girls. But, gentlemen, this is only a down payment."

"Those men are really costly," exclaimed Doblado. "We are mere amateurs in monkey business."

Governor Doblado gaped at the last entry for 'fifty' after a name which he could not read.

"What animal is this?" he asked aloud. General Bayoneta looked at Montero's memo.

Montero did not answer at once.

"Is it Mac or Wac?" asked Doblado with some envy. He couldn't believe anyone would receive more than him.

Montero grinned.

"Is there a Wac worth fifty thousand?"

"Then…" Doblado said, "Tsk, tsk."

"Yes, gentlemen," admitted Montero without mentioning the name. "You know the miracle, so you also know the saint."

"Our corporation is really number one," chuckled Doblado and Bayoneta.

Son Tua's eyes narrowed as he smiled.

Before the laughter subsided, Son Tua started to leave. Bayoneta offered to drive his father-in-law home.

"Just a minute," Montero held back Bayoneta, "I'd like you to look into the affairs of my hacienda. Both of you know that I can't rest with what's happening. The unrest continues although I have changed the overseer with your recommendation, General. I told you about the agitators, didn't I?"

"I know," answered Doblado.

"I want peace in the hacienda," said Montero emphatically.

"That can be done if the General and I work together," promised the governor.

"What's bad is the alliance of the city laborers and the farmers," General Bayoneta worried. "And they are being goaded by the *Kampilan*."

"The backer of the *Kampilan* is a friend of your Dolly," Doblado said mockingly

"So, do everything possible," insisted Montero, ignoring Doblado's remark. "I want to drive out all those who don't want to abide by the old terms. Replace them with those ready to obey. Captain Pugot says he can get replacements from Ilocos. The Ilocanos are good, industrious, and thrifty. If you could put away the troublemakers," Montero whispered so that Son Tua wouldn't hear.

"Leave it to the General and me," the Governor said. "Sleep well. We know what to do."

Montero handed Doblado a roll of paper bills. "That's for the two of you. For poker," he said, smiling. "For the hacienda."

The clock struck eleven o'clock when two cars passed through the gate. The mansion was like a giant suddenly wrapped in darkness.

XLIV

A charity benefit was on the agenda at a merienda meeting of prominent women at the Manila Hotel.

It was half an hour behind schedule; yet not even the invitation committee had arrived. Right after lunch, Doña Julia rushed to get ready. She opened her wide built-in cabinet for afternoon clothes and looked over the dresses on the left. Then she looked at the ternos on the right. She could not decide between a terno and a dress. After a while, she got a dress with pastel colors; most would be wearing dresses. Actually, she wanted to wear something different, but she would run short of time if she wore a terno. She had to have her hair and nails done.

Reminding Dolly to be ready at four, Doña Julia hastened to her favorite beauty salon. After two hours, she returned looking ten years younger. Her hair was newly set and shining with perfumed pomade. Her nails newly trimmed and painted blood red. Her lips were as bright as her fingernails and toenails.

She started dressing at three thirty and finished at four fifteen. Dolly had been ready for some time. She was alluring in her red dress with white fleur-de-lis prints. Both wore step-ins with glass heels.

Doña Julia came late, but she was still the first to arrive. She saw the committee's secretary giving final instructions to the head waiter about the table arrangement. There would be a table for the special guest and the committee. Arrangements for food and decoration had been made several days before.

After another half hour, the guests came. All women, almost all were guests at the blessing of the Monteros' mansion.

Arriving together were Mercy Mahabaguin and Mrs. Conchita Pantoche who had fetched the First Lady. But the guest of honor asked to be excused. She had another appointment. There was no explanation why both invitations were accepted. Naturally, the absence of the honored guest dampened their spirits. At such gatherings, the status of the guests was more important than the purpose. Mercy apologized to the group for the absence of the First Lady. All were disappointed; each had her own request to make to the President's wife. Now they had to wait for another rare opportunity.

Balbinitá Cuatrovientos, Blancanieve Cienfuegos, and Maggie Siemprejoven were all dressed up as if for a fashion show. They had been planning hard where they would place themselves for the picture taking. Balbinitá had asked Mercy to let her pin the orchids, while Blancanieve and Maggie had asked the photographer to take their picture with the guest of honor.

The committee decided to go on with the meeting as planned.

The first number of the program was merienda. The guests grouped themselves at the tables spread out in the hall.

The waiters were used to such conversation which sounded like a thousand bumblebees. They were used to waiting on groups of women at such gatherings held on various pretexts.

At a group of wives of important officials, the "dessert" was the news of the separation of a department secretary and his wife.

"They have been estranged for a long time," said one.

"But they lived under the same roof," remarked another.

"For appearances," stressed the informant. "Besides, their children are grown-up. But they don't eat nor sleep together—separate beds and separate tables," she emphasized in English.

"Is that possible?" asked a third. "That's hard. Better to be separate outright."

"Hoy, woman," said an older one, "if all estranged couples in Manila since liberation were to live apart, we would worsen the housing shortage."

The remark was met with loud laughter.

"Aba, I have many vacant apartments," said one. "No scandal. Only we know what happens inside the house. If that should happen to common people, it's a sure fight. Bloody, too."

"Scandal is due to gossip," said the first. "The gossips keep talking about people who should separate. If we had divorce laws, the…"

"What for?" objected the advocate of the status quo. "In Hollywood, where every three days someone changes their spouse, divorce is needed. But we are different; couples who don't speak to each other live together. Give the right medicine for the particular illness. Besides, we can manage without divorce. It was Quezon, I think, who said, 'If you can eat it raw, why cook it?'"

Louder laughter met the remark attributed to the late President Quezon.

At another table, the topic was the merits of various Manila couturiers. Some complained of the few who did not fulfill their commitments, the lack of skill of some, wrong measurement and wrong style, and the greed of others who had charged too high and demanded advanced payment.

"I have an easy solution for a bad dressmaker," bragged a matron who looked like a bulldog despite her elegance. Her nose was like a flattened cashew nut and her upper lip like an ashtray.

"What do you do?" eagerly asked the others.

"Why, don't pay. Let him try to collect."

"Then you can't go back to him."

"I certainly won't. Dressmakers are a dime a dozen."

"Ah, I have no problem with our dressmakers," bragged another who looked like a foreigner except for her color. "I don't have my clothes sewn here. I have a dressmaker in Hong Kong."

"I thought it was Paris."

"Chica, Hong Kong is the Paris of the Far East. You have no idea how many Manilans make regular trips to Hong Kong. Many go there for mah-jongg."

"About dressmakers. Who is really better, a male or a female?"

"Men, of course," chorused two in the group.

"Why?"

"Because women dress up for men. If there were no men in the world, women wouldn't even wear clothes. If fine clothes are for men, then it's an advantage to have a male dressmaker. That's why Paris has a Christian Dior."

"Then why aren't tailors women, following your line of reasoning?"

"Because of men's pants. In taking the measurements, one always asks: right or left? Can a woman ask this?"

At the other table, the talk among businesswomen was not so loud. They were discussing the black market value of dollars and the peso, the smuggling of diamonds and blue seal cigarettes, ways of getting allocations from government agencies.

"The lower our dollar resources, the lower the value of our peso," explained one. "In Manila, the exchange is one to three, but high in Hong Kong."

"What about the wives of big shots? All expenses for trips, good times, and purchases come from profits from the dollar. Even those without dollars earn by being dummies of foreigners, who control eighty percent of our dollars."

"It is said that trade in diamonds is slow."

"Why not, when there is an oversupply? At first, the smuggler brought in diamonds and sold them to the wealthy, to the wives and mistresses of sugar daddies. Now, it's the reverse. The wives

of big kamotes have become smugglers and sell diamonds to
wealthy Chinese."

"Maybe the baggage of the big shots is not opened at the
pier and the airport."

"It's suicide for the agent to inspect the baggage of one with
a diplomatic passport, a bigwig. And these people always travel
with a special or diplomatic passport."

"I read that even a maid was given a diplomatic passport."

"You'd do the same in their place, chica."

"You can believe it. That's why my husband wants to run
for senator."

"On which ticket?"

"Any ticket. He's not choosy, just so he gets squeezed in.
If you're a senator, the party does not matter. It's easy to get a
diplomatic passport."

At one table were Balbinitá, Blancanieve, Maggie, Betty,
and daughter Betsy. Balbinitá told the waiter that she didn't care
for *puto, kalamay* and *goto*,[1] because they would ruin her figure.

"Just give me orange juice and a pack of Camels."

For these five, the only worthwhile topic was how to stay
young and beautiful, how to care for their complexion, stay slender
and avoid white hair.

Maggie said that hair nowadays is dyed any color. "It should
match the eyes. Some are unbecoming because they don't match
the skin. Ruby for the fair complexioned and white for those
above seventy."

Betty Labajita passed around a picture of herself and her
daughter to get the others' comments.

At another table could be heard the gripes of younger matrons
about maids. They ask for high salaries, are choosy about their
jobs, and even want privileges of common employees.

"They are getting stuck-up," said a young pregnant matron.

---

1 puto…—native dishes served as snacks

"Just because they have learned to read and write, unlike their grandmothers. Now they are imposing conditions on their masters and want to be señoritas."

She related that the maid who had just left was from the North. She had been given thirty pesos a month, free food, with no other duty but to wash the dishes and clean the house, no laundry, no cooking, and she wanted to be allowed to go to church on Fridays and see a movie on Sunday.

"They become maids only to get to Manila," answered another.

"When they get here, they look for other jobs—waitress, vendor, or salesgirl. But their real aim is marriage."

"What should they come to Manila for? In their barrio, they can also find husbands."

"They want someone better. If they become waitresses or salesgirls, they might marry a Chinese."

"Better a Chinese than a Filipino good-for-nothing."

"A thousand times better. With a Chinese, you won't starve; with our countrymen, you don't only starve, but get beaten up. So you can't blame the poor girls."

"Times have changed. I prefer the maids we were used to—no complaint about work. Just like members of the family, they don't think of leaving and stay until their old age. Whatever you give is appreciated, no complaints, no questions. Even this attitude was changed by the war."

"And the ones with the looks and figure become hostesses," one said, pouting. "And once a hostess, she becomes a congressman's mistress."

The merienda was over after two hours. Mercy stood up and announced that the aim of their meeting, as stated in the invitation, was to hold a benefit for charity.

Several proposals for fundraising were given—mah-jongg, bingo, a dance, a movie, a fashion show, or a rummage sale, etc. The women didn't lack ideas but could not agree.

At last they thought of asking for a sweepstakes race, but didn't reach a decision. When they adjourned, they resolved to hold another meeting which they would make sure the First Lady would attend.

XLV

The strictness of the new overseer of Hacienda Montero was the last straw that broke the camel's back. Don Segundo replaced Pastor with a former constabulary captain notorious for his ferocity and his zealous support of the Japanese conqueror.

The new overseer was not known by his real name, Caballero, but by the epithet Captain Pugot. According to Charles Darwin's theory of "The Origin of the Species and the Descent of Man," one could trace Caballero's ancestry, not to the noble knight errants or an agile jockey, but to a stubborn donkey. He had a long face, a wide mouth, and an odd way of showing his teeth and kicking his feet. It was said that as a feared collaborator in Central Luzon, he surpassed even the head of the Kempeitai in the number of people he beheaded—guerrillas or non-guerrillas. At the slightest suspicion that a peaceful citizen had some dealings with the bandits, refused to collaborate with Japan, or refused to give what he asked for, he would be lucky if his head was not severed within seventy-two hours.

Just as lucky was Captain Pugot who was swallowed up by the earth during the two uncertain days between the departure of the Japanese and the coming of the GI. He was next heard from when he voluntarily surrendered to the American forces in Manila.

Otherwise, the furious guerrillas would have given him a dose of his own medicine—beheading.

The tenants and sharecroppers at Hacienda Montero considered the hiring of Pugot a slap and a challenge. It was obvious that Don Segundo would not only insist on the old system and a one-sided policy but had no plan to meet the farmers halfway.

Pastor, who was sympathetic, being one of them, was replaced. Captain Pugot was a soldier who knew nothing about agrarian relationships and cared nothing about the tenants' plight. All he cared for was blind obedience to the Japanese. He was a good follower but a bad master.

The fears of the farmers soon came to pass. Their requests were completely rejected; all debts, even with those whose fields lay idle, were being collected. Those who couldn't pay were given an ultimatum. Meanwhile, he insisted that the tenants submit to the old system of sharing expenses and harvest; this was better than having no land to till.

The strict overseer announced this harsh decision. To prove that he wasn't joking, Captain Pugot built a strong fence around the yard of the hacienda house left by Pastor and his daughter Puri. At the entrance stood an armed guard, an ex-soldier under Pugot during the occupation. He formed a troop of armed civilian guards to whom he promised to lease all the farms taken from the stubborn tenants. In addition, the new overseer contacted workers from Ilocos and Isabela who were ready to accept the conditions rejected by the old tenants. They felt that the laborers' situation in their provinces was worse.

Pastor and Puri had moved to their own land in a barrio not far from the hacienda. Puri had inherited part of the land from her mother. Pastor bought his brother-in-law's share.

Ever since he returned to farming, Pastor devoted his time to improving his farm and strengthening the farmers' union. The members often met at his place.

In answer to Captain Pugot's harshness, the tenants decided to fight for their demands. They stubbornly stuck to their right to the land bought by Don Segundo's money, but in which they had invested sweat and blood. Many of the tenants had been born on the hacienda when Montero bought it from the first buyer of the friar land. The ancestors of many had been on the vast land when it was claimed by the friars who asked them to clear it without pay, supposedly as a service to the church, and therefore, a service to God. The only payment was the granting of indulgence to those who hewed and plowed the land should they commit sin, like not going to mass on Sunday or to confession at least once a month, slaughtering or consuming meat on days of abstinence, and so on.

For example, Mang Tumas and the parents of Danoy, both leaders of the farmers, grew up on the hacienda along with the tall trees around it. They didn't care to adjust to a new place. "Our roots are buried here," Mang Tumas told a gathering one night. "This is where we will stay no matter what happens. We respect the owner's right to his property, but he should learn to respect our right to life. For a long time we have enriched the hacienda and the Monteros, while we wallow in poverty. Who among you is without debts? Who among you has any savings? If you should die of hunger, who among you would have money for the mass and the coffin? Tell me. Therefore, if we ask the landlord for new terms, if we request the government to buy the hacienda and divide it among us who have sacrificed for it, it's because we too have a right to live without misery. No matter how much Don Segundo paid for the hacienda, he has been repaid many times over."

All felt the same way. Danoy added that the armed sentry and the civilian guards would not scare them.

"We know Captain Pugot and his men," Danoy declared heatedly. "They have not yet paid for their old crimes. Only lightning is safe from vengeance."

"What happened to our petition to the governor?" asked a tenant.

"As expected," said Mang Tumas.

"The governor is two-faced," accused Danoy. "He gives us promises because he needs our votes. But, in truth, he is tied to Don Segundo. I have no more faith in the political chameleons."

The civilian guards and the farmers often had their near skirmishes. There appeared a dividing line between them, the same line that had divided the collaborators from the guerrillas in the past, when courage and loyalty were tested between the opportunists and the nationalists.

The grass along the way to the hacienda house grew tall. The fields lay idle. The guns of the civilian guards were clean and shiny, while the farmer-guerrillas brought out their old weapons. They were alert and prepared for any eventuality. The cold war was serious throughout the hacienda.

Fortunately, Don Segundo sent word to postpone the picnic because of a slight ailment of Doña Julia. Montero was aware of his farmers' discontent and he backed up Pugot's move to hire sentries and civilian guards, thinking that this would be effective in maintaining peace.

"Everything under control, sir." This was the overseer's regular report to Don Segundo. In Pugot's mind, the situation was good whenever the farmers were frustrated in their petitions.

One day, Rubio and Iman went to the barrio. Rubio was the leader of a huge labor federation in the city and Iman was a reporter of the *Kampilan*. The labor leader and the farmer had met several times since they joined forces the past year.

Pastor quickly sent for Mang Tumas, Danoy, and the others.

When the rest arrived, Rubio told them that the laborers were fed up with widespread unemployment, with meager wages which were not enough for their family's food, with the exploitation of thousands who work overtime but are underpaid, with the prohibitive cost of goods controlled by the blind administrators who should enforce the law but who receive bribes, and the apathy of the government and the politicians who cared only for their personal welfare.

"If those who control the nation's economy are too opportunistic and the government officials close their eyes, the people should act," Rubio declared harshly.

"Our troubles in the fields are also grave," said Mang Tumas. "You must have seen the guards at the hacienda."

"When conditions are serious in the city, they are also serious in the fields and probably everywhere," said Rubio. "Prosperity can't be divided; at any rate, it shouldn't be. It is anomalous to let a small part of the union live in comfort while the majority starve. This is not the fruit of our victory against the Japs, against cruelty, against evil. No! We did not spend lives and blood to let the traitors gorge themselves again, the greedy and the heartless. I don't know, but my friends, in our hands, in the hands of the farmers and laborers, lies our salvation. Let us protest and fight…"

Rubio was carried away by his emotions, for at such time, he remembered his own life, his sufferings from when he was orphaned until he was blown by fortune like a leaf, as a newspaper boy, a driver, a cigarette vendor, until he was mauled by some Japanese who left him almost dead while a thousand countrymen watched in a plaza; his slaying of his betrayers, his hiding in Manila and in the provinces like a hunted animal, until he joined a band of guerrilla-outlaws, which he immediately left; his return to Manila at the end of the war, when he joined the waves of the jobless and was elected leader of the workers' federations. These thoughts rose in Rubio's heart and mind and fired him up to seek relief for himself and others like him.

Rubio urged the farmers to attend a mass rally in Manila which would call for a general strike—the declaration of the nation's protest against the worsening hardships of the poor.

Iman brought Mando's message to Pastor and Puri to come early and drop by the *Kampilan* office.

Since his return, Mando had visited them. He stayed almost the whole day and was alone with Puri when Pastor fetched the other leaders. So Mando was fully aware of the latest happenings at the hacienda. Once more he noted the difference between Dolly and Puri.

On their way back from the barrio to the national road, Rubio's group passed by the hacienda and were stopped by two civilian guards who asked where they were coming from.

"Where are your passes?" one asked.

Iman explained that they went to visit someone and weren't going to the hacienda.

"Even then," roughly answered the guard, clutching his gun. "Next time, ask for a pass there." He pointed to the hacienda house.

The newspaperman and the labor leader did not argue, but when the two civilian guards had turned their backs, Rubio said:

"When we return, you might be gone."

The two hired guards of Captain Pugot looked back and fumed on hearing the laughter of the two men in the departing jeep.

XLVI

In all the barrios and neighboring towns of Hacienda Montero, the farmers prepared for the trip to Manila. They were eager to attend the meeting at Plaza Miranda. This was a hundred times more important than a town fiesta. The oppressed would decide whether to launch a general strike.

But when it was time to leave, only those who could be accommodated on the single bus could join.

After lunch, the farmers gathered in front of Pastor's house, but only one hundred could be accommodated. Many decided to go by passenger bus.

Before starting, Pastor and Danoy were chosen to be the farmers' spokesmen at the meeting. Pastor would relate the history of the hacienda from the time it was taken by the friars and transferred to different owners until it was bought by Segundo Montero before the war. Danoy would describe the oppression of the farmers and relate how their petitions were ignored by the present owner.

The farmers were in high spirits as the bus proceeded to Manila, not because they hoped for instant solutions, but because of their eagerness to meet their comrades in the city, the small employees, the laborers, and the jobless. Besides, their spokesmen would be heard by thousands regarding the injustice that cried for immediate redress.

Puri, Pastor, and Danoy sat together, with Pastor in the middle. After a while they were silent, each occupied with his own thoughts. Pastor planned what he would say at the meeting. He had the history and conditions of Hacienda Montero at his fingertips. For many years, he had been a tenant, a sharecropper, and an overseer. But in his talk, he had to condense the whole in a clear, orderly, and effective presentation. Pastor had often heard speeches which were so long that, like an unrolled string, they got the speaker entangled. Instead of capturing the goodwill of the listeners, the speaker became a dragonfly caught in a spider's web. Pastor wished to avoid this.

Puri's thoughts were more on the meeting with Mando. True, she was concerned with the farmers' welfare. She was Pastor's confidante regarding his position at the hacienda. She listened to the tenants' discussions and served them at home or in the field. She was regarded as one of the intelligent women at the hacienda.

But above this, she was a maiden in bloom. Like a budding flower living for the whisper of the bee and the kiss of the butterfly, both of whom offered the honey of dreams. Thus, her thoughts were more on Mando than on the concerns of the farmers.

Puri had lost her former serenity since Mando wrote to her, "I failed to see in my travels a woman who can compare with your virtues, and I rejoice in this failure." In her heart, Puri feared that Mando was flattering her, but it was a sweet lie. Between a man and a girl, the truth often serves as an arrow that wounds the heart, but white lies are always sweet and serve as balsam to heal wounds so that love and joy can sprout.

Puri was pleased with Mando's words although his hints went no further. Puri was not sure if there would be anything serious between them. Because of the upbringing and natural ways of the country lass, Puri would remain hoping and waiting. She hoped that when they met that night, they would have a chance to talk more seriously.

Danoy who sat at Pastor's right stole glances at Puri. He knew what he would say at the meeting and felt he also knew Puri's thoughts.

Unlike Mando, Danoy had long gone beyond mere hints and had proposed. Puri liked Danoy, but that was all. She felt no buzzing in her ears, or fluttering of her heart when she was with Danoy. Perhaps if she had not met Mando, she would have been moved by Danoy's perseverance but Puri was sure that such was not likely. Danoy saw a certain smile and a gleam in her eye only when Mando was around. Danoy was hurt, but he learned to accept the inevitable. He had enough experience to know that the pot could not clash with the jar and stay whole, even in love.

Besides, Danoy's esteem for Pastor was as great as his love for Puri. He felt obliged to respect the girl's happiness even at a personal sacrifice. When Mando began to frequent the hacienda, Danoy felt that it was not for the *Kampilan*. He saw where Puri's happiness lay and bowed to his cruel fate.

After two hours, they reached the capital city. After a while, the bus stopped before the *Kampilan* building. Mando came down to greet the guests. Most remained seated. Mang Tumas and Danoy said they would proceed to their meeting place, the headquarters of Rubio's federation. They would see each other at the meeting that night.

Mando led Pastor and Puri to his office on the second floor. Magat greeted them and introduced Andres. The reporter Iman was out.

Construction had begun on the new building which was to be the permanent home of the media under Mando—a modern newspaper, a radio and television station.

Mando proudly showed his guests the blueprint of the building and pictures of the press which he bought abroad. It would soon be installed in the basement.

"In three to four months, you won't recognize this place," said Mando. He was sure that the work would be finished by then.

He said that the three branches of media—newspaper, radio, and television—would bring the public accurate and honest news. They would also present wholesome entertainment on the air.

"That's a big task." Pastor was awed.

"A big task and a big service," Mando answered.

He explained that his organization did not aim to earn from public service. He referred to other groups which often wore masks and pretended to be nationalistic, humane, and Godly. But despite such disguise and window dressing, their real aim was to gain money, fame, and power.

"The sincerity of professed aims can be seen in the result. You can count on this—the forge of the nation's sentiments will not be used as tools by politics, business, or even religion. These forces are too strong. While the country is weak and in want, we should search for one who will faithfully speak the truth."

"You," said Pastor.

"We," amended Mando.

Sometimes, Pastor wondered why Mando was concerned with the workers. He supposed this was because Mando was a man of principles, and truth and justice were on the side of the poor.

Puri was more impressed by Mando. She listened to Mando and her father, hardly saying anything, but savoring all words that revealed Mando's nobility. She was fully convinced that Mando had no equal.

Pastor left the office and went to Andres' desk. Puri could hardly hear Mando's soft words as they looked at an album.

"Don't you want to live in Manila?" he asked.

Puri was taken aback.

"I didn't know Tatang planned to leave the farm," she answered coyly. "With God's grace, we are living peacefully on our small parcel of land."

But her heart was beating fast. She could not bring herself to ask Mando why he asked that question. Mando's explanation was not satisfactory.

"Just asking," he said evasively. "No one can guess what will happen."

Puri replied, "A person can adjust wherever fortune brings him. We saw this during the war. Thousands of families were uprooted. With God's grace, they survived."

"Man knows how to adjust," agreed Mando. He added, "Just the same, the place where he is should also be adapted to his needs. This is only right."

"Yes, that is ideal. But the farmers are used to adapting themselves. They are like the bamboo that bends with the wind to keep from breaking."

"Tonight we shall announce the beginning of the end of such humility," he said. Puri noticed that his earlier gentleness had vanished.

"Tonight's meeting," Mando continued, "is the shout of the oppressed that they shall not always be forgiving."

"Forgiveness is not a virtue, but neither is it cowardice," said Puri. "We peasant folks have a saying—if the ganta is full, level it."

Mando was pleased that Puri had not only the virtues of a barrio maiden but also a deep understanding of life. She had a deep concern for the problems of her fellow men. Evidently, Puri was not just a lovely gem to look at but a rare woman.

Like her father, Puri also wondered at Mando's difference from other rich men. She recalled Don Segundo's ways.

"Let's talk again about my question about your living in Manila," Mando roused the girl who seemed lost in her thoughts. "I'll explain why I asked you that question," he added.

Puri did not answer, but her heart beat faster. Just then, Pastor looked in through the door and reminded them that they might be late.

"Why, I didn't realize how late it had gotten," Puri managed to say.

Mando brought the two to supper before they proceeded to the meeting.

XLVII

It was a fifteen-minute drive from the *Kampilan*. Mando stopped the jeep in a yard with an ordinary house.

"We're here," said Mando, helping Puri alight. "This is our home."

It was only then that the guests realized where they were going. They thought they were going to an eatery in the suburbs. Could this be the house of the wealthy publisher who was constructing a large building in Manila?

"This doesn't look like the house of a...Don," Pastor observed jokingly.

Mando laughed and answered that he would rather be called anything but a Don.

"The best way to make Don Segundo mad is to remove 'Don' before his name."

"Tata Pastor, Don Segundo and I are opposites." Mando smiled.

"Very few in your situation live in this kind of house," insisted Pastor.

"This house is right for one person—a bachelor," explained Mando, glancing at Puri who quickly looked away. "I remember that the philosopher Socrates once said when a friend asked why he lived in a hut, 'I am lucky if this small hut is filled with good friends.' So, come in, my dear friends." He stressed the word 'dear,' looking steadily at Puri.

The bungalow was in the middle of a lot surrounded by a low wall. Around were a few large trees. It had two parts divided by a passageway that served as a garage. There was no other vehicle but the jeep. The right was made up of the living room, dining room, library, two bedrooms, and a bathroom. The rooms were small. In this part lived Mando and Tata Matyas.

The second part on the left was the kitchen, the quarters of the two helpers, and a closet. Both helpers were male, a cook and the lad Kiko who came to Manila with Mando and Tata Matyas after the war. The cook did the marketing and cooking and attended to other chores for Mando. Tata Matyas hardly worked except to tend a few plants and read. Kiko cleaned the house and the yard. Once in a while, he would drive Mando's jeep, especially when he came home at night with Mando. Kiko went to night school and proceeded to the *Kampilan* after class.

Mando asked the cook Mang Simo to get supper ready. Earlier he had told him that he would have guests.

He introduced the guests to Tata Matyas.

"He is my foster father," said Mando. The old man knew the two by name, for Mando often talked about them. Mando had also told Tata Matyas that Pastor was his mother's brother but asked him to keep this a secret. Mando kept nothing from Tata Matyas.

Tata Matyas and Pastor sat facing each other and were soon engaged in conversation. Mando showed Puri the various parts of the house of "a bachelor."

The library adjacent to the living room was small, but Puri was fascinated. She looked at the pictures, some books, and some of Mando's precious mementos. Mando showed her the old copies of *Noli Me Tángere* and *El Filibusterismo*, which had new binding. He told her that these copies were kept by Tata Matyas from the time of the revolution against Spain until the end of the Second World War. Also in the library were most of Rizal's writings, the complete collection of *Epistolario Rizalino*, the collection of the newspapers *La Solidaridad*, *El Renacimiento*, and *Muling Pagsilang*. There were also some copies of the Bible in Tagalog, English, and Spanish, history books like world history, the histories of Europe, the United States, Britain, Spain, Japan, Mexico, and Latin America, the history of the conquest of China, India, and Africa. There were also three or four histories of the Philippines.

"Philippine history should be rewritten," said Mando.

"Why?" asked Puri.

"Because it is full of errors and lies."

"But is there a history which is not so?" asked Puri, repeating what she often heard from the farmers during the war.

"That's why Philippine history should be rewritten," Mando said firmly. "The one who should write it should not be one author but a committee of Filipino experts. The publisher should be the government. Many things should be changed," he added, "but not all at the same time."

"Is that not the dream of all movements even before the birth of Christ?" Puri asked. "Change and more change. What happens to the leaders?"

"The blood of the martyrs glorifies the history of mankind," said Mando. "The story of our country should relate honestly the history of the Filipinos, their economic life, situation, society, civilization, culture, and faith, many centuries before the landing of the Spaniards. It was not a race of Negritos which was found by Magellan and Villalobos. The latter, out of respect for the people living here at that time, named the islands after his king. The history taught in schools during the last fifty years is the story of conquest by foreigners, their government and their deeds. These ask to be straightened out."

Puri understood, but at that moment she would have been more pleased if he would explain what he had said about her or about them. For example, why he was happy that in his travels he found no girl with Puri's qualities; his question of whether Puri would like to live in Manila someday, the… So when she sat on an easy chair in the library, she said that Mando's house was nice because it was neat, clean, and peaceful.

"No one would say there was no woman to fix it," she added.

"Are women the only…" But Mando cut himself short. Instead, he said, "That is what this house lacks. That's why I asked if you wished to live in Manila." He stopped abruptly.

"And I answered that I didn't know if Tatang had any such plan," Puri replied. "I don't see the connection between that and what this house lacks."

"I'll tell you straight, Puri," Mando took courage. "What this house lacks is a woman; no, not just a woman, but you, Puri, only you. If you will agree to leave the farm."

"Right away, you impose a condition," she reproached him. "That's putting the plow before the carabao."

"The reason, Puri, is my timidity. I thought I was brave, with all my experience, but now I realize that I am fainthearted. I am afraid to tell you that…"

"That you want me to be a maid in this house?"

"To be my queen."

For a while, both were silent; both were at a loss for words while from each heart to the tiniest vein in their finger flowed indescribable emotions.

"Now that I have confessed to you," Mando broke the silence.

"When did you think of this?" Puri asked softly.

"Ever since I first visited the hacienda and talked to you."

"Years?"

"Centuries."

"Then perhaps you will not expect an immediate reply."

"Please don't prolong my suffering."

"You placed the condition that I should live in Manila," Puri said. Mando felt the sting of her mockery.

"I don't place any condition, for I'm pleading."

"That's why," she insisted, "my living in Manila will mean not only a change of address. I was born and grew up on a farm. Throughout my life, I have mixed with barrio folks, the poor like us who live in huts and know nothing except how to till the soil. I'm used to their ways, their relationship, their beliefs. You want me to move to the city. Shall I leave all that I'm used to? Can I change all those, my life, myself?"

Puri looked steadily at Mando as if to read his answer in his eyes.

"You won't leave nor change anything," Mando declared. "All that you are Puri, I shall be proud of. I shall not ask for any sacrifice or change. You will do nothing but love me as I love you."

"That includes all I have said," objected Puri. "Your situation will force me to change. You are a publisher, an important man in society. I read in the papers, I see in pictures the life and ways of society people, especially the women. I don't want to be a Cinderella nor a mannequin of luxury, of the beauty parlor, or of fashion. I'm not afraid of change if this is progress."

Mando could see that Puri was blushing. This made him admire and desire her more.

"You have nothing to fear," Mando promised. "I love you because you are you. Different from others. I don't want you to be like them in looks, in manners, in dress. Besides, I don't belong to society, Puri. I don't belong. The people's organization, the masses are different from the society of the few; society is different from high society."

"Then, you are a fish out of water," Puri concluded with misgivings.

"What you see is the surface," Mando said. "You don't see the real me, my origin. I was not always like this. I am a farmer's son. I have tasted all kinds of hardship. I worked as a servant in order to study; I studied to be free from servitude. During the war, I joined the guerrillas. I lived in the mountains and fought. I gained good friends like Tata Matyas, Professor Sabio. After the war, we pooled our resources to establish a new life. You know the rest, Puri. That is my story."

"It does not show, Mando. You have changed. Why should I not also change if it will help you?"

"Change is the first law of life," Mando agreed. "But change for the better. When I said you wouldn't change, I meant the inborn goodness of country folks. For example, who would want to replace modesty with immodesty, humility with arrogance, industry with useless activities, thrift with wastefulness? On the other hand, who would not want to learn the right way of living in the city, to gain knowledge, to do more good?"

Puri was about to answer when Mang Simo peeped into the library, reminding them that supper would grow cold.

Mando and Puri saw Tata Matyas and Pastor still discussing the ills of the country.

"No one denies that we were misled by our conquerors," declared Tata Matyas. "What we should do is return to the past. When I was a child, if I thought I was misled by goblins, I turned my clothes inside out and retraced my footsteps. Sometimes, a child is wiser than many of our leaders."

"In the field, a new idea is spreading," said Pastor. "You are right, sir, but many farmers feel that more is needed. They say that we should follow the carabao which breaks its rope and uses its horn."

"An empty sack can't stand," declared Mando. "Let's continue our talk at the table." They went to the dining room together.

XLVIII

The meeting at Plaza Miranda opened with mass singing of the national anthem.

One couldn't even drop a needle through the thick crowd. Mando, Pastor, and Puri had to inch their way to the stage on one side of the plaza.

The makeshift wooden stage was wide and well-built. It was well-lit. One could clearly read the posters with the aims and petitions of various groups.

There was a plan to have a preliminary demonstration in the afternoon around the city streets, passing by Congress and Malacañan and ending at Plaza Miranda.

But the officials refused permission. Even the meeting was only up to midnight.

Rubio was speaking when Mando arrived. Among those seated were Senator Maliwanag, Danoy, and Mang Tumas with delegates of various groups.

Rubio was just starting with his opening remarks. He said that the meeting was for the welfare of thousands of people from all walks of life. He wanted to ask leaders of government and business to take immediate steps to curb widespread poverty. And should those concerned fail to move, to launch a nationwide strike.

"This crisis burdening the poor is not divinely caused," Rubio said. "It is the work of a group of greedy men, those in power—the power of politics and of money. Let us not blame the Nazarene there in Quiapo church. Let us demand accounting from government leaders and big businessmen, because the present crisis is the result of their management. They are the birds of prey of our times."

The labor leader minced no words. Like a boxer, he pleased the crowd with his short, straight jabs.

He continued:

"Unemployment and high prices are not decreed from heaven, I repeat. They are the means to further enrich the wealthy and to impoverish the poor. Look at them. They wallow in luxury while the nation starves. What do we ask for? The right to live like men. To eat three times a day, food from our own sweat. Only this. But we cannot have it. For the leaders love only themselves. For the wealthy love only their gold. What shall we do? Speak up and tell us what we must do. Should we not stop the strangling of the nation? Let us strike and oppose this."

Applause and shouts of "Change! Change! Strike! Strike!"

But not all in the plaza came to support the meeting. In truth, the hired detectives of the government and business were spread out, listing and recording names and remarks in their memorandum pads, twisting their meanings. Rubio's words were written by the hired detective as "Let us demand a confrontation with the nation's leaders and big businessmen. The situation strangling the nation should be replaced with something better."

Rubio was unperturbed, for he was used to such tactics by law enforcers. He was known as a true labor leader. He knew that in the spy's vocabulary, any worker who can't be bought is an enemy of peace and a friend of disorder. Rabble rouser, red, communist. This treatment was only for workers and their sympathizers. Businessmen, bankers, politicians in power were not spied upon, no matter what they said or did. The so-called heralds of peace had an odd belief that they were the only ones concerned with peace and order.

At any rate, the majority of the crowd at Plaza Miranda were prepared to listen, to understand and to support the aims and decisions of the movement. They ignored the detectives whom they considered the scum of the fallen Japanese militarism. In their veins flowed the courage and pride in knowing that they had not been mere onlookers in the past, nor would they be mere yes-men in the future. Their nationalistic spirit remained a flame in countless hearts.

Rubio introduced a student who started to speak in English. The crowd protested and told him to speak in Pilipino.

"We don't need a foreigner in this meeting," said a few who were standing near the stage.

"Speak in Tagalog so we can understand one another," shouted others.

"Our country is free. Don't talk in the language of our former master. The *Kano* (Americans) have gone."

The student apologized, explaining that he was Visayan. He tried to speak in Tagalog and was applauded.

He said that the students could not fold their arms indifferently in the face of alarming events. According to him, ninety percent of students were children of poor employees and laborers. A large number were working their way through college.

"If the cost of living is high, so are school expenses," he declared. "Then who among the poor will have the chance for an education? Is education like canned food which is paid for in dollars? If the poor have to choose between rice and books, you know, gentlemen, what the answer will be. Therefore, the coming generation will be an army of ignoramuses."

The detectives noted down the student's name and his school.

A delegate of the women workers, a worker in a cigarette factory, faced the mike. She described the pitiful conditions of the workers.

"The best cigars are made in Manila," she said. "But the Filipino cigar makers are starving. Why? Because most of our countrymen smoke American cigarettes, the contraband blue seal."

"True! True!" agreed her listeners.

"Ours is excellent, yet we patronize others," she continued. "We think we are modern, progressive, if we wear foreign clothes, eat foreign food, speak the language of foreigners, ape their vices. We have no unity, no mind of our own; we have no self-respect."

"Bravo!" many shouted again and again.

The woman said that the mothers shoulder most of life's hardships. "The women hold the purse, but what can you do if the purse is empty?" she asked.

The analogy brought laughter.

She asked for a campaign against indecency and ostentation among the rich, especially the women.

"Actually," she pointed out, "wealth is not due to these orchids of society. They have no right to live like goldfish in an aquarium. Why should workers who help in producing this wealth always remain in want? It is our right and our children's right to receive social justice."

"That's the girl!" came from the pleased listeners.

Puri shook hands with the woman and graciously moved to make room for her.

Rubio introduced Pastor, then Danoy.

The two convincingly presented the alarming conditions in the rural areas. The conditions at Hacienda Montero aroused the ire of many. Pastor spoke calmly and slowly, but his words were as sharp as bolos which cut deeply. Recalling the story of Cabesang Tales, Pastor declared that the farmer who is robbed of his earnings is often branded a bandit, an enemy of the law.

"We till the soil, we harvest the rice, corn, sugarcane; but we always lack these very products. We toil in vain because of the greed of the exploiters. We must have change, we must have social justice," Pastor said. "Let them not force us to leave the plow for the bolo."

"Tatang!" Pastor overheard Puri's voice above the applause.

"I was calm," said Pastor. He believed his speech was quite mild.

On the other hand, Danoy's speech was fiery. His delivery was like the sound of a machine gun. He protested that on top of oppression, the landlord used violence, gave guns to civilian guards. Danoy stressed that they were God-fearing, but they were not afraid of the sword.

"We fought the Japs after the armed forces surrendered," Danoy declared. "If the farmers had helped the enemy, the course of the war would have been different. Not only are we workers but loyal Filipinos."

The crowd applauded the courage of the Filipino farmers.

"We fought, not against the color of the Japs, but against evil," Danoy went on. "We shall not stop fighting evil. Ka Pastor who spoke before me was right. We ask for change, for justice. Not only that. We shall also ask that the existing arrangements be stopped. We should not have equal share with the landlord who does nothing but grow fat. It's time we owned our land, for ourselves and our children, the fields which we enrich with our sweat and blood. Unless this is done, all talks of justice are but flowers of the tongue and for show."

There was a hearty applause. The detectives listed down the names of Pastor and Danoy and the passages from their speeches.

There was also some commotion when two detectives roughly climbed the stage in a menacing manner. They were stopped by three husky men assigned by Rubio at the stairs. The detectives resented the reminders of Rubio's men and insisted on having their way.

Rubio intervened and allowed them to go up. They claimed that they were only after the safety of those on the stage. There was a report that there would be trouble at the meeting.

"This is a meeting of the poor," Rubio explained. "There will be no trouble, unless the enemies of truth and justice hired troublemakers."

"We are just doing our duty," said the two and they stayed behind.

Rubio proceeded to introduce the next speaker: Mando Plaridel.

XLIX

The meeting was at its liveliest at ten in the evening. The sky was clear, and the stars vied with the blazing lights in the plaza.

The crowd was increasing. It seemed that all were prepared to stay the whole night. Rubio introduced Mando as a "friend of the oppressed." He mentioned that Mando was the publisher of the *Kampilan,* which was a true defender of the poor. Rubio said that in a country where the newspaper is not a tool of the mighty, it does not last long; the birth of the *Kampilan* and the vows of Mando Plaridel are a heroic sacrifice. Mando waited for the long applause to die down before he began.

Mando acknowledged that he was the publisher of the *Kampilan*, which was owned by an association of men with noble principles. He pointed out that the *Kampilan* was a defender, not only of the poor, but of truth and justice, which happened to be on the side of the majority.

"The war has long ended and for years, the Philippines has been independent," Mando declared. "It is sad to say that up to now, there has been no improvement in the lot of the common man. The country gave all for democracy. Does the nation enjoy the fruits of democracy? Let us look around us. The fortunate are in palaces, the unfortunate in barung-barongs. The haves are

feasting; the hungry pick trash cans. Is this the tomorrow promised during the war? Is this the reward of those who sacrificed?"

Mando explained what a free nation should enjoy. Without
adequate means, there is no freedom, for the slavery of poverty
and hunger is the worst kind of slavery.

"All should have means of livelihood, schools, hospitals,
and medicine for the sick," said Mando. "In short, equal opportunity for all."

Mando was interrupted by hearty applause. Continuing, he
reminded the crowd that the country should depend on the people
if they want to be freed from their burden of poverty.

"My brothers, the fruits of democracy are not tame doves
which voluntarily alight on our hands. Not even a ripe guava falls
by itself into the mouth of a Juan Tamad. We have to work, work
hard, coupled with bravery, brains, and unity. Under the present
setup, it is a mistake to depend on the government completely.
The government is a tool of the people; what it cannot do should
be done by the people themselves."

Mando added that it is the people's duty to learn, to create
their own means of livelihood, if the administration is helpless.

"Our land is rich. You shall not starve if you strive," he
emphasized.

Protest resounded. Some shouted that the land is owned by
the powerful.

"We have no land, but the dirt on our body." All laughed.

"There is land," Mando declared. "Land for those prepared
to move to new places and clear forests. The Philippines is vast
and won't lack land for hands willing to work."

Mando commented on the wrong preparation of the youth
who flock to the city looking for office work.

"Instead of enjoying freedom and health in the fields, they want
to work as employees in business firms. We need more mechanics,
electricians, carpenters, plumbers, technicians for radio, printing,
factories, mines. But what kind of workers abound? Clerks, mes-

sengers, stenographers, salesmen, agents, other white-collar jobs. Actually, we don't lack jobs, if the nation would keep in mind that we are in a period of reconstruction and beginning industrialization. We lack skilled laborers, such as those I mentioned, and not those who are choosy about their work."

Then Mando took potshots at party politics, which cares only to rise to power or to stay there. He pointed out that in the past fifty years, politics became the opium of the masses.

"In all these, we are going in circles. The nation seems to remain unmoved. It is a common remark that our land is rich in natural resources, but why are the Filipinos beggars? Two parties vie for power, but whoever is on top takes advantage of his position to steal from the country. The nation has long been a victim of this system. Strangled by a two-headed monster. It's high time the nation freed itself from the sharp claws of this monster, formed a strong union, and waved its own banner towards the emancipation of the oppressed."

Mando's speech was followed by prolonged applause. Rubio stood up, glanced at his watch, and said he would introduce the last speaker.

Rubio had not yet mentioned his name, but the plaza stirred with expectations. Everyone knew Senator Maliwanag as the champion of Philippine nationalism.

"He was orphaned as a child," said Rubio. "His grandfather was killed in the revolution against Spain and his father fought against the Americans. He was in the Death March after the fall of Bataan and imprisoned at Capas. One day, he escaped with a friend, who was then slain. He joined politics and proved to be a courageous leader. My friends and comrades, I give you the poor man's candidate for President of the Philippines."

Deafening applause and shouts of "Mabuhay" greeted Senator Maliwanag. He stood for a long time before the microphone before the crowd quieted down.

The Senator began with the story of the Arab and the camel.

"The Arab let the camel put his head inside the tent. Then his whole body. In the end, he killed the Arab and got the tent to himself. That is our country and the foreigners who sought shelter here… What should we do with the camel?" asked Maliwanag.

The plaza was filled with angry suggestions.

"Lash him!"

"Drive him out!"

"Slaughter him."

"That is only right," answered the lawmaker. "But until now, we have not decided to lash, drive away, or slaughter the camel. Until now, he is inside the tent, and we are outside. My country-men, I do not want us to be like the camel, but neither do I want us to be like the Arab."

Laughter followed this last remark.

"In Rizal's time, the patriot was exiled or shot," Maliwanag continued. "It was forbidden for a slave to desire freedom. A Bon-ifacio and his Katipunan were needed to free the Philippines. As a result of our own weakness, we were conquered by the Americans. For half a century, Americanization was forced on the country. The English language, clothes, products, vices, tastes, our way of life. The day came when the Filipino forgot his own and became a lowly follower and imitator of his master. For a Filipino, there were only two constant ambitions: to become fluent in English and to have lots of dollars in his pocket."

The Senator drank water, then continued.

"Now that we are free, a democracy, a republic, we should change many things. Let us cast off the ugly uniform of a pris-oner, of a slave. Let us truly be free, a real nation in our mind, in economy, in reality."

"We have no bonds, we can move freely," Senator Maliwanag spoke forcefully. "We are no longer blindfolded; we don't have to work blindly."

"Our leaders are all blind," shouted a shrill voice.

"It's up to you, the people, to change the blind leaders and drive away the shameless camel," declared the Senator. "When we revived the nationalist movement after Rizal and Bonifacio, many protested and insulted us. Most were foreigners, but not a few were Filipinos in complexion, it is shameful to admit—Filipino slaves and lackeys. But let us pity these unfortunates. That is to be expected; what one eats, one burps."

Senator Maliwanag repeated some parts of his speech delivered in Congress about the pitiful plight of the Filipinos.

"The foreigners control the big banks, the rich mines, industry and trade, transportation, electricity, and communication services. Must we remain water carriers and hewers of wood?"

"No! No!" shouted the crowd.

"Then we should heartily support Philippine nationalism. Every powerful country is nationalistic. The United States, Britain, Japan, Germany. Look at their products. Made in the U.S.A., made in England, made in Japan, made in Germany. They are proud of their own trademark, the name of their country. Look at the progressive movements of the independent countries in Asia and Africa after the last world war. China, India, Indonesia moved against the foreigners. Even Indonesia, Burma, Malaya, and Ceylon awakened. They no longer idolize the whites, who now treat them like human beings. Soon, the dividing line between races will be erased, and each will enjoy his inherent right to live according to his own principles, faith, and desires.

"We Filipinos should not be left behind by the sweep of history. Let us ride with the times. Cast aside the slave's mentality, superstition, and fear. Let us keep studying and working. There is no race or country favored by God. No race or country is more intelligent than another. Rizal was brown, but no white man of his time could compare with him in brains, in courage, and in nobility.

"Philippine nationalism is the key to our country's prosperity and progress. If our natural resources on land and sea are owned and developed by the Filipinos, all its riches—gold, iron, oil, pearls, rice, sugar, copra, tobacco, abaca—all our harvest and our finished products shall benefit the citizens. I repeat what Quezon once said—that we do not need millionaires in the Philippines; what we need are millions of Filipino families living in prosperity and comfort.

"It is obvious that if the country achieves economic independence through nationalism, surely the army of the unemployed and the hungry will disappear. Instead, we shall see a contented and happy nation which is truly free."

The applause was like the sound of a hundred rockets.

"Long live our candidate for President!" many shouted.

"Long live Philippine nationalism!" the crowd shouted back.

The distance from Plaza Miranda to Hacienda Montero was more than a hundred miles. While the people at Plaza Miranda were fired up by their ardor, a mysterious fire suddenly broke out in the farmlands in Central Luzon. The fire quickly spread to the warehouses and the granary as fast as the shout of an irate farmer.

There were only a few men at the hacienda, most were at the meeting in Manila. Even the overseer Captain Pugot was away; supposedly at the capital. He left before dark.

The civilian guards came late. The women and old people were hesitant in trying to control the fire. The people in the barrio got ready to safeguard their homes. The fire was controlled at the edge of the hacienda.

After an hour, Captain Pugot arrived breathlessly, accompanied by soldiers. He quickly gathered the civilian guards, asked the sergeant for an immediate report, then issued strict orders.

The fire started at the old warehouse, according to the sergeant. In a moment the large granary was also ablaze.

The mouth of the granary was still smoking, and no one could give any clear testimony, but Captain Pugot was certain that the fire was caused by troublemakers. His hunch could not be wrong, he said loudly.

"Those men won't stop until there is complete chaos," said the fierce Japanese collaborator. "Let them hide behind their dead ancestors; they can't escape," he threatened.

Captain Pugot knew who the "troublemakers" were. In his vocabulary, all leaders of the farmers' movement were "bad men," and all their followers were "lost" or "crazy." He had a list of their names and identity, starting with Pastor, Danoy, Mang Tumas.

He ordered their arrest. He knew these persons had gone to Manila, but in his mind, this was the very proof of their guilt. When the sergeant reminded him that he saw Pastor leaving, Pugot answered that he was aware of this.

"I know," he said with a nod. "They were not at the scene of the crime, but they were behind it. They hide their hands, but their heads can be seen. Can there be better evidence than the fire itself?"

There was no doubt in Pugot's mind that the fire was intentional, that it was not due to carelessness or caused by others.

He had not changed his old ways as a petty lord under the Japanese Army. For him it was enough that a person was suspected. Evidence was not important; if there was none, it could be planted or created.

He should have paid for his war crimes, for his brutality and savagery. He was saved from the electric chair or life imprisonment by surrendering and ingratiating himself with the Americans until the granting of general amnesty. The rural folks' hatred for him had cooled off and was revived only when he repeated his brutality as overseer at Hacienda Montero.

The soldiers and the men sent by Captain Pugot returned in high spirits. They had gathered some rifles at Pastor's house, documents at Mang Tumas', and a kerosene can and rags at Danoy's.

"No doubt, it's them," Pugot exclaimed as he examined the objects gathered by the searchers. There was no court order to search and confiscate.

"This would have been used to cause trouble at the hacienda.

If that had happened, blood would have flowed. For sure, they plan to kill me, perhaps Don Segundo and others. And here," he said, pointing the rifle towards a document. "We can read their dastardly plans."

It was learned that the document was nothing but the printed constitution of the farmers' association.

Captain Pugot posted a hundred more guards near the entrances to Hacienda Montero to await the farmers who were coming from Manila. He also placed special guards at the suspects' homes. Meanwhile, he ordered the old folks and the women at the hacienda and the barrio to stay in their respective huts and not to leave without permission from the soldiers or civilian guards. He ordered a real "sona."

It was almost dawn when the guards heard the sounds of a vehicle coming. One looked out and saw two bright "eyes" approaching. In a few minutes, a bus came speeding by.

The guards were sure this was the vehicle of those who came from the meeting in Manila.

The passengers were talking and laughing noisily. The women were singing. They thought nothing of it when the guard stopped the bus. But they got worried when the guard ordered the driver to stop in front of the headquarters of the civilian guards. All the passengers were told to get off.

Captain Pugot stood at the door. He threw away his lighted cigarette and threw a fierce look at the farmers. He immediately ordered a search of all except the women. Puri remained beside her father.

"Why, Captain?" Pastor asked, puzzled.

Pastor and the civilian guards knew each other, as a collector knows a creditor. Pastor was the former overseer who was replaced because of his good dealings with the tenants.

"Don't pretend to be innocent," Pugot hollered. "Don't you know?"

"Know what?"

"The hacienda was burned, and you, your group, planned it. You are bad men."

Captain Pugot's words were like a grenade exploding. Some of the men moved, ready to escape. The door was blocked by rifles.

"Captain, you are mistaken," protested Pastor.

"Prove it in court," the Captain shot back. "Meanwhile, I arrest you in the name of the law."

Upon hearing Pugot's words, a husky farmer grabbed a rifle, but a guard quickly hit him on the mouth. There would have been a free-for-all had Pastor not calmed down the farmers.

"Keep calm, comrades," Pastor called out. "There are women."

"Go on, dare us, fools! The bullets won't shy away from you."

An uneasy peace was restored. Pugot separated the men on one side and the women on the other. In the dim light, he looked over the farmers. It was only then that he noticed Danoy's absence.

"Where is Danoy?" he demanded.

"He stayed in Manila," a man answered, "at a friend's house."

"Ah, he deserted you. We found a kerosene can and rags similar to those used in the fire," Pugot declared. "He can't go far."

After searching the men and asking the women to take out what they carried, the guards took down their names, ages, and other information. The law enforcers took whatever they—daggers, certificates of membership in the association, etc. The clothes taken from the bus were piled on one side.

The sun was high up when the women were released.

"Don't let them leave the houses," Captain Pugot told his men.

Puri told Pastor that she was going to bring him food, but he told her not to do so. He could not eat alone, and it would be hard to prepare for a hundred people.

Puri saw a civilian guard on the stairs of their house. The furniture was all topsy-turvy and the dresser was open. The box of letters from Mando was missing.

Captain Pugot questioned Pastor and Tumas, but the two eluded the noose which he tried to place around their necks. They knew that any talk with the captain, anywhere, at any time, would be used against them.

"Confess that you are the brains behind the arson," Pugot urged Pastor and Mang Tumas.

The two leaders remained silent, pretending not to hear him.

"Where did you get the rifles found in your house?" he asked Pastor who remained deaf.

"Where?" Pugot stamped his boots.

"There are no arms in my house," Pastor said firmly.

"There they are." Pugot pointed to the top of the table. "You dare deny it?"

"They're not mine."

"They were found in a room in your house."

"If you say they were found in my house, maybe you put them there," Pastor said angrily.

A slap struck his mouth, causing his face to jerk back. The women screamed. Mang Tumas made a move. Some farmers sprawled on the floor stood up.

Captain Pugot quickly drew his .45 and almost simultaneously the civilian guards raised their rifles. Some soldiers watched closely. The farmers gritted their teeth.

"Don't make a false move," shouted Captain Pugot. "Unless you want to be buried here."

Not new to such a tight situation, Pugot breathed easily when he sensed that the farmers would cause no trouble despite their fury.

"You, Pastor." Pugot faced the farmers' leader. "You want to be known as tough. Let's see if you won't soften up. I have lost my patience with you."

Pastor kept silent but he looked steadily at the fiery eyes of the captain.

"Why do you keep these documents?" Pugot turned to Mang Tumas, showing a pamphlet in his face.

"That is the constitution."

"This is bad. Subversive. Anti-government."

"It says nothing except how to unite the farmers."

"It says that one of your aims is to remove social classes. There should be no rich or poor."

"The exploiters and the exploited," interrupted Mang Tumas. "What's wrong with that?"

"That is communism," Pugot accused.

"It was Christ who spread such a principle—equality of men, improvement of the conditions of the oppressed."

"Liar!"

Mang Tumas said no more, for he saw that Captain Pugot was at a loss. Because their exchange had reached such a point, he knew the captain would no longer use reason but force. Mang Tumas had no desire to taste what Pastor had. But the chief investigator would not leave this alone.

"Why did Danoy stay in Manila?"

"I don't know."

"He won't stay without a reason."

"Maybe."

"What reason?"

"I don't know."

Mang Tumas received the slap he was avoiding. The old man's face jerked back. Pastor made a move. Once more the farmers got on their feet. But that was all. Pugot had a tight grip on his revolver.

"Never mind," he sneered. "Where would that Danoy hide anyway? If he does not come today, I will hunt for him myself and bring him back in chains."

Pugot's threat was met by silence. He might as well have been talking to the wind.

Then he went out and signaled the sergeant of the civilian guards to follow. He said he would consult the governor and the PC Commander at the capital. He instructed the sergeant to gather evidence.

"Don't allow any visitors," he ordered sternly. "If someone brings food, accept it, but don't give it to the prisoners. Let them starve."

"Yes, sir."

It was morning, a morning different from the preceding night. The sun shone on the ashes of the hacienda fire, but it did not brighten the fate of the farmers confined in the civilian guards' quarters.

LI

Dolly was far more alluring when she returned to Manila and shone once more in high society. She had an added glamor which was the envy of other women, young or old. They felt that her charm was enhanced by her long stay in Paris, her experiences, and having everything she wanted.

But they were wrong to think Dolly got everything she wanted. One thing she could not call her own was Mando's heart. An elusive heart. She often thought he didn't care. He seldom had time for her.

Their affair in Paris was not rekindled in Manila. True, they met. Sometimes, he would take her to a nightclub, invite her to the movies or theater and escort her to some gatherings. But she wanted more.

Not once did he invite her to Baguio where she longed to breathe the clean air and watch the moon behind the tall pine trees. Once she wanted to see Zamboanga City. Couldn't Mando leave his office for a few days to fly with her to the famous pearl of Mindanao? Her boyfriend simply said that perhaps her only reason to go was to prove what some Yankees claimed: that "monkeys in Zamboanga have no tails."

Nevertheless, it was in neither Dolly's nature nor her up-bringing to give in to frustrations. She accepted that Mando was very busy supervising the construction of the new building and managing the newspaper. When Dolly looked at herself in her large bedroom mirror as she powdered her body after bathing, or put on an elegant dress, she could not see how Mando could help wanting her.

How many men, all distinguished—bachelors, widowers, or married—were crazy about her? Some gave hints; others openly declared their intentions; still others kept their hopeless desires smoldering in their breasts. Pong Tua-Son, son of the Chinese millionaire Son Tua, was kept dangling hopelessly. She merely laughed at the proposal of the head of the Bachelors' Club. A wealthy widower, a congressman from the Visayas, was crazy about her, but she often made fun of him.

Dolly realized that she had fallen hard for Mando, not because she had given herself to him. This had happened with Colonel Moto during the Japanese occupation and with Lieutenant Whitey during the liberation. Dolly had experienced other loves, but this was different. With Mando, Dolly felt a love that was like a burning flame. Her desire raged even more now that they both were in Manila.

Mando's seeming coldness served as fuel to Dolly's desire which became a flame of impatience and jealousy.

Dolly was at her most beautiful when she got out of her car in front of the *Kampilan* building. She went to the office on the second floor. Mando was alone reading his mail.

He stood up and greeted Dolly. He was expecting her, for she had called up earlier.

"Sit down, Dol," said Mando, leading her to a chair. They sat facing each other.

Dolly reproached him. "If I had not come, I wouldn't see you."

"Dol, you know I'm very busy. Don't you know that…"

Dolly pouted. "Maybe you're not too busy to give me a kiss, or don't you have the time?"

Mando stood up, but stopped on hearing her dry laugh.

"I came to invite you to lunch. We have to discuss something."

"Where do you want to go?"

"Anywhere. Some place private. Papa spoke to me about Pong."

"The little Chinese is persistent, isn't he?"

"He's ready to wage war to have me."

"And how do you feel?"

"As if you don't know."

"If you can wait, I'll just finish my work. You read in the meantime." Mando got a woman's magazine and gave it to Dolly. "Care for a drink?"

"No, thanks."

Mando returned to the table and Dolly started to leaf through the magazine. It was eleven o'clock in the morning.

Suddenly Magat entered, followed by Puri. Hearing Magat's voice, Mando raised his head and saw Puri.

"Puri," he called quite loudly, standing up.

Dolly glanced back and saw the guest, a young girl who looked quite poor. Perhaps a factory worker or a fruit vendor. That was Dolly's first thought. So she turned her eyes again to the magazine.

"What brought you back, Puri? Or haven't you gone home?" Mando asked after Puri was seated. Magat remained standing behind a chair.

"There was a fire at the hacienda. Tatang was arrested."

Although the two newspapermen were used to big events, both were startled by the news. It was only then that they looked at her closely. Her cheeks were pale and her eyes hollow, her hair was uncombed, and she had not changed her dress. Her hands and feet were dirty. She looked tired but seemed unmindful of fatigue. She was a picture of anxiety.

Puri related what had happened. How Captain Pugot stopped the bus upon their arrival and the arrest of the passengers who were blamed for the fire. She was afraid of what might happen to her father who had already been slapped by Captain Pugot.

She had escaped from the civilian guard by passing through the *batalan*[1] and the backyard. She crossed the field to the road and took a Manila-bound bus.

Mando and Magat asked questions about the fire, Captain Pugot's behavior, the arrest of Pastor and his companions, and the supposed evidence leading to their arrest. She mentioned the rifles said to be found in their house, the kerosene can and the rags in Danoy's house, and the papers in Mang Tumas' house.

"Danoy is in Manila," said Mando. "He should know this at once." He told Magat to get in touch with the young leader.

"An old trick," Mando exclaimed after a while.

"The usual tactics of ex-convicts," declared Magat

Mando and Magat concluded that the crime was not done by the farmers, but their persecutors.

"I would know if father was hiding guns," Puri declared, "for he would ask me to keep them. Just like during the Japanese times."

"Don't worry, Puri," said Mando. "We shall not let Tata Pastor and his group down."

Mando looked at his wristwatch.

"It's almost twelve," he said. "Magat, better call Danoy in Rubio's office. Tell him to come right away. We have important matters to discuss."

Magat went to his office.

Mando approached Dolly who appeared impatient.

"Shall we go?" she asked before Mando could speak.

"Dolly," Mando said gently, "may we postpone our date?"

"Postpone! And why?" she asked, surprised and annoyed.

"Something's happened. I should attend to it."

---

1 batalan—a working area at the back of a nipa house (house on stilts and made of organic materials like nipa palm leaves and bamboo), usually without a roof

"Why don't you postpone that? I've been waiting for two hours."

"This is urgent."

"Is it because of the cigarette worker?" sneered Dolly, pointing with her lips at Puri.

"She's not a cigarette worker," Mando explained. "She came from the province."

"Oh, a *provinciana*.[2] And why should you care that much for her?"

Dolly had raised her voice, but Puri was not aware that Mando and the woman were arguing about her. Thinking of her father's problem, she seemed unaware of anything else.

"Please, Dolly, I'll see you tonight," Mando begged.

"Now, I'm sure of what I suspected all along," she accused. "I mean nothing to you. A provinciana is more important."

"You're wrong, Dolly. She's my cousin."

"Oh, your cousin," she jeered. "Who else then will receive all the pleasure?"

"Dolly!"

The phone rang. Mando left Dolly to answer it.

Dolly stood and approached his desk. She glared at Puri who was looking at the picture on the wall, taking no notice of Dolly who had sat facing her.

Dolly noticed the face and attire of Mando's "cousin." A girl obviously from the barrio, but lovely. Comely face, smooth dark cheeks, languid eyes now clouded with grief, naturally wavy thick hair, rosy lips, firm breasts, and shapely arms.

She wore a flattering *balintawak*,[3] but Dolly's sharp eyes saw that it needed washing.

Miss Montero also noticed that the girl was younger than she. She would not admit to herself that she was lovelier.

---

2 provinciana—country lass

3 balintawak—a traditional Filipino dress for women

When Mando hung up, he hurriedly left his office and went to Magat. The two women were left facing each other.

When Puri noticed Dolly, she smiled in greeting. But Dolly gave her a suspicious look.

LII

Dolly's hatred-at-first sight was not because of the provinciana's rare beauty nor her freshness and youth. Many beautiful young girls could be found everywhere. Dolly had been to famous cities in the world, and she had seen much. Not everyone who was young and beautiful was noticed.

A girl should have class, personality, and individuality. Like a diamond or any other precious gem, quality could not be faked.

In Dolly's eyes, the girl quietly sitting opposite her had no class. One could tell from her manner of dressing, her dirty fingernails, and her hairstyle. If Dolly had met Puri elsewhere, she would probably be sympathetic instead of annoyed.

However, the girl's arrival in that office had spoiled Dolly's plans with Mando. Could she possibly overlook that?

Even though Mando said that she was his cousin, Dolly could not bring herself to like her. If it had been someone else, she would probably try to befriend Puri, a relative of the man she loved. Dolly could only think that Puri was the reason she could not have lunch with Mando and have their serious discussion. Nevertheless, she tried to contain the small storm brewing in her mind for Mando's sake. Dolly decided to coat her usual coarseness in dealing with her inferiors.

Instead, she aimed to obtain more information about this cousin of Mando's.

Without any pleasantries, she addressed the girl in a familiar tone. "Your errand seems important." She was fishing for information, for Dolly felt the girl could not have any important purpose. Probably, she wanted to borrow money or was looking for work or a close relative had just died. But then, why should Mando put off their date? Why did Mando say that this girl's business could not be put off? Why should Dolly be the one to give way? Dolly was getting furious. She waited for Puri's answer.

"I had to see Mr. Plaridel, ma'am," Puri answered. Looking up, she saw Dolly's frowning face. Puri's eyes widened, for the face was familiar. Seeing the cold reaction to her words, Puri decided not to reveal her purpose in coming.

"Where did you come from?"

"From the barrio outside Hacienda Montero."

Dolly held her head higher when she heard Hacienda Montero. So the girl was from that place. From the farm. It showed in her appearance. Probably the daughter of a sharecropper or a tenant of her father.

"Papa owns Hacienda Montero."

"Don Segundo. Then you are Señorita Dolly, ma'am?" Puri realized why the face was familiar.

"Yes, and who are you?"

"Puri, Pastor's daughter."

"Pastor? Does Papa know him?"

"He was the overseer of your hacienda during the war, ma'am."

"Ah, I remember now. He is no longer there, is he?"

"No, ma'am."

"And you are his child?"

"His only child, ma'am."

"Oh, are you the girl whom he brought along to the house? What are you doing now?"

"I help Tatang in the field."

"Your father is foolish. Papa offered to take you to live with us; then you could have gone to school. Did you get any schooling?"

"A little," Puri said humbly. "I know how to read and write."

"Of course, that is enough in the barrio. But it's a pity. Like our houseboy, I can't remember his name – Papa sent him to school... But he was also a fool. He left suddenly during the war. The fool was already in college."

Puri realized that she was referring to Andoy. It did not occur to Montero's daughter that Pastor was the youngest brother of Andoy's mother. Therefore, Andoy was related to Puri. Those who lie in luxury are naturally forgetful of the names and the services of their lowly servants.

"You too. You should not be just a provinciana."

"There is nothing wrong with being a provinciana."

"What I mean is, you would have received a better education if you had lived with us, and got better opportunities."

"Farmer folks like us enjoy life on the farm."

"Of course. To each his own. As the saying goes, each has his own destiny. With your looks, you could have lived in Manila and married a man of some importance."

"What do you mean?"

"Why, a professional, a lawyer, a director or one like Mando, or a wealthy merchant."

"Barrio girls don't see what you call men of some importance. For us, it is enough for a man to be good, to know how to make a living, and to love his family."

"Then you would be content with a farmer, a laborer?"

"I would care for the person, not his occupation."

"Even if he can't give you a life of ease?" Dolly wondered.

"Farmer folks are used to hard work. It is true we want to live better lives, but more important is the happiness from faithful and peaceful relations."

"There can be no happiness and peace without the necessities of life."

"We have a saying – learn to curl up when the blanket is small."

"That's why you barrio folks won't progress," said Dolly, getting bored. She stood up and looked at the door that Mando had passed through a while ago. "What could be taking him so long?" she wondered.

But Puri would not let her mocking remarks pass and answered sharply, "The barrio people don't progress through no fault of theirs. This is what the landlord wants."

Dolly was jolted by the pointed remark. She had thought the girl stupid and timid.

"What do you mean?" The Montero heiress frowned.

"Because they are not given the chance to live in some comfort. In the landlord-farmer relations, only the landlord gets rich."

"Why, is there a law against getting rich?"

"None, if the wealth does not come from another's blood."

"Everyone has his capital – the landlord his land, the tenant, his labor. The law is clear on the conditions and share of the harvest. Do you mean that the owner of the land and the money should have no share?"

"All the farmers ask is justice."

"What justice? Isn't there a law that decides all these?"

"Laws made by proprietors and landowners."

"That's the trouble with you peasants. You refuse to recognize the law. If you aren't satisfied, work for changes. Change the lawmakers, if you can, since you too can vote. But use reasonable means, not violence."

"Those who use force are the powerful. It is absurd to argue that the weak are the ones who use force."

Dolly was not aware of the latest happenings at Hacienda Montero and Puri felt it best not to tell her. She could tell that Dolly's outlook was like a hard rock which could not be plowed or sown on.

"Even you women listen to bad advice," Dolly said after a while. "An unreasonable mother can only have insolent children."

"Insolent because they have learned to reason, because they protest against oppression." Puri raised her voice and also stood up. Dolly was standing behind a chair. "The first lesson a barrio woman teaches her child is to live by the sweat of his brow and not to covet what belongs to others. We know that taking advantage of others is the source of all trouble."

"And who is taking advantage?" demanded Dolly.

"If there were no opportunists, the world would not be divided between the rich and the poor; there would be no mothers working the whole day in the fields, washing, doing heavy work, and lucky women who spend the whole day at socials, in pleasure and luxury."

Dolly felt the sharpness of Puri's words and wanted to leave. It would be a shame to be drawn into an argument with a common woman. Dolly was sorry she had bothered to talk to the lowly provinciana, who was now acting like an agitated wasp. Nevertheless, she answered sternly.

"The trouble with you plebeians," she said like a snake spewing venom, "is that you are a horde of envious persons. Just because you are ignorant, you envy the educated; because you are beggars, you envy the rich. It's impossible for all men to be alike."

Puri could imagine Don Segundo Montero abusing his tenants. At that moment, she could not see the beauty of the popular society belle but the ugliness of a Fury. Pastor's daughter defiantly denied that the worker's plea for justice was urged by envy.

"Your argument is farfetched," she declared, no longer giving deference to the haughty girl. "Why should we envy you? What should we envy? Your greed, your coarse manners, your wasting time and money on useless things? The country women are real wives, real mothers; they work and care for the home, day and night. They raise their children, not nursemaids; they prepare their families' food, not servants; they help and accompany their husbands, not their husbands' friends or their friends' wives. They are poor because they are cheated, but they are happy and peaceful in the midst of poverty. Why should they envy those whose fingers are covered with diamonds and whose bodies are wrapped in silk but who don't find happiness under their roofs and search and buy their pleasure in parties, nightclubs, gambling, and other worldliness? Envious! We would never exchange our purity of life for the glitter of your hypocritical society."

"You see the faults but you are blind to the virtues," Dolly shouted. "Our works for charity, religion, health... Those are nothing to a stupid person like you."

"Don't insult me." Puri raised her right hand.

Dolly retreated.

Dolly was more experienced and better informed than Puri, but in that encounter, she was dumbfounded. She could insult her for her situation and her poverty, but Puri's arguments were like arrows hitting their mark. And she seemed ready to fight. Dolly told herself that she really is Pastor's daughter. And she remembered that this same Pastor had been removed as overseer for his insolence. He was more loyal to the outlaws than to the governor during the Japanese times and more sympathetic to the tenants and sharecroppers than to the owner of the hacienda.

Dolly decided that it would be useless to argue with the girl whose mind had been instilled with antisocial ideas. So, after throwing her a dagger look, she went to the door without a word.

Near the door she met Mando. "Are you leaving?" he asked.

Dolly left without answering. Puri was standing by the desk looking at the two.

LIII

Mando was caught in a dilemma. Of course, he was used to being caught between a wall and a dagger; between the devil and the deep blue sea. How many times did he encounter Japanese soldiers and false guerrillas during the war? The large shark when he and Karyo dove into the Pacific Ocean for Simoun's wealth. Other dangers in the mountains and on the plains. And in foreign cities during his travels. But he lacked experience being caught between two women who both loved him and needed him at that moment, demanding his time and attention. Mando was not used to the chess of hearts. So he hesitated when Dolly left in a huff, while Puri was anxiously waiting.

Nevertheless, Mando overcame his confusion. He motioned Puri to sit down and followed Dolly. He caught up with her on the stairs.

"Dolly, wait a moment," Mando called after her.

She stopped, looking vexed. Her pride was hurt by Mando's neglect and Puri's discourtesy.

"Please forgive me," he entreated.

"Is that all you have to say?" Dolly made a move to go down.

"I admit I neglected you because of an urgent reason.

"Yes, your cousin's business is important."

"I'll go to your place tonight."

"Never mind, don't trouble yourself."

Mando went with her to the car and helped her get in.

"Tonight, Dol?" he repeated.

"I'll be out. Goodbye!"

When Mando returned to his office, he told Puri who had just left.

"That's Dolly, Don Segundo's daughter."

"We had a talk," Puri answered. "She seemed offended."

"She came to invite me to lunch. But how could I go?"

"So, that's why she seemed annoyed with me."

"Your business is many times more important than her invitation."

After arranging the papers on his desk, they left.

"Come along, Gat," Mando invited Magat when they passed by his desk.

"I'll wait for Danoy. We'll go together."

When Mando and Puri reached his house, Dr. Sabio was there talking to Tata Matyas. From Mando's phone call, the professor had an inkling of what had happened.

Soon Magat and Danoy came. Anxiously, Danoy asked Puri what the civilian guards did to her father, Mang Tumas, and the rest. Puri told him that they were hunting for him, and Captain Pugot threatened to come to Manila if he didn't return to the hacienda within twenty-four hours.

After lunch, Dr. Sabio asked Puri to relate all the events at Hacienda Montero since they arrived from the meeting in Manila. The girl repeated what she had related earlier, adding some details she had overlooked, and answering Danoy and Dr. Sabio's questions.

Puri related how Captain Pugot had hit her father when he would not admit that he had anything to do with the fire and accused the captain's men of planting the guns found in his house. Puri said that if it were not for the farmers' concern for the women, blood would have flowed. The farmers who had been maltreated were ready to fight.

"They are in danger," she said. "Captain Pugot threatened to kill anyone who made a false move. He shouted at Tatang and threatened to soften him up."

Mando calmed down Puri's fears and said that the tenant could no longer be treated like a carabao. Now there are laws that recognize every man's rights. One could sue a landlord or chief who commits abuses.

"Many laws are as worthless as wet paper," Danoy pointed out. "Often the law is applied according to the place and the person. In our experience, justice is elusive to the tenants of the haciendas."

"Because you have accepted such conditions," answered Mando. "The law should be given life, not only by the officers but by the affected citizens. A child who does not cry is not fed."

"In our government offices, the small fry are small fry." Danoy insisted. "In our courts, justice is on the side of those with money."

"For an even match, both sides should have the same weapons," Mando said. "I said there are laws, and anyone who commits abuses should be made to answer for them because the small fry are no longer alone. You saw their strength at the meeting last night; they have unions, a mouthpiece like the *Kampilan*, friends like Senator Maliwanag, Dr. Sabio…"

The president of Freedom University nodded. Then he looked into the legal aspects of Pastor's case, Captain Pugot's use of physical force and illegal detention, and the steps they should take to free the detained men as soon as possible.

"Captain Pugot is not alone in this," Magat surmised. "Pugot is only a hired tool. Who gave him orders? Who would profit most from such a plot?"

"The answer is obvious," said Danoy. "But besides Don Segundo, without a doubt Governor Doblado and General Bayoneta are involved."

"Captain Pugot was supposed to be at the capital during the fire. When he returned to the hacienda, he was accompanied by soldiers," Puri told them.

"See?" exclaimed Danoy, for Puri's statement seemed to confirm his suspicions.

"Now they have met their match," Mando declared.

Then he asked Dr. Sabio to tell Puri and Danoy about his plan to buy Hacienda Montero and other lands with tenancy problems.

"As you know," began the professor, "the farmers have long been asking the government to buy the land and to administer or sell it on installment to the tenants."

"That's what we ask," Danoy agreed, "but this request has fallen through a basket full of holes."

"Either will be hard for our government at present," Dr. Sabio said. "First, there is no money in the treasury. Second, it does not want to have any more white elephants. There is hardly a government corporation that is not losing money because of poor management and corrupt administrators usually chosen because of their political influence. Besides, many big politicians are landlords. Will they agree to a sale where they won't make huge profits?"

"In other Asian countries, the tenancy problem was solved," Mando answered, "because the government knew that peace was impossible until this problem was solved."

"True," Dr. Sabio agreed. "But before that happened," he added with a slight smile, "the former government of landlords and businessmen were overthrown by revolution. The new government took over the lands held by foreigners and their tools. This happened in China, Egypt, Burma, Indonesia, Cuba."

"There are no signs that we will see this here in our lifetime," Mando answered dryly.

Tata Matyas spoke for the first time. "That was one of the aims of Supremo Bonifacio," the former revolutionary said softly, "but he was slain and the revolution passed to the hands of the bourgeois. When the republic was set up in Malolos, Aguinaldo was surrounded by the tentacles of the status quo. Their only concern was their own welfare. So that when the Americans won, they became the first collaborators."

After saying this, Tata Mayas remained silent. But what he said clarified Dr. Sabio's views.

"I talked to Segundo Montero," Dr. Sabio continued. "I told him that Freedom University wanted to buy the hacienda. At first, he said that it was not for sale. Then he mentioned an offer from a foreign millionaire. He would not reveal the name, although I think it is his friend Son Tua. I reminded him that a foreigner could not own land unless he used a dummy. I also said it was better for Freedom University to own the hacienda for it would not be used for profit."

Don Segundo was annoyed and asked what was wrong if the land should yield profit when it involved a large capital. He wondered why Dr. Sabio, a scientist, was such an idealist, whereas he, Montero, was a practical businessman. Dr. Sabio corrected him about his wrong concept of the aim of Freedom University.

"There are many gains other than money," said the professor. "For example, the additional know-how of the farmers."

Finally, Don Segundo said he would sell the hacienda at the current market price. Dr. Sabio offered to add thirty percent to the assessed value.

"It would be good if we were to buy your land," Dr. Sabio added. "You will have no more headaches arising from conflicts. Don't you get tired from the trouble in the fields?"

According to Dr. Sabio, Segundo Montero stood up and banged his table with a fist.

"That is the chief reason why I don't want to sell," he shouted. "Those shameless farmers might say I'm afraid of them. Let's see who is stronger."

Dr. Sabio's associates were more bent on buying Hacienda Montero because they felt that the attitude of the present owner was a real stumbling block to order and progress.

"It's sad that we still have the likes of Montero," Dr. Sabio sighed. "His way of thinking dates back to the days before the printing press."

Dr. Sabio made an apt comparison between progress and the people who enjoyed its benefits.

"It's been one hundred fifty years since the first steamship," recalled the sage of Freedom University. "We have had electricity for half a century. There are many railroads and streets crowded with cars. The air is crisscrossed by planes. In a minute, radio brings the latest news around the world. Atomic force has been harnessed, no longer to destroy, but to serve mankind, to explore the moon and the planets and to promote civilization and man's happiness."

Dr. Sabio rubbed his forehead with one hand, then continued.

"What has not changed is man's greed, his cruelty to his fellow man, his blind self-love. There is Montero as an example."

Puri served hot coffee. Mando asked Dr. Sabio to allow Puri to stay temporarily in the girls' dormitory at Freedom University. Danoy would stay at Mando's house.

"I can't rest until Tatang is free," said Puri.

"He will be free by hook or by crook," said Danoy rashly.

"We shall do all we can," Mando said calmly.

They finished their coffee.

LIV

The captive farmers endured fatigue, hunger, and anxiety at the civilian guards' quarters in Hacienda Montero. The guards closed the windows and doors after Captain Pugot rushed to the capital. They were no better than sacks of rice bran dumped in a warehouse.

His men followed the captain's orders and more. No visitors were allowed. Food brought by relatives was accepted but eaten by the guards themselves.

They were stingy even with water, bringing in only one pail from the brook before noon. How could this suffice for twenty-five men who neither ate nor slept?

Puri had planned to bring food, but her father told her not to bother. No food would have reached him anyway.

Many sat on the floor and leaned against the walls. Many dozed off. Pastor, Mang Tumas, and two or three others remained awake. Pastor urged Mang Tumas to rest, but the latter said he could not sleep. When the guards left, they spoke softly about their grave situation.

"They did this because of last night's meeting," said one.

"No, this had been planned for a long time," answered Mang Tumas. "Those people have no solution but violence."

"And they blame us for their crime," answered another.

"That has always been the tactic of the exploiters since the time of Christ," said Mang Tumas. "May the news reach our friends in Manila."

"For sure," said Pastor. "They have not captured everyone in our barrio and the other towns. Puri is neither ignorant nor a coward."

"Puri and the others have guards," said the first speaker.

"They can place daggers in her path; she will find a way," Pastor said proudly. "Puri has a man's heart."

"It's a good thing Danoy stayed behind," said Mang Tumas. "I'm worried about his rashness. When he learns of the plot against us, there's no telling what he might do."

"He often says, 'Only lightning can't hit back,'" agreed Pastor.

The captives barely noticed that the day had passed. It was dusk. They did not complain. Hunger was not new to them, although they tried to avoid it like an unwelcome kin.

Several times, they asked for water, but the door remained locked. Only the echo of their own voices answered them.

It was seven in the evening when Captain Pugot returned. He did not tell his men about his mission at the capital. He usually kept such secrets to himself. That day he had met Governor Doblado and the prosecutor, made arrangements with the commander of the MP headquarters at the capital, and reported to Don Segundo and General Bayoneta by long distance. Bayoneta was his backer for becoming overseer.

"How's everything?" Pugot asked the sergeant of the guards on his return.

"Okay, sir."

"No visitors?"

"None, sir."

"No one was fed?"

"No one sir."

"Good. We shall transfer them to the capital tonight."

The captain thought a while, then told the sergeant to prepare the rice gruel.

"Yes, sir."

Then Captain Pugot ordered the opening of the door of the headquarters. He entered followed by the sergeant and some guards. He looked haughtily at the captives.

"Why aren't you sleeping, Tumas?" he asked the old leader sitting next to Pastor.

"And you, Pastor," he sneered. "You are tough, ha?"

Receiving no answer, he went out.

After an hour, the guards brought in a large can of thin, plain gruel which was still steaming.

"Eat your fill," mocked the sergeant and locked the door again.

There was no ladle, cup, nor plate, but after an hour, the sergeant saw that the can was clean. He could not imagine what the captives had done with the boiling gruel. He looked at the floor, but nothing had been spilled. He didn't show his amazement. Pastor and Mang Tumas laughed secretly over their small victory.

Out of revenge, the sergeant ordered the guard not to give them water.

That night saw the transfer of the farmers charged with burning the hacienda and planning trouble.

Pastor and his companions were loaded in a covered MP truck. The truck sped from the headquarters of the civilian guards accompanied by a weapons carrier loaded with guards and soldiers. They firmly gripped their rifles, showing their fingers were itching to press the trigger.

The two vehicles entered the fenced MP headquarters. It was past nine in the evening.

Upon reaching the yard, Captain Pugot went ahead in his jeep, motioning the truck driver to follow. He stepped before a low building shaped like a granary and made of wood and stone and a galvanized iron roof.

He told the farmers to get off and enter the granary. It was two hundred yards from the barracks and the office of the Commander. It was obviously a prison for special captives.

The granary, which was like an inverted tortoise shell, had several parts. At the entrance was the office of the sergeant of the guards. Beyond this was the prison, behind which was a secret room with no opening by a permanently closed narrow door. Opposite was a combined toilet and bathroom. There was a guard at the door between the sergeant's office and the prison and another guard at the door leading to the secret room that was covered by thick walls. The bathroom had no water. Water had to be fetched from a well outside.

The dark prison was fifty square yards with no light except a small bulb. The dusty cement was cold, a strange coldness that could cause rheumatism. The swarm of hungry mosquitoes buzzing and the ugly cockroaches crawling all over were hardly disturbed by the guests. Under the roof without a ceiling, the tangle of cobwebs added to the darkness.

The twenty-five farmers were dumped like lifeless objects. In Captain Pugot's list, they were the ardent supporters and followers of a dangerous movement; these people were his enemies, and they would show him no mercy if their positions were reversed. So his conscience didn't bother him for his cruelty.

The sergeant told the farmers to keep quiet.

"You are in jail, not at a meeting," he snarled.

Mang Tumas found an old sack in a corner and mopped the dirty floor. There was no cot nor boards to place on the cold floor, no mats nor mosquito nets.

Nevertheless, many fell asleep from exhaustion. They had no rest for almost forty-eight hours. Their bodies were weary, and their minds confused.

Pastor and Mang Tumas lay down side by side without speaking.

When many were snoring and Pastor was dozing off, he felt the end of a hard object on his neck. Opening his eyes, he could discern the mouth of a rifle. A guard was rousing him.

Pastor got up. Mang Tumas pretended to be asleep. He opened one eye to see what was happening.

Mang Tumas saw Pastor taken by the guard to the end of the prison beyond the door. The old farmer was sure his friend was not being taken to the bathroom, for he had not called the guard.

Mang Tumas imagined what could happen in the secret room. He knew that the investigation had not ended in the quarters at the hacienda. He had heard Captain Pugot's threat to soften up Pastor and the other tough ones. Pastor was firm and was known for his fearlessness. Mang Tumas also knew that there were limits to human endurance, but no limit to the cruelty of the tools of the enemies of justice and right.

Mang Tumas listened intently, cupping his hands over his ear. He thought he could hear thuds and groans, but these were only in his thoughts. The strange silence of that horrible night disturbed old Tumas.

There was no light in the hidden room where Pastor was brought. The only light, the guard's flashlight, fell on the face of the farmer's leader, blinding him. Two strange men kept grilling Pastor. He could not see their faces, but they seemed as young as Danoy. He had not met these men before. They seemed to be investigators from the intelligence branch of the armed forces.

At first, they tempted Pastor with the siren's song, praising him, his war record, his loyalty to the workers. Then, they reminded him that if he had not been "lost," he would now be enjoying a good time. If he would only help the landlord or the officials, he would receive what he asked at once – land or money.

Pastor defiantly answered that he could not be a tool of exploiters. The hand of the guard hit his mouth. Then he was told by the two investigators to choose between prison or freedom.

The evidence against him would surely put him behind bars if he would not cooperate.

"Choose!"

Pastor didn't even wipe the blood from his lips.

Finally, they tried to make Pastor admit that he owned the guns found in his house, that he was the brains behind the burning of the hacienda, that he threatened to start a bloody uprising in the fields, but he would not admit their lies.

Pastor again received hard blows from the husky guard, and he staggered. For two hours, the two detectives left Puri's father at the mercy of the guard, a real executioner who bravely played his role. When the two returned to the hidden room, Pastor was sprawled in a corner, unconscious.

LV

The two detectives were not concerned about Pastor's condition brought about by the beating.

"He is really tough," said the guard as the two looked at Pastor, who was like a crumpled bag in the middle of the room.

"I'm getting tired of that devil," said one detective, shaking his head.

"He won't listen to reason," said the other.

"He can't get away with his foolishness," bragged the guard. "He will rot here."

"Don't give him all; he might not wake up anymore."

They had asked the guard to fetch water, which they poured on Pastor's face. The blood flowed through his veins; he regained consciousness and sighed. Then he opened his eyes. His eyes lit up, a sign that he recalled what had happened.

Pastor tried to get up, but all his bones ached. He remained seated on the floor.

"You only want to get hurt," one investigator said.

"If this had been another time or place, you'd be dead," added the other.

Pastor felt it was useless, arguing with these men. They were men only in appearance and were worse than destructive machines fixed on their targets.

Meanwhile, Mang Tumas was uneasy as he lay. He was attacked by mosquitoes, but he took no notice of them. He was afraid his companion would be killed. After several hours, which seemed like a year, he could make out two shadows coming out of the door at the prison's end. He recognized Pastor led by the same guard who took him out. He could not bear to look at his companion's face. He was sure he had changed a lot. Pastor could not walk unaided. Mang Tumas was sure Pastor sustained broken bones during his stay in that cell.

"We're not through yet," Mang Tumas heard the guard say.

Pastor sat down without a word, but he could hardly lie down. Mang Tumas got up and helped him lie on the cold cement floor. The old man asked in a whisper what was painful. Pastor complained that his whole body felt like a swollen boil. Mang Tumas gently rubbed Pastor's hips and arms. His tears fell out of pity.

It was almost dawn. Other than the whispers of the two farmers, nothing broke the tomb-like silence of the dark prison. Even the guard outside seemed to have dozed off in his wooden chair.

Soon Pastor's soft groans ceased. To Mang Tumas, they seemed to come not from his lips but from his very soul. These were not ordinary groans from physical pain, but the recoiling of the soul against nameless cruelty.

Perhaps Mang Tumas was the only one who had not slept. He thought of Pastor and the guard, their similarities, their differences, their goals, the reason why Pastor was a prisoner who was abused and why the guard became the cruel henchman.

Mang Tumas found only one answer – the desire to search for a livelihood. They had the same goal, but different means. Pastor was a farmer living off his own sweat and fighting for freedom and justice in order to live a better life. The guard also lived on wages paid for fulfilling his duty to quell or keep Pastor from his goal and bore the attractive title of law enforcer, herald of peace, and other such titles. But if he were to analyze the events and actions of each, he would see that the guard was the enemy of the law and Pastor, the victim.

Mang Tumas figured that the guard was only a tool, a hireling. Evil was not inborn; he was overcome by the desire to make a living, even by a means contrary to his conscience.

If the guard would shed his uniform and join a group of farmers, he would appear to be one of them, thought Mang Tumas. Perhaps he was the son of a farmer. If Pastor should wear the uniform, he would appear to be the guard. The dividing line that created the difference between Pastor and the guard was very thin, but the gap was very wide in the actions, so that they became opponents instead of helpers.

The hands of the clock may be slow, but time moves inexorably.

Several loud whistles roused the farmers. It was six o'clock. The morning was hot and humid.

Most had been awake for some time but didn't stir. They remained lying down, alert. Each was thinking of the past two nights they had been locked up at the quarters at Hacienda Montero and in this prison at the MP headquarters in the capital.

What would happen to them? What had befallen their families? What was in store for them on this day? They could foresee that they would be subjected again to questions and more cruelty from the guards and soldiers.

They felt intense hunger and thirst. But the wounds in their souls were even more painful.

Pastor was awakened by the whistle. He had fallen asleep after he had been brought back from the cell. Opening his eyes, he turned to Mang Tumas, but he was not there. He had slept with Mang Tumas on his left, but he was not there now.

Pastor looked at the others, but Mang Tumas wasn't there either. In their situation, a moment's separation caused anxiety.

Pastor tried to calm himself thinking that Mang Tumas must have answered a call of nature. He thought that Mang Tumas would suffer most from the hardships because of his age.

When the guard saw that the new sergeant had entered, he ordered them to fall in line.

"One line," he hollered.

In the sergeant's hand was a list of the detainees' names. He was short and squat, dark-skinned, and seemed ill at ease in his clothes. Surely his parents must have come from their dwelling place in the trees and forests to buy dogs for slaughter. Unlike his ancestors, the sergeant was learning to walk upright; in fact, the heels of his boots were six inches tall.

He threw the row of farmers a sharp glance and looked at his list. But before starting, he gave them another dirty look and delivered a short speech.

"You are prisoners," the sergeant began, although no charges had been filed against them. "You have been jailed because you are enemies of the government. But even if you are bad men, we shall treat you well. You will not starve, for you will have chow twice a day – at ten in the morning and at five in the afternoon. Here you won't be hurt, unless you lie. Here your life is safe, unless you try to escape. You know that a bullet is faster than your feet. Now, perhaps that is clear."

Then he read the names which were in alphabetical order. Everyone called answered, "Hep!"

Several times he stammered and was forced to spell the name which he could not pronounce. The detainees kept quiet every time the sergeant read a name of more than three syllables. He was like an unskilled acrobat on a flying trapeze. After reading Pastor's name and casting a furtive look, he said, "So you are their leader, ha?"

"I am a farmer," answered Pastor who could hardly stand straight.

"It's too bad we did not meet earlier. I heard of you during the Japanese times," said the sergeant.

"Because I was with other Filipinos," retorted Pastor.

When the sergeant approached Pastor, all eyes were on them, but he did not raise his right hand.

"You are a hero; that's why you're here," he sneered. "Just wait, I'll pin a medal on you." And he turned away abruptly.

Pastor just looked on and said nothing. The sergeant went on calling the other names. Up to the end, he didn't read the name of Mang Tumas. Pastor thought the old man's name must not be on the list.

The sergeant went around the jail, proceeded to the hidden cell, then returned and went out the front door. His chin was raised, and his shoulder twitched with every step.

When the door closed after the sergeants and the guard, the farmers immediately rushed to Pastor. Mang Tumas was not the only witness to Pastor's trip and return from the cell. A part of Pastor's face was swollen, both sides were black and blue, and he felt that his ribs were broken. The guard had hurt even his most sensitive parts.

The farmers were hurt and very angry.

Some recalled the cruelty of the soldier-collaborators and the civilian guards during the last war. They were worse than the enemy in torturing the guerrillas, the townsfolk, and the farmers.

"Just thinking of it makes my blood boil," said a farmer. "When a guerrilla was captured by those beasts, his tongue would be cut off, his ears and his fingers and his genitals, before he was beheaded. I saw this with my own eyes, and I barely made my escape."

"Not only that," said another. "Sometimes they would slice off the flesh on the thigh or arm of a fellow Filipino, roast it and make him eat it. If he refused, they would knock out all his teeth. It was horrifying."

They became more worried by the disappearance of Mang Tumas. They asked each other, but no one had seen him taken out. They were all sound asleep. Pastor surmised that this must have been when he dozed off. No one could tell if Mang Tumas was brought to the torture cell or outside the jail.

Before ten o'clock, some soldiers brought a can of boiled bran with some small fried fish and hot ginger tea. That was the first "delicious" food tasted by Pastor and his companions in three days. The grumbling of their stomachs stopped.

LVI

Mando and his associates took the necessary steps right away. After leaving his house that afternoon, each did his own part. They could not take their time because of the urgency of the situation.

Dr. Sabio brought Puri to the dormitory.

When Mando reached his office, he immediately conferred with his reporter Iman and asked him to gather all information about the events at Hacienda Montero. He bade Iman to rush to the hacienda and get photographs. He provided Iman with a car and money.

After bringing Puri to the dormitory, Dr. Sabio asked the law officers of the university to take steps to free the farmers and to file charges against Pugot and his men.

Andres and Rubio joined Mando, Magat, Dr. Sabio, and Danoy at the professor's office the following night.

They discussed other problems of the workers besides the case of Hacienda Montero. Andres was well-informed on troubles regarding the ABCs of industrial strife in the city.

"Any progressive program should be supported by the labor force in order to succeed," said Magat. "So the blow against unionism is also an attack on progress."

Rubio said that the foreign capitalists and their official tools always give way to the sprouting and growth of company unions.

He explained that it was easy to spot the company unions and their leaders because, while the members could not hold their heads up against oppression, their leaders lived in grand houses and rode in flashy cars.

"It is treachery for the leader to wallow in wealth while the union is impoverished," declared Rubio vehemently. "The union should provide a living for the leader, or he will be bribed by the capitalists. But neither in poverty nor in luxury."

Danoy declared that the union leaders were lucky because they enjoyed greater security than the farmers' leader.

"There we are always plagued by the landowners and their hirelings." Danoy said. "We always have a foot in jail or in the cemetery."

Magat pointed out, "In this country, there is no difference between the landlord and the factory owner. They have but one capital and one outlook. Both will dare anything and oppose any movement that will reduce their profit. This truth never fails."

After this exchange of views, Dr. Sabio brought the discussion back to Pastor.

"Are you sure, Danoy," he asked the young leader, "that you don't own the kerosene can and the rags said to be taken from your house?"

"Do you have any doubt, Dr. Sabio?" asked Danoy.

"None, but I wanted to hear it from you."

"It's also certain that the guns don't belong to Tata Pastor," added Danoy. "Regarding the papers found in Mang Tumas' house, if there was anything other than the constitution of our association and the list of members, it must have been brought by the civilian guards."

"They have been jailed in the MP camp for two days now," Dr. Sabio recalled. "I wonder if they are safe."

"As safe as a canary guarded by a cat," Danoy answered, clenching his fist. "Oh, if it were the Japanese times and our guerrilla troops were intact," he sighed.

"If it were the Japanese times, Tata Pastor would not be in jail because Captain Pugot would be in hiding," Magat said bitterly. "Now we former guerrillas obey the law and the collaborators are back in power."

"While they are detained, we should not rest," Danoy said.

"That's why we are working overtime," answered Mando, who had been listening silently. "This is being done without even suspending habeas corpus."

Then he asked Dr. Sabio about Puri. The professor said she was settled at the dormitory.

"But she insists on going back to the hacienda or the town. She is anxious about her father."

"If she is at the hacienda, there's no telling what could happen to her," Danoy declared. "The men are mauled by the civilian guards; the women are raped. It was lucky Puri escaped."

"I could see that Puri has presence of mind and does not panic," Dr. Sabio remarked.

"From childhood, Puri has been used to hardship," Danoy commented with admiration. He looked at Mando as if to say, "There's a lucky guy."

They were about to end their discussion when the phone rang. Iman wanted to talk to Mando or Magat.

"Big news!" The reporter's voice was loud.

Mando asked him to come right away.

In a few minutes, Iman rushed in.

"Mang Tumas and another farmer were slain," he blurted out. The news hit them like a grenade. Danoy stood up, waved his fists in the air, slumped onto his seat, and covered his face with his hands. He cried as Iman related the latest news.

According to the MP report, the two had tried to escape. This report was based on Captain Pugot's account. Mang Tumas and his companion were said to have escaped but were caught and fired upon when they refused to halt. Both had wounds in their backs.

"And Tata Pastor?" asked Mando.

"Tata Pastor is in jail, incommunicado. We could not go near the detained farmers," Iman reported. "But I have pictures of the corpses which are now in the barrio outside the hacienda."

According to Iman, the civilian guards forbade them to take pictures and tried to confiscate their cameras, but the Lieutenant intervened. The Lieutenant explained that there was no need to be afraid that the public would see the pictures of the slain men. Was it not the practice of the constabulary and some officials to parade the corpses of the "outlaws," some of whom were headless, with their arms tied at the elbows? There were those nailed on the cross or hung upside down on the pointed bamboo poles in the plaza as a warning against crime and treachery.

So the sergeant agreed and posed with other guards who were looking at the corpse of the old leader of the farmers.

"The unrest at the hacienda is serious," said Iman. Soldiers and civilian guards swarm all over the place as if the barrios were under martial law. The people appear calm, but they are seething within like a boiling cauldron.

"No one we talked to could believe Mang Tumas was killed while escaping," Iman went on. "He was slain, they said. Old Tumas was tough, they said, but he would not try to escape. If it had been Danoy, maybe. Many fear that they will do the same to Tata Pastor. He is also tough, according to the barrio folks."

"Did you talk to Captain Pugot?" asked Magat.

"Captain Pugot was away," said Iman. "He did not appear at the hacienda. Nor in the town. Some said he was called to Baguio by Segundo Montero."

"He can't hide forever," Danoy threatened.

Andres left after hearing Iman's full report. He hurried back to the *Kampilan* to prepare the latest edition of the paper, which would come out the first hour of the morning.

"Use the pictures on the front page," Magat instructed. "The corpses of Mang Tumas and the other farmer."

After Andres had left, Magat groaned that long after the war, conditions were still similar to the Japanese times. He asked who should answer for such happenings.

"That is the foremost cause of the conflict dividing people," Dr. Sabio said. "Many want to start where the war left off, which is as it should be. Those in power want to restore everything and thereby fix the world."

He declared that almost everywhere, especially in colonial countries, the social revolution had triumphed, and a great social and economic change had taken place to reduce inequality among citizens.

"Except this country," stressed the professor, "which goes on kissing the boots that kick it. As the Spanish saying goes, '*El mismo perro con diferente collar*.'[1]"

"There is unrest in the barrios, but what can be done?" asked Rubio. "Will they be content to weep over their dead and bury them?"

"And how can we teach and establish the correct philosophy, beliefs, and system…?"

"By ceaseless struggle."

"By the power of the tongue or the sword, Doctor?" asked Danoy.

"Whichever is effective at the proper time," Dr. Sabio admitted with a smile. "At times, the mouth and the pen are effective; at other times, the sword. But at all times, they should be guided by the mind."

Even the hotheads, Danoy and Rubio, agreed.

"Very well." Mando stood up and suggested, "It's time we rested, because we have much to do tomorrow."

The first rays of a new day were beginning to appear.

---

1 El mismo perro con diferente collar—The same dog with a different collar

LVII

Everyone complained of the intense heat of early summer. The grand cars of Manila's four hundred families of high society vied with each other in scattering dust along the length from the capital to the cold Mountain City.

Among the earliest to go was the Montero family. They opened their new bungalow along the row of vacation cottages in an exclusive place near the Mansion House.

From the latter part of February until the first weeks of June, when the winds signaled the coming rains, Baguio was more exclusive than Little Baguio in Quezon City or Forbes Park. Here were society's elite; hence, the latest fashion, ostentatious gatherings, costly pleasures, and also vices. The festivities at the Mansion House, popular amusements, the Pines Hotel, and even the churches which were crowded with the Sunday saints – all became shows for clothes, jewelry, and cars of elite Manilans, the small circle of the mighty.

Gathered after supper in the poker room of the Montero bungalow, were the usual cronies. But that night, they were not thinking of poker or drinks. Don Segundo had invited them to discuss more serious problems.

Seated at a round table were Son Tua, the Chinese millionaire now known as Tua-son, his son-in-law General Magno Bayoneta, Senator Botin, Governor Oscar Doblado, and Montero.

They were joined at supper by Captain Pugot, who had been summoned by Don Segundo to report on the latest incidents at the hacienda. Afterwards, the head of the civilian guards left and didn't join them in the poker room.

Doña Julia and Dolly were invited by the architect Pong Tua-son to a gathering at Pines Hotel. Ever since Dolly left the *Kampilan* office in a huff, Pong noticed that the girl no longer avoided him nor answered crossly when he would speak of love. The Chinese mestizo's ardor had not cooled off.

When Don Segundo's guests had settled down, sipped their drinks, and lit their Sumatras, the host announced that they needed the help of Senator Botin very badly. The lawmaker was the angel of the mysterious Montero-Son Tua corporation, a client who never said no to his needs. During his whole stay in the Senate, Botin had proved that influence peddling was a rich spring. A senator's salary was not enough for the expenses of his office. Montero declared that public feeling against graft and corruption and the upsurge of nationalism would become big stumbling blocks for their corporation. The noise of the newspaper campaign and the bigger noise of the unions and other national movements resulted in strictness at the port, investigations, and bills. Their illegal businesslike contraband would not find rich soil under such conditions.

He asked Senator Botin to oppose all radical measures and policies. He considered radical any change in the status quo which would reduce the profits of "free enterprise." The free enterprise of the Monteros and Son Tuas was not freedom of capital and honorable business but unlimited greed and license to amass blood money through intrigue and deceit.

Senator Botin was a professional politician whose only desire was to remain in office by fair means or foul. For him, faithful service to the nation was not the key to political strength but skill in manipulation coupled with sharpness of mind, a smooth tongue, and agility. He tried to get along with everyone. He burned candle offerings alternately to God and to Satan. But every minute, he did not neglect to serve himself. Montero knew the Senator's weakness, and this served as the bond of their relationship.

However, Senator Botin hesitated regarding Montero's suggestion. Times had changed and it was difficult to go against the tide of nationalism. He confessed that Senator Maliwanag could do a lot together with men like Mando Plaridel to overcome ignorance.

"Let us admit that they light up the people's minds like a flashlight in a dark room," the legislator said.

"Dangerous people," remarked Montero.

"We Chinese have a way to handle dangerous people," said Son Tua meaningfully.

"Our army solution never fails," declared Bayoneta.

Montero and Doblado smiled, but Senator Botin disagreed.

"The silken gloved hand is effective," he said.

"An iron hand in a silk glove," Bayoneta amended.

"There are many ways to kill a chicken," said Don Segundo. "What we want to know, Senator, is if you're still with us."

"Did I say otherwise?" the lawmaker quickly answered.

"Can you stop the radical proposals in this session?" Montero suddenly asked the Senator who was caught unaware.

"For a fee." The Senator pursed his lips, pointing his nose upward.

"Of course," said Son Tua. "When have we ever said no? How much?"

"Very well, I shall canvas and let you know."

"You take care of it, Compadre," agreed Son Tua.

After another glass of whiskey, Senator Botin left. As a parting gift, Montero gave him a sealed envelope.

When the four stockholders of the corporation were alone, Montero reported that the situation was alarming.

"You know this without my saying so," he stressed. "You, Magno, as general, and you, Osky, as governor."

"There's a storm brewing," Doblado answered.

Montero continued, "These are bad signs. The meeting at Miranda and the fire at the hacienda."

"The fire?" Governor Doblado exclaimed.

"We just beat them to it," answered Montero, "or else worse could have happened."

"Aren't things bad enough?"

"We are still on top." Montero was confident.

"Until when?"

"As long as those in power like you don't lose heart and while those with money know how to pay."

"We are not afraid and we have no complaints against you," declared Bayoneta. "But Senator Botin was right; times have changed. Before, a general was like a king; now an officer is treacherously shot by a soldier. Before, a millionaire could buy anything; now, the millionaire is afraid of a newspaper's attack and an investigation."

Son Tua agreed with his son-in-law and related how in the blissful past, he walked on a red carpet wherever he went because of his money. How many times did he travel in Asia bringing his flashy car? Then, he would buy diamonds and other precious gems in Hong Kong, Bangkok, Singapore, and other cities, and contraband goods worth hundreds of thousands. He would hide them in the gasoline tank of his car. This was why he brought it on his trip. Upon his return, his car would zoom out of the pier. Who would suspect that his gasoline tank was full of diamonds? In Manila, the jewels cost five times as much without taxes. "Where would the department stores on the Escolta get their diamonds?" he boasted.

He paused for a while and rubbed his hand over his pale face.

"Now, give bribe, left and right, still much fuss," Son Tua sighed. "Men very bad these days, very bad, very greedy."

And the Chinese multimillionaire once more reclined in silence on the cushions of the easy chair.

On the other hand, Segundo Montero recalled the happy days soon after the war, when his orders were brought by an American official who made frequent trips. When he and his wife traveled, they were met at the pier by the wife of a Malacañan official; so, no one inspected their hand-carried valises which were full of contraband goods. Often their influential friends even asked the examiner to place their baggage in their car.

"A pat on the shoulder or a small gift was enough," said Don Segundo. "Now they are too strict and want a very big share. The examiners get rich faster than the smuggler who invests capital."

"As long as they accept bribes, that's not too bad," said Doblado. "Those that can't be bribed are harder to deal with."

"Like the *Kampilan* and Senator Maliwanag," Son Tua added.

"But there is no pot without its matching stand," said Bayoneta. "If I'm not mistaken, the *Kampilan's* publisher is a friend of Miss Montero."

"Wa?" Don Segundo was taken aback. "What do you mean, General?"

"Is it wrong for Miss Dolly to use her influence on Mando Plaridel?" asked General Bayoneta.

"Bad, *hijo*, very bad," Son Tua quickly answered. The General remembered that his brother-in-law Architect Pong was courting Montero's daughter. He took back his first suggestion and said that if Mando won't listen to reason, one should try other tactics.

"I still believe that every pot has its match," he repeated and drank his whiskey.

They agreed to push through their operations despite obstacles.

"We're still on the side of those in power," Montero said. "And we should not waste this opportunity."

"The more risk and expense in business," said Son Tua, "the greater the profit."

Go on with the transactions on arms, jewels, and other contraband; increase bribes to the helpers in the government; get more helpers; take the necessary steps against the enemy, the "radicals" in the administration and outside; and prepare for any eventuality. In short, the corporation was prepared to confront those who favored change.

When Doña Julia and Dolly were brought home from the Pines Hotel by Pong, Don Segundo's guests left.

It was very late. From the height where the bungalow stood, they could see the drowsy lights around Burnham Park and smell the fresh air which, like delicious wine, gave energy to the body and soul.

LVIII

The next morning, Don Segundo had finished breakfast and was reading the papers on the terrace. Doña Julia had gone to market in one of their cars. Don Segundo was waiting for Dolly because he wanted to talk to her.

As he read the front page, his mind was on General Bayoneta's suggestion. "Is it wrong for Miss Dolly to use her influence on Mando Plaridel?" Bayoneta had asked. With distaste, Don Segundo had rejected such an idea, but this morning he gave it a second thought. After thinking it over, he asked himself, "What's wrong with it? Why not?"

Dolly was a good friend of Mando Plaridel. Of course, he could not refuse her. Mando's paper had rapidly gained a wide readership because of his policy of truth without fear or favor. An ardent exposure of anomaly, in politics, business, or society, the *Kampilan* kept attacking anti-nationalism, smuggling, graft and corruption, influence peddling, and other dirty deals. One word from Dolly would be like a red light on the speeding *Kampilan*, which would surely run over the corporation of Montero-Son Tua.

Don Segundo was aware that Dolly was no neophyte in using her charms on a man's heart. During the Japanese times, the strict Colonel Moto became putty in her hands. After liberation, she caught the elusive Lieutenant Whitey. In terms of silver, greedy

Don counted his gains from urging Dolly into friendship with the two foreigners. He could not measure the loss for Dolly, who was a hundred times more precious than any material thing. He had no idea that the very room of his daughter in their old house was witness to the Colonel's collection of debts from Dolly in exchange for the favors he gave Montero. He had no idea why Doña Julia and Dolly had a vacation in Hong Kong before she proceeded to Paris to study in Sorbonne. Also unknown to the haughty Montero was the extent of Dolly's intimacy with Mando in Paris.

The father thought his child was still chaste, although mischievous as a butterfly and as elusive as a moonbeam. He thought the playful Dolly was amusing herself with her suitors. He thought Dolly's relationships with the other men were similar to Pong, that Colonel Moto's and Whitey's kisses meant nothing. Kisses were washed away by soap and water. What girl during these times did not kiss her boyfriend?

Moto's and Whitey's days had passed. Don Segundo saw nothing wrong with Mando. He looked honorable. Also, he knew that Dolly could make Pong sit in a corner. So, he thought Mando could hardly say no to Dolly.

Dolly came out on the terrace in fine spirits. Seeing her father, she hooked an arm around his neck. Then after looking at the society pages, she sat down. The maid served breakfast.

"Pa, where's Mama?" Dolly asked.

"She left awhile ago to go to the market."

"Why didn't she take me? I said I'd go along," the girl sulked.

"She didn't want to disturb your sleep," the father said fondly. "Don't you have a date, hija?"

"Pong asked me to a banquet for architects."

"It looks like Pong can't stay away," remarked Don Segundo.

"Here in Baguio, it's convenient for a girl to have a regular escort."

"And how is your publisher friend?"

"Him? Always busy. It's annoying."

"Isn't he coming here?"

"I wouldn't know."

"Why don't you ask him to come up here for a few days?"

"What do you want from him, Papa?" Dolly became curious.

"Nothing. I just want to get to know him better."

"What for?" Dolly insisted.

"Isn't he courting you? It's only natural for a father to want to know the man interested in his only child."

"You've already met him, Papa. Didn't you talk to him at my bienvenida and other gatherings? Before that, I mentioned him in my letters from Paris."

"But I don't know his character, his ways and likes, his..."

"What for? He's not courting you."

"But you are my child."

"Even then, Papa. You're not me. Suppose you find fault with him, but I like him. What then?"

"I would advise you."

"And if I don't listen?"

"You are the queen of your feelings, Dolly. But then, I would have done my duty as a parent. Anyway, you are of age."

"Thanks, Papa." The girl was pleased. "Okay. I'll invite him, but I can't promise he'll accept."

"Can he refuse you?"

"You really don't know that man."

After breakfast, Dolly called Mando long distance. Luckily, he was at the *Kampilan*. This was the first time he'd heard her voice since she angrily left his office.

"How's Baguio?" Mando asked.

"Cold and shivering."

"Isn't that what people go there for?"

"I want to feel heat amidst the cold," the girl answered meaningfully. "If you come, Mando, then I shall find heat amidst the cold."

He gave a low whistle.

"It's really hot in Manila," he answered evasively.

"When will you…find the time to come?"

"Is that an invitation?"

"Why do I even bother calling you?" Dolly whispered. Then she added, "I'm always doing the calling."

"Let's see. There will be a meeting of editors there," said Mando, ignoring her reproach. "Maybe Magat and I will go."

"I know you won't come because of me," Dolly reproached him. "But thank you for coming up here. Maybe when you are here, you'll remember to visit me."

"For sure, Dol."

"Can I count on it?"

"Not only a visit, but…we'll go out and have fun."

Dolly's voice was happy once more. Mando could imagine the girl smiling at the other end of the line.

"Is Magat your only companion?" she asked.

"Who else?"

"Won't you bring your cousin…the barrio maiden?"

"Now, Dolly…"

A restrained laugh resounded on the other end of the line.

LIX

After two days, Mando and Magat arrived at the Pines Hotel. The next few days would be the national meeting of newspaper editors.

The publisher and editor of the *Kampilan*, the fighting Tagalog newspaper, decided to attend to back up their aims. First, their stand on free reporting. Then, respect for the citizens' constitutional rights without fear or favor.

Above all, the *Kampilan* staff agreed to launch the move for the Filipinization of newspapers in the Philippines. They wanted Congress to pass a definite policy on this. Not a few lawmakers agreed with it. Senator Maliwanag had once discussed it in a speech in the Senate.

A newspaper is a powerful tool, shaping the national sentiment through the news, editorials, and other features, pointed out Maliwanag. It was not right that this democratic force should be entrusted to the hands of foreigners. A newspaper is different from any ordinary business which is allowed to non-natives. Rather, a newspaper is a strong influence on the mind and heart of a nation; it can be used, and is actually being used, by a few foreign publishers against the nation itself, especially in political and international issues. This is not only a grave insult but a despicable treachery of a guest against his host. Such anomalies go on unnoticed under the guise of freedom of speech and of the press. These freedoms are provided to the Filipinos by the nation's constitution, but should these also be enjoyed by foreigners who use them to sabotage and betray their host country which has shown them goodwill?

Mando and Magat discussed the pros and cons at length with the *Kampilan* staff before they went to Baguio. They firmly believed in the Filipinization of newspapers, some of which are controlled by foreign capitalists.

On the other hand, high government officials often presented obstacles to free information, opposed easy access to records and official documents, refused to give information especially about scandals, denied accurate news if they were involved as a result of their corrupt ways.

Also, those in power often committed abuses in investigations, searches, arrests, and detentions. Their illegal acts were often accompanied by threats, violence, and brutality—especially in remote areas, where the people were poor and ignorant.

"The newspapers should take a united stand against these evils," said Mando. "I can almost see many editors who will lose their tongues when this resolution is brought up."

"Of course. The more money goes to the publisher, the more he will lick the boots of the mighty. Those who pose as the nation's newspaper fool no one but themselves," added Magat.

"I bet this resolution won't pass," Mando surmised.

"If the Filipinization of retail trade is still pending in Congress, how can this one on journalism be approved by editors of papers owned by foreigners? They are afraid to lose their jobs."

"Have you ever thought, Gat, that the newspapers themselves are strangling a free press?"

Magat agreed. "Look at the biased treatment in some papers of some advertisers who are their gods; news of strikes at large companies, demonstrations, pickets, and the like are cut or not published. As long as it is against the advertiser, or a bad product like harmful medicine, the readers don't learn about it."

"It's no surprise that some newspapers and journalists should lose their prestige," added Mando. "Often the rotten politicians and the crooked newspapers are compared because both get rich suddenly without apparent sources. So, it is the duty of the press to cleanse itself. Some are used to throwing stones while they themselves are wallowing in the mire."

"Let us make the *Kampilan* a model," said Magat. He felt that if he could not cleanse a vast corral, he could keep his own house clean. "We should be honest and courageous."

"Honesty and courage used for good," Mando explained. "Used for crookedness, loyalty is stupidity, and bravery is evil."

Magat was sure that the nation would hear their voice because the *Kampilan's* circulation was growing.

"More than a hundred thousand copies," he said with pride.

"Still too small," Mando said. "I won't be satisfied with less than a million... I'm not kidding. A million copies are not enough for twenty-three million people. Look at the newspaper circulation in Japan, England, the United States, Russia, and Germany."

"As long as the nation is only used to reading news about crime and the comics," Mando went on, "but not about the economy, science, and world events, that nation will not be well-informed. It will remain a victim of propaganda. The reader should know that atomic force is now many thousand times more horrible than the bomb exploded by the Americans in Hiroshima and Nagasaki. They should know about the Cold War and why countries burn wheat and cotton while millions of people in poor countries die of hunger and cold every year. They should understand and join the campaign for peace, for the disarmament of strong nations, for raising the standard of living, eradicating disease, and saving mothers and infants from early death."

"Mando, we need a hundred years for such a campaign to bear fruit," Magat observed. "Besides, we should not deny nor forget that society makes the government and, of course, also the newspapers."

"Right," agreed Mando. "Changes cannot be done in one generation, but in several. True, we shall not enjoy its fruit, but we should support the movement for our children's future."

Mando paused as their car reached a narrow wooden bridge. Then he continued, "In our own time, it's a sin to be indifferent. Have you heard the story of the ignorant old man in China who hewed down two mountains that stood in his path?"

Mando related the story. The old man who was called a fool was blessed by God because of his strong determination.

Mando explained his plan to develop a taste for reading. They would send free copies of their paper to schools, public libraries, clubs, national organizations for language, social and charitable purposes.

"If we send them free copies, yes, we can develop their love for reading, but are we not teaching them the bad habit of not spending for their own good?" Magat objected.

"If they have no money for rice, how can they buy news-papers? Up to now, a newspaper is still a luxury to thousands of poor families."

"The *Kampilan* will be bankrupt."

"The country will benefit," Mando faced Magat before going on. "The *Kampilan* was not established for profit. Besides, the free copies are only temporary."

Both lit cigarettes, each engrossed in their own thoughts. It was soon lunch time.

After lunch, they had time to tour popular places in the Mountain City. They passed by the Mansion House, but did not enter its elegant garden, went up Dominican Hill and tested their legs on the long stairway to the shrine of the Blessed Virgin, proceeded to Camp Allen to see the campus and buildings of the Philippine Military Academy. Before dusk, they alighted before the big marketplace. Mando and Magat were fascinated by the Igorot handicrafts—wooden images, brass implements, and objects made of stone. They bought a few items.

"This is a wonderful city," said Magat, "but it is sad that the beauty, climate, and joys of Baguio belong only to the rich and are denied to the poor."

"What do you want," asked Mando with a smile, "bring Baguio to Central Luzon?"

"I would like the law to help the poor and enable them to spend a few days every year in Baguio. Or Los Baños, Tagaytay, or other resorts," Magat explained.

"I have read it is hard to change the world at once," said Mando. "But we should not shirk the responsibility of working for change."

"That's what we have begun, isn't it? And we found out right away how few we are."

When they returned to the hotel, many editors and reporters from Manila were on the patio, in the lounge, and the dining room. A big group was around the bar.

They joined their colleagues in the usual conversation— about the VIPs in Baguio, which gatherings of professionals, businessmen, and officials were scheduled for summer, and what pompous gatherings of high society were being planned. The two did not hear of any plans to launch the timely Filipinization of mass media, freedom of the press, and respect for the rights of the citizen as provided by the constitution. Or that someone would notice the condition of the Igorots who were deprived of land and driven to remote places at the instigation of some in the name of civilization.

"Just think," Mando pointed out to Magat, "the Igorots are the race that made the rice terraces, which are considered one of the world's wonders. The pharaohs used millions of slaves to build the pyramids, which symbolize their pride. But the Igorots built the rice terraces for their food. They are truly admirable."

Before getting dressed, Mando phoned Dolly.

"Have dinner here," the girl urged him.

"Alone?" asked Mando.

"I want to see you."

"Really?"

"And I want to be alone with you," Dolly answered.

Dolly was worried about her relationship with Mando. Until now, the lovely Montero heiress could not tell if the *Kampilan* publisher was her sweetheart, her fiancé, or just a boyfriend. Because they had no definite agreement, and she could not blame him for it because he had always been elusive about such commitments.

But now Dolly longed for Mando and was anxious to be clear on their relationship. Time was passing her by, and many matrons were younger than her.

Dolly realized that their affair in Paris was mostly due to her. First, because of her extreme annoyance with the foreigners who hovered around her, especially upon learning that she was the only child of a millionaire. Second, because of her eagerness to have the exceptional Filipino bachelor who was the object of glances and sighs of the white women in the famous city. In Manila, it was common for society girls to boast of escorts with aquiline noses and cat's eyes. But in Paris, Dolly saw that a man was not judged by the color of his skin, but by his manliness and personality. No Westerner could surpass Mando in the eyes of the hard-to-please Manila girl.

Now that they were both in Baguio, Dolly expected to feel Mando's love and ardor. She looked forward to stolen moments of happiness, a mere sip of one dying of thirst for love.

In the face of the uncertain attention of the man she loved, she would be obliged to accept Pong. She didn't care for Pong and often brusquely answered the coaxing of Doña Julia. She said she would rather be an old maid than take the Chinese mestizo seriously. But she said this only because there was Mando Plaridel. Actually, Pong was not bad-looking, and was educated, a favorite of the Bachelors' Club, distinguished in his profession, the son of the millionaire partner of her father. Pong was also wealthy in his own right.

"Let fate decide," Dolly told herself, thinking of Mando's coldness.

She thought of all their circle, men and women, who got married without love. Name, money, ease, and other factors were considered more important than love.

Fickle by nature and without firm convictions, Dolly was tired of such depressing thoughts. What she planned was not because she didn't love Mando, nor did she care for Pong. Rather, it was her hurt pride for which she sought a remedy, a revenge in which she would be the first to get hurt. She would see how her talk with Mando would turn out tonight.

On the other hand, Don Segundo looked forward to a serious talk with the publisher. He wanted to come to an understanding with Mando whom he heard to be a man of principle and a radical. Don Segundo could not understand how a man with such opportunities could be a radical. The landlord was afraid that neither his money nor Dolly's beauty could change his mind. He felt that he and Mando were worlds apart and could not be reconciled. Mando would not shy away from issues contrary to Montero's interests; Montero and his colleagues were not prepared to change or retreat.

It would be good enough, Don Segundo thought, if he and Mando could agree to disagree.

Like Dolly, he was eager to meet Mando at dinner tonight.

LX

From the window in his room at Pines Hotel, Mando looked at the famed zigzag road, which was coated with silver moonlight. He could see the seemingly endless intestine-shaped and horseshoe road at the height of five thousand feet, starting to weaken and lie prostrate at the foot of Benguet. At first glance, this wonderful road, a creation of modern engineering, was like a giant snake coiled on the breast of the mountain with its head hanging over the mouth of the ravine. Mando recalled stories he had read as a child. Such paths, caves, and hills were supposed to be crossed by a knight-errant before he could reach the castle of a beautiful princess on top of a mountain.

Mando smiled to think that he had only to take a car below at the hotel. In a few minutes he would reach the house of the girl waiting for him. The doors of her home and of her heart would be open. So after fixing his tie and putting on a woolen suit, Mando went down with zest. He talked a while to Magat in the lounge and said he would not be back for supper.

"A night in Paris," Magat kidded him on learning that Dolly had invited his friend.

Mando left without commenting on the insinuation. He was thinking of other things.

Dolly greeted Mando at the door of their beautiful bungalow.

She pressed his arm.

"I'm glad you had time tonight."

"I had to come and see you."

"So you have not completely forgotten about me."

"We have had no quarrel, Dol."

The girl led Mando to the living room. Don Segundo was seated in an easy chair.

"Papa, Mando is here," said Dolly.

The old man stood up and shook hands with the guest. Doña Julia came in and also shook hands with the publisher.

"When did you arrive?" asked Don Segundo when they were seated.

"At noon, sir."

"Will you be staying long?"

"The newspaper editors will meet for two days starting tomorrow. Today's Friday, so I shall leave Monday morning."

"You seem to be in a hurry."

"It's hard to stay away from Manila for too long," explained Mando. "The new press is being installed. Soon we shall inaugurate a radio station."

"Oh…"

"I hope you and your family will come."

"Let me know and I'll attend."

Doña Julia announced that supper was ready. They all went to the dining room. There was no other guest.

"It seems to be very quiet here," Mando observed.

"Not really," answered Doña Julia. "Pong Tua-son often comes," she added, throwing a glance at Dolly. "The other night, the Governor and the General were here. Also Senator Botin. Dolly here keeps receiving invitations."

"I often decline, because it's tiring. I came here for a vacation, didn't I, Papa?"

"But Baguio is not a place for rest," Don Segundo corrected her. "During summer, it replaces Manila. Here are the government, business, and society. How can you rest?"

"In fact, expenses in Baguio are double," Doña Julia remarked.

"Of course, because everyone is here," said her husband. "The capacity of public services is limited. They are meant for a small group of special guests, but now, who does not come for a vacation in Baguio? Imagine! One day Burnham Park was filled with buses of excursionists—salesmen and salesgirls of Chinese bazaars in Manila. Each had his bundle of food, too. So, after lunch, the food wrappings of leaves and envelopes were scattered everywhere. I don't know why people who do nothing but throw garbage are allowed here. They bring along their bad manners."

Doña Julia sneered.

Mando made no comment on Doña Julia's haughty complaints or on Don Segundo's belittling the lowly employees who had come to see Baguio. He did not remind them that the government had spent the people's money on the city of the pines, and no one had the right to consider it their private preserve. Mando was used to the ways of the Monteros. Once more he saw that the glitter of gold and diamonds could not cover up their ugly behavior, but made them even prouder. Mando wondered how they would react should they know who he was. Would they insult him as Andoy the houseboy or would they fear him as Mando Plaridel? He thought this might be a good opportunity to find out.

After supper, they returned to the living room. Don Segundo removed a wrapper from a Corona cigar. Mando and Dolly lit cigarettes. Doña Julia stayed behind to give instructions to servants. Then Dolly went to her room.

"I read in your newspaper about the incident in my hacienda," Montero began, when he and Mando were alone.

"The news in the *Kampilan* is a result of our investigation," Mando answered.

"Often that result is according to the intention of the one investigating, isn't it?"

"Our only interest in the issue, sir, is to print the truth. We have no side but this."

"Has it ever occurred to you, Mr. Plaridel, that the truth has many shapes, that reason has two or more sides? What can have complete certainty?"

"What you say is true, in many cases," Mando said. "But regarding the happenings at the hacienda, some facts can't be denied. First, the fire was not caused by the accused. Second, the arrest and detention were urged by vicious revenge. Third, under your management and your overseer, peace is impossible in your hacienda."

Don Segundo lighted his cigar again. Then he said calmly, "You judge hastily. Do I have any arrangement that is not followed by other landlords? Whether for tenants or sharecroppers, I ask nothing except what the law provides. If the law is bad, change it first, but I won't be the first to change. I invested money. Is it wrong to profit from my capital?"

"No one says that," Mando replied. "But if you know that the law is biased, a law signed and made by the powerful, why don't you take the initiative to improve the lot of your tenants? They are always in want, while you..."

"My wealth didn't come from them. Since the war, I have been losing money on the hacienda. The farmers are hard up because of their stupidity. They are a swarm of stupid people. They prefer to loaf rather than work, and what they should save, they throw away on vices."

The landlord puffed his cigar and after inhaling the gray smoke, he added.

"Perhaps you don't know the ways of the farmers. What do they do during the months between planting and harvesting? What do they do with their share of the harvest? What should be spent in a year is gone in a month. Don't blame the landlord if the tenants who don't know any better should live from hand to mouth, instead of having plenty of rice, chicken, eggs, and vegetables. The way I see it, they are their own enemies."

Mando let Don Segundo recite the farmer's weaknesses, because he knew they were true, but not for all. Many tried their best and worked day and night to support their families, but they could not make both ends meet despite their efforts. Mando felt that arguing with Montero would only end in unpleasantness.

"Granting your reasons, Don Segundo, one fact will surface: that the haciendero and the tenants are like oil and water. Because of the fire and the arrest of their leaders, the bridge of real understanding was also burned. I believe that you are now losing money. It is also true that your tenants are dissatisfied. But the land is extensive and it's a waste to have them lie idle. The land will remain even if you are no longer the owner and even if it is tilled by other hands. There is a corporation that is ready to buy your hacienda, Don Segundo."

"Not a few have made offers. The government itself… The Chinese multimillionaire Son Tua. To get rid of my headache, I have thought of giving up that hacienda. If those who wish to buy are ready to pay my price."

"If it is reasonable…"

"A reasonable price is the market price. The land will not grow stale nor rot."

"Perhaps Professor Sabio had talked to you in the name of Freedom University which will manage the hacienda if he buys it."

"Yes, we have talked about it," Don Segundo replied. "He mentioned his plans for the university, the planned research and experiments and the supposed advantages to the students and the farmers. But his offer was low. So my answer was like that of the Archbishop to some Catholics who were working on a transaction: 'I am happy that you are Catholics, good Catholics, I hope,' said the Archbishop. 'But in this transaction, religion is out. This is business, and as the American saying goes—business is business.' That was the end of the discussion."

"You are a good businessman, and it's not for me to advise you that it is better to sell and convert into cash a land that is causing you losses."

"That's true, I guess. But some losses become gains."

"How can that be, sir?" The publisher was amazed

Don Segundo saw his chance and followed with a barb.

"For example, your newspaper. You can't deny that the *Kampilan* is losing a lot. But you continue to print and finance it."

"But the newspaper is not a business, but a service," objected Mando.

"Don't fool yourselves."

"Don Segundo, I'm sure the *Kampilan* is not a business."

"If you insist, I won't argue," the Don conceded. Then he added, "Your newspaper is unusual."

"What is your basis for comparing the *Kampilan* and Hacienda Montero?"

"I invested in Hacienda Montero to help produce food for the nation," Don Segundo said steadily. "You invested capital in the *Kampilan* to offer services, as you see it. Is that not so?"

"In a way…"

"So your paper is a harsh critic of the incidents at the hacienda."

"A critic of anomalies," Mando corrected. "Of graft and corruption, smuggling, cheating…"

"Very well," the haciendero cut him short. "You fan blind nationalism, radicalism, goading the poor against the rich."

"Mr. Montero." Mando was put on the defensive.

"Your friends want to buy my hacienda," Don Segundo went back to their topic. "I have a proposition for you."

"I am listening, sir."

"If someone wants to buy the *Kampilan* at a good price, will you sell it?"

"Certainly not."

"Would you agree to an exchange?"

"With what?"

"My hacienda for your newspaper." the landlord said each word emphatically.

Mando stood up, surprised, but he quickly saw that the foxy Don was only baiting him and did not mean to make good his offer.

"And what would you do with the newspaper?"

"A newspaper is a powerful weapon in anyone's hands." Montero's smile was sour.

"Oh, you will reverse the policy of the *Kampilan* if you own it." Mando's face was flushed with anger.

"A newspaper is a property like any other," Montero declared.

"Not the *Kampilan*." Mando stood up, disgusted. "Never."

When the discussion was getting heated, Dolly entered, followed by a servant carrying a tray with a coffee pot, sugar, cream, and cups.

Dolly poured coffee and served her Papa and her boyfriend. The coffee aroma was overcome by the perfume of the enticing Miss Montero. Mando recalled their happy nights in Paris.

Dolly reminded Don Segundo.

"Papa, it's past ten. You should rest. Besides, I didn't invite Mando to debate with you the whole night."

Then Dolly left after whispering to Mando that she would watch the moonlight from the terrace.

The old man was obliged to stand.

"Mr. Plaridel, I feel I have come to know you."

"That's good, sir, but you could be mistaken."

"I have learned that we don't have the same beliefs," he said with a hint of reproach.

"Perhaps so, sir."

"And you don't wish to come to terms with me."

"Even if I wished for it, that would be hard."

"Even if you are interested in my child?"

Mando was taken aback, like an actor when someone deviates from the script. Nevertheless, he spoke calmly.

"It seems, sir, that there's no connection."

"Really? ...And why not?"

It was the right moment. It could no longer be avoided, Mando told himself. He faced Segundo Montero.

"Because, if you should know who I am, either you would curse me or you would curse yourself."

It was now Don Segundo who was taken by surprise. He moved back a few steps. It seemed to him that Mando Plaridel had changed appearance.

"Who are you?"

"Don't you remember me?"

"Who are you?" repeated the landlord.

"Then you will know it a few hours before I leave Baguio."

Segundo Montero controlled himself. He was filled with fear and anger on hearing the mixed reproach and threat of Mando Plaridel. He stared at the young man, the ugly scar on his left cheek, his dark glasses, his body that seemed to possess unusual strength. As when he first saw this man, Don Segundo once more searched his memory. Who was this mysterious man who was suddenly thrust in his path?

He left the room without saying goodbye, as if he were fleeing from an evil spirit. Mando was left standing beside a table.

Then he went to the terrace. He was met by a strong breeze, which wafted the perfume of the girl waiting for him. Dolly went to him and clung to his arm. The moon was bright and the myriad of stars were diamonds twinkling in the sky that hovered above. Some stars were like lights hanging from the branches of the tall pine trees on the hills. Mando expected that his conversation with Montero's daughter would not be different from his talk with Don Segundo.

"Did you have a quarrel with Papa?" she asked.

"We never got along well. *Never.*" Mando's harsh words decreased the coldness. Dolly could not imagine what he meant by "never."

"Mando!" The girl was puzzled.

"Dolly, perhaps, after tonight, you will not wish to see me again."

The girl was even more astounded.

"Mando, what's wrong?" She guessed that her boyfriend had quarreled with her father.

"I shall repeat what I told your father—that if you knew me, you would either curse me or curse yourself."

"Who are you?"

Mando removed his dark glasses and covered the scar on his left cheek with three fingers. Dolly stared at him but could not remember. She took two steps nearer and looked closely. She removed the hand covering the scar and her wide eyes almost touched that face which she had kissed a thousand times, the face which had pressed against her breast and lay in her lap, the face which in the midst of happiness she would not let go of, as if it were a dream that might suddenly vanish. Then she moved back and asked, filled with anguish.

"Who are you?" Dolly insisted.

Mando put on his glasses and held Dolly by the shoulder.

"Have you forgotten your servant, your slave, before the war? The wretch who was often hit by your father and mother, the one you often insulted and rapped on the head, the one who, in your desire to please the Japs, was betrayed to the Kempeitai? Don't you remember…?"

Dolly seemed rooted to the spot, then…

"Andoy!" Dolly exclaimed, ashamed and afraid. It was as if she faced a ghost.

"Yes, Andoy."

"You…traitor! Cheat!" Dolly was overcome by great shame, frustration, and remorse that she had entrusted her honor, and all—

everything—not to the exceptional Mando, but to the wretched and lowly servant Andoy, the peasant, the vagabond. She could never forgive herself. She would never forgive this snake that had fooled her completely. Curse of hell!

Then she covered her face with her hands and wailed. When Mando moved towards her, she turned and like a fierce lioness, she screamed:

"Leave me alone. I don't want to see your shadow. Traitor! Slave!"

It was not the lowly Andoy who left quietly but the honorable Mando Plaridel. For a long while, Dolly remained in her pathetic position, unmindful that the moon had descended and the cold was like needle pricks.

LXI

The nation was horrified by the atrocities that took place at the hacienda and the adjoining barrio. When the public read the news and saw the pictures in the *Kampilan*, it became the talk everywhere. Senator Maliwanag delivered a resounding speech in the Senate, suggesting an immediate investigation of the renewed terrorism in the farmlands. Rubio called for a resolution of protest supported by an army of laborers in the city.

Meanwhile, Dr. Sabio and some lawyers pushed through the court battle. They asked for the release of Pastor and the others detained in the MP headquarters.

On the other hand, Pastor and his group were charged by the MP with arson, possession of deadly weapons, and conspiring in a rebellion. They fabricated evidence to justify the farmers' detention.

Nevertheless, at the first court hearings, the farmers were granted bail. The court declared that they had cause to sue those who had illegally detained them.

Captain Pugot was charged with the slaying of Mang Tumas and another farmer. But what justice could the old man hope for, now that he was in his coffin?

Mang Tumas was not buried at once. The farmers had his remains embalmed and laid him at the union house in the barrio.

They felt it best to wait for Pastor and the other detainees. They wanted to render proper homage to Mang Tumas, a martyr to the farmers' cause.

What Mang Tumas used to say came true. Whenever he talked of the poverty of an oppressed worker, he would ask, "Who among you, if you should die of hunger, could afford a mass and a coffin?" He proved it with his death.

But Mang Tumas' poverty didn't deprive him of an expensive coffin. Day and night, the union house was full of people attending the wake. There was a continuous supply of food.

Despite the rumors that Mando was answering for all funeral expenses, the farmers wanted to do their bit. They took up a collection. Those who had no cash contributed rice, viands, drinks. Many volunteered for any chore.

His relatives wailed when they first saw the face of the dead man, but an old man calmed them down.

"We should not weep over the death of Tumas," he said. "He died with honor. He seems to be asleep."

Others said he had never looked more serene. His thin silver hair was combed back; his lips and cheeks were pinkish from the slight rouge used by the embalmer. In his becoming attire, he seemed to have dozed off after speaking at a meeting. He wore a white barong-Tagalog, white pants, black socks. The old man said he had known Tumas since childhood, but he couldn't remember seeing him in socks. His socks were the mud from the fields.

Two tenants noticed that Tumas' clasped hands held the small cross of a rosary, which was like a small chain tying his hands. It was placed by a female cousin of Tumas with whom he had never gotten along.

Among the wreaths, which were already starting to wither at the foot of the coffin, stood out the names of Pastor and Puri and of Mando. The two wreaths had been sent from Manila.

"Tumas is fortunate; he is at peace," said an elderly woman.

"My husband is still detained with Pastor," complained another, but her face showed relief because her husband was still alive.

"We shall all die," the old man said. "What matters is how we live. Tumas led a noble life. In death, his is nobler than Segundo Montero who has not started to pay for his many debts."

Unlike in the usual wake, there was no cheerful sound of a ukulele or guitar and of gambling, no teenagers drinking and quarrelling.

There were various groups quietly talking, no loud laughter nor improper behavior. They talked of the life and deeds of the dead man, his beliefs and principles, his courage and loyalty to the farmers' cause. They exchanged views on the nationalist movement, the rising prices and widespread unemployment, the filth of party politics and political opportunists, the exploiters among government bigwigs and their many schemes.

"We are also to blame," declared one. "In a democracy, the majority should be followed. The poor are the majority, but we aren't followed. We tolerate what's happening. Whom should we blame?"

"The leaders are at fault," another protested.

"Who chose the leaders?"

"Many leaders rise to power through money, threats, cheating."

"Truly, we never learn our lesson."

"But if you oppose them, you end up like Mang Tumas or Pastor."

"Sometimes, the dead are better off."

"I prefer to be alive," remarked a woman. "You manage to eat, somehow. When you're dead, you're eaten up by worms."

It was a day before the funeral when Pastor and Puri arrived at the barrio. The detainees had been freed by a court order. Pastor had fetched Puri at the dormitory and brought her home in a car Mando provided. Mando had planned to attend the funeral, but he had to attend an editors' conference that Saturday. Nevertheless, he had paid for all the expenses and asked Andres to take his place.

Mang Tumas was brought to his resting place by a long and solemn procession. The farmers' union took charge. As ordered by Governor Doblado, the MPs and civilian guards did not interfere nor watch. The Governor, the Commander, and Captain Pugot had all left. It was learned that they went up to Baguio.

The funeral procession was more than a mile long. The mourners were farmers, laborers, common folks not only from the hacienda and the barrios, but also from the towns and Manila. Senator Maliwanag, Rubio, and Danoy came. Andres came with Pastor and Puri.

Before the funeral, Danoy clung to the coffin of Mang Tumas for a long time. He did not shed tears but in the veins of his clenched fists flowed boiling lead instead of blood. Danoy was closest to Mang Tumas and was trained by the old man to be a leader of the farmers.

Danoy was sure Captain Pugot was behind the slaying of Mang Tumas. Pastor had related to him the mysterious disappearance of Mang Tumas from their room after Pastor's third degree treatment in the secret cell.

"I wonder why they killed Mang Tumas instead of me," Pastor grieved.

"If I had not stayed behind, for sure you would also be burying me," said Danoy.

Both were sure of the dark days to come, as long as the problems of the hacienda were unsolved and the civilian guards stayed.

"Will you return to Manila after the funeral?" Danoy asked.

"That is the advice of Mando and Dr. Sabio. They want Puri to stay at the dormitory and to study domestic science at the university. You, what are your plans?"

"I shall not be far from here, but the enemy shall not get me. We cannot abandon the tenants and the barrio people."

"Danoy, my staying in Manila for a while does not mean I'm neglecting them. Only…"

"I know, Tata Pastor, I know…"

Some touching eulogies were delivered at the grave of Mang Tumas. Danoy, Rubio, Andres, and Senator Maliwanag spoke. They compared the life and martyrdom of Mang Tumas to a fertile seed from which would sprout a luxuriant, healthy plant that would bear delicious fruit for the orphaned comrades in due time.

Senator Maliwanag vowed that he would strive to realize the ardent wish of the slain leader, to transfer the ownership of the hacienda to the present tenants or to a corporation that would practice real social justice. The Senator could not make the promise in the name of the administration.

It was dusk when the people left. Senator Maliwanag rode in his car together with Rubio. Andres led Puri to their car, which was parked on the narrow road.

But Pastor and Danoy remained standing beside Mang Tumas' grave, speaking quietly.

"They have killed Mang Tumas, but his beliefs will spread," Pastor repeated. "It is our duty…"

"It's not enough to spread his teachings," Danoy disagreed. "The criminals who killed him must pay."

"As soon as possible."

"I shall not rest, I swear… Even alone."

"Then you shall not be alone," Pastor answered fervently. "Many oppressed people will join you… Let's go."

Pastor walked towards the waiting car. He looked back and watched Danoy moving away until his shadow was completely lost in the dark that shrouded the whole graveyard.

LXII

The soil had hardly settled on Mang Tumas' grave when blood flowed once more at the border of the hacienda. Two of Captain Pugot's civilian guards, noted for their ferocity, were ambushed one night on the wild path between the hacienda and the next barrio. The unknown assailants disappeared.

Someone who answered the cry for help found the two guards with deep bolo wounds in their necks. They were dead on arrival at the town hospital. The investigators got few clues, inasmuch as the victims could hardly talk.

Nevertheless, they said there were six to seven men who stopped them. Upon learning that they were civilian guards, the men raised their arms. The chief told them to repent their sins.

One of the assailants suggested they shoot the civilian guards with their own rifles, but the leader decided to save on bullets.

"Just cut off the heads of the beasts," was his harsh command.

"Let the dogs tear their bodies apart," added another.

After hearing the snatches of stories from the two civilian guards, the investigators asked a few questions.

"Was Pastor the leader?"

"His face was covered."

"Was it Danoy?"

The dying guards could not tell, but they could identify them if they should see them. But they died on the way to the hospital.

The next day, an uneasy silence reigned over the whole hacienda and the adjoining barrios. No group gatherings, no discussions, only a few walked on the streets.

Civilian guards patrolled in threes, with an MP sergeant or a private. They went from house to house asking the residents to come out.

New checkpoints were added between the hacienda and the barrios. Guards were added to the entrance to the hacienda from the provincial road. All the guards carried rifles and steel helmets as if for a real battle.

All the farmers and townspeople were questioned by the civilian guards and the soldiers. They were asked if they had seen Pastor or Danoy within the last twenty-four hours. Each one said, "No." Some said they had seen Pastor and Danoy at Mang Tumas' funeral Sunday afternoon. That was the last time the two were seen. They probably went to Manila after the funeral. Pastor and Puri were in the *Kampilan's* car. Rubio rode with Senator Maliwanag.

During the interrogation, the barrio became a locked chest. They had seen nothing, heard nothing, knew nothing. Yes, sir, they were ready to cooperate with the authorities. Yes, sir, they would help catch the criminals. Yes, they would report any news to the law enforcers. That was all.

Captain Pugot returned from Baguio and could be seen in his jeep going back and forth between the hacienda and the barrio. His jeep was full of his men and was always speeding.

Curfew was imposed throughout the troubled area. From eight o'clock, no one could go out without a pass. Lights out by nine o'clock. Nothing disturbed the silence and the darkness but the sound of the boots of the civilian guards patrolling in groups.

Captain Pugot's suspicion was right. His two men were slain not by the tenants of the hacienda nor by farmers in the barrios.

Nor did he suspect the farmers he had detained except Pastor and Danoy.

This was the work of the outlaws, Captain Pugot told himself. His eyes flashed and he gritted his teeth as if grinding the bones of a skeleton.

After the war, many guerrillas did not return to the towns. They stayed away for various reasons. Some were not willing to return to pre-war conditions; some were evading punishment for crimes; some decided that they were better suited to the free life in the forest, with no masters but themselves and not bound by laws made by those in power for the good of a few, to the detriment of many.

Sometimes, the outlaws came to the town when they needed something. They had some alliance with the radical farmers who supported them in return for protection. This started during the Japanese times and continued after the war. That was why the farmers had the nerve to defy the landlords and government officials. They had the support of the tough ones in the forest.

Captain Pugot had no doubt that the killing of the two civilian guards was connected with the death of Mang Tumas. The two incidents were linked. The ones who slew Mang Tumas were his men; they were the ones who'd been made to pay. The captain was enraged. He was positive that either Pastor or Danoy and their associates were behind the latest killing. Without a doubt, they had given the word and goaded the others to avenge the luckless Mang Tumas.

"The devils are asking for trouble!" Captain Pugot exclaimed when the next day they brought no arrests nor a definite report from the investigators. The MP report was also vague.

"Why didn't you arrest anyone?" Captain Pugot snarled at the head of the civilian guards. "He will confess when he is ripe with bruises."

The sergeant reminded him of the court order to release the detained farmers. Besides, those who detained them were warned.

Captain Pugot and his men were charged with the willful killing of Mang Tumas despite their report that the old man was trying to escape.

"You're a bunch of cowards!" Captain Pugot shouted at the sergeant. "You are easily scared. Two of your companions were beheaded, and you have not avenged them. What runs in your veins? Coca-Cola?"

That night the barrio people retired early. They had supper before dusk so they would not need a light. They avoided their practice of relaxing downstairs after meals and exchanging views about the day's events. They were thinking of the curfew and knew the consequences of breaking it, even unintentionally. They had no wish to give an excuse for the enforcers to make them pay dearly. So they spread their mats early and tried to sleep, acting as if they had heard ghost stories.

It was midnight when the barrio was startled by continuous shots. Shouts, curses, groans, and weeping answered the snarls of the bullets. Some nipa huts burst into flames. Some fleeing shadows suddenly stopped, staggered, and were swallowed by darkness.

The confusion lasted for hours. It was almost morning when quiet reigned. The sun shone on the corpses of men, women, and children and the ashes of houses burned to the ground. Many wounded could not walk. Instead of being given first aid, they were arrested by the soldiers and civilian guards.

The civilian guards were the first to report what happened the previous night. They claimed that a group of armed bandits attacked but were repulsed by law enforcers and suffered many casualties. In the crossfire, some citizens were killed.

But some farmers who had stayed awake saw what happened. No outlaws raided the barrio. There was no encounter at all. The shots came only from one side—the civilian guards and their soldier accomplices. It was a deliberate killing of the farmers who were asleep, unarmed, and defenseless.

And the farmers knew who plotted this despicable atrocity.

This was Captain Pugot's vengeance for the death of two of his men. He did not take it out on the outlaws but on the poor families of the innocent farmers.

"That is the answer to the bandits' challenge," Pugot told himself. "A lash at the carabao, a welt on the horse." Some guards were startled by his loud guffaw.

LXIII

On their trip back to Manila from Baguio, Mando told Magat to implement his plan to send free copies of the *Kampilan* to institutions and national organizations. Mando learned from the circulation office that they might have to double the number of copies. It was a sure loss and quixoticism, according to Magat. Mando insisted that, being a real service to the nation, it could not be a loss.

However, Mando was aware that it was not the volume of the newspapers that was important but the contents—news, pictures, columns, and public opinion. Many reading materials were being circulated by different movements, full of propaganda, obviously in favor of their vested interests. These materials often reported the reverse of facts.

The *Kampilan* was full of features that could not be seen in popular commercial newspapers. Their only concern was the truth.

After the editors' conference in Baguio, the *Kampilan* became bolder and more militant. It vigorously attacked the abuses, graft, exploitation, greed and pride, oppression and callousness of the very people who should be the role models because of their high position in the government, in industry, and in society.

The *Kampilan* unmasked the officials on the blacklist, publishing their names. Big names.

It published a long "White Paper," which listed these names along with the means by which they enriched themselves overnight.

It pointed to the sharks, the crocodiles, and other monsters inside and outside the government. It proclaimed that if the county should prosper, these despicable hordes should be put behind bars.

Naturally, the articles resulted in a furor, anonymous letters, and threats. Many hired lawyers who dug for possible charges that could be filed against the *Kampilan*, its publisher, and its editor.

"Don't go out without bodyguards," Senator Maliwanag jokingly warned Mando as they had snacks one afternoon.

Mando merely shrugged his shoulders, saying that although he didn't wish to die, he could not do his work if he was afraid.

Then the Kampilan followed up with an exposé of the abuses in agricultural lands and demanded the punishment of the leaders in the slaying of the farmers. It published news of the actual incidents, contradicting the reports of the MP and the civilian guards. The paper explained why the farmers remained poor. They were always the victims of unjust systems—usury and a meager share of the fruit of their toil. It also pointed out why there could be no peace on the hacienda under the present owner, who clung to old and unjust law. Finally, it suggested remedies: sell these fields to be converted into cooperatives managed by the administration or by a corporation, with safeguards for implementing social justice.

The newspaper also featured the declaration of the farmers' union, which included the signatures of Pastor and Danoy. The landowner and the law enforcers were blamed for the latest incident in the hacienda.

What is the farmers' union? After the last war, the tillers of the soil united. They had to, because otherwise they would remain weak and oppressed. They formed their union according to law. Their activities on behalf of the workers were open and legal.

We challenge those who are sworn enemies of the poor people to prove that we are the enemies of peace and order. The charge that we are communists worshipping a foreign ideology is an old tune that dates back to Christ. Was not the Nazareth teacher hit with mud by the scribes and pharisees and called a rabble-rouser, a fake, a violator of the laws of the temple and of Rome, a destroyer of peace and order? Jesus, meek as a lamb, was sentenced by Pilate and nailed to the cross between two outlaws, whereas the murderer Barabas was freed.

The false gods of politics and business know that we cannot be threatened nor bought. We are free Filipino citizens, unafraid to present our ideas and convictions on different national issues. This country was continuously enslaved for four centuries by foreigners, but we are descendants of Filipinos who strove to be free of bondage. In our veins flows the blood of Lapulapu, Rajah Soliman, Dagohoy, Diego Silang, Burgos, Gomez and Zamora, Rizal, Bonifacio, del Pilar, Luna, Jacinto, Jose Abad Santos, Crisanto Evangelista, and others who preferred prison, death, or exile to a life of ease in the cage of the master.

We are always behind the independence movement. We want our Constitution to be amended so that our Republic shall have complete independence and erase the ugly marks of our former colonialism. We are against wasting lives of Filipino soldiers in other lands to keep foreign dictators on the throne in the name of democracy. We are against raising and adding new taxes while worsening unemployment and the black market exist. We are for a living wage for our workers in the field and in the factory. We are not against cooperation between labor and capital in a just manner, but not like the cooperation between the rig driver and his horse.

We possess the spirit of sacrifice and courage, because we believe that we have on our side the na-

tion, justice, and God. They should be on our side. A wise man said that one may hold back the waves of the ocean, but not justice for the common man.

The union of labor under one confederation, one society, and someday, under a real political party, is part of the inevitable spread of the brotherhood of those with a common fate. It should be encouraged and supported. It is better that the poor use the ballot rather than the bullet. But it is sad that in the eyes of a blind administration, this is a crime.

Those in power often declare that the people should be loyal and serve the government. These people forget themselves. They think we have a dictatorship or a monarchy and not a democracy. In a real democracy, one does not have to ask who has the first duty to be loyal—the people or the government. If the latter is true, as it is undoubtedly, how little is the disobedience of a citizen to the administration compared to the treachery of a whole administration against the whole country and people!

Our sacrifices are only an example of the untold sacrifices of the many. Thousands, millions, all over the country, farmers like us, laborers, employees, soldiers, ordinary citizens, the old, women, and children live in misery and want. Those pitiful ones live in an unending night, without a tomorrow, orphaned even inside a dazzling, noisy city; they are hungry in a land of plenty; they are thirsty while surrounded by water; they are the victims of misery caused by men and a government duty-bound to promote their welfare.

If our voices are heard now, it's because we are part of the oppressed many, imprisoned, abused, and always persecuted, not because we are criminals or enemies, but loyal Filipinos, defending our four freedoms, which we wish for the majority. For this noble principle and vow, we are ready to suffer more if necessary. And the tears, sorrows, and poverty of our lives

*will not weaken our resolve but will add courage and
fervor to continue, head up, until bright times smile
upon us, when our motherland will be truly free and
prosperous—freedom and prosperity for the Filipino
people now and in the next generations.*

The *Kampilan* was praised in gatherings of the common
people, but not in the higher councils.

"This is sedition; it urges rebellion! That Mando Plaridel is
a dangerous man," said an influence peddler.

"He is digging his own grave," answered a stout politician.

LXIV

The new moon rose early, like a golden bow across a gray violin. The night was bright, the diamonds glittering in the thick hair of the sky.

Mando was leisurely driving his car. The wheels of the car were slow compared to the beating of his heart. Mando was visiting Puri at the girls' dormitory of Freedom University. He had called ahead, so Puri was waiting.

They had not seen each other for more than a week. Only two or three times since Puri rushed to Manila until Mando went to Baguio. They had talked on the phone, but only for a short while. Both were eager for their meeting that night.

Puri stood up when Mando appeared at the door of the visitors' hall on the ground floor of the dormitory. She wore a white dress with blue bias trimmings on the neckline, sleeves, and hem.

Mando's eyes showed his surprise and admiration.

"I came to see a barrio maiden, but I am met by a coed."

Embarrassed, Puri hastened her steps as she led Mando to their seats.

The hall was wide. Some girls were with their guests talking quietly and laughing once in a while.

"I think you are getting along well here," Mando remarked when he and Puri were seated.

"What makes you say that?"

"It shows. You seem healthier and even lovelier."

"Can my appearance still change? I still look like a barrio girl even if I'm dressed like a coed."

"You are more beautiful than all of them."

"Oh, no. You're too kind."

Mando was not flattering her. There were many young girls at Freedom University from different provinces; many were really pretty. But surely none could surpass the innate beauty of the girl from the barrio adjoining Hacienda Montero.

When Mando and Magat first saw Puri a few years ago, Magat remarked that she was a rare orchid hidden among the leaves of a forest vine. Mando said she was like a pure pearl whose whiteness was enhanced because it had been kept in Simoun's jewel chest, watched over by the waves at the bottom of the sea.

Puri's dreamy eyes met Mando's gaze and her dimples appeared on her light olive cheeks as she smiled sweetly.

"Any news?" she asked.

Mando didn't answer at once, but continued to feast his starving eyes on her loveliness. He remembered Dolly, who was like sparkling champagne in an amber cup, tempting one to drink it in one gulp. Puri's beauty was different; it was enticing and enchanting in its purity and modesty, not intoxicating nor satiating; rather her beauty grew on the beholder. The few years that passed were like a dab of powder that gave her greater allure and sweetness.

"What's new?" again Puri asked her guest, who was staring at her.

Mando appeared to hear her for the first time. Slightly embarrassed, he laughed softly. He referred jokingly to Ulysses who asked to be tied to the post of a ship as he sailed near the island of the sirens. Then he told her the latest happenings not yet related by her father or Dr. Sabio.

"After the massacre of the farmers, the situation at the hacienda worsened," Mando said. "This is not the end. Officials like the governor and some MP officials are washing their hands of it. It's hard to expect justice. The President should step in to prevent more bloodshed."

"Tatang wants to return to the barrio," Puri said anxiously.

"I told him not to," Mando said. "He said he could not let down his companions and Danoy. I told him it would be suicide. He and Danoy are wanted at the hacienda. The civilian guards won't go easy on them."

"I asked him to stay," said Puri. "But if he insists, I shall go with him."

"You too."

"Why should I hide here?"

"This is your place now," Mando said emphatically. "You are not hiding, but waiting for the storm to pass. In times like these, the hacienda and the barrio are not for a beautiful girl, the daughter of Pastor at that. Dr. Sabio and I want you to stay. We are not mere observers in this fight. We are involved and we are with you in the fight against evil. And Puri, you are precious to us. I need you. When peace is restored, I want...to..."

"That makes me more afraid," Puri whispered.

"About my intentions?"

"Your safety."

"Thank you, Puri." Mando was perfectly satisfied. "I know you have some regard for me. But I won't come to harm. No. Fate saved me from the Japanese bullets. Good fortune shall spare me now for the sake of the national issues and for you."

"I am frightened at times," Puri confessed. "I don't know if I'm becoming a coward. I don't understand. I'm used to struggle. During the Japanese times, although I was still in my teens, I surprised many with my daring. I was a guerrilla courier. I brought food and medicine to their hiding places. I learned to give first aid to the wounded. When I grew up, I helped in the campaign of the union. I spoke at meetings. But now, Mando, I can't sleep at night…"

"Puri, you're not a coward. You are still steadfast. Your resolve has not weakened, but…"

"But what…" Puri searched his eyes for the answer.

"Your heart feels a new emotion."

"Mando!"

"Yes, Puri, my love for you is not a stone flung into the desert."

"Not a stone flung into the desert," Puri repeated softly to herself.

"Is it not true, Puri?"

Puri bowed her head, then raised her face. Mando held her gaze, like a small dove suddenly hit by an arrow. Mando took Puri's hand and the dove felt its strength returned by the warmth of the hand, which caught it.

Later, she asked what Mando thought of Dr. Sabio's suggestion that she take up domestic science as a special student.

"Good; of course, you have graduated from political science."

"You're mocking me," Puri protested.

"I mean, you know much about housekeeping and earning a living, also about citizenship. You will attend classes because you're here anyway, and to supplement your knowledge, to polish any roughness. You have learned political science from your experiences in the farmers' movement, their teachings, goals, and strategies in the struggle, whether against the Japs or against the landlord. For example, the relationship between politics and economy. Because while their lives influence the decisions of the policy makers, their decisions or politics also affect the economy. We see this every day, everywhere. We are witnessing it at the hacienda, in Central Luzon, in the city, in Congress…"

"I have ideas about political science, about the government and its branches and its relation to the people and the country. I have heard of modern political economy, of capital and labor, wages and profit. About domestic science, I know how to sew and mend, cook rice, sinigang, and chicken adobo… Isn't that enough?" Puri smiled and raised her eyebrows, waiting for Mando's answer.

"Very good," he agreed heartily. "You'll be not only a good wife, but an ideal mother."

"And Dolly Montero?" Puri shot the unexpected question.

"I don't remember that name," Mando said innocently. "Written in my heart are only four letters: P – U – R – I."

LXV

Mando's and Puri's hearts were full of joy when they parted at the girls' dormitory. More than at any of their other meetings, Puri got a specific answer to her doubts and worries. Only she and no other was Mando's love.

Although he did not receive a categorical answer because of her inborn modesty, Puri showed her feelings in various ways. A girl's love cannot be hidden. As the saying goes, "One does not have to declare or announce what can be seen from one's actions and looks."

Of the two, it was Puri who was unsure that Mando would be faithful. Mando was confident, because only Danoy was his serious rival. Even Danoy had waved the white flag when he saw that the good-looking and intelligent Mando Plaridel seemed to be the awaited prince who would awaken the sleeping heart of the princess of the fields.

Puri was happy to hear Mando's white lie that Dolly Montero was erased from his memory. Nothing was engraved in his heart but her name and image. In love's language, white lies are not sins, but they add savor and color to enhance the sweetness and beauty of courtship.

Say that the loved one has all the wealth on earth, the fragrance of flowers in Proserpine's garden, and the brightness of the myriad of stars in the sky. This gladdens the heart if ardently said by a loved one. The one praised believes and is pleased. Not because the analogy is true, but because the loving heart sees in her such fascinating beauty.

As he had done earlier, Mando drove leisurely on his way home. It was only ten in the evening. He was still full from the heavy merienda and he had no urgent business.

He would pass by the *Kampilan* and probably see Magat and Andres about their paper's campaign and the disorder in Central Luzon. Mando was aware that in addition to the threats, the *Kampilan* was the subject of talk in gatherings. This was a common question: Have you read the *Kampilan*? This took place in the coffee shops, barbershops, marketplaces, offices, and schools.

Mando smiled when he overheard this. He knew that they were just beginning. As soon as the radio and TV stations were inaugurated, then things would really happen. Then they would see how thick the hides of the enemies of truth were.

Mando's car was moving slowly when he reached a dark section. The moon seemed to have closed her sleepy eyes. The road became darker because of the shadows of the agoho trees on both sides.

Mando almost hit the vehicle parked in the middle of the road. Had he not easily swerved and stepped on the brakes, it would have been a serious accident.

Mando stopped and got out. He saw that the stalled vehicle was a jeep. The two men were bent over the motor, which was exposed, and were tinkering with something. A third man walked towards him.

"It stopped, Maestro," he greeted Mando.

"That was close," Mando answered.

"It stopped in the middle, Maestro," the man repeated. "Can you help me?"

The man looked intently at Mando and his car and stared at the number.

Mando approached the jeep. The two men looked up.

"What's the trouble?" asked Mando.

"I don't know; the connection seems to have been cut off."

"Don't you have a flashlight?" Mando asked, bending toward the motor.

"Here." One of the men held a flashlight. However, instead of pointing the flashlight towards the motor, he hit Mando's head with it.

Mando had not approached the jeep like an innocent child. He was suspicious from the start. The stopping of the jeep in the middle of the road at that time and place while he was passing might not be an accident or coincidence. Those men were after something, probably something not good for Mando. Just the same, he stopped and got off instead of remaining in his car and driving off.

But his eyes were open and his senses were alert. He didn't like the faces and looks of the three strangers. Although their actions didn't give them away at first, Mando's intuition warned him.

Senator Maliwanag's reminder flashed through his mind.

"Bring a bodyguard whenever you go out." That was what his lawmaker friend had said. He shrugged his shoulders, but he knew it was no joke.

Now it had come. And he was alone.

Luckily, Mando was always ready. He had a purpose in asking for a flashlight. Mando quickly dodged so that the man missed his mark. The flashlight broke on the motor. There was no time for explanations. Quickly, Mando turned and socked the man with the flashlight, hitting him squarely on the jaw. The flashlight was flung afar.

Mando turned to the next. The man tried to wrestle with Mando. He was shorter but well built. Using his skill in judo-karate, Mando pressed his Adam's apple. When he was about to push him, Mando looked back. The third man, the one who first approached him, had a gun. He seemed to be just waiting for Mando to be free of his companion with whom he was wrestling.

"Cowards," Mando shouted so that the man would lose his cool.

As they wrestled, the third man pulled the trigger. Mando felt a fire blaze on his side. Suddenly, the second man's hawk-like hold loosened and his body sagged. The bullet, which had whizzed by Mando, had gone through his chest and was embedded in his opponent's heart. The man's eyes were staring lifelessly when he let go. Both were bloody.

The gunman was dumbfounded. It was a hard blow—he had killed his own companion. Mando took advantage of the short moment and went for the gunman. But the man got over his surprise and fear. His trembling fingers angrily pulled the trigger of the Colt. Once more a gunshot roared. Mando grabbed the gunman and pinned him down like a nail caught in a wrench.

Mando was as strong as he was in his younger days in the Sierra Madre, unafraid of the Japanese, the man-eating shark, the criminal Martin, and others against whom he had pitted his strength. He tightened his grip until the man's skin turned black and blue and became swollen. The gun fell and the man tottered as if he had been constricted by a python.

The man who was hit by Mando's fist regained consciousness and tried to crawl away. But before he could get far, he heard Mando's voice warning him and ordering him to lie face down or get shot. Mando held the Colt dropped by the third man.

Mando fired two shots upwards to get attention. Meanwhile, the new moon shone again on the grim view of a corpse, a man sprawled, and another lying face down with his hands clasped on his nape. The last two were alive.

Mando lit a cigarette as he looked at the scene. It occurred to him that if he had just been a bold publisher and not an experienced fighter, he would surely be the corpse, instead of the unfortunate gangster.

Two police patrol cars rushed to the scene. They found Mando sitting, pressing a handkerchief on a bleeding wound in his right shoulder, a newly lighted cigarette between his lips and a revolver in his right hand. He was obviously weakened by the loss of blood, but he did not take his eyes from the two prostrate men.

The law enforcers helped Mando into a police car. While Mando was being rushed to the hospital, the two gangsters and their dead companion were brought by the other car to the police headquarters.

LXVI

Mando's wound was not fatal, but he had to undergo surgery. The bullet was embedded in his shoulder blade. The wound on his side could easily be treated.

That same night, Magat and Andres rushed to the hospital. Dr. Sabio came as soon as he heard the news. After learning that the publisher was out of danger, Andres returned to the office. The morning edition of the *Kampilan* should include news about the attempt on Mando's life.

Magat and Dr. Sabio stayed in the hospital lobby during the operation. They waited until Mando was brought back to his room. According to the Doctor, he should be in bed for about two weeks.

The professor and Magat analyzed the root cause of the violence against Mando.

"He has no personal enemies," Magat said. "For sure, this was not personal."

"No doubt," Dr. Sabio agreed. "All those hit by the *Kampilan* are his enemies. Those who waylaid him were only hired men."

"As long as evil is widespread, those who do good are in danger," Magat declared.

"This is true," said the professor. "Mando, you, Senator Maliwanag—you are all playing with fire."

"And you too, Doctor," Magat added.

"Hasn't Mang Tumas already paid with his life? The fight will become more violent."

"Until they are defeated," Magat said forcefully.

"And while those in the right do not retreat," added Dr. Sabio.

"What's the use of living in a society where evil is the master?" grieved the ex-guerrilla leader. "The Japanese were driven away, but evil was not vanquished. Now evil is committed by the Filipinos themselves."

Then they pinpointed who would gain from Mando's death. Who had reason to hate him enough to have him put away?

Magat told Dr. Sabio about the heated argument between Segundo Montero and Mando. The millionaire landlord and head of the smuggling syndicate learned that neither his gold nor the beauty of his daughter could change Mando's mind. Mando had let Dolly's father know that he would go on supporting the campaign, which went against Montero's interests. This must have convinced him that if Mando would not listen to reason, then it was up to him… There were other, more effective means.

"That group will stop at nothing to remove any obstacle," remarked Dr. Sabio, after hearing Magat's story.

"They are worse than criminals." Magat clenched his fists.

"To think that those people are thought honorable, regarded highly, and are the top of society," remarked the president of Freedom University. He added, "They are the worst birds of prey."

"Idols with feet of clay," Magat added. "But their days are numbered."

"I wonder," Dr. Sabio said doubtfully.

They stopped when Mando was wheeled out of the operating room. A doctor and two nurses transferred Mando to his bed in a private room.

The patient was fully conscious but was forbidden to move or talk. After a while, Dr. Sabio made a sign that he was leaving. Magat stayed to watch Mando. A private nurse had been assigned, but Magat decided not to leave his friend. He knew that the plotters would not rest if they learned that Mando was safe.

Mando had a fever and was restless the whole night. Magat didn't sleep a wink.

The next morning, Dr. Sabio returned with Puri and Pastor. It was only that morning that the professor told the girl about the incident. She insisted on going to the hospital right away. They fetched Pastor. Tata Matyas was informed but he was only going to be brought over once Mando was able to talk. They reassured the old man that his foster son was not in critical condition.

Puri forgot her shyness. When she entered Mando's room, she sat on the side of the bed and held his hand. The young man opened his eyes and his pale lips smiled slightly. He saw that the girl was tearful.

Andres came with Iman the reporter. He brought a copy of the *Kampilan* with news of the attempt on the publisher's life. They were unable to include the more explosive report from the police that the incident was a plot to kill Mando Plaridel. The investigation showed that the slain man and two captured men were civilian guards at Hacienda Montero and had revealed the mastermind.

"Our suspicions were correct," Dr. Sabio told Magat after Andres told them about the investigation by the Manila authorities.

Some members of the police department went to the hospital. They confirmed that the two men who shot Mando had signed a confession.

That day Senator Maliwanag called, together with Rubio and some friends. Old Matyas also came but was taken home by Pastor after he saw Mando and was reassured that he was all right. The old man was very angry, but he just gritted his teeth.

"Lord, please don't let anything happen to him," he whispered.

Senator Maliwanag shook his head and reminded the patient of his advice to have bodyguards.

"Perhaps when I go home," Mando said softly and secretly motioned towards Puri and winked. The Senator smiled. Puri, who was talking to a nurse, was unaware of the byplay.

"If you need bodyguards, just tell me," Rubio offered. "If it's force they want, we are ready."

On the other hand, Mando received no message from Dolly, not even a telephone call or a letter. She had not yet returned from Baguio.

Puri asked her father's permission to stay at the hospital to help Mando's private nurse. Pastor agreed, but Mando would not hear of it. He said he would be happy to have Puri visit him every day, but he didn't want her to waste her study time. Mando was pleased with this new proof of Puri's love; but he felt she should not stay. Anyway, there were doctors and nurses assigned to him.

"Thanks, Puri. If I were seriously ill, but I'm not. Use your time for your studies, because you're pressed for time."

She did not insist. She wanted to show Mando that she was ready to serve him and look after him. She forgot that they were not yet engaged. She didn't think of what others would say about her offer. In moments of danger for a loved one, a girl's coyness bursts like a pricked balloon.

Nevertheless, as Puri was leaving after the others had gone, she showed some reproach.

"Are you coming tomorrow?" asked Mando.

"Didn't I want to stay? But you don't want me to. Of course, your nurse is efficient and pretty, too."

"Do you really love me?" Mando asked, ignoring Puri's insinuation. "You're not answering… Do you really love me?"

"Do you still have doubts?" The girl smiled and bowed her head, then she walked out.

At that moment, Mando felt completely well. He wanted to get up to run after her. But the nurse took his temperature and observed that it had risen.

"You are tired because of too many visitors," said his doctor when he saw the nurse's report.

Only Mando knew why his temperature suddenly rose.

That night after supper when Mando was alone, he had an unexpected guest.

"Danoy!"

It was Danoy, the missing leader of the farmers. Danoy said that he was in a remote barrio outside the hacienda and was observing everything. He had joined forces with the outlaws. They had heard of the attack on Mando. So he secretly came to find out how he was. He was relieved to see that Mando was all right.

Danoy would return to the barrio that night.

"We shall settle our accounts," he said grimly.

When the nurse returned to Mando's room, the mysterious caller was gone.

LXVII

Within a few days of hearing the news about the failed attempt to kill Mando, the small circle of big "gentlemen" left Manila almost simultaneously. Only recently, the group had met in Montero's Baguio cottage. Was it only a coincidence or were they hiding something? This coincidence did not escape the notice of the publisher's friends. Magat and Dr. Sabio discussed it.

Senator Botin hurriedly left for abroad. The congressional session was over. It had really become the sickness of congressmen to follow up the hundred days of idle meetings with a junket. Thus, they were able to travel at the government's expense with some kind of excuse. But Senator Botin was not considered among the distinguished lawmakers who were sent to international conferences. Just the same, Senator Botin sailed, supposedly to stay away for several months.

Governor Doblado went for a vacation in Hong Kong. His invalid wife had died; an event which brought him two good fortunes: money and freedom. They were childless. Since he became a widower, Doblado seldom went home to Quezon City. He stayed two or three times a week in the town next to the capital.

Doblado was not a stranger to the house of Tindeng and her two children. When Doña Ninay was still alive, he used to have lunch and rest there after office hours. The youthful Tindeng was said to be related to Doña Ninay who had sent her to school. But her neighbors, especially those who hang around the nearby store, said that the relationship between the playboy governor and the middle-aged woman was not that of uncle and niece. The two children, they were sure, were born from the affair. And when the governor was released from the bonds of matrimony, whom would he fear? Now he could expose not only the head but the whole body of his "albatross."

But when Doblado went to Hong Kong, he didn't take Tindeng along. Among the passengers on his plane were Doña Julia and Dolly. Was it a coincidence? For the new widower and the youthful matron, this was a rare chance. Before Doña Julia married Segundo Montero, her boyfriend was Oscar Doblado. The only obstacle were Oscar's parents, who wanted him to finish his studies. Then Montero saw his chance. He won over Julia's father. So she married the man who became Dolly's father.

"We had gone the whole way, Dolly," Doña Julia confided, when she discovered her daughter's affair with Lieutenant Whitey. Dolly had developed a fondness for unripe fruits when the American pilot was assigned to Iwo Jima. To console her daughter, the mother revealed her own youthful indiscretion. To make Dolly feel better, Doña Julia added:

"I told you of my experience to show you what fate does not mean to be, won't be. You weren't meant for Colonel Moto, nor Lieutenant Whitey. Why should you crack your head? Are they the only men in this world? You are young and beautiful. You won't lack suitors."

And the two had gone to Hong Kong without a send-off. Their present trip was for a different reason. Now they were going on a tour and to do some shopping. Although Dolly was hurt by her breakup with Mando, her earlier experience had given her strength. She had taken means to prevent her affair from growing out of season. In the city of Paris, a girl could learn anything she wished to know.

From Baguio, Pong Tua-Son proceeded to Hong Kong to supervise the construction of a modern building. He invited Doña Julia and Dolly to show off the architectural masterpiece. The two women would be guests of the Chinese mestizo who had long been lighting candles to the Montero heiress.

From the coquettish glances of Doña Julia to Governor Doblado and their exchange of off-colored jokes, especially when Dolly was not around, it was obvious that they would not be lonely in Hong Kong.

Their early affair would likely have a sequel.

Meanwhile, General Bayoneta suddenly decided to rush to the Visayas and Mindanao to "investigate rampant smuggling in the south." Ocean traffic was supposed to be open from the ports between Jolo and Borneo. From Jolo, smuggled goods were freely distributed in Zamboanga, Cebu, Iloilo, etc. Naturally, they also reached Greater Manila.

Although his real aim was to avoid the "heat" in Manila, he also wanted to know the new groups of smugglers who were lording it in the south. For a long time, the syndicate of his father-in-law Son Tua and Montero almost monopolized the field. Now, it was over. Therefore, there were other officials, political and military, who were helping themselves to the pot. There was no definite news about Montero and Son Tua. They could not be found either in Manila or Baguio. It was said that they were resting. Actually, they had gone into hiding.

The newspapers, including the *Kampilan*, did not mention it, but Magat and Dr. Sabio observed that the privileged group was thrown into flight by the failed attempt on Mando's life. Perhaps they would not be so uneasy if Mando had been killed and his attackers had not been caught. The dead don't talk. But Mando was alive and safe and the criminals "sang." Only the investigators knew whether they had revealed the mastermind of the plot or not. But one could not mistake "the sum of two plus two."

Mando was out of danger. He might not have to stay for two weeks as expected earlier. After a few days, he could sit up propped by pillows and have the nurse read to him. Sometimes he would listen to music over the radio.

But he often had visitors. Everyday, Magat and Dr. Sabio never failed to see him. Also Rubio and Tata Pastor. Mando knew the latest events, the progress of the investigation into his assailants, the trips of the members of the Montero syndicate, the obvious hiding of Don Segundo and Son Tua.

He showed no signs of being hurt by his complete break with Dolly, not even to his confidant Magat.

Only a sigh escaped his lips. This could mean relief.

But when Puri came every afternoon, he could not hide the glow of joy in his eyes, and the color that came to his wan cheeks. He was bored when Puri was away. It was not the skill of his special nurse nor the head physician that made him feel better. It was obviously the presence of the girl, which he always looked forward to.

When Puri came, Mando seemed well. He asked to be propped up on the pillows and would talk lovingly to Puri, inquiring about her studies, life in the dormitory, her needs and problems. Puri would remind him that she was the visitor and not the patient.

Dr. Sabio brought some books and Andres, some magazines. On the small table were copies of *Reflections of the Revolution of Our Time* by Harold J. Laski, *Atomic Age* by Bertrand Russell, *Toward Freedom* by Jawaharlal Nehru, *The Good Society* by Walter Lippmann, *Residencia en la Tierra* by Pablo Neruda, some works of Jean-Paul Sartre, and the latest editions of *Science and Society* and *Dissent*.

Mando looked at the books and smiled at Puri.

"How can a sick man read those?" He shook his head regretfully.

"Perhaps Dr. Sabio wants you to read them when you get well…"

"Maybe. The truth is I lack time to read. What can I do? I have to work day and night."

"Do you want me to read for you?" offered Puri. She was about to get up from the side of Mando's bed.

"No, let's just talk."

"Aren't you tired of talking to me? I'm here every day and we have been talking all the time."

"Call me 'dear,'" the patient asked.

"Answer my question first. Don't you get fed up?"

"If I were a poet, Puri, I would tell you that the butterfly would tire of the flower's nectar, the stars would tire of shining in the sky, but I would not tire of talking to you."

"But, what shall we talk about now?"

"Many things, Puri. There are many things I have not told you about my life."

"Would they change my feelings for you?"

"I don't know. Maybe not, but I don't want to have any secrets from you."

Mando was thinking of telling Puri who he was before he became Mando Plaridel.

LXVIII

One late afternoon, Puri was pushing a wheelchair on the hospital grounds. Then, she stopped before a wooden bench under a shady tree.

"Let's stay here," the girl said, looking at the patient. "Aren't you tired?" she asked lovingly.

Mando smiled. This was the first time he had left his room. He was brought from his room by elevator and the nurse and Puri brought out the wheelchair to the garden.

"You're the one who might be tired. Even if I have lost weight, I'm still heavy."

Puri rubbed her arm and smiled.

"I'm used to hard work. Don't forget, you're with a country girl."

Then she helped Mando to the wooden bench. She dusted the seat and they sat side by side.

The golden breeze was cool and gentle.

For some moments they were silent. Mando was watching two birds chasing each other on the branches of a banaba tree while Puri was looking at the golden rays of the afternoon sun, blending radiantly with the bright green of the thick grass. Mando was thinking that he and Puri would be like the lovebirds, not only playing among the branches, but also building a special nest and living happily. On the other hand, Puri was thinking that the breeze combined with the color of the grass created a new loveliness, like their love, which brought forth a new person in her —a being pure, filled with song, sweetness, and joy.

Puri was eager to hear Mando's secret, which he had mentioned the day before. But Puri felt it was not right to ask. Anyway, Mando did not keep her in suspense.

"Puri, it's time you knew this," said Mando, breaking the silence. "You should know who I really am."

Puri quickly looked up and stared at his face intently. She could see no one but Mando Plaridel. Her lips parted slightly, but she said nothing. Her eyes showed her bewilderment.

"I am Andoy," Mando said abruptly.

Puri was startled, although at first the name meant nothing. "Andoy?"

"Yes, Andoy, the son of Tata Pastor's sister."

"My cousin!" she said, unbelieving. "Can this be true?"

Mando placed his right hand on hers, then related his experiences.

He recalled the wretched life of his family under the Monteros, his life as an orphan, and a servant who was sent to school by Don Segundo. He related his escape when the Japanese occupied Manila, his flight to the mountain, the dangers and hardships he encountered among the guerrillas, his meeting old Tata Matyas and his finding of Simoun's treasures. Puri already knew about his experiences since he first went to Hacienda Montero and about his travels in foreign lands.

Puri withdrew her hand and said with hesitation, 'I should be happy to know you, the real you, because Tatang and I have no other near relative except you, but…" She could not go on.

"We are first cousins," Mando finished for her.

"Why did you keep it a secret this long?" There was a trace of reproach in her sad voice, implying that she would not have let herself fall in love with the only child of her father's sister.

"For two reasons, Puri," answered Mando. "First, because my story had to be kept a secret until I had fulfilled my mission; second, because I fell in love with you the first time I saw you."

"But..."

"Are you changing your mind, my dearest?" Mando took her hand again.

Puri looked into the distance. The two birds playing among the branches were gone, and the golden glow had disappeared from the grass. Instead the green had turned to gray as the mantle of darkness quickly spread.

Puri was sure that her feelings would never change even with the truth she had learned. If Mando was Andoy, what then? To her, Mando was Mando and no other. This was the man she knew from the start, the man she would continue to love.

"But Tatang?" Puri objected, not knowing what to answer.

"I shall tell him everything."

When Pastor learned that Mando was his only sister's son, he embraced him and was thankful for his good fortune.

"No wonder I felt drawn to you at once," he said, very pleased.

"That's why I called you Tata Pastor right away."

When Mando mentioned his love for Puri, the face of the old man changed and he thought for a long while.

"What will happen to the two of you if you should be parted?" he asked after a while.

"It would be a punishment we could not bear."

"Of course," Pastor said after thinking about it. "Who else would care for each other?"

Mando's eyes expressed his thanks.

"Don't worry, I shall talk to Puri," Pastor added. "I can't give her happiness."

After a few more days, Mando left the hospital.

When he was stronger, he invited Pastor and Puri, Dr. Sabio, Magat, and Andres to a gathering. He told his guests that it was not only for his recovery but to plan and launch a program, which had been his goal since he came from the Sierra Madre after the war.

"Tata Matyas knows about this," said Mando, looking at the old man seated in one part of the living room.

Mando explained a comprehensive program for education, the press and information, research and agriculture, and other branches of knowledge in support of the aims of charity and society.

"We have funds for all these. We shall not use these for business or politics but for humanitarianism. We shall not work singly or by twos or tens. We shall form a corporation which shall manage and implement our program through several branches."

Mando declared that money and capital used selfishly were like a monster that preys on animals and fish, but doesn't give life. He recalled what the fantastically rich steel magnate Andrew Carnegie once said—that the time would come when one would be ashamed to die a rich man.

Included under the extensive corporation were the *Kampilan*, and the radio-TV station, Freedom University, and the hacienda, which they planned to buy.

He asked Dr. Sabio to explain the long-range program of the university regarding studies related to the common welfare. It pledged to develop intelligent and nationalistic youth, attuned to the scientific age.

"The university will never become a diploma mill," said Dr. Sabio. "We shall support students who will become the pillars of the nation."

Mando told them the findings of the last investigation by a congressional committee headed by Senator Maliwanag. It was discovered that Hacienda Montero and other agricultural lands had been bought by the government from the Mitras and other former owners. But after some years and because of schemes of the greedy and the ignorance of the famers who had been awarded the land, the partitioned lands were recovered by the powerful.

This case would be brought to court. Based on the strong evidence, the government was expected to confiscate these lands. Although Don Segundo had bought Hacienda Montero, the sale was illegal, and he didn't have to be repaid but would likely be taxed for his excessive profits from the hacienda under his management.

At this point, Dr. Sabio explained why he did not pursue his university's plan to buy the hacienda from Segundo Montero. Senator Maliwanag had mentioned the congressional investigation of the former friar lands.

Mando and Dr. Sabio had agreed to wait until the property was reclaimed by the government.

'Therefore," Mando concluded, "we may buy the land from the government, supervise it for the tenants, and contribute to agriculture."

All approved the plan presented by Mando.

Before they started dinner, Pastor asked permission to make an announcement.

"I am honored to announce that my only daughter Puri and Mando Plaridel will be married soon."

The news was happily received and the guests shook hands with the betrothed. Tata Matyas approached Puri and affectionately kissed her on the cheeks.

"I have no doubt you and Mando will be very happy," he told the radiant girl.

After the other guests had left, Mando gave his fiancée Maria Clara's medallion. Mando told her the story and value of the jewel. "It was supposed to have brought bad luck to its first owners," he said. "But I'm not superstitious. Take care of it because it is precious and because of its link to the history of Maria Clara, Huli, Simoun, and Cabesang Tales."

"I shall value this as a token of a past which should always live in our memory and as a symbol of our love," Puri said happily.

LXIX

Early one morning, two children gathering wood were horrified to see a corpse hanging upside down from the branch of an ancient tree. The sun's rays had hardly pierced through the thick woods between Hacienda Montero and the barrio.

The frightened children ran back to town and told the first person they met about what they had seen. Right away many farmers rushed to the spot.

They exclaimed when they saw the horrible appearance of the corpse. Although the slain man's face was black, his red eyes staring, the tongue caught between his teeth and his jaws rigid, they could still identify him.

"Captain Pugot!" one shouted.

"Yes, it's Captain Pugot," agreed the others.

Some sighed, some made a sign of the cross. The women offered prayers.

A farmer hurried back to town to report to the barrio lieutenant who would report to the authorities.

One wanted to cut off the rope binding the feet and tied to a branch, but he was dissuaded. They decided to let the law enforcers take over.

The corpse was in khaki uniform and wore boots, had a crew cut, Japanese-style. Instead of his former ferocity and usual sneer, now severe pain and grief were registered on his face.

"At last he has paid," said one of the older farmers.

There was no need to explain the fate of the ferocious overseer. If they had anyone in mind, they just kept their mouths closed. No one dared offer an opinion on who drew the curtain on the bloody story of the notorious collaborator of the Japanese, who had earned a frightful reputation for his black conscience. His record as collaborator was repeated as overseer of Hacienda Montero.

The noise over Pugot's slaying was drowned out by the sensational exposé of the powerful smuggling syndicate, which included many of the big fish in politics, business, and society. The *Kampilan* used up the whole front page with names and pictures – Segundo Montero, General Bayoneta, Governor Doblado, Son Tua. There was also an insinuation that Senator Botin was also involved. He was now traveling abroad.

The charges against the syndicate were serious. Some were also charged with individual offenses. Montero for the plot to kill Mando Plaridel. Also involved were Captain Pugot and the hired men who agreed to turn state witnesses. Son Tua faced possible deportation for various illegal operations.

The *Kampilan* published a hard-hitting editorial on the sudden fall of the idols who had exploited, sucked, and abused others while enriching themselves.

> *Like Antaeus, the birds of prey have a hidden weakness. The moment they are separated from their perch of intrigue and deceit, they will be hit and overthrown by the bullets of truth, and their beaks and claws can no longer tear up and devour their hapless victims.*
>
> *Once we said in this editorial: Gone is the cursed creature using the disguise of the Eagle, the Vulture, the Owl, and the Vampire Bat, but he has left his de-*

scendants and those of his tools and accomplices. They
can be found, not only in the mountains, but on the
plains, in the fields, on the sea, in towns and cities, in
large buildings, among high government officials, in
important enterprises where their sharp beaks, teeth,
and claws are used in the accustomed gobbling up of
lives and sucking of the victim's blood.

But one day, that day will surely come, no longer
the mysterious hand of fate writing on the wall, as with
Belshazzar, but the hands of the oppressed will give
them justice. We shall live to witness that day.

Who knows if the editorial of the courageous *Kampilan* might have been a prophecy? Its warnings were speedily realized.

One night as the millionaire Son Tua was returning to Manila from Baguio, his car was waylaid by a group of armed men in a secluded spot in Central Luzon. They kidnapped the wealthy Chinese, but let his driver free. The driver reported it to the authorities.

"They didn't look like bandits," declared the driver to the PC. "They looked more like farmers than criminals. They didn't know me but they took my master. I heard their leader say, 'Son Tua, you have many sins against this country.'"

The PC suspected that the ones who slew Captain Pugot were also behind the kidnapping of Son Tua.

After a few days, three famous Manila doctors rushed to Baguio. They had been fetched to examine Don Segundo Montero who was stricken with paralysis. He was unconscious, but his life was not in immediate danger because his heartbeat was normal. Should he live, he would be a vegetable, according to the doctors' diagnosis.

It was learned that Don Segundo was on the phone when he had his attack. He was talking to his lawyer in Manila about the cases against him. The most serious were the unsuccessful attempt on Mando Plaridel and his being head of the smuggling syndicate on arms, jewelry, and blue seal cigarettes. He also wanted to know if the *Kampilan* could be charged with libel.

"Why wasn't that animal killed?" was Don Segundo's last remark when he suddenly collapsed.

On the first flight from Hong Kong were Doña Julia, Dolly, and Pong the architect. They returned as soon as they received the cable about the kidnapping of Son Tua and the attack of Don Segundo.

Meanwhile, there was no letup in the troubles at Hacienda Montero and the adjoining barrios. The conflict was worse than during the war. The Filipino soldiers and civilian guards were more despicable than the Japanese.

The bloody abuses were links in a long chain starting from the takeover by the loathsome Captain Pugot as overseer. A fire broke out at Hacienda Montero at about the same time as a meeting of workers in Plaza Miranda in Manila. Then the farmers and their leaders were arrested, detained, and starved for several days. Mang Tumas, a veteran leader of the farmers, was slain. To avenge his death, two civilian guards were beheaded.

But the revenge of Captain Pugot was far more brutal: a raid on a whole barrio where even women and children were not spared and the innocent and defenseless were shot. Finally, Captain Pugot paid for his villainy with his life. He was found hanging upside down from the branch of an old tree in the forest, like a new Judas who died, not at his own bloody hands, but at the hands of those whom he had sinned against.

Like a fire in the heat of summer, the flames did not stop after burning down a group of houses at its source, but spread, devouring the whole surrounding area because of the strong wind. The flames could not be quenched until all had turned to coal and ashes.

The death of Captain Pugot did not restore peace. Those who sought justice did not believe that this killer in soldier's clothes was the root cause of all the trouble and conflict at the hacienda.

He was only a tool of the greedy and heartless proprietor.

There were other skirmishes between the civilian guards and the farmers and there were casualties on both sides. The farmers resorted to their guerrilla tactics of surprise attack, attack-retreat. Thus, they were able to collect weapons and sow fear in the hearts of their persecutors.

Later on, the farmers joined forces with the outlaws and occupied Hacienda Montero. By then the hacienda lay almost idle, because Captain Pugot had been put away and his notorious troops were dispersed. No new overseer was appointed by Don Segundo, who had lost his faculties.

"Let us look after the hacienda so that it won't turn into a wilderness," said Danoy. "The land should be used to serve those who till and care for it."

A large group of farmers now prepared to work on the vast Hacienda Montero and the adjoining barrios – former tenants and sharecroppers, people who used to be peaceful and docile, but had been driven to the forests and mountains by the inhuman treatment of the landowners and the cruelty of the officials. Now they got ready to defend, by any means, their right to work and live by their toil.

The armed troops were alarmed at the report of the provincial commander.

"The rebellion of the dissidents in Central Luzon has spread," was the report from the provincial capitol, which was quickly picked up by the newspapers and the radio.

"Banditry and anarchy reign," said an additional bulletin.

It was worse than the signal for an approaching storm.

"This kind of propaganda is an omen that the army intends to solve a social problem with an iron fist," Mando prophesied, as he and Magat were having coffee at the *Kampilan*'s canteen.

LXX

Mando's fears were not unfounded. The next day he received a telegram from the President, inviting him to a conference at the palace. He learned that Senator Maliwanag and Dr. Sabio were also summoned. The telegram did not state the purpose of the conference.

They guessed that it was connected with the latest news from the army in Central Luzon.

More than once, the President had warned against so-called instigators of the farmers. Although no names were mentioned, the three instigators were called radical leaders.

Several times, the palace had attacked the activities of an "ambitious senator" and his allies, "a university professor," and a publisher of a radical newspaper.

The three men agreed to meet in Mando's office the same day. Senator Maliwanag and Dr. Sabio arrived together late in the afternoon.

"The President's telegram is an ultimatum," the Senator began.

"What shall we do?" asked Mando.

"Face the lion in his den," answered Maliwanag.

"First, let's analyze the President's intentions," Dr. Sabio suggested, "and let us give a tentative answer, an analysis of a serious problem and the steps the administration should take to solve these problems peacefully."

"Good," said the legislator. "We shall not be accused of criticizing without proposing a remedy. Perhaps, no one wants trouble except General Bayoneta."

The three brought a prepared statement when they went to the office of the President that day.

When they were seated, the Chief Executive spoke.

"I invited you, gentlemen, because the situation is critical. If you don't help me, what I wish to avoid might happen."

He glanced at the *Spoliarium* by Juan Luna on the wall of the office. The painting showed scattered corpses being dragged by the centurions.

"I don't want trouble and I don't want to use an iron fist." The President looked at each of his three guests. "That is why I called you. Here is the Army's report."

He handed the report to Senator Maliwanag who looked at it and passed it on to Mando and Dr. Sabio. The confidential report stated that serious trouble would erupt at any time. At the end, their names were mentioned as instigators.

"This report is biased, Mr. President," the lawmaker said angrily.

"My aim is peace and order," the President stressed, ignoring Maliwanag's protest. "If the Army would have its way, you know its solution. The authority of the government should be obeyed. I don't want it to reach that point; so, I invited you."

"On that point, Mr. President," answered Senator Maliwanag, "perhaps we have no quarrel. Every good Filipino is against disorder. We are prepared to help, because we know that in every disorder, the first to be hurt is the nation and the government. We are the nation and the government is us. So it is everyone's duty to be concerned with peace and order."

The Senator presented their paper to the President.

"This is a short paper which we prepared," he said. "Sir, here is a list of problems, the grievances and petitions of the farmers and laborers and, according to our studies, effective solutions, if you will agree and accept them."

The President scanned some pages.

"Some petitions are reasonable," he conceded. "But most cannot be granted right away. They are neither in our hands nor in the hands of the government." Then he reread a page. "Besides, it includes a warning, a threat. The government cannot be threatened, gentlemen…"

"We have done nothing but let you know the feelings of the oppressed," Mando answered. "No more, no less. It is different from the Army's report, sir."

"Very well. This, a barrio school, okay." And he slowly looked over the petitions. "This one, construct roads in some barrios, okay. This one, put up a hospital, later; we shall look for funds."

He stopped and stared at his guests.

"This one, ban civilian guards," he continued. "On one hand, the landowners' right should be protected. This one, remove the PC from the vicinity of the hacienda. Gentlemen, it is the government's duty to keep peace and order. And this, take the hacienda, expropriate, and divide it among the farmers. Our government is a democracy, not authoritarian; here the landlord and the tenant have equal rights. The law does not forbid a citizen to own a piece of land or a hacienda."

"Then, sir," Dr. Sabio tried to cut in.

"I advise you to go to the barrios in Central Luzon, especially Hacienda Montero. Many listen to you. They are ready to obey. Talk to the farmers. Advise them. Tell them to be more patient, because my administration is not sleeping on the job. I am doing everything under the law. I care for them; my heart is with the poor, because they are among the five million who elected me to this high office, but I am not God, nor a dictator…"

"They have been forgiving and sacrificing for too long," answered Senator Maliwanag. "They are on a hacienda which has amassed and is still amassing wealth for the landowner. But they are starving, their wives are sickly, and their children can't go to school."

"Don't forget that the war has just ended." The President was evasive. "The Japanese robbed us for three years and the returning Americans destroyed everything… Don't expect me to restore all of these in two years. Especially if I don't get your cooperation."

"The oppression of the farmers is older than two wars, sir," Dr. Sabio pointed out.

"If they are still disappointed in your administration, no one can say if…" Mando was unable to finish, because the President had cut him short.

"I know what you mean," he said violently. "If the farmers lose their trust in the government, they will take matters into their own hands. That, my administration cannot allow. Mark my words. I don't want to follow the Army's advice, but if they don't respect the law…"

"Sir, they are fed up with the ways of those in power," Senator Maliwanag reminded him. "Promises, threats, more promises, threats, violence. Please change the tune, Mr. President. This is a chance to be different from your predecessors. Help the poor country by action. Come down from the palace, go out to the fields and barrios; look at their lives and their conditions first-hand; let your feet get muddy from the pot-holed roads; let the tears of mothers and children wet your hands when you extend your charity."

"You are said to be surrounded by a cordon sanitaire by your staff who seek to keep you from the people, by the favored elite who are only after wealth, position, and personal power. They get you drunk with feast and pomp, they burn incense, they praise your mistakes and shield your eyes from the sad truth."

The President reluctantly calmed down after the successive arguments from Senator Maliwanag and Mando Plaridel. He rubbed his right hand over his closed eyes before speaking.

"We shall see," he said slowly, as if talking to himself. "It appears, the President of a country is the most powerful leader, the chief executive. It appears that he has the power to do whatever he wishes. Ah, sometimes, I want to exchange places with a professor or a publisher."

He paused a while, ran his hand over the thick pile of papers on his table, then continued. "But gentlemen, I confess my hands are often tied. You can't imagine the pressure of various forces and varied interests. There are politicians, the foreigners through their embassies and communities, the newspapers and other mass media, and the citizens themselves.

There is also nepotism, the temptation to give jobs to relatives and friends. You know I am not rich, nor am I enriching myself even though I could become a millionaire within twenty-four hours. Oh, Maliwanag, put yourself in my place." He hit the arm of his tall chair with his right hand.

"What you said, Mr. President," Mando answered in a sympathetic tone, "are problems that go with the position. For one who is weak-willed, these are reasons for drawing away from the people. The common people don't come to this palace, and you have not gone to them except during election campaigns. Forgive me, honorable President, but inasmuch as we are talking heart-to-heart, your image among the people won't please you, sir."

"What image?" The Chief Executive frowned.

"If you'll pardon me, sir, your image is different and far from how your followers have painted you."

"*Aba*, my image is good in our press and in the American press."

"They are using different colored glasses," replied Mando.

"Certainly different from the glasses of the *Kampilan* publisher," the President said mockingly.

"Sir, the *Kampilan* is committed to the truth, not to profit by pleasing those in power. Sir, look at the business enterprises of some foreign publishers. The *Kampilan*, sir, does not claim to be the paper of the nation, nor the clarion of freedom and truth. It is known for its daily publication."

"You were the first to report a threatened coup d'état of my administration, weren't you?"

"It's my honor, sir, whereas the other newspapers were mute," replied Mando.

"You also heard about the planned coup d'état, Senator Maliwanag, before it was published, didn't you?" the President asked.

"Like a man whose house is burning, Mr. President, you are the last to know," the Senator answered enigmatically.

"And where did these traitors come from?" the President gloated. "Those men said the same thing. My image was ugly. The people were angry with my administration, the nation whose five million elected me to this position." He took a deep breath after repeating his favorite statement about his election. "What is the suggestion of those close to me? That I should establish a dictatorship. If I were a dictator, many heads would roll in the mud."

"Maybe the nation will not allow the President to become a dictator," respectfully reminded Dr. Sabio, an expert in political science.

"Even to save the republic?"

"Not for any reason, sir. The aborted coup d'état was a plot of ambitious military men who were instigated by foreign agents. This is common in Latin America. They are easily prodded and bought but just as easily quelled."

Mando added after Dr. Sabio, "When the executive loses his patience and calm because of the problems of a democratic system, he might be tempted to become a dictator. Just like Hitler. For sure, the nation will fight and revolution will break out. Such a revolution can't be stopped because it is a general uprising of the people and not a coup d'état of a few Judases in the administration.

The aim of a revolution against you, for example, Mr. President, is not only your removal from office and a change for another, but to destroy a termite-eaten building and to eradicate a system which harbors evil. It aims to establish a new government structure which answers the hopes and desires of the whole nation."

"You speak boldly, Mr. Plaridel." The President was annoyed.

"I want you to feel the gravity of the situation." Their eyes met.

"You think you are always writing an editorial," the President said more heatedly.

The dialogue ended. Mando did not answer the direct insult.

"Señores," The President broke the silence, no longer concealing his anger. "I called you not to ask for lectures on how I should perform my duties. No one can teach me this. I see that it will be difficult for us to understand each other, because you don't want to help in keeping peace and order. That's up to you. You have read the confidential army report. So don't blame me."

"Mr. President!" protested the three visitors.

The Chief Executive brushed aside their shocked protest with a wave of his hand.

"Let us lay our cards on the table," he challenged sternly. "Either you stop your followers or accept the consequences."

"Whose duty is it to stop disorder, ours or yours here in this palace?" asked Senator Maliwanag.

"Are you challenging me?" demanded the Chief Executive.

"Or are you threatening us?" retorted the legislator.

"Señores, I wish to avoid bloodshed, but if you…" And he stood up angrily.

The three also stood up, red-faced in contrast to the President whose lips were pale and whose eyes were ablaze. Like a final blow, Senator Maliwanag said these words:

"Honorable President, you will make the decision. Nevertheless, remember this: the three of us can be killed, a hundred or a thousand farmers, but the nation can never be destroyed by those who betray her."

"I hold the list of traitors to the country and to the government." The Chief Executive's voice trembled. "I am sure they will not escape the punishment of the law. Good morning, señores."

His aide entered and was told to lead the guests downstairs. But before Senator Maliwanag left, he made a meaningful parting remark.

"Mr. President, remember that King Belshazzar did not heed the handwriting on the wall."

"The moment there is disorder in Central Luzon, I shall suspend the writ of *habeas corpus*," shouted the President.

"Stop the waves of the ocean first."

Without a word, the three got into Mando's car and asked to be brought to a restaurant outside Manila.

"Let us eat first before we are arrested," joked the young publisher.

At that moment in Hacienda Montero and the neighboring barrios, the farmers were uneasy. They were talking about the tense situation. Many recalled their valuable experience during their fight with the Japanese during the occupation. They were confident that they would not be subdued and could defend themselves against those who trample on their rights and dignity.

Rubio arrived at Hacienda Montero with a letter from the industrial workers in Manila and other cities. They vowed that they would not allow their brother farmers to be oppressed and were prepared to offer men, money, and other needs during any difficulty.

"We are free farmers and laborers who have the right to live as human beings and not like slaves," said the declaration in part.

Early that afternoon, crowds of farmers and barrio folks flocked to the hacienda. Pastor lit a torch and set fire to three large effigies, which looked like scarecrows. The faces were those of Segundo Montero, Governor Doblado, and General Bayoneta. Being made of rags and straw, the three ugly replicas of even uglier characters were soon ablaze and were devoured by fire amidst the merriment of the village folks.

"Death to the monsters. May they die like the executioner, Captain Pugot," shouted the noisy crowd.

"Long live social justice!" was the resounding answer.

"Long live the Filipino people!" The chorus was deafening.

But their joy was short-lived. All became silent when they saw what was coming. Without warning, two trucks dashed towards them, full of soldiers and civilian guards. Close behind was a tank. The feet of the raiding soldiers hardly touched the ground before they rained bullets on the farmers. The three burnt effigies were still smoking.

Like chicks scattered by the gunshots, the surprised farmers and village folk scampered at the soldiers' attack. Many ran. Some sought cover. The few who had weapons were forced to fight; that was better than being killed without a fight.

The zealous soldiers who jumped from the two trucks were like tigers chasing mountain cats. The scene was a reenactment of similar cruelties in different places in Central Luzon during the Japanese times and after liberation when the military and civilian guards returned to power.

Holding a .45 revolver in his right hand, the captain fiercely looked at the dead and wounded farmers. He counted twenty-seven. Not one of his soldiers had a scratch.

He approached a prostrate body, turned the head with his boot so it faced upward. He saw that the dead man was Pastor.

The captain was pleased and said, "Now, it's you Pastor. Yesterday it was Tumas. Tomorrow, Danoy. Not one of you will remain. You will all be wiped out by bullets."

Meanwhile, the earth was stained with the blood of the wounded. No one came to their aid.

That night in a secret place outside the city, Mando and Magat conferred with Rubio and Danoy the whole night. The first two were tested fighters against the Japanese. The last two were true labor leaders in Greater Manila and of the farmers in Central Luzon.

Before they parted at dawn, Mando declared fervently, "We shall use all our strength and do everything we can so our nation will be truly free and independent, and the Filipino people will be the true masters of their own land. A just democracy; equality before the law and in opportunities in life. This is our vow and ultimate goal, for which we shall lay down our lives."

The End

Acknowledgements

We, the children of the late Estelita Constantino-Pangilinan, wish to thank everyone who made this publication possible and our mother's wish a reality. When she presented her master's thesis to the graduate school faculty of the University of Santo Tomas (UST) in 1976, Estelita wrote:

"To all who have contributed to the completion of this work through their encouragement, support, constructive criticism, helpful suggestions, and prayers, many thanks. An extra measure of gratitude goes to:

My adviser, Dr. Alejandrino Q. Perez, and my reader, Dr. Ophelia A. Dimalanta, for their kind but critical guidance.

The chairman of the panel of examiners Dr. Ophelia A. Dimalanta and members Dr. Eduardo Deveza and Professor Norma G. Tiangco for their incisive questions that demanded a re-examination of statements and judgements made in this study and led to their clarification and reinforcement.

The Faculty Development Program Committee and the administrators of La Salle Green Hills for my study leave.

My family and friends for their steadfast faith and unfailing support, especially to my sisters Misses Lourdes and Norma Constantino.

My children for their understanding of my need for personal growth and relieving me of countless chores, especially to Karina and Clarissa for helping out in the tedious proofreading and for patiently following up on my papers.

The high school office staff for the preparation of the manuscript, Misses Adela Daygo and Cora Cruz, Messrs. Christopher Garcia and Ambrosio Batanes."

More than four decades later, we continued to receive help and support from many individuals.

First and foremost, we sincerely thank Attorney Virgilio (Gil) delos Reyes, who was Estelita's student at La Salle Green Hills High School and was inspired by *Mga Ibong Mandaragit* even as a young man. As fate would have it, he later met Estelita's youngest daughter Joann when they were both members of the University of the Philippines Student Catholic Action. Since 2009, Gil has helped us immensely every step of the way, from tracking down a copy of Estelita's manuscript to giving invaluable advice and even connecting us to potential publishers and reviewers.

We thank Nonoy Bonzon who took the time to get a copy of the hard bound 700-page manuscript from the UST Library and ship it to us from Manila to New Jersey before online document sharing was possible!

Our heartfelt appreciation to our friends who supported us along the way, especially:

- Marcy Pedraza, UST alumna and former faculty member, and Kaori Fuchigami, UST librarian who helped us track down some missing pages from the manuscript.

- Dr. William (DokNet) Billones who shared his artistic talent and gave us permission to use his artwork for the book cover.

- Francis Edward Bayon who went out of his way to print and arrange the delivery of our book proposal to a potential publisher.

We are very thankful to Philana Wang who lent her time, skills, and creativity to format this book and help us navigate the self-publishing platform.

Thanks to our spouses Tonee, Tom, Daisy, and Noel for their moral support. To Noel Bansil, we give our special thanks for his critical suggestions and insights. Sadly, Noel passed away before the publication of *Birds of Prey*. We dedicate this book both to him and to our mother Estelita.

We could not have done this project without the help of Estelita's grandchildren Andrea, Samantha, Nicole, Michael, and Anna who assisted in getting the typewritten manuscript into a Word document and in proofreading. We have no doubt their grandma is smiling down from heaven.

We give our additional thanks to these individuals whose help, advice, and support have been invaluable to the process of releasing this translation: Michelle Magno-Puentespina, Patricia Boyle, Cha Coronel Datu, Susan Romero Vidal, Rita Alampay Davis, and Lisa Liddane. We also thank Lindsey Cohick for her clear editorial eye.

Finally, we are forever grateful to our mother Estelita for her love and her legacy. She will forever be our little star, our guiding light.

About the Author

Amado V. Hernandez was a Filipino journalist, patriot, poet laureate, activist, labor leader, guerrilla fighter, and educator. Besides his newspaper work, he wrote about the working class, social injustice, oppression, guerrilla activities, political intrigues, and corruption. Because Hernandez's works were influenced by his own experiences and strong beliefs, it has been said that the artist and the man were one.

Mga Ibong Mandaragit is one of his best works. It was written between 1951-1956 while the author was imprisoned for crimes of rebellion. It took thirteen years before he was acquitted of all charges in 1964 by the Supreme Court of the Philippines.

As newspaper editor and columnist, Hernandez was widely read and respected for his nationalistic, pro-labor views. He declared in the preface to *Mga Ibong Mandaragit*, "My involvement in the labor movement and in politics was a direct fulfillment of my principles and beliefs. I don't wish to write from an 'ivory tower;' the writer is not a mere observer in a democracy."

He died in May 1970 and later received several posthumous awards, the most prestigious of which was the award of National Artist of the Philippines on June 12, 1973 in recognition of his rare excellence and significant contribution to literature.

Other Award-Winning Works:

Isang Dipang Langit (An Arm's Stretch of Sky) – Poem
(Republic Cultural Heritage Award, 1962)

Kayumanggi (Brown) – Poem
(Commonwealth Literary Award, 1940)

Pilipinas (Philippines) – Historical Poem
(Commonwealth Literary Award, 1938)

Luha Ng Buwaya (Crocodile's Tears) – Novel
(NPC-ESSO Award, 1963)

Pili sa Pinili (Chosen from the Selected) – Poem
(NPC-ESSO Award, 1964)

Report sa Indonesia (Report from Indonesia)
(NPC-ESSO Journalism Award, 1965)

Muntinlupa – Play
(Palanca Literary Award, 1958)

Hagdan ng Bahaghari (Rainbow's Ladder) – Play
(Palanca Literary Award, 1959)

Ang mga Kagalang-galang (The Venerables) – Play
(Palanca Literary Award, 1960)

Magkabilang Mukha ng Isang Bagol (Both Sides of a Coin) – Play
(Palanca Literary Award, 1961)

Wala nang Lunas (No Remedy) – Short Story
(Ilaw at Panitik, 1932)

About the Translator

Estelita Constantino-Pangilinan was an educator and a published author. She graduated Magna Cum Laude from the University of Santo Tomas with dual degrees of Bachelor of Arts in English and Bachelor of Science in Education – English. She later earned her Master of Arts in English also from UST. The translation (from Tagalog to English) and critical analysis of *Mga Ibong Mandaragit* was Estelita's master's thesis which she submitted in 1976. The UST panel of examiners gave Estelita a grade of Meritissimus for her oral defense, something she was very proud of. In her translation work, Estelita took care that whenever there was a conflict between word or literal translation and thought, it was the thought that prevailed. She taught English at the Manila Central University and at La Salle Green Hills High School where she became assistant principal. After a long and successful career in academia, she worked as a speech writer for the Philippine Tourism Authority.

Other Published Works:

Journalism Handbook (National Book Store, 1974)

Speech and Drama (National Book Store, 1991)

"The Hospital That Never Was" (*Sunday Times Magazine*, July 1968)

Freshman Readings (Manila Central University, 1966)

"So You Want To Be A Writer?" (*The Varsitarian* [University of Santo Tomas], 1963)

"Courage, Ladies" (*Ubiquitous* [La Salle Green Hills], 1963)

"Beatriz" (*The Varsitarian* [University of Santo Tomas], 1948)

Various Essays (*The Pharos* [Manila Central University])

Glossary

A

Aba. An exclamation of protest or surprise

Agatsonas. A kind of bird

Anahaw. A kind of palm

Anitos. Spirits of ancestors

Ate. A title of respect for an older sister

Atis. Sweetsop

Azucena. Dog meat

B

Balasubas. Derogatory word for those who refuse to pay their debts

Balintawak. A traditional Filipino dress for women

Bangkuwang. A coarse, fibrous aquatic herb used in mat weaving

Barong-Tagalog. A native Filipino long-sleeved shirt for men—usually made of embroidered material, and worn for special occasions

Barung-barong. Shanty

Batalan. A working area at the back of a nipa house (house on stilts and made of organic materials like nipa palm leaves and bamboo), usually without a roof

Bataw, sigarillas. Vegetables with pods

Bayong. A large rectangular bag of woven material used for marketing or carrying things

Bienvenida. Welcome party

Bilao. Flat native basket

Binatog. Boiled corn kernels eaten with grated coconut and salt

C

Cacique. Spanish word for a local political boss

Cavan. Measure of rice; a sack

Chabacano. Pidgin Spanish

Cogon. A kind of grass

Colorums—Tanggulan, Sakdalista, Hukbalahap. Names of groups that revolted against the government

Corredora. Agent, usually of jewelry

D

Death March. An infamous event when prisoners of war were ordered to march from Bataan to Capas. Many died from fatigue, hunger, and illness.

Despedida. Farewell party

E

El mismo perro con diferente collar. The same dog with a different collar

Entresuelo. Mezzanine

F

Filipinista. A Filipino nationalist

G

Ganta. Unit of measurement equivalent to around three liters

Genuwain. A corruption of "genuine" that became widely used during the Japanese occupation

H

Hara-kiri. Japanese form of suicide

Herbolarios. Unschooled men who prescribe herbs, fruit, etc., as medicine

J

Jueteng. A game of chance

K

Kaingin. A burned clearing in a forest

Kalaw. A bird

Kaldereta. A kind of meat dish with sauce of tomatoes and coconut milk

Kalumbibit, etc. Kinds of medicine

Kamagong. A kind of reddish-brown hardwood

Kamote. Sweet potatoes

Kamoteng-kahoy. Cassava, a root crop

Kangkong. A kind of vegetable that thrives in swampy places

Kastaniyog. Coined from castañas (chestnuts) and niyog (ripe coconut)

Kempeitai. Japanese military police

Kura. Japanese term used for giving orders

Kuya. A title of respect for an older brother or male cousin

L

Lapu-lapu. A kind of fish

Lechon. Roasted pig

M

Macapuno. A glutinous type of coconut used for sweets

Merienda-cena. Heavy snacks or light dinner served at about 6:00 pm

Mickey Mouse. Money with little value issued by the Japanese in the Philippines

Miss Pilipit, or Miss Pilit. Miss Twisted or Miss Forced; a pun on Miss Philippines

O

Operation of the saw. Double-dealing, suggested by the forward-backward movement of a saw

P

Padulas, Parating, Pabagsak. Various terms meaning bribe

Palay. Harvested rice with its husk

Pandanggo sa Ilaw. Candle Dance, a folk dance

Pareng. A corruption of compadre, denoting relationship between the godfather and the parent of the godchild; used loosely to show camaraderie

Pelotari. A player of Jai Alai

Pinipig. Newly harvested rice that has been pounded flat

Pinoy. Slang for Filipino

Pinta. To take a peek at playing cards

Provinciana. Country lass

Puto, Kalamay, Goto. Native dishes served as snacks

R

Relleno. Stuffed chicken

Republic of Barasoain. A government formed in Barasoain, Malolos, Bulacan by the Filipino leaders after they overthrew Spanish rule

S

Sari-sari store. Convenience store

Sinigang. A dish with sour broth

Sona. The Japanese practice of cordoning off an area and rounding up the residents

Suman. Glutinous rice wrapped in leaves

Supot. Not circumsized; literally, "encased"

T

Taksan. Japanese word for many

Talahib. A kind of weed

Talakitok. A kind of fish

Tampipi. A native suitcase

Tapa. Dried beef

Tatang. Father

Tayu-tayo, atin-atin. Just us, among ourselves

Terno. Traditional Filipino dress with butterfly sleeves

Tong. A gambling den's percentage of the winnings

Tuge. A kind of root crop

Tulya. Small shells/mollusks

W

Weeds don't die. Philippine proverb; rough equivalent of "Only the good die young"

Made in the USA
Middletown, DE
02 October 2021